The Onion Files *is an extraordinary fictional spy thriller written by a true intelligence professional. In this novel, General Pattee utilizes his vast experience and wide-ranging international intelligence contacts to provide a riveting, imaginative, easy read story line. The novel revolves around a post 9-11 plot by al-Qaeda terrorists to devastate key nodes of the U.S. electrical power system utilizing cyber warfare as the key instrument of this effort. While* The Onion Files *is a fictional novel, it provides a very accurate tutorial highlighting the growing challenge for current international intelligence agencies. It dramatically reflects the critical need for close cooperation between worldwide intelligence agencies to maximize appropriate counter efforts as the threat continues to grow. In that regard, I strongly recommend that intelligence and homeland security personnel at all levels read this fascinating novel.*

– Lt. General Leonard Perroots (Ret),
Former Director, US Defense Intelligence Agency

Osama is alive and well in this fast paced thriller about the next major terrorist attack in North America. The destruction of their targets of choice would be much more devastating than the loss of the Twin Towers on 9/11. The author's background makes his descriptions of events all the more credible. Val Pattee retired as a major general having spent the majority of the time following his fighter pilot career in the highest levels of the intelligence world during the Cold War. One can't help but think that some of his 'imaginary' crises are based on similar events from his past. A chilling thought.

– Major General Lewis MacKenzie (Ret),
CM, OOnt, MSC and Bar, CD

Val Pattee brings a lifetime of real world experience to writing this page turner. The Onion Files *has an intricate, compelling and credible plot. One wonders how close to the brink we really are.*

– Gordon Smith,
Former Canadian Deputy Foreign Minister

THE ONION FILES

THE ONION FILES

VAL PATTEE

151 Howe Street, Victoria BC Canada V8V 4K5

For information and bulk orders, please contact
info@agiopublishing.com *or go to*
www.agiopublishing.com
Visit this book's website at www.valpattee.com

ISBN 978-1-897435-05-2 (trade paperback)
978-1-897435-06-9 (casebound)
987-1-897435-07-6 (electronic edition)
978-1-897435-08-3 (audio book edition)

10 9 8 7 6 5 4 3 2 1

Printed on acid-free paper made without fibre from old growth forests.

ACKNOWLEDGEMENTS

Many of the characters in this story are mosaics of people with whom I was associated over the years and a few events come close to some of my morning briefings, but this story is a work of fiction. Any hint that our infrastructure is vulnerable in the way portrayed in this story is straight from my imagination.

To my family, who bring great joy into my life, to Richard for technical computer expertise and creativity, and to Joan, Ross and Dominique for ideas and drama. Faith Gildenhuys provided exacting editing. Bruce Batchelor made publishing *The Onion Files* not only possible but exciting.

The International Islamic Front for Jihad against the US and Israel has, by the grace of God, issued a crystal clear *fatwah* calling on the Islamic nation to carry on *jihad* .... The nation of Mohammad has responded to this appeal.

– Osama bin Laden,
quoted in *TIME* magazine,
December 23, 1998

PROLOGUE

Woodhaven is a small, idyllic town nestled in the low valleys of New Hampshire. Although the region's primary industry is dairy farming, people had started moving in from the big East Coast cities, buying up land and creating picturesque hobby estates. The newcomers often spoke about how Woodhaven felt calm and safe compared to the bustle they had left. You could forget about troubles in the rest of the world, they said with a touch of pride. Cottage industries developed, and more modest homes began to dot the countryside, with Woodhaven becoming the cultural and commercial focus for the new rural sprawl.

Jeremy Thorpe, an assistant bank manager at the local branch of New England Trust, was just finishing his meal with his wife, Selma, and their five-year-old daughter, Chloe. Coming home every day for lunch was a delight, with just a short drive through the beautiful town to the office. He loved the opportunity for the personal touch that his job now offered. Jeremy knew how lucky he was. Two years ago, after Jeremy had completed eight exhausting years toiling at a large national bank in Manhattan, Selma and he had decided to quit the hubbub of big city life. They chose Woodhaven, a small town where they could raise Chloe away from urban temptations. The sale of their New York condo provided the capital they needed to relocate and Selma was able to give up her job as a dental hygienist to devote herself to Chloe full time. Their house was only minutes from the center of town, yet right beside the network of wooded pathways that they enjoyed almost daily. They knew that they had settled into a wonderful life in a beautiful part of New England.

"Honey, can you pick up some big garbage bags so I can rake the leaves this weekend?" Jeremy asked Selma, and glanced at his watch. "I gotta go—don't want to be late for a one o'clock meeting."

Chloe's eyes instantly welled up in tears. "Don't go, Daddy! You promised you'd take me to the park."

"My darling, tomorrow is Saturday." He smiled at Selma. "Maybe a picnic? The weather looks great and we could enjoy the fall leaves at their very best. Chloe, I promise I'll swing you as high as you can go."

He leaned over, kissed his wife, then gave his daughter a pat on her curly head before bounding out the door. Jeremy jumped into their cherry red Ford Taurus station wagon—the color was the closest thing to a flashy red sports car that he could afford at this point in his life. There were no regrets about their mid life career choice, he thought and said out loud, "I'm a *very lucky* man."

He backed down their privet-lined driveway, giving a wave to Chloe watching from the living room window. It was 12:50 on a gorgeous Friday afternoon with Indian Summer in full swing.

Beth Simmons had worked at the New England hydroelectric dam since construction on the massive structure was completed in 1979. At the time, it was the largest infrastructure project in the northeastern United States, its huge reservoir providing a recreation area extending for eighty miles above the dam. The power plant's massive dynamos fed electricity to the eastern seaboard and formed an important part of the integrated grid that covered the continent.

Beth had settled into the comfort of a well-paid union job, with little stress and a steady daily routine. She especially liked the fact that she could sit for most of her shift in a reclining chair. At 224 pounds, Beth Simmons weighed exactly twice the recommended ideal body weight for a 5-foot tall, 47-year-old woman.

Pipes and wires, all regimentally aligned, crisscrossed one long wall leading into the operations control room, before running somewhere deep into the structure. As she walked by them every day, the neatly ordered lines were a constant and favorable comparison with her previous life—haphazard, unstructured, without real purpose. She remembered well this opportunity of a new job in what to her was a new world, and she'd seized it. Like Jeremy and his family, she was content with her quiet life in the tranquil village.

Beth had just completed her regular 1:00 p.m. call to the main power distribution center to confirm that all the circuits were up and running.

From across the control room, her partner yelled, "Hey, Beth, we got an earthquake or something going on here?"

She had heard the low rumble and scanned the control panel stretched across one wall of the operations room. The slight vibration felt the same as when the gates on the big dam opened, but the panel told her nothing was happening—no red lights, no amber lights. Everything looked okay. Then Beth did a double take. Something wasn't right here—*nothing moved.* All the gauges that normally oscillated and jumped were locked, frozen between the green lines on the dials.

"It doesn't feel like an earthquake, but I can't figure out what's happening." Beth swiveled in her chair to face the open window that framed the normally placid lake above the dam. The air was still. She could hear gulls squawking as they soared above a sailboat. The lake which had been placid just moments ago was roiling. The choppy waves came out of nowhere, not a breath of wind. Beth could not take her eyes off what was going on. Now the lake came to a fast boil, the swirl of a whirlpool starting to form. Beads of sweat poured down Beth's forehead as she realized that the sailboat was in trouble, for now the whole lake was moving, the waves creating a vortex centered where the boat was starting to lean precariously. She could faintly hear the screams of fear from the children on board. The surface of the lake churned as other boats also became caught up in the circular current. Beth knew these people were going to die.

Hoisting herself out of the recliner, she moved as quickly as she could across the control room. Pulling the main power switch to OFF, Beth thought about the notice that she had read three days before: "In the event of unexplained anomalies, immediately turn off all power to the equipment." She had thought at the time, "Oh sure, who's going to be the jackass that shuts down power to New England? And who's going to answer for the humongous cost of restarting the system? How likely is that?" Now, with her hand still on the switch, she thought, "Well, I guess I'm the jackass. Boy, I sure hope whoever wrote that order is there to back me up on this."

Reaching for the emergency phone she knew her efforts were too late for the small boats, capsizing and disappearing, one after another.

Far away, hands began pulling the main power switches at control stations across the continent. It was already too late in Woodhaven. The wall of water, now fifty feet high, thundered down the valley tearing through the first village below the dam, carrying away everything in its path. Jeremy's cherry red Ford Taurus station wagon had just turned left onto the bridge that separated East Woodhaven from the downtown core. The covered bridge across the lazy Woodhaven River that had served the community for over a century became instant kindling as the wave caught it. Houses, cars, people, Jeremy, his cherry red wagon, everything tumbled down the river valley, and little Chloe never did swing in the park with her dad.

In the wilds of Afghanistan, Osama bin Laden placed his hand on Kazim's shoulder and said quietly, *"Bada'a"*—it has begun.

CHAPTER 1

Not even Jim Buchan saw it coming, and he had been a spy all his life, the best in the business. It was his amateur son who ran rings around the experts, leading the race to head off the al-Qaeda disaster.

Jim, a Cold War veteran, a former senior director of the Central Intelligence Agency (known simply as 'the Agency' to those in the business), had over the years done it all, from early Cold War days in Berlin and Vienna to helping accelerate the Soviet collapse. Leigh, Jim's wife of over forty years, had accompanied him on his far-flung, often dangerous postings, and Jim had promised that when he retired they would settle in the Washington area so that she could complete her PhD degree. Leigh had done that and was now a top analyst with the Strategic Analysis Center, a prestigious strategic think tank in the Georgetown area of Washington, D.C., contracting to business and government agencies worldwide. Two of their three sons were settled on the West Coast, married with families, which included three grandchildren who filled Jim and Leigh with joy on yearly family get-togethers. Mark, their younger son, had been a happy accident, coming along after his brothers were teenagers. He had lived at home through college, and now he and Jim found themselves not only as father and son, but also as close friends.

This morning Jim and Mark would be having their weekly coffee together at their favorite café in Georgetown near Mark's office. It was a ritual they'd observed dutifully since Mark finished his postgraduate studies in computer science and moved into his own apartment a few blocks away. As Jim approached their rendezvous, he saw Mark striding toward him, a long, loping gait, arms swinging, taller than most of the pedestrians, his large horn-rimmed glasses glinting in the sun. He could have been an academic or a student, rather than the up-and-coming businessman that Jim had seen emerging over the past few years. They met at the doorway of Small Beans.

Both father and son eschewed the fashionably-branded coffee shops, to support local small business owners. Jeannie, a large, friendly woman was both owner and operator of Small Beans and her regulars came not only for the outstanding food and coffee, but for the relaxed, personal service and atmosphere. She greeted them with enthusiasm, "How y'all doing?" and "What can I get ya? The usual?"

Jeannie brought the customary chocolate scone for Mark, blueberry for Jim. Just as their steaming hot cappuccinos appeared, the door to the coffee shop swung open. Warm summer air wafted in as a very striking lady arrived on the scene, a bright smile on her face, amber eyes flashing, short auburn hair bouncing. She wore a stylish summer suit, with a shocking pink blouse, the smart attire accentuating her regal appearance. Though now in her sixties, Leigh could pass for someone twenty years younger.

Leigh had never conformed to the dark, pinstripe crowd, and today was no exception. She carried the stylish black leather brief case that Jim had given her as a graduation present, saying to her, "From now on you can carry the weight of the world." Leigh and Jim had been married for forty-five years, yet seeing her come through the door still made his heart flutter. In early years he had been slightly jealous of the attention that she elicited from every man she met. Now he was just plain proud.

"I'm on my way to a meeting and thought I'd see what I'm missing every Friday morning. Looking at the coffee and scones, maybe I'll have to lay down the law for this old guy."

"Or try some yourself, my dear. Hey, Jeannie, one non-fat extra tall latte and a cheese scone for Doctor Buchan, or I may never be allowed in here again."

She ignored the taunt, saying, "What do you two find to talk about at these weekly confabs?"

Before Jim could answer, Mark said, "Hold it a minute."

The big screen television was tuned to CNN, the sound muted. Like many customers, he'd had one eye on the news trailers running across the bottom of the screen, beside the read-out showing today was 30 June 2001, with 186 days left in the year.

"Hey, Jeannie, can you turn the sound on? We should hear this," Mark called out. He grabbed his cappuccino and walked toward the TV. The news item took only minutes, everyone watching in silence. When it was finished the room erupted, everyone talking at once.

"Well, Dad, I see that bin Laden is at it again, making more threats. After the debacle in Somalia and blowing a hole in the *USS Cole*, it's hard to imagine what might be next. What do you suppose he plans to do this time?"

People around the world had watched this latest broadcast from the Dubai station, Al Jazeera, which CNN had just relayed. As in the previous tapes, Osama bin Laden had ranted against the infidels, calling on the faithful to martyr themselves in the name of Allah. Then the talking heads, the commentators, the experts, had done the usual analysis, weighing risks, each predicting disaster, but no one really knowing what to do, what action to take. No doubt the many security agencies in the USA and abroad would crank up activity levels without really knowing where to focus.

"You know," Mark continued, "I see a lot of discussion about cyber terrorism these days. I think there's a real risk that al-Qaeda might somehow succeed in figuring a way into a critical system. Knowing what I could have done when I was only thirteen doesn't give me a lot of confidence that a determined hacker couldn't trigger a disaster."

Jim thought for a moment about what Mark had said, his memory flashing back to his own career and to Mark's childhood. "Well, I can tell you, you were already into it at a very young age, very clever, and for sure, you had me worried for quite a few years. Now, with the life that I had, you likely won't be surprised when I say that I happen to agree with you. I had an experience when you were, let's see, twelve, which makes me very skeptical about feeling too confident about security processes. Most of my ex-colleagues feel that the big advances that people like you have made in computer security systems pretty much rule out serious risks. Of course, they didn't go through what I did in '89."

"That's when you got shot, isn't it?" asked Mark. "Wasn't that about a Soviet computer virus, part of the Cold War?"

Leigh had been sitting quietly listening to the conversation, enjoying what was indeed an outstanding latte.

"Yes, Mark. In all those years of being an agent's wife, that was the worst. I guess in retrospect it was a good thing that I didn't know what was going on," she said. "It wasn't till he was on his way home on a stretcher that I even knew that something had happened."

"It was a KGB operation," explained Jim. "Just at the tail end of a long and complicated era. It might have been called the Cold War, but sometimes it was way too hot! With this episode it's not widely known how close we came to financial disaster. The guy who organized it was a KGB computer genius named Kazim. I had the misfortune of meeting him at the receiving end of his gun. He's the one who shot me. He called his operation лук, which is Russian for *onion*. That was the KGB code word for the file. It was a fitting name, because each layer that we peeled off revealed another layer. When we found one answer it only led to another question. At the time I thought that whoever allocated code words to their operations had a sense of the dramatic. It was only later that I learned that Kazim had named it himself. A bit risky on his part, but I guess too subtle for his KGB colleagues at the time."

"Why's that?" Mark asked.

"It turns out that Kazim's 'onion' was his secret reference to the onion domes on Islamic mosques, his way to pay homage to the religion that he was not permitted to practice, and his way of silently stating that he was doing this for Islam. None of us, not in the Soviet Union nor in Washington, were aware then that religious fanatics like Kazim were going to emerge by the thousands in the not too distant future."

"As a kid I can remember hearing whispered references to 'the Onion.' I could never figure out what you and Mom were talking about."

"Well, that was it," Jim said, taking a sip of his cappuccino. "Kazim had designed his computer program so that, once started, no one would be able to stop it, to peel it apart. I suppose this is all still classified, but what he did was design a virus-like worm that would go into banking systems. He used a hack, a ruse, to get passwords from bank managers and then inserted a worm. When activated, it would have erased data throughout the financial world. Remember, this was in the late '80s, with banking system security in its infancy. Heck, most people weren't even aware that there could be a breach that could infect across the entire network, passed from one machine to the next."

"I can understand that," Mark added. "Even today most people are pretty blasé about security on their own computers."

"Kazim's bug would have migrated through credit card depositories and the banking system, then through the major companies. It would have erased financial files worldwide."

They were silent for a minute, reflecting on how close to financial disaster the capitalist system had come.

"Thank goodness that threat was foiled," Leigh said. "But in the reports I'm now reading, there's no doubt that the world is still a dangerous place, with different dangers, perhaps less predictable, and coming from so many parts of the world."

"Yes, because the old Soviet Union tended to keep the lid on their part of the map. It kept a lot of anger and frustration bottled up," Jim agreed.

Leigh continued. "I've just read a report on Islamic terrorism. There are several good analysts examining the whole issue, but they aren't getting much traction in official circles. The group I'm with would agree with you, Mark. We think we are at substantive risk, but we have no idea where. There are just too many possibilities."

By this time they had finished their coffee. Leigh suggested, "It's a beautiful summer day out there. Let's cross to the park where we can talk for a while. I want to hear where you two think this is going."

Jim signaled Jeannie for the bill, but she shook her head saying, "Catch you next time."

She gave a wave, smiling and called to Leigh, "So now you know their secret! I'll expect to see you with them on Fridays."

Leigh was right. The park was indeed beautiful, some of the trees still in bloom, temperature climbing to 74 degrees, the sun streaming through the foliage. As they walked toward a bench Mark was deep in thought.

"You know," he said reflectively, "one of the first ever computer viruses was in the banking system, so you must have been in on these threats right at the beginning, Dad. If I recall correctly, the first virus was for changing a system to fix it, at a university in the mid-'80s. Kazim's would have been one of the first viruses, in this case a Trojan, to get the passwords. The worm would have been the one he plugged in, awaiting the 'go code' to destroy the system. Dad, you have to admit you aren't exactly a world class nerd, so how did it happen that you were there before anyone had begun to think about worms and viruses? I'd sure like to hear about that."

Jim and Leigh settled on a bench and Mark perched on a rock, while nearby a couple of swans swam lazily on the small pond, their reflections shimmering on the smooth water.

"Hmm, and, you know, I'd like to be able to tell you everything," Jim replied. "It is a pretty good story, but I don't expect that those files will be declassified for years, if ever. The Onion revealed huge vulnerabilities in our financial systems, some of them too close for comfort. Some heads still around would roll if those files were released. Maybe even worse. Our whole system for doing business would need a major overhaul. Keep this confidential: I never understood the details, but I was told that what Kazim did was replace the transport communications protocol—"

"—Yeah, some call it the transmission control protocol. It's TCP in the business."

"Well, okay. He replaced the TCP in the computers of bank managers so that it would trap accounts and passwords. It was so dangerous, especially when we learned that he had sold the hack to others, that we had the industry generate a 'cert,' a warning, to all UNIX users."

"Well, it's not as if his hack would have been that difficult. I can see how he could have done it. A worm is a program that has the ability to copy itself from machine to machine. They move around and infect other machines through computer networks, in the case of your Onion, the financial system. He would have set it to go off, pulled the trigger, by entering a password through a port, a door into the system. As the worm replicated itself, it would have destroyed the data. Pretty sophisticated for those days, but definitely doable. You're lucky you caught it."

"That's for sure, and it was luck." After a pause, Jim added, "The other aspect that's still classified is my role in the whole affair. I wound up dealing directly with the enemy, the Soviet Union, long before it became fashionable."

"We're going to have to figure out a way for me to get that story!" Mark was thoughtful. "So, if Kazim could do it then, why aren't we worried now? It seems to me that, as networked technology reaches into more and more of everyone's lives, there is even more opportunity to create chaos."

"Some of us are worried," replied Leigh. "In the business you're in, you'd know better than I, but I think people feel safe now because of the closed systems that are used for the really critical infrastructure programs."

"Yeah, I guess that's true," Mark conceded. "If only authorized people can get into the systems, that does protect them from outside attack. No one's supposed to be able to break in from outside."

"At least that's the theory," said Jim. "But you know, Mark, that's exactly what the experts were saying in '89, and it still happened. Even on the inside, in closed systems, it's possible for a determined adversary to find an opening, and people like Kazim and the terrorists are determined! Unfortunately, in my time, we had several bastards who were on the inside. All with full security clearances, in as tightly closed a system as we could devise. So we still wound up with the occasional disaster. Some of the big ones have become public knowledge, like Aldrich Ames and the FBI's Robert Hanson—or Walker, the guy that let the Russians know about our submarine cable taps. These people cost the lives of some of our best agents, our most valuable spies, or compromised really good, hard-won technical intelligence. It took us years to build those foundations, to lay the groundwork for those networks, to develop the technology and put it in place, and they were gone just like that." Jim snapped his fingers.

"And, Dad, you people were paranoid about security. I've always wondered how anyone could get away with spying in an outfit that went to such pains to protect its secrets."

"One thing I learned over the years is that even with the best security arrangements that anyone can dream up, a determined enemy will eventually succeed in breaking in. People get into a routine and forget to be vigilant. Moreover, all the security checking in the world can't always get around human nature—greed, love, sex, philosophy, maybe even more important these days, religion and ideology. It is certainly these last two, religion and ideology, that are the drivers for the Islamic fundamentalists, for bin Laden and his thousands of disciples. Even knowing the root causes that create spies doesn't prevent people from falling into traps. Of course, the terrorists we are facing are fanatic; they don't need lures to trap them to do what they do. The bottom line is that I learned long ago not to underestimate a determined enemy."

"Yes, that's for sure. Certainly, spies have been around forever, from ancient history to today," Mark noted. "And it wouldn't be the first time that religion and ideology have got in the act. Al-Qaeda even refers to us as the new crusaders."

"The intelligence papers I'm looking at these days worry me," Leigh added. "The fundamentalists are adding more converts every day. The madrassas are churning out disciples whose only education is the Koran and hatred of the West."

"Mark, I'm more than a little skeptical about anyone who says infiltration can't be done today. When I think about the wide range of support that al-Qaeda has generated in so much of the Islamic world, it really scares me. Muslim fundamentalism used to be concentrated in the Middle East, but now the hatred extends worldwide. Bin Laden has done a good job in spreading the word, in calling out to the faithful in terms that generate hatred—enough hatred to turn them into martyrs for the cause. They've got a lot of committed people out there working to cause us harm."

"I'd agree with you, Dad, at least on the computer side of things. As the systems become more complex, the experts and the hackers just keep dreaming up new stuff. Also, the complexity itself makes it more difficult to plug all the holes. It's becoming more challenging by the day. The large systems have to do upgrades almost on a daily basis. If the systems had stayed with UNIX it probably would have been easier to debug the code, but the new systems introduced dynamic link libraries. It makes it really difficult to debug now—and it's just that difficulty that generates business for a consultant like me. It's the challenge of making sure that systems are secure that earns me the big bucks I'm now raking in."

"For sure," Jim replied. It never ceased to amaze Jim that his geeky, computer-crazed son was now earning more than he ever had with the Agency. "Things have certainly worked out well for you. Your business seems to be going like gangbusters. I guess the downside is that you haven't got time to enjoy that rocket you got yourself," Jim said with a twinkle in his eye.

"That's true, but I do get out for a drive in it occasionally. I was doing fine, with a lot of work from industry, but now I'm even getting some big government contracts, work that was always done in house. It never used to be done by contractors."

"Apparently, all the security agencies have been cut to the bone. They can't do everything in house anymore."

"You know, Dad, maybe I'll have some fun, play around with this a bit. Revisit my teen years and do a little hacking myself. Any suggestions where I should look, where I should start?"

A mother with twin children had stopped and was throwing bread crumbs to the swans, the kids laughing with delight as the heads on graceful necks bobbed in stately fashion for the goodies. All three Buchans were lost in thought in the midst of the tranquil beauty of the scene. Jim broke the silence.

"Well, if I were al-Qaeda I'd be looking at our infrastructure, maybe take a lesson from the Soviets and hit us where it hurts—in the pocketbook. But then again, these guys, the terrorists, want to see death and destruction on TV. If they were going to do something I'd put my money on infrastructure operating systems, systems that could cause real damage if they got derailed."

"Maybe industry, like nuclear plants?"

"I'd agree, and I'm sure that they are a target. But because they would be so attractive to terrorists, they're watched pretty closely these days. They'd be hard to break into, although that's everyone's worst nightmare. Maybe the transportation system, but it's so decentralized that it would be really difficult to coordinate a major disaster. Certainly, they could play havoc with local areas, like a city subway."

Jim smiled as he watched Leigh's note pad getting fuller and fuller. She had been doodling from the beginning of the conversation and he could see circles and boxes linked by lines as she captured the conversation, diagramming infrastructure, underlining vulnerabilities. She had been listening with interest, not wanting to break into the dialogue between father and son, but now she looked at her husband and said, "You've been reading the papers I'm working on. The meeting I'm on my way to is to discuss the vulnerability of our infrastructure. Mark, I tend to agree. I think we are at risk. We don't do a whole lot to protect our systems."

By now she was visibly excited. "We've looked at the whole range of infrastructure, starting with the financial side of things because I knew about your experience in '89, Jim. Even a cursory examination of the transportation system shows how very vulnerable it could be: trains, subways, tunnels, ships. Thousands of containers go in and out daily, cruise ships traveling the world. Air traffic is huge, arrivals from everywhere. Finding a common thread in any of it really is looking for the needle in the haystack. I think you'd have to narrow it down, one sector, or one component of a system. For example, how about the electrical grid? You remember the blackout in New York a while back, and that was just a minor screw up, just finger trouble."

"Hmm, can you imagine what would happen if al-Qaeda could figure a way into the power grid? Man, that would do some serious damage."

Jim added, "It would take pretty clever planning to find a way into the system. There'd have to be vulnerability, some central common denominator, which would cause more than just major inconvenience, like in the last power failure. I feel certain that the terrorists are looking for a way to see American blood and guts on television. It would take more than just the lights going out to satisfy their holy war."

Mark's face lit up with the challenge. "I could run programs to monitor sectors, look for anomalies across systems, find a link. What about the hydroelectric dams? Turning off the power *and* flooding the areas downstream. That would sure get people's attention!"

"Yeah, I guess if I were bin Laden I'd find myself a guy like Kazim and set him loose to figure out how to hijack the system," Jim agreed.

"Dad, your old outfit is surely working on that kind of stuff. With the emphasis we have on security everywhere, I can't imagine that the experts aren't on top of it."

"Oh, they'll be working on it, I'm sure, but all the resources in the world can't cover all the bases all the time. It is all about minimizing the risk with the available resources."

"Maybe I'll play around a bit, just to satisfy my curiosity." Mark was clearly excited by his self-imposed challenge. "Yeah, I think I'll give it a go, see if I pick anything up. You know, not knowing what you're looking for is half the fun of hacking."

"Well, if you are going to do some looking I'd start by surveying various systems to see which ones cover enough infrastructure, ones that would have a wide enough impact if they went off the rails. If al-Qaeda is going to do it, they'll want to do it big and dramatic."

"I'll do that, set up some programs to track some systems, see what I can find."

"Let me know how you make out, Mark. I must say, though, that I genuinely hope you don't come up with anything. The destruction those terrorists want is almost too scary to contemplate."

"Don't hold your breath. This could take some time. See you in a bit, folks."

Mark was lost in thought as they left the park. Leigh watched her son climb into his brand new, shiny black Corvette. "You know, my husband, our son is kind of like those swans over there, serene and unruffled on top, but peddling like Hell underneath."

As Mark accelerated away from the curb, Jim and Leigh continued to marvel at how their son was driving the car of Jim's own dreams, and at the tender age of twenty-four.

CHAPTER 2

Almost a month later, Mark casually scrolled down his computer screen. He had been getting casual about it, but still had done it every day since talking with Jim about cyber terrorism, searching for anything that his scanners might find that would indicate vulnerability. Banks of computers whirred softly, the heavyweight air conditioning package needed to cool the array making more noise than the machines doing the work.

Mark didn't conform to the popular image of a hacker. He was one of the new generation of Washington specialists. Knowing that in the computer security business he couldn't let the hippie inside escape, he had to settle for an elegant casual look if he wanted to get the big contracts that he was drawing in. His auburn hair and mustache were neatly trimmed, the glasses giving him an I'm-a-serious-guy look. He wore slimline DKNY jeans, an open-neck white shirt, loafers, with socks; his only concession to the corporate world a blue blazer hung on the coat rack ready for any unexpected summons or visitor. He was relaxed and easygoing, classical music playing softly in the background in both his condo and office, leaving customers impressed with a sense of quiet competence and confidence.

Perhaps because his dad had been really closed-mouthed about his career over the years, Mark decided that he'd have to find out for himself what Jim did in that secret world. He had always enjoyed reading and read widely, but particularly any history to do with the Cold War. As a clever and precocious teenager, it didn't take him long to figure out that few secrets could survive some subtle hacking, and from then on the computer really captured Mark's attention. As the internet started to catch on and more closed systems linked in, he found that he didn't have to wait for the history books to be written. He could read history on his screen as it happened, not exactly what his dad did every day but at least the broad outlines of US actions as the Cold War evolved.

That was likely why girl friends didn't last long. With his lanky good looks and eye-catching head of auburn hair, they latched onto him with high hopes. But most couldn't stand the concentration and attention that he lavished on what really turned him on. They lost him to the computer screen while twiddling their thumbs. In recent years, some had been encouraged by a beef fillet on his barbeque accompanied by a smooth Shiraz, only to have their hopes crumble when Mark disappeared behind their rival, his huge array of machines.

Mark always kept up a running dialogue with himself when he was hacking, but now his voice was loud and excited. "Aw, this can't be!" he muttered, as he reran the logs on his screen. He reached for the phone. "Hey, Dad, you've got to come over and see something. I don't know what to make of this!"

"Why? What's up?"

"Well, you know I'm still working on tracking systems, trying to see if there is a chink in the armor, and I may have found something."

Jim Buchan had always been proud of his son's expertise with computers, although in earlier years he had been a bit concerned about the hacking. He knew too many stories in the past of the havoc that hackers could cause. He smiled as he remembered Mark saying to him years ago, "Don't worry, I'm a white-hat hacker, a netizen, one of the good guys."

"So I assume that's as opposed to a black hat—the bad guys?"

"Yeah, they're script kiddies for the most part," Mark had said with a smile.

Jim knew that Mark had taken their conversation about cyber-terrorism to heart and was looking for back doors that might place programs at risk. When Mark called, he had an inkling that something important was going on.

"I'm on my way."

A half hour later he was at Mark's Georgetown condo.

"Hey, Mark, I should have known better than to think you would forget to follow up on our discussion in June about cyber terror. I'd guess from your call that your hacking must have borne fruit. It's been what, a month or so? I was just starting to relax. To tell you the truth I had almost stopped worrying about it."

"Well, I must say that I was devoting less attention to it until I ran some logs this morning."

"Okay. Let's have a look."

As they entered Mark's home office, Jim again marveled at the equipment that filled the room. Every space was bulging with computers and parts, lines running into a rack of routers, lights blinking everywhere, each array alive with activity, a virtual cornucopia of processing power.

"Careful of those cables—they're all over the place."

"You're telling me!"

Mark picked up a voltage tester and motherboard from a chair, depositing them on a stack of technical books to clear a spot for Jim to sit down.

"You've added a fair bit since I was here last. How in the world do you keep track of all this stuff? You must be able to talk to the world from here. Jeez, Mark, it looks like the ops room at the Johnson Space Center."

"Well, this is my rec room. It's where I have my fun. From here I talk to friends, people in the business, whatever. The real work gets done at the office. I can't begin to spend the time at work that real hacking takes and, believe me, I've spent a lot of time in here since we spoke last month."

"I can believe it. And I guess since the break-up with Alicia, you've had lots of time."

"Dad, I'm over Alicia. It was great while it lasted, but she wasn't the girl for me."

"I must admit your mother and I are not sorry to see her go. We were getting a bit concerned about how serious you might be about her. I expect that maybe she'll miss your Corvette more than she'll miss you."

"Okay, okay, down to business. I don't think you're going to like this. I took your advice and left the nuclear stuff alone. I started by researching systems with central controllers, and I couldn't find much in the transportation sector. Someone who really worked at it could probably find some vulnerabilities, but they'd likely be localized."

"I'm not surprised, and that's why the local authorities everywhere worry about it. Even so, though, not a whole lot of security dollars are thrown that way, and the municipalities sure can't afford to cover all the bases."

"So, from there I looked at the electrical generating and distribution system. Across the country the whole thing is huge. The distribution grid is so complex that it's hard to imagine anyone being able to hijack enough of it to cause extensive damage, although it could be done. We saw that in the feedback loop, the power outage that we spoke of that caused such havoc across the eastern US and Canada. That is what got me thinking that it wouldn't be too hard to generate an outage like that if you knew the grid. There'd be lots of local, even widespread, disruption, but not the blood and guts on TV that you spoke about. On the other hand, a quick overview of the major hydroelectric dams convinced me that Mom's idea could be right on the mark. I started taking a serious look at how the whole thing works."

"So, you have my attention. What have you found?" Jim asked. "And don't tell me that in all that mess you found a common denominator."

"Well, I think maybe I did. The dams are almost all independent, operated by a whole range of different agencies, businesses and independent operators. Not surprisingly, they all use similar engineering to generate the power. There are many computer programs to run the equipment, to operate the dams and the turbine generators."

"So, it wouldn't be too easy for anyone to gain enough control to make a catastrophic difference?"

"That's certainly what you'd think. It took me a while, but it turns out that a company in California has the contract to supply and maintain the software that operates a fair number of the generating stations, by my best guess maybe about 40 percent of our hydroelectric capacity. What really caught my attention is that the ones controlled by this outfit include the big dams out West. The systems are pretty well automated. The company that handles this set of dams has got the software market sewn up, with a sole-source contract. Operating a dam is pretty complex and there's no demand for the programs other than from the generating stations, so there's not much competition. It is a common denominator in what is otherwise a real hodgepodge, and it seems to me that if someone could gain control of that software, they could do just as you said, they could hijack that part of the system."

Jim's thoughts were running ahead. "I would guess the company that has the software contract must be pretty closely monitored, given how critical the infrastructure is. All the staff would need security clearance and the company would be monitored and audited regularly. Still, that doesn't make it foolproof. What is it that you've come across that makes you suspicious?"

"Well, I set up a bank of computers to scan and log activity. They've been running for a while now, and when I checked through the records I noticed that a port opened for one minute at midnight. I ran it again last night and, sure enough, the same thing."

Jim blurted out, "Don't tell me. It wasn't Port 5000, was it?"

Mark looked at his father in astonishment. "Dad, you amaze me. How in the world would you know that? It's not as if you're into computers! … But, of course, you saw it in '89, didn't you?"

"I sure did. That's exactly what Kazim did with the Onion!"

"From your description when we spoke about all this, I thought I'd see if I could find the kind of anomaly that might do what you suggested, provide a key to the back door. It looks like I might have found just that."

As Mark scrolled through his screen, it didn't take Jim long to recognize that something was seriously wrong. He couldn't believe what he was seeing. There it was, over and over on the screens in front of him, Port 5000 on each of the computers controlling the dams, open for one minute at midnight, two nights in a row.

"Mark, I saw this more than a decade ago. It's like my past coming back to haunt me. This is really alarming."

Jim recognized the configuration that became the Onion File, which had come so close to bringing unimaginable financial disaster, and so close to killing him. He could not know that he was about to see history rerun, with all the same risks, twists and intrigue.

CHAPTER 3

Early on in Jim's career, it hadn't taken the Agency long to realize that Jim Buchan was not cut out to succeed in the undercover side of things. It wasn't only his size and his appearance that made him stand out. At just over 6 feet and 190 pounds, with rugged good looks, he didn't easily blend into a crowd. The real challenge was that when it came to one on one, it wasn't going to work. It was his eyes that gave him away. Anyone paying attention was struck by the intensity that burned in that blue-gray gaze. He projected a sense of strength and confidence that caused people to take a second look—and that second look sent the message that this quiet man could walk through brick walls. For the good guys, for friends, that toughness generated trust and confidence. But for adversaries the result was caution and fear.

His hair now silver gray, Jim was still in the same solid physical condition as when he had joined the Agency all those years ago, his appearance only enhanced by the age lines that had developed over the last few years. He had put on a few pounds toward the end of his career in the spy world, but now that he was retired he was working his way back to his old fighting weight. After wearing a shirt, tie and jacket just about every day since university, to his surprise Jim now felt very comfortable in jeans, loafers and tee shirts. Of course, Leigh did the shopping and she made sure that these casual clothes were smart and right up there with the latest trends.

Jim had always been a man of few words, almost to the point of being taciturn, but colleagues had learned early on that, when he spoke those few words, they should listen. He had worked his way through the Agency ranks and had been recognized as an analyst who cut through the bullshit, who called it like it was, and an operations guy who did not hesitate on the front lines. The slight limp that he had inherited from his encounter with Kazim in '89 was hardly noticeable, but it had put a stop to the tennis and squash that he had played regularly since high school. Now he had to work to stay fit. Every morning after Leigh left for work, Jim went through a thorough workout routine in the gym he and Leigh had added to their home, looking out to the Potomac River.

They had met while she was still in university. Jim was doing a stint as a recruiter at the eastern universities. He hadn't convinced Leigh to join the Agency, but they often joked that while he may have been a failure as a recruiter for spies, he had been one hell of a success in recruiting a wife. Jim knew from the moment that she walked in for the interview that this was a girl he wanted to know—smiling, eyes sparkling, confident, full of life, auburn hair cut short, a tall girl, maybe five-ten, irreverent enough to catch his attention. It didn't take long to establish that she had filled out the forms and gone through the application process as a lark, a challenge, one that she had no intention of pursuing.

"So tell me, Miss O'Reilly, why did you apply and come for this interview if you had no intention of accepting a potential offer?"

"I was curious. Some of my friends were doing it and I thought I'd have a look."

"And what did you find?"

"No surprises. You have a reputation for hiring good people, and your selection process should produce them for you, but it's not for me."

Jim looked at her thoughtfully and made the type of decision that he later became known for throughout the Agency, bold and direct. "I expect I might get fired for this, but I won't tell if you won't. I have your phone number right here in the file, so let's pretend I'm asking you for it. How about I give you a call?"

"And may I presume this call would not be to continue the interview, Mr. Buchan?"

"That would be correct. It would be to ask you for a date. How about dinner and a movie?"

And the answer came, just that quick: "I accept."

They had been together ever since.

In his last position before he retired Jim had been so busy that Leigh had taken the opportunity to fulfill a lifelong dream. Her dissertation to complete her PhD was on the use of open-source literature to assess threats, and she was now one of the foremost experts, heading the risk analysis section of a small outfit that rivaled Henry Kissinger's lucrative group. She thoroughly enjoyed the work and the change from being known and respected as Jim's wife to being sought after in her own right. Leigh's effervescent personality had always stood her in good stead. Jim credited her with the happy family life that they had enjoyed, and he knew that her discrete support had not hurt his own career either. She was a happy, optimistic woman, still good-looking, still passionate in their lovemaking. "I sure am one lucky s.o.b. that's for sure. How could I have been so fortunate?"

This morning as he walked uphill on the treadmill, Jim's thoughts ranged over the irony of Mark's discovery. He was almost afraid to think where it might lead. Could Mark be right? In his heart he knew the answer. He had seen it all before.

Since his retirement, he and Leigh had settled into a very pleasant life. He was thrilled to see Leigh doing so well, loving her work and her stature as an independent researcher and analyst, and he knew that after all the years of tension over his work, with a constant concern for his safety, she was now at ease, happy to see him quiet and at home. Where was Mark's computer research leading them?

When he retired, they had discussed whether they should scale down from the home that they had bought forty-three years before, the home in which they had raised their three sons. With Mark now gone, did it make any sense to stay in such a big house? They had bought what had been a rambling cottage on the Potomac River north of McLean, Virginia, close enough for Jim's commute to the office. In fact, in his early years before gridlock traffic and an official car and driver, Jim had ridden his bike to work. The place had been ideal for the kids' schools, in an area that then was somewhat run-down. Like many of the new owners in the area at the time, Jim and Leigh couldn't afford to build anew, so they had renovated the house continuously, improving it little by little until now they had an old-world, gracious home with all the modern amenities, a little enclave of country living with easy access to the city. Over the years the family had spent many of their best hours relaxing and talking on the deck, with the tranquil view across parkland to the river as a backdrop.

The mortgage was paid off, the equity huge. He smiled to himself. The only reason that they had even considered buying the place was because Leigh had just received a small inheritance from her grandmother, enough to cover the down payment, and they had fallen in love with it before they had even got through the front door. When they had bought the property as youngsters all those years ago, everyone thought they were nuts. It had meant going in debt for a place far beyond their means, but over the years of frugal living they had loved ever minute spent there. And it had turned out to be their anchor, even as Jim's moves made them gypsies, roving from posting to posting, wherever the job took them. Now the house was the best investment they could ever have made, prime real estate in a sought-after neighborhood.

Besides, the place had played a starring role in Jim's career, not intended or planned, certainly not anticipated, and in retrospect humorous in the way that it had focused the limelight on him. In the '60s, on Jim's posting to Germany, they rented the house to a pleasant young couple, professionals, he a scientist, she a business consultant, both recently out of a Czechoslovakia in turmoil. About six months after their return from their posting in Berlin, Leigh decided to renovate the bedroom and en suite bathroom. She won the argument about changing the location of the sink and toilet, even though it meant opening walls and floors to redirect the plumbing. Jim wasn't concerned about the work; they had a good contractor and, no question, this was Leigh's domain. Jim's interest was casual. He knew that when it was finished it would be just what Leigh envisioned.

When she insisted on showing him the project, he reluctantly stepped over the debris in the bedroom to see the progress. It was April 4, 1966, but Jim recalled the conversation as if it had happened yesterday.

“Just a minute. We can’t see a thing in this light. I’ll turn on the extension. This is going to be great, Jim. You just wait till you see the finished product!”

Walking in the glare of the work light, Jim suddenly stopped dead in his tracks. He was in the business and had seen with his own eyes the arrangements for secretly wiring a room, the concealed wire that snaked where no wires had a right to be. He grabbed Leigh by the arm, a finger to his lips as he led her out the door to the patio.

Leigh was flabbergasted. “What are you doing?”

“Now that I see it, I guess I should have thought of the possibility. We’ve been had big time. The place has been bugged.”

“What do you mean bugged? How could that be?”

“I expect it was on our last posting, that beautiful young couple. I’ll bet the bad guys were just waiting for the opportunity. I’ll arrange to get the place swept tomorrow. Tonight we’ll act as if nothing is wrong.”

Leigh started giggling. “Well, they sure wasted their time and effort here! You wouldn’t betray a secret if your life depended on it, not even to a passionate lady who looks after your every desire. Whoever had the misfortune of having to listen to those tapes must have demanded a bonus to make it worthwhile!”

“That’s true. I guess it is kind of funny, isn’t it,” Jim admitted.

He walked to the neighbor’s and used their phone.

“Roberto, it’s Jim Buchan.”

“Yes, sir, what’s up?” Roberto was that shift’s duty officer in the Ops Center 24/7 watch.

“Roberto, I’m calling from my neighbor’s house. I need you to arrange a sweep of my whole place. Unfortunately it looks as if the house has been wiretapped.”

“What’s happened? What do you mean?”

“We’re doing some renos and I see wires where there shouldn’t be any wires, and they aren’t 14/2 electrical wires I can tell you!”

“Okay, sir, I’ll call the team right now. Then I’ll call back to let you know what time to expect them.”

"Great. I expect the whole place is wired so tell them that it'll take several hours."

At four o'clock the next afternoon the phone rang in Jim's office. It was Roberto. "They did the sweep. This one will go down in the books, the most thorough job they've ever seen. The whole house was fully wired for sound with bugs in every room."

"Still working?"

"No, the main power feed to the bugs had been cut where the wall was opened for the new pipes."

"Good, that makes my next decision a lot easier. Many thanks, Roberto."

The summons was waiting for Jim when he arrived at the office the next morning: 'The Director of Operations, 9:00 a.m.'

Jim was there, outside the office at 8:50, and at 9:00 sharp the door opened.

"Come on in, Jim." The senior Agency staff was seated around the table.

After brief introductions the boss led off. "So, Jim, I understand you had some excitement in your life yesterday. This is an interesting report that we've just read," he noted, putting down a file folder.

"Yes, sir, it is." With a twinkle in his eye Jim continued, "I expect that all of you are on their list, but your homes are likely swept regularly, so in desperation they're really stooping low."

Then, as the director started to speak, Jim interrupted, saying, "Sir, I would like to say something before we start." Jim glanced around the table, taking in the looks of surprise at this young officer's gall, cutting off the boss in mid-sentence.

Then, after a pause, the director said with a smile, "Okay. Let's hear it."

"Gentlemen, I've thought about this all night, what I'm sure you are going to talk to me about. When I learned about the bugs the first thing that came into my mind was the opportunity we have at hand. We leave the bugs in place and feed the bastards whatever we want them to believe, but I can tell you that was only for a split second. There's no way that I'd subject my family to that. Can you imagine asking my wife and kids to live in that kind of a fishbowl, knowing that their every word would be heard in Moscow? I don't think so. In fact, I know we aren't going to do it."

The silence around the conference table was stunning, although it only lasted seconds as Jim held his breath.

Dennis, the senior analyst, broke the ice. "Besides, folks, they're smarter than that. They'll know that the house is torn up with the renovations and that the wires would likely be seen. Even if they didn't, they'd recognize a change in your patterns and they'd know something was up."

"Sir, that's the only thing that makes my decision easier for me to live with. It turns out that the power was cut a few days ago, so the listeners know that we're off line and examining the house. Reconnecting their lines and coming back on now would be pretty transparent."

This time there was no hesitation. The director ended the discussion. "Well, Jim, you're right on the money. That is just what we had in mind, what we were about to propose. But you've made your case and it sounds reasonable. Gentlemen, why don't I just let our Soviet friends know that we know what they've done, that we've caught them in the act and that it's one strike against them toward the next round of diplomatic expulsions?"

As heads nodded around the table, Jim was dismissed with a "thank you."

As he left the room, the door closing behind him, Jim heard the director laugh and say, "Now there is a young man that we'll have to watch. That took some guts, and did you see those eyes? You don't argue with him!"

Without Leigh's renos, they would have been living in the fishbowl for decades. Jim smiled to himself, remembering their talk. The discussion about whether to sell the house had not lasted long. They loved the place and besides, it carried some interesting baggage that no other home could ever match. When he looked out the window from his treadmill, Jim knew they had made the right decision.

As he worked up a sweat, his mind roamed over that period in his career that had been on the front lines of Cold War action, action that could not be shared fully with Leigh or his kids. But Leigh had understood his motivation from the start, even before she had committed to a life with him. After the first couple of dates, she knew that he was a complex man, devoted to his life with the Agency. He recalled the wonder of the first time they made love, nothing tentative about her, and afterwards the deep questioning, no beating around the bush.

"So, you big, gentle giant, what is it that drives you to such zeal? If I'm going to spend my life with you, I need to know that you'll be coming home occasionally from God knows where."

They had talked for hours, Jim putting into words thoughts that until then had been unfocused, in his subconscious, since he was a kid when his father hadn't come home from the war. His mother had told him what she knew, which wasn't much. He had to read between the lines of the little that had been released about Wild Bill Donovan and his Office of Strategic Services. All he knew was that his father had died in occupied France and he could only guess at what that meant. When the CIA was formed from the remnants of the OSS, Jim knew what he wanted to do, and a quiet overture made at university was immediately accepted.

Now as he finished his fast walk on the treadmill, his sweating face clouded over as he thought about what Mark was discovering. Jim knew that Leigh was not going to be pleased with him putting himself on the line yet again, this time with their youngest son at his side.

CHAPTER 4

Two months before the 9/11 World Trade Center tragedy, on the other side of the world, a fateful event took place, one that would inadvertently set the stage for a separate al-Qaeda attack.

"Cobra Two, break left, break left, chaff, chaff go. Stargazer, this is Cobra Lead, over."

"Go ahead, Cobra."

"Stargazer, Cobra has a visual on the launch. They're firing at us. We've got missiles on the way, with our names on 'em."

In a heartbeat, the quiet atmosphere of boredom on board the big airborne command center, the AWACS, switched to excited action. As it circled at 35,000 feet over the Arabian Peninsula, the dozen operators received an unbelievable view on the screens that covered a good portion of the Middle East. This big airplane was there any time there was action, serving as the eyes and ears of the fighter aircraft that were taking the brunt of any trigger-happy Iraqi gunners.

Lieutenant Sheila Alverez, the radar controller on the screen focused on southern Iraq, spoke into her headset. "Cobra, affirmative, we see it on our screens." She watched as the fighters curved rapidly to the left, taking evasive action, the chaff trailing behind to distract the missiles coming at them.

"Stand by one, Stargazer. Okay, we've got it wired. They're smoking by us on the right. Am I cleared in live?"

Lieutenant Alverez's response was immediate, the rules of engagement clear: if fired on, shoot back. "Affirmative, Cobra, go get 'em."

"Cobra's in live. Cobra Two, take the right complex. I'll go after the building on the left."

The crew in Stargazer waited anxiously for the call to come.

"Okay, Stargazer, Cobras are off the target. Two good hits. We're bingo and headed home."

"Roger that, Cobra. Have a good day. Stargazer out."

Lieutenant Alverez had flown dozens of missions. She had done many dry runs, computer-generated on her screen, but this was the first live engagement. Her clenched fists were white; sweat ran from her brow and down her chest, soaking her bra through to her blouse. The guy on the consol next to her watched the tension, and said laconically, "Kinda exciting, isn't it?"

He was a retired US Air Force staff sergeant, now on contract with one of the many high tech companies that supplied the sophisticated equipment that made it possible to watch Cobra Flight's close call. He had spent his life looking at radar screens, and had seen this kind of action a long time ago on comparatively primitive equipment.

"You know, back in the Cold War days, I was a young fighter controller in Europe. My little screen covered about a hundred miles of the East German border, fuzzy enough so that I could hardly see the blips, the little green dots that were live returns from the radar signals. Nothing like what you have here today, Lieutenant, computer-processed, all the garbage removed. Our job then was twofold, first to try to pick up any bad guys trying to sneak across the 25-mile buffer, the 'no-fly zone' that we had established on our side of the border. Maybe even more importantly for our fighter jocks, it was to warn our own fighters when they were getting in harm's way. Radio and navigation aids didn't come close to what you're used to, and the jet stream often was stronger than forecast. It didn't take much for a young pilot to find himself blown much further east than he could imagine. And the Ruskies helped."

Lieutenant Alverez listened with interest. She was new to the game but had heard some pretty hairy stories of things that had gone on in the early days of confrontation—the Berlin Airlift, reconnaissance flights penetrating the Iron Curtain, probing at the borders. "What do you mean, the Russians helped?"

"They used to beam high-powered radio signals into NATO airspace, signals that overrode our own navigation and radio frequencies, to trick a pilot into believing that he was heading home when he was actually being lured across the border. Our young jocks sometimes found themselves close to disaster because the Russians shot down anything that strayed over the line. I actually saw it happen. I'll never forget. I kept calling on the emergency frequency, trying to turn him back, but he just didn't get the message. Then the MIG streaked up on my screen and, zap, my little blip, a real live fighter pilot in an F-84 jet disappeared off the radar. Lieutenant, we got away easy today."

The two F-16s had launched their laser-guided 500-pound Mark 82 Snakeye bombs, rolled up and off the targets and, their fuel at a minimum, headed for home, another mission over the no-fly zone in southern Iraq successfully completed.

Cobra Flight's experience was just one of many in a long line of skirmishes in Iraqi skies. After Desert Storm, when the coalition forces had thrown Iraq's army out of Kuwait, no-fly areas had been unilaterally set up by the US in both northern and southern Iraq. The term 'no-fly' referred to Iraqi aircraft, to ensure both that Saddam Hussein did not resume his territorial ambitions and that his military capabilities were kept in check. These zones were patrolled regularly by US and British war planes to ensure compliance. As time went on, Iraq tested the Allied resolve by first turning on their target acquisition radars, and then went further by actually firing missiles and anti-aircraft guns at the patrolling fighters. It didn't take many near misses to convince the US to shoot back. After a few years of this, intelligence analysts began to wonder about the decision-making process in the Iraqi Command. Why would any commander order offensive action when the result was assured destruction? And yet the response and the destruction continued. Cobra's excitement that day was just one of many skirmishes in an ongoing exercise of bombing practice for the American and British pilots, and suicide for the Iraqis.

This Cobra mission took place well before 9/11, at a time when the US still felt secure in its borders, when suicide bombers and explosions were confined to TV pictures of far-away places.

What no one involved in the intensity of the patrols that day could foresee, though, were the unintended consequences of Cobra Flight's success, for in that building on the left, David MacIntyre's father and three brothers were having lunch. Unbeknownst to the world, their deaths would complete Dave's conversion to the al-Qaeda cause. Dave MacIntyre was vulnerable, his emotions still in embryo, unfocused, ready to be molded.

Thus another key element in the al-Qaeda's plan for *jihad* had just fallen into place.

CHAPTER 5

With his Anglo-Saxon name and California upbringing, Dave MacIntyre was a most unlikely al-Qaeda sympathizer. So much so, in fact, that he had sailed through his many high-level security checks without a ripple. Like the events of 9/11 itself, it was only after the fact that anyone might see some of the dots, let alone the connections between them.

Dave was American born, American educated, a history buff with a postgraduate degree in computer sciences from UCLA. He was working for Microsoft when a colleague mentioned that a little outfit called Intelligent Solutions & Security was recruiting for a programmer for some classified work. During the interview it became clear to Dave that the job might be right up his alley. He'd be the main man, from concept to design to application. It would be his baby, all that he had trained for and loved doing. The fact that it was classified intrigued him. Yes, he definitely wanted the job. When he was advised that a security clearance was a condition of employment, he didn't give it a thought. After he was offered the job and filled out his first personal history form to start the long security clearance process, the fact that he had been adopted was simply not an issue, not relevant, not even noted on the forms. The initial clearance gave the MacIntyre family a clean bill of health, and each subsequent update started from that base. Dave had easily masked the subtle changes in his views that he had experienced over the past few years at college, and then more seriously, as bin Laden's message took root.

What was known only to Dave was that his real parents were Iraqis. Dave had been born just after their arrival in Southern California. After his mother died, his father and older brothers returned to the Middle

East, leaving Dave behind. In doing so, Dave's father was honoring the vow made at his wife's deathbed. It was a difficult decision, one which he wrestled with for some time. He could not bear to leave his son, but at the same time did not want him to experience the turmoil that he knew they would be returning to in their homeland. After much thought, the father put together a file containing the family history, some treasured photographs, and his explanation for this decision to put his son up for adoption. He closed the file with a letter.

> *My dearest son,*
>
> *I pray to Allah that what you find in this file will help you to understand the most difficult decision of my life. We came to America so that you could be born into a new world. When your mother died, I did not have the heart or the strength to make that new life. Her dying words were to ask a promise, one that broke my heart. She wanted you to have the opportunity that would be denied to you if we returned home. That is why, when your three brothers and I left to return to Iraq, you stayed to start a new life in America.*
>
> *These photos are of our family, three generations, your grandparents, your parents and your brothers.*
>
> *I am leaving this letter with my cousin who will watch over you in your new family. I have asked him to translate this letter into English, to find you, and to give it to you on your sixteenth birthday.*
>
> *May Allah have mercy on my soul that I have made the right decision for you.*
>
> *Your loving father*

The first 15 years of Dave's life had been pretty normal. He was a smart kid at school, winning the math prizes, fitting in well with his peers, no real teasing about his somewhat swarthy complexion. It was the Latinos who got most of the unwanted attention; however, his unwillingness to join in such taunting tended to separate Dave from the pack. Dave knew deep down that he appeared and felt different, but was unable to understand why.

This all changed at the end of a school day fifteen years after that letter had been written. Dave was bent over unlocking his bike for the ride home when a shadow fell over him. Looking up, he was surprised to find a bearded man, clearly Middle Eastern, holding out a package.

Before Dave could speak the man said, "David MacIntyre, do not be afraid. I wish you no harm. I have kept this message to you safe since it was entrusted to me so many years ago. I have watched your childhood from afar, and have made the reports that you will understand when you read the letter. You should do that in private. May Allah be with you."

Then, before Dave could even gather his thoughts to protest, the parcel was thrust into his hands and the man was gone.

Dave tore the package open. Faded photographs spilled to the ground. He read the letter and looked at the black-and-white photos of people he didn't recognize. On his way home from school he found a quiet spot for a slower read of the extraordinary letter. In turmoil that night he confronted his parents, but for reasons he did not understand or think about, he did not reveal the package that had been handed to him. He told his parents that someone at school had teased him about his dark skin, about being adopted. Dave had passed through the difficult early teen years without apparent discrimination from his peers, so his father was somewhat surprised that the issue had now come to the fore. He and his wife made a special effort to reaffirm their love.

"David, you've been our son since you were a baby. We've never thought of you in any other way."

"But I am adopted?"

"Yes, Dave, you are. The question has never come up—there was no reason for it to. When you were born we desperately wanted a baby, and God brought you to us. You have been our son from the beginning."

"What about my real parents? What happened to them?"

"We never knew. We just knew that we were fortunate to have found you. And we love you."

By the end of the long evening of discussion and explanation, Dave's parents had confirmed their love, reassuring Dave of his place in their life. But it was that little file, which he looked at often in the privacy of his bedroom, and his interest in history, that had led him at the age of sixteen to start to trace his ancestral background. Little by little, Dave began to understand why he had always felt different, and that his roots actually lay in another world entirely. As he uncovered his true heritage, he found his views slowly changing and his beliefs in American values unraveling.

In school he had been a computer whiz, and now he used the internet to connect to people in the Middle East, particularly in Iraq. It was not easy finding a way through Saddam's security blanket, but like youngsters everywhere, the kids in Iraq found detours around the roadblocks. Dave could hardly believe the different perspectives on history and politics that came to his screen. One of the chat groups spoke about religion, about Islam as the path to salvation. For Dave, it was a revelation that there were views so radically different from those of his sheltered upbringing. He had just never thought much about religion before.

The more Dave read and the longer he spent on the internet, the more he became revolted by what appeared to be hypocrisy in the news commentary and on television, about wars, politics, society and the economy. Like thousands of other Americans, his parents had invested their savings in the dot com bubble and, like many of those thousands, Enron got a big chunk of their pie. For the MacIntyres the prospect of a comfortable retirement didn't fade, it vanished overnight. Dave just could not understand how financial scandals such as Enron were allowed to ruin so many innocent people. Where was the justice in this capitalistic society?

When, with so much turmoil in the Middle East, more Arab kids immigrated to America and moved into the neighborhood and into the classroom with their heavily accented English and Arab dress, attitudes toward Dave began to change. With Dave's newfound knowledge of his heritage he became more aware of and sensitive to what until now had been only mild ridicule.

"Hey, Dave, I see a lot of your friends are arriving in the neighborhood," one of his classmates said, a note of derision in his voice.

"What do you mean, 'my friends'? I don't know any more about them than you do."

"Oh, and here I thought they were your cousins, come to visit you. They look just like you."

Then the schoolyard fights began, with the newcomers invariably on the wrong end of the beatings.

"Come on, Dave, are you with us or with them? "

"Yeah, Dave, Arab or American? Whose side are you on?"

Dave felt he should do something, but what? Some of the bullies were his friends.

One day he watched as a young Saudi boy was taunted and ridiculed for his foreign dress and accent; Dave was afraid to step in but unwilling to accept what the other kids told him was the 'American way'.

"These guys are Aaa-rab scum—and you're one of them."

Dave was too frightened and ashamed to do anything, but it fed his confusion about how this could be happening in a nation of immigrants. He began to understand how fear of the unknown, of the strange religion infiltrating their community and the minaret that had materialized overnight at the edge of town, could create hostility towards the foreign newcomers. He read more about Islam.

In the eleventh grade, Dave experienced real rejection for the first time. He fell head over heels for a girl two rows over in history class. After weeks of agony, dreaming about how he could gain her attention, smiling at her in class with no hint of response, her blond head not moving, in desperation he had summoned the courage to shyly approach her.

"Hi, Elizabeth, I see you're a whiz in history. I like it, too. Uh, maybe we could get together and talk about the project?"

"Get lost, Arab. I wouldn't be seen dead with you."

With the images coming to him on the computer screen in his bedroom, he began to question US policies. Was the Middle East really all about oil as so many commentators said? And what about the war going on in Iraq, with Desert Storm pitting his country of birth against his real family? Surely that wasn't just to keep the oil flowing. How could so many innocent Iraqis be fighting and dying if they were being freed from oppression? Dave found himself hating what the US had done to his people, to his homeland, Iraq, not even aware of the irony of imagining Iraq as his homeland. The more he learned about the history of his ancestors, the more disillusioned he became. He began to read the Koran, which struck a cord deep within his awakening spiritual soul.

The first time that he went to the local mosque he was amazed at the comfort that the visit brought him. The local imam spoke to him quietly and encouragingly, and his visits became more frequent. Little by little, Dave became a convert to Islam and began to understand the deep hatred that drove the radical Islamic groups. His own radicalization crept up on him. He didn't know it was happening, nor recognize that it was being subtly and very carefully nurtured.

One day on his visit to the mosque, the imam said, "Dave, I want you to meet someone. This is Silvio. His background is similar to yours and you will find that he will be a good friend."

Dave felt an immediate bond. Silvio was obviously Arab, yet American, like Dave, a rotund, casually dressed guy in jeans and sneakers, with wire-rimmed shades and a trimmed beard and mustache like the pictures Dave had seen of the Saudi royal family.

"Hey, Dave, pleased to meet you. The imam has told me about you, your father and brothers fighting for their freedom with you caught in the middle unable to help them. You are not alone. I have found peace through Islam and, with Allah's blessings, you too will find your way."

With this introduction, Dave's conversion to the cause began in earnest. Dave and Silvio became instant buddies, sharing concerns and ideals. For Dave, Silvio was a savior, able to explain and justify the terrible thoughts that tormented him, that his country had betrayed him, that he was a stranger in his own home. Silvio was good at it. Along with how to shoot an AK-47 and construct an improvised explosive device, he had been trained in undercover techniques by Osama and Kazim at a camp in Afghanistan. Since returning to the US, Silvio had worked at blending in, becoming part of the scenery, invisible. Although what little money he needed was provided by bin Laden's backers, as his 'inheritance', to build his cover Silvio hired out as a house painter. His real task had been searching the Southwest for some time for an appropriate pawn, and not long after meeting Dave, Silvio realized that his long search was over. He had found his man.

Silvio and Dave spent hours talking about religion, about Islam and about the injustices in the history of the Middle East. Silvio's every move was designed to ensure that Dave would unwittingly provide Kazim with what he needed, what Mark had uncovered in tracking Kazim on a computer screen in a Georgetown condo.

Early in the relationship Dave said, "Silvio, you should be concerned about your weight. I jog and hike."

Silvio looked at him in alarm, and Dave added with a grin, "Don't worry, I won't invite you to join me on the jogging circuit, but I know a great hike. We could start slowly and work up to it. I guarantee that you'll love the view."

Silvio would do whatever it took to reinforce Dave's trust, even if it meant going hiking, so his agreement was immediate.

"Sure, Dave, but, really, I will slow you down."

From then on they had spent many pleasant days together hiking in what became their personal spiritual sanctuary, the beautiful Elbow Canyon. And Silvio thought that Dave was right, that this truly was wonderful, as they enjoyed the steep trail extending up the valley, encountering stunning vistas of the mountains ahead and river far below. In this paradise-like environment, Silvio nurtured their friendship and laid the foundation for all that was to come in Dave's short life.

CHAPTER 6

Kazim had been recruited into the KGB as a teenager in the 1970s. His duties included some mild spying on his fellow Turkistanis. For a boy from an impoverished family, the rewards were enormous, and for Kazim the largest of those rewards was the chance for an education. He managed to make up for his small stature through cunning, recognizing that his unassuming appearance could be an advantage. In a society where physical strength still equaled power, he chose to emulate Lenin. He bolstered their similarity in stature with a little beard, trimmed like the one in the photographs that were revered and displayed everywhere in the Soviet Union.

Less than a decade later, he found himself in Moscow with a post-graduate degree in computer sciences, following the same professional path that Dave MacIntyre on the other side of the world would one day pursue. He was so good that his fellow Soviets overlooked the fact that he wasn't really one of them. Even though he was a hick from the outback, the official Soviet policy of embracing the republics made it possible for him to become one of the KGB team. He was smart, quick-witted, wily as a fox, and a whiz on a computer, soon gaining a reputation in an organization and a country that was slow in getting started in the connected world.

"Hey, Lenin, get your skinny ass in here. We've got a job for you." His boss called him Lenin, not at all derisively, but as a mark of respect for Kazim and his abilities, and as a sly jab at his slightly ridiculous similarity in appearance, temperament and ruthlessness to the real thing.

"Lenin, you're going to build a program that will win us the war without firing a shot. When we pull our trigger, it will bring the capitalists to their knees."

"It will be my pleasure."

Then, after a broad outline of the concept, the boss asked, "So, Lenin, can this be done?"

"This I can do, Comrade. You have trained me well, but I will need some Western equipment."

"Tell me what you require and you will have it."

Thus, by the late '80s, Kazim found himself as the key programmer on a small, highly classified KGB project. His role was to draw the blueprint for the лук, the Onion, the software that would lie sleeping, ready to invade financial systems in the US if the Cold War turned hot.

For many of the Soviet old guard, Gorbachev's opening to the West went against all their convictions, all they had spent their lives working for. What was happening was nothing less than betrayal, a squandering of Soviet power for an unknowable future, with their own leader, Gorbachev, in bed with their archenemy, Reagan. They could not allow the disintegration of their Russian Empire. It didn't take much convincing for Kazim's cell of programmers to decide that their secret system should stay in place, ready for activation when the leadership finally came to its senses. While the Soviet Union collapsed around them, Kazim's bug became the center of a power struggle between the hardliners who wanted to turn back the clock to the heady days of power and those who were prying open the Kremlin piece by painful piece. It was clear to those who had special clearance to the Onion that it would survive the storm battering their country only if the old guard won the struggle, because the Onion would not be allowed to live through the changes that perestroika was driving.

And it was Kazim's task to ensure that it survived. "Lenin, you are to protect our Onion with your life."

"No worry there, Comrade. My small team and I are the only ones who even know it exists. I'll be ready when you give the word."

"You'd better be. Your future depends on it!"

Like most of his fellow Soviet citizens, Kazim kept his personal and religious views to himself over the years. The alternative, particularly in the Soviet southern republics, could bring a quick and harsh reprisal. With the implosion of the Soviet Union, so clearly signaled by the sledgehammers at the Berlin Wall, the floodgates were opened. But people in the far-flung republics were still cautious; people like Kazim had seen the results of the Chechnyan efforts toward independence and they weren't going to make that mistake. They knew that they couldn't face Russia head on, that any overt rebellion would be brutally crushed. They didn't like it, but they recognized the reality that they would have to work clandestinely to build support to escape the Russian yoke. And for many it wasn't only the Russian political yoke, it was the suppression of their Muslim religion that most hurt them, which made them feel oppressed. Like many in the Islamic world, they wanted a state governed by sharia law, by Islamic religious decree.

Then, after years of chaffing under Soviet rule, a prophet's words found fertile ground. "Rally the Arab world. Throw out the infidels, with their corrupt Western morals. Establish Islamic rule and sharia law throughout our lands."

Russia didn't really fit the description of a land of corrupt Western morals and values, but it was close enough in their eyes. Osama bin Laden was the hero and the messenger, al-Qaeda the way to a glorious future. Kazim's people had found an ally in their fight for freedom, not only from the Soviet yoke but for an Islamic land. For the peoples of Kazim's world, the thought of an Islamic nation easily overcame any differences within the Arab world, confirming the old adage that 'the enemy of my enemy is my friend.'

When Kazim's Onion was destroyed in a night of bullets and betrayal, he fled Russia, just one short step ahead of his pursuers, his zeal for freedom for his homeland renewed and reinvigorated. He traveled to Afghanistan to join the fight against the Russian occupation, and it was not long before he whole-heartedly embraced bin Laden's vision of the future. With Kazim's expertise in computers and his ex-KGB knowledge of the Russian and Western worlds, he quickly became a valued senior member of bin Laden's inner circle and their top advisor on technical and security matters.

CHAPTER 7

Kazim's second Onion was born in 1999, in a camp in Afghanistan, at the same time that the plot was hatched for 9/11, the attack on the World Trade Center and the Pentagon. The Taliban, with clandestine US help, had thrown the Russians out and were now in firm control of the country. Al-Qaeda and the radical Islam of bin Laden had found a home, a place from which the *jihad* he promised could extend across the world. Training camps received recruits, and millions of dollars flowed in, from the faithful across the Muslim world and from those who straddled the fence.

Eight men sat cross-legged in a circle on a magnificent Persian carpet in a comfortable home on the outskirts of Kabul, not lavish, rather simply furnished in accordance with the leader's unassuming, soft-spoken persona. The weather was sweltering, and they wore robes and turbans, the age-old dress for combating the heat and respecting their faith. The ritual teapot was now empty. At the ring of a bell a fully-veiled woman came to clear away the remains of the meal, her eyes glowing through thin slits in the burqa.

Discussion had ranged over several potential plots to hit at the infidels' heartland, Osama bin Laden listening quietly while his senior advisors debated the merits of each. Risks were not much of an issue given the army of soldiers ready to give their lives for the cause, nor were costs, with a seemingly endless supply of donations to fund this holy war. Despite this strong financial backing, their efforts to acquire nuclear and biological weapons had not yet been rewarded.

After a long dramatic pause, as he looked out over the dry expanse of arid land, the leader closed his eyes and spoke in low, deliberate tones, "And what about our main quest? What success are we having in gaining our ultimate weapon?"

He was a tall man, gaunt, his flowing beard and robe adding to the aura of mystery and authority. The man to his right, a Pakistani who had been with him from the start, replied, "Osama, we have paid my countryman, Khan, one million US dollars to deliver a suitcase bomb. He has not done so, and I begin to despair that my efforts are in vain. He has assisted and provided many nations with nuclear expertise and equipment. I do not understand why we do not yet have a bomb."

He was referring to A.Q. Khan, the Pakistani revered at home as the father of Pakistan's status as a nuclear power. Unbeknownst to world powers, Khan had created a worldwide net of trading in nuclear technology and, despite the best nonproliferation efforts of the UN and the US, had delivered to Libya, North Korea, Iran and any other would-be member of the nuclear club that was willing and able to pay the prices that he demanded. Khan had no shortage of clients, and was wealthy indeed.

Osama bin Laden responded derisively, "I expect it is because of the turmoil going on in their country, the divisions in their beliefs in Islam, and the balancing act that they play with the United States. They are cowards, afraid to support our cause, crushed under the American thumb. But we will continue our efforts, continue our quest. Only a nuclear explosion will bring the entire Arab world to our door, and only the threat of nuclear weapons will bring Israel to the table with our Palestinian brothers."

Banging his fist into his hand, he rose from the carpet. "The infidels understand only power. Their rhetoric about peace is useless! We must redouble our efforts, both with Khan and in Russia."

The man generally acknowledged as number two in the al-Qaeda hierarchy, al-Zawahiri, agreed. "That is so, my brother. By the blessings of Allah, we will raise the stakes so that they cannot refuse."

Talk of action that could be more immediate than a mushroom cloud ranged around the circle of robed men. The leader said, "We must keep the pressure on in Europe, in France and Germany, in Spain, to energize our followers, and in Asia, where support is building for our cause, but our priority must be the infidels' heartland."

One of the men who had sat quietly through most of the discussion now spoke up. "We have an imam in the United States who believes that it would be possible to hijack airliners and crash them into cities. I have spoken with him and I agree. It could be done."

The concept of using commercial airliners as bombers quickly gained support and agreement, and planners were sent off to make it happen. Funds were allocated to infiltrate twenty martyrs into the US and to sponsor flying training for some of them. Financing was not a problem. Al-Qaeda used the US banking system to transact their clandestine business and to invest their funds, and ironically the interest earned would pay for the flying school courses. One of the robed men laughed as he said, "Imagine, using the infidels' own weaknesses to bring them grief and suffering. This contribution to our *jihad* will bring special pleasure, special martyrdom to our fighters."

And, as one, they went out to the terrace, saying "Praise be to Allah." Kazim shot several rounds from his Kalashnikov into the air toward the setting sunset. After making themselves comfortable, looking out over the arid valley toward the peaks shining in the last rays of light, all eyes now turned to Kazim.

"And what have you been planning, my brother?" asked bin Laden.

"Allah willing, my offering would take a different path," Kazim said quietly. "We have many eager martyrs for the cause, willing to die in the glorious explosions. What I offer is disaster of a different sort, cyber terrorism, which will bring fear and destruction to the infidels from coast to coast, action that will hit them in their heartland."

"So, what would this be?" asked a robed man sitting beside bin Laden.

"I will take control of the dams that generate electricity across America. They will open on my command, flooding large areas of the country, destroying everything in their paths. Then the loss in capacity to generate electricity will bring the country to its knees."

"But America has nuclear generators. Would the loss of the dams cause that much harm?"

Kazim had done his homework well. "Yes, you are correct. Turbines are only one of many ways that they produce electricity, but the loss all at once will cause the circuits to overload and destroy their system to distribute the power. It will take much time for them to recover."

Bin Laden added, with obvious pleasure, "Yes, the economic impact will be great, but for our cause the destruction caused by the enormous flooding will bring more glory to our *jihad*. What would you require to achieve this attack?"

"All I need is one brother who is already in America, free to move about, who could recruit the martyr who will bring me the keys to the Kingdom."

"And do you know this martyr, this person who carries the keys?"

"I know of him. He is an American citizen who is the son of an Iraqi. It has taken me two years with the help of our friends in Pakistan to locate such a person. I believe that, with Allah's blessing, he could be converted to our cause."

A dissenting voice came from the other side of the circle. "Your plan is complex. It would take some time to recruit this martyr. We want to see results now."

After considerable discussion, weighing the pros and the cons, bin Laden spoke softly. "Yes, that is true. We do want action now. But our cause is eternal and can take many paths. We will fight with all our means until the infidels leave our lands."

Spreading his hands wide, bin Laden continued, "My brother, how could we convert this man with the keys to our cause? Where is this brother you speak of who could bring him to us?"

"I trained in one of our camps two years ago with him. His name is Assad. He is above suspicion and is waiting in America for the call to do his part for our *jihad*. We must contact him and he will bring the man with the keys to us."

"With the blessing of Allah, we will find Assad and put him to work. Kazim, you do the preparations that you will require to bring terror and destruction to our enemies."

Assad was a man caught in the middle, a committed Muslim, the American citizen known to Dave MacIntyre as Silvio. Years before anyone had heard of al-Qaeda, he had committed himself to a holy man, an imam, in a mosque in California. This imam was a radical Wahhabi, a fervent believer in a new caliphate, an Islamic land ruled by the sharia, religious law. The imam quietly supported the cause, recruiting converts wherever he could find them. He had converted Silvio, who had gone to Afghanistan to train as a *mujahidin* to help in the holy war against the Russian occupiers, returning to the States long before anyone was interested in potential terrorists. And that imam in California later became the link between Kazim, Silvio and Dave.

When news of Cobra Flight's fateful bombing mission in the no-fly zone in Iraq reached al-Qaeda, Kazim knew that he had found the proverbial straw that would break the camel's back. The message was passed to the imam that Dave's father and brothers had been killed in Iraq by American bombers. The imam met with Silvio. Silvio saw that message as a gift from Allah, and knew this gift would seal Dave's commitment to the cause. He was on the phone immediately.

"Hello, Dave, it's Silvio. I have some important news that you should know about."

"What's that?"

"I can't tell you over the phone, but it's really important that we meet. Could you make it at our normal spot about nine tonight?"

"I'm heading out for dinner and to a computer meeting with some friends tonight. How about tomorrow?"

"Dave, you need to hear what I have to say. It can't wait."

"Well, okay, I guess. The guys are going to be disappointed. I was going to lead a discussion on some new software. I'll cancel that, though."

"Good. Tonight then?"

"I'll be there. See you at 9:00."

Dave had never heard Silvio so agitated and so persistent. Their conversations had always been so rational, with gentle suggestions that Dave found comforting, helping him understand the turmoil that roiled his personal world. As he drove toward the rendezvous he wondered how all those people on the streets could seem so content when their country was killing people, people who believed in God, who prayed five times a day, who wanted only to live their lives in peace.

"These people have no idea what I am feeling," he thought. "It's as if I'm in a different world."

By the time he arrived at their coffee shop he was both concerned and anxious to hear Silvio's news. Silvio rose to greet Dave, kissing him on both cheeks, his face a mask of sorrow.

"Allah be with you."

"And with you, my friend. You look as if you have the weight of the world on your shoulders. What is this terrible news that has you so upset?"

"Dave, we have spoken with the imam about the injustices that America is inflicting on your homeland and on Islam. Yet, to Americans all of the many faithful who have been killed and injured are just pictures on television, statistics, meaningless."

"That's for sure. Most people don't pay any attention to the slaughter they see on the screen. I just don't understand it. It's like when I was in school and Arab kids were beaten up as if they were nothing. The same people who did the bullying wouldn't treat a dog that way. And the same thing with the bombing. It's as if the people being maimed and killed weren't human."

"That's true. But the injustice that I am about to tell you is personal, not kids in a schoolyard. You are aware of the bombs that rain down on Iraq, against people who cannot defend themselves, bombs dropped on a nation at peace."

"Yes, I have seen the news, the pictures of the air force using my homeland for bombing practice. I do not understand it."

Communications with al-Qaeda was not difficult. Through the use of anonymous proxies that disguised the internet provider address of the originating computer, emails were routed via anonymous remailers, making the email impossible to trace. The accounts at either end were anonymously signed for in places of free internet access, where no identification had to be used.

As Dave was talking, Silvio reached in his pocket and pulled out six photographs that had been emailed to him the day before. He handed them to Dave.

"What's this?" Dave asked. "It sure is gory—blood and guts all over the place. This must be one of the bombs that you're talking about."

A look of horror crept over Dave's face. "You said this was personal. What did you mean?"

"Dave, we've seen the pictures of your family, your father and your brothers, the ones your father left for you. Those pictures were taken a long time ago. Unfortunately, these photographs are more recent."

"Oh, no! This is my family? They were bombed?"

"Yes, Dave, they were. US warplanes killed them while they were having a peaceful lunch. They were sitting on a balcony enjoying the view over a valley when the planes roared in out of nowhere. The bombs whistled as they tore though the sky, then the tremendous explosion, flames and smoke everywhere. This was what was left when the planes departed. Your whole family is dead, killed by the US government."

"This can't be true," Dave gasped, his body shaking. "I only found them in the last few months. Finally I was able to get to know my real heritage. I've thought so much about them. I feel I know them."

Silvio and Kazim had not been leaving anything to chance. The brothers that Dave thought he had met on the internet were really only one man and that was Kazim. He had dreamed up the idea of reinforcing Dave's doubts and confusion by impersonating Dave's brothers in email exchanges. Dave took the bait, amazed that fate had allowed him to connect with the roots that he had missed all those years growing up in America. Dave and his 'brothers' had spent hours on the net, the descriptions of life, of society, of Islam so at odds with anything that Dave was reading in the Western media.

The fertile ground was now sown with the seed of revenge. Silvio had only to complete the cultivation that had so painstakingly been undertaken.

"You know that your father loved you, Dave. He gave up so much for you and he has watched over you, watched you grow up over all these years. Now they have all died in the US war with Islam."

"I need to think. I hate this country for what it is doing to our people. I want to be doing something, but I don't know what to do."

In his soft voice Silvio set the stage. "We need the comforting words of the Koran. We need to pray for their souls. Come with me to the mosque. The imam will bring peace to you in your time of trouble."

Later that evening, the imam spoke gently. "All peace be upon he who follows the Guidance. The Koran guides us in our lives, Dave. You must avenge your family. Their memory must be honored. They cannot have died in vain, for nothing."

"But what can I do? I have no tools to avenge them. I will pray for them."

"We will help you in your time of sorrow."

Dave thought back to an evening a few years ago. The MacIntyre family had been in their living room watching the news as a tape showed an F-18 dropping laser-guided bombs on Iraqi targets. It was the same sort of image that Dave had in his mind when he looked at the photos Silvio had just shown him, now spread out on the floor in front of him. As the view through the gun sight tracked the target, the bomb dropped from the wing pylon, the reticule switching to a close-in view of a direct hit. The explosion threw up debris as the fighter pulled away. Dave's father had clapped, smiling with glee. "That's my baby, right on the money."

"What do you mean, Dad? I know you work for Hughes, but I didn't know you were involved in that kind of thing."

"It's classified, so I don't talk about it, but yes, I design those guidance systems."

The imam could read the confusion on Dave's face. One of his adopted father's designs had killed the father that he had never met, the one he was now mourning.

"How can I live with myself?"

As they sat in the quiet sanctuary of the mosque, the real conversion began in earnest, gently but firmly, and it wasn't long before all those doubts, all the disillusionment that had been nurtured so carefully brought Dave to the cause.

Silvio and the imam had exchanged many emails with Kazim setting up the plan. On Dave's next visit, the imam said, "I have heard from your father's friends. They have a way to bring justice for your family."

"What would this be? What can I do from California?"

Silvio held Dave's gaze for a minute, and then said, "A brother in Iraq is a computer expert like you. I will give you instructions on how to contact him."

Silvio certainly did not begin to understand the computer terminology that he had been given, which, for Kazim, was probably a blessing. It meant that it would be passed verbatim, uncorrupted, and he was right. His instructions were specific, precise, passed on to Dave by an uncomprehending Silvio. As a fellow techie, Dave immediately recognized the ingenuity of Kazim's plan. He had no trouble taking home the backup discs of his software for the dams that evening, slipping them into his pocket, and giving a wave to Wally, the night security guard as he left the office.

When he got home he turned on his computer, and looking at Kazim's instructions, loaded the peer-to-peer (P2P) file-sharing application. He went through the setting up of the blowfish encoder/decoder that would encrypt all the communications. Before he did anything else, Dave used an application to compress the Intelligent Solutions & Security software, the controller program, so that it would be faster to send. While he was waiting for the compression of the files he looked at the P2P.

"Very nice," he thought, "a distributed server for encrypted sharing." He set the proxy in, just as he had been instructed. The proxy was in Bahrain. "Odd," he said to himself, as he wondered what the island nation was like. He inserted the nickname that Silvio had told him to use, using the correct ASCII bytes, logging onto the P2P net and entering the chat room. He was shocked to see so many ppz (people) in the room all talking away. He had no difficulty reading through the computer jargon as it appeared on the screen.

<TheCoz> lmao

<¤¥¤Metal¤¥¤> phewwwwwwwwww

<¤¥¤Metal¤¥¤> i can relax now 8 bloody teens just left

<Çå$îm*> [Dave knew that this was Kazim's nick-name] metal, you ok, or did ya let one go? LOL [Laughing out loud, in the jargon]

<Çå$im*> j/k

<¤¥¤Metal¤¥¤> lol

< Çå$îm*> geez, no wonder

<¤¥¤Metal¤¥¤> bet that was pooky

<TheCoz> damn 8 kids?//

<¤¥¤Metal¤¥¤> 4 where mine

<Áñgè£_of_Death> jesus metal boy..4? quit w/ the sex already lol

<¤¥¤Metal¤¥¤> lol

<Çå$îm*> LOL

<¤¥¤Metal¤¥¤> i did nearly 4 years ago

<Çå$îm*> the man's a MACHINE, i tell ya...LOL

¤¥¤Metal¤¥¤ plays like a virgin

<Çå$îm*> LOL

<¤¥¤Metal¤¥¤> :D

<bug¤> hi bytes

<¤¥¤Metal¤¥¤> yo bytes

<bytes> [this was Dave, joining the chat group] hello?

<Çå$îm*> Ahh I see u made it bytes ... guys meet an old friend of mine

<Áñgè£_of_Death> pleased to meet u

<bytes> hy ca$im

<Çå$îm*> did u get me that movie?

<bytes> yes how do I send it

<Çå$îm*> right click on my name in the user windows> choose send file navigate to the file click on it
<bytes> got it
<Çå$îm*> ty [thank you], I see- it's incoming
<bytes> I must go to bed now I will leave the computer running so that u can get the movie ill leave the room but leave the server on good night
<Çå$îm*> sleep well my friend
<bug¤> good night bytes
<¤¥¤Metal¤¥¤> nite bytes
<bug¤> sleep tight bytes ;)
<bytes> has left

David looked at the screen for a moment, watching all the data uploading and wondered how Kazim could be so bold. The encoded bits went up to the internet and through the proxy and were relayed to Lahore, Pakistan, where a wireless router sitting alone on a table near a window broadcast to an unseen computer. Kazim sat across the street in another apartment watching the incoming data, having lost interest in the chat room for the moment. The long, painstaking quest had paid off. Kazim reached to a table behind him, picking up his well worn copy of the Koran and his prayer rug, both of which were with him always, carefully arranging the blanket towards Mecca, and sank to his knees.

The plots discussed by those robed men sitting around a Persian carpet so many months before were now becoming a reality. Non-pilots with enough training to steer airliners, flights and targets selected, support troops with box cutters were ready to book flights. Terror was about to strike in New York and Washington. Soon afterward, by the time anyone in the US started to pay any attention to the enemies in their midst, the devastation that Kazim had planned would be realized. Dave was converted and Kazim had his keys to the Kingdom. He had Dave's software and would re-write the code.

It would be only after 9/11 that Dave began to question what he had done.

CHAPTER 8

Now came the hard part. There were not many people anywhere with the ability to do what Kazim was about to undertake, but he had laid the groundwork well. He required a team—not just any team, but one of experts, and Kazim had access to that resource.

In the remote wilds of Afghanistan and Pakistan, tribal lands have been ruled by chiefs since the dawn of history, and the present-day rulers were just the most recent in this long history. They were happy to lend support to bin Laden, not only for the significant income that came their way, but because al-Qaeda would protect their turf. The Taliban and al-Qaeda were a team and, Kazim, his simple Arab clothing and demeanor concealing his sophisticated knowledge and expertise, was one of them. He had no difficulty fitting in. Though the wonderful days in St. Petersburg, the Hermitage and Winter Palace were a dim memory, he saw the irony of his high tech work in this 'Lawrence of Arabia' setting, with primitive huts alongside lavishly furnished tents.

Kazim bowed low as he entered the abode, greeting the chief with deference.

"Praise be to Allah, and peace be upon you."

"And upon you, my brother."

As in so much of the world, no business in this setting could be contemplated until the formalities of hospitality and respect were complete, the more important the guest, the more elaborate the protocol. Kazim was anxious, but he covered his usual frenetic nervousness well and remained relaxed during the compulsory ritual. When the meal and prayers were finally complete, signified by a nod from the tribal chief, Kazim got down to business. He had arranged with the tribe to set up an elaborate system of couriers to carry messages from the wilds to Kabul, and he now made arrangements for a delivery. This package was not one that could be sent to its destination over the internet, both because it had to be encrypted and because its destination was as secret as its contents. Its destination would have raised alarms had it been known.

The local tribal chief dispatched his courier, and a day later Kazim's package was in the hands of a staffer in the Russian mission in Kabul. It then went by encrypted message to an office in St. Petersburg. There, three of Kazim's old KGB colleagues were in business for themselves, doing sophisticated computer work for the highest bidder, and now for Kazim. The St. Petersburg team was good. They had the optimal experience of working for the KGB, and the finest equipment, initially stolen from their old employer, now updated with bin Laden's money. They followed the instructions they had received.

The coded mail was very simple. It instructed the team to meet in a chat room, giving them the time that they should log on. They signed onto the P2P at the appointed time. No one else was in the room, just Kazim.

<£èè† Håxº®$> [standing for elite hacker] has entered

<Çå$îm*> I need u to tinker this as was planned.

Kazim right clicked on leet's name and sent the application to St. Petersburg.

<£èè† Håxº®$> ok its incoming, any ideas on how u want us to approach this

<Çå$îm*> no I think u r thoroughly capable ;) ... if u need help u know where to get in touch with me c u l8r [meaning see you later]

<£èè† Håxº®$> has left

They went to work immediately, reworking the software code and, as they began to look at it, they thought, "Very nicely done."

It was a SCADA (supervisory control and data acquisition) that used PLC, programmable logic controller, interfaces for controlling equipment, including the dams.

On the second day of hard slogging, one of the programmers said, "Hey, this part of the code is almost the same as the one for our systems—it's the timing sequencing. Why don't I save time and splice it in? No use reinventing the wheel."

"If you can do that, great. We're going to be hard-pressed to meet Kazim's timeline. That'll save us close to a day."

They needed the time, because they were not only reprogramming the software that controlled the dams, they were also writing the code that was going to erase all of Kazim's tracks.

What they didn't know, though, was that their decision to save some code-writing time would turn out to be a stroke of serendipity for the US.

Three days later Dave got a call.

"Hey, Silvio, what's up?"

"I have some information for you. Can we meet?"

"Sure, one hour, same place?"

"See you there."

Silvio was already seated when Dave arrived. "Our friend has sent a message for you. He has asked that I give it to you exactly as he dictated it to the imam. I sure don't understand all the computer jargon."

Kazim's instructions that Silvio passed to Dave were indeed detailed and specific, and Dave followed them to the letter. The next day he stayed at the office working late. After 11:00 p.m. he logged onto the server as root account (the administrative level) in the computer room. He first turned off the automatic backups, and then opened a browser, entering the IP address that Kazim had given him. Sure enough, an ASCII site came up, with only one file. He then proceeded to overwrite the main dam control application update file with the hacked package that Kazim had sent him. Dave's regular monthly software update was always sent out at midnight to the dams, and Dave had given Kazim the root password for the month, the password that was changed each time on the day before the scheduled update.

Dave knew that he was safe. He did the update every month, as regular as clockwork, and no one was going to question him, but he still found himself shaking as he punched the keys.

When he finally logged off, after what turned out to have been a fairly long day at the office, he breathed a huge sigh of relief. He got in his car and pulled up to the security gate, rolling down his window, knowing that the time would be entered in the log.

Wally, the pudgy retired cop, woke up with an embarrassed start. "You're later than usual, Dave. No trouble, I hope?"

"No, just running a bit behind. I had a bit more work than usual. No problem. Good night, Wally."

On the drive home he realized how tense he had been, and thought to himself, "Relax, it's over." He was sure that no one would notice the time discrepancy and, if they did, he could easily explain the extra hour. His thoughts were jumbled, elated that he was taking the steps to hit back at the society that had caused him so much sorrow, but at the same time anxious about what he had done. He wondered what Kazim was up to. He was sure that it was doing something big because Kazim had specifically told Dave not to turn the automatic backup system back on until the next morning, which meant that Kazim needed access to the computer for a long time. Dave knew that he would have to get in early to reactivate the backup before anyone else arrived.

At the same time, on the other side of the world, Kazim had driven around a city in Pakistan, not far from the Afghan border, his laptop loaded with a net stumbler, an application that allowed him to find wireless access points. He was looking for ones that he had already tested with 'air snort', a package that captured interesting keys and packets thus allowing cracking of the encryption required to access the wireless router. This time, though, he found an unprotected wireless router.

He retrieved an empty Pringles chip can from the back seat which he inserted over the antenna through a little hole in the bottom of the can, making a barrel so that the radio waves were directed toward the router. The purpose of the can was twofold. It increased the distance the signal would traverse in the direction that the barrel and antenna were pointing, and it also reduced the footprint of the radio signal so that no elint (electronic intelligence) watchers could spot his surreptitious transmission.

"Hmm," Kazim said to himself, "this makes things easy."

He logged onto the site, opening proxies in Iran and in France, calling up the Intelligent Solutions & Security servers and waited with satisfaction to see his files download properly, and then watched the successful upload of his hack to the dam servers across the country. As he checked the file sizes to confirm that his hack had been the one loaded to the dams, a smile crept across his face. He next overwrote the hacked update at IS&S by replacing it with the original update that was supposed to have gone out to the dams, effectively covering his tracks.

Kazim's next task was the crown of the kingdom he was creating. He inserted a hack on the main server that would allow him to destroy most of the data on the server and, if all went as planned, was supposed to cook its chips in the process. All he had to do was call Port 5000 and enter his password. He was like a kid, wiggling in his seat with joy—he was just so damn good. This one was going to work. Politics weren't going to get in the way this time.

Kazim then went to the internal logs for Intelligent Solutions & Security, deleting his tracks with false entries. Once satisfied that all his code had been inserted, he logged out, shut the laptop, withdrew the aerial from the window of the truck, threw the Pringles can in the back and drove off into the brilliant afternoon sunlight.

Dave was at the office bright and early the next morning, the first one in, nervous as he approached the gate.

The morning guard raised the barrier. "Hi, Dave. You're in early. Wasn't last night your monthly marathon?"

"Yeah, but I have a couple of things I need to finish first thing this morning."

He went directly to the computer center and logged on as root, the administrative account. He quickly scanned the logs and messages. "Hmm, nothing here." He looked at the xferlog, the file containing the logged information from the ASCII—not a trace that anything had been done. It all looked like the normal monthly update, even the size of the file was correct, no sign of the large package that Kazim had cooked up for the dam servers.

Next he looked at the wtmp log, the file that records all logins and logouts. There was not a sign of any suspicious connections. It was as if Kazim didn't exist, had never been there. Dave knew that Kazim must have entered the system, but there sure was no record of it. He smiled with relief as he turned on the automatic backup system, the one he had disabled and left off the night before.

Stanford Cartwright had started his little company in the late '70s, and early on decided that he wanted to keep it small and specialized, focused on operating software. He was a tall, laconic, easygoing guy, trusting in human nature, effective and competent, and over the years, he had been very successful in hiring people on the same basis. He just couldn't conceive that anyone would abuse his trust. His office worked on personal initiative and independence. He surrounded himself with people who were self-starters, and in all his years running his little company he had been proved right. His business was successful enough that he even thought the buyout discussions underway with a large conglomerate might provide for his retirement. When he arrived for work that morning, Cartwright was not surprised to see his star programmer already on the job.

"In early this morning, Dave? Weren't you in doing the update last night?"

"I was. It was a big one and I had a little cleaning up to do before we start the day."

"Good man, Dave. That's the kind of initiative I like to see."

"Unfortunately, I must have been a bit tired when I finished. I forgot to turn on the automatic backup system when I finished the computer run last night."

Without a second thought the boss smiled, patting him on the back, "That's okay, Dave, no harm done. The logs will pick up last night's activity, no problem."

And when Seth, the chief of security for Cartwright's little company, arrived a few minutes later, Dave completed the job of covering his tracks. "Morning, Seth. The update last night took quite a bit longer than usual, and when I left I forgot to switch on the backup. I did that just now, so if you run across anything, that's what it is."

"Okay, Dave. Thanks for letting me know."

Dave breathed a sigh of relief. He was safe, home free. No one could ever trace what he had done.

CHAPTER 9

The next morning, September 11, 2001, the whole world watched in awe. The images, the horror, the death and destruction seared into the consciousness of hundreds of millions of people around the world, the lives of every American instantly and intensely altered in so many ways. Those in charge of security and intelligence knew that their worlds had undergone a seismic shock, one that they had not foreseen, the damage reaching to the depths of each of their agencies. And the Buchans now knew with certainty that the dams had to be next.

On the other side of the world in al-Qaeda territory, Kazim had anticipated that 9/11 would complicate things. They had had pretty much of a free ride in preparing for the aircraft hijackings, but now he was certain that the US would retaliate any way it could, tightening the screws everywhere. He was pleased that his preparations were well underway and that he had the software in place, yet he knew that life had just become infinitely more complicated.

CHAPTER 10

Among the many changes in the US after 9/11, for Kazim the biggest was the intense scrutiny that came to bear on everything that al-Qaeda did. He was not particularly worried. His Onion was ready to go, so this would just make things a little more difficult, more of a technical challenge. When the US started to take the problem of al-Qaeda seriously in their homeland, it became clear to both Silvio in the US and Kazim in Afghanistan that a new way to communicate was required. Some al-Qaeda members had already become martyrs through the extensive monitoring of their communications that got underway after their glorious victory in New York.

Mohammad, a brother who had been one of the robed men at that fateful planning session two years ago, was in Yemen organizing another hit at the US Navy fleet in the Gulf. The US had made some progress with the Yemenis following the *USS Cole* disaster, when a small boat loaded with explosives blew a large hole in the *Cole*, killing 17 sailors and injuring 39. Unfortunately for Mohammad and al-Qaeda, intelligence had quietly been obtained that an al-Qaeda leader was traveling through Yemen, and the US had just the technology to test. A Predator drone, an unmanned airplane with a Hellfire missile strapped under its belly was launched, waiting for the signal. When the cell phone signature was picked up by the listening post, a button was pushed. The missile dropped off the Predator, ignited and streaked its way to its target. Moments later, the car and its occupants disappeared in the fireball.

Kazim had established an elaborate system that gave bin Laden communications links around the world. He could talk to his far-flung converts in Indonesia, the Philippines, Thailand, Malaysia, Europe, London, and New York. Kazim's security measures were almost obsessively solid because it was a traitor, one of his own cell, who had caused his only failure—the first Onion. As for the infidels, the Americans, he just knew that he was smarter. He could turn their technology against them. He could talk to the world, using his old Russian employers as a communications link—stuff the US technology up their asses.

However, one botched detail almost caused the $25 million on bin Laden's head to be paid out.

The al-Qaeda hierarchy was reasonably comfortable in a tribal village near the Pakistan border, nearly invisible in quarters near the mosque. Kazim had his equipment set up in a nondescript garage tucked under the trees.

"Osama, I will be out for the morning sending our messages."

"May Allah be with you, my brother."

As the chief and only communicator for the group, Kazim had sole charge of one of the few remaining vehicles, a Toyota truck like the ones that had been the universal vehicles of the *mujahidin*, serving all the military functions: transport, gun platform, command and communication center. This particular truck was rather simply equipped with some computer and radio gear.

This morning Kazim was delivering al-Qaeda messages to cells on three continents. He backed out of the garage and set off on the dirt road that led up the valley to the mountains above the town. It was only about a twenty-minute ride to the remote village where he had installed a base station computer. Kazim parked the truck at a point close enough to the base to communicate the messages that Osama wanted sent. He set the laptop on the dashboard of the truck, pointed the aerial out the window and aimed at the barn window near the edge of a town a short way up the valley from Feyzabad. He reached around for the Pringles chip can.

"Now where is it? Omar must have cleaned out the truck again."

He couldn't find it and the prearranged time was minutes away. Well, they were in the wilds of Afghanistan and he wasn't far from the barn. After all, how big was the risk? He pointed the antenna at the base station and turned it on. In the barn a laptop booted up, warming a high-power antenna attached to the wireless router. Kazim began to transmit the coded message and its routing instructions to the laptop that was the base of the system. As the transmission was in progress, the laptop dialed up the internet service provider, an anonymous account. The package was sent to a remailer in Iran, a nation hostile to the infidels. Kazim figured that even if the US searchers found the package, they'd never get the source or the destination. They might decode the headers to determine the route his package took, but they'd never get cooperation from the host country of the remailer, Iran.

Kazim didn't hear the plane overhead. He was lost in readings from the Koran playing from his laptop, plugged into the vehicle's stereo. What Kazim simply did not anticipate was that the US also had some pretty good, even elite, techies, and one of them was sitting in front of a bank of consoles in the back of that US Army airplane. This guy was apparently not a soldier. He was in civilian clothes, white Polo shirt, khaki cargo pants, Nike sneakers, and this was his domain. Stephen Smith was well traveled, but his extensive trips were not to the hot tourist spots of the world. His duties had taken him to places like the outback of Australia, above the Arctic Circle in Canada and Norway, the remote borders of Russia and Iran, places that provided the ideal geography to catch the signals that the National Security Agency wanted to hear.

When his equipment was in use, only Stephen was allowed in the compartment in the back of the plane, and he was the boss of the operation. He told the pilots where and when to fly. The NSA had mounted their most modern and sophisticated scanning, listening and video equipment on board this small aircraft, and it was now flying through the rugged mountain passes that traversed Afghani tribal lands. It just happened to be in the right place at the right time, but it was not all by accident. It was exactly as Stephen had planned. He had done his homework and figured that this had to be the right part of the world, remote, invisible. This was his third try at this particular valley.

The comms in the cockpit sprang to life, interrupting the copilot who was bragging about his conquest in Kabul the night before. The civie locked in the back monitoring the screens broke into the conversation, and the pilot never did hear the outcome of the copilot's lucky night on the town.

"Captain, I've got a contact from that scruffy town we just passed."

The pilot responded in a bored drawl. "I suppose you want me to go around again, Stephen, another wild goose chase, some farmer on a CB calling in to tell them to have dinner ready." But he did the circuit, and the plane flew through the signal once again, recording packets from Kazim's computer.

"Captain, this is the real meal deal. They are coded computer packets, exactly what I hoped to find."

"Mountain Base, Ears has something for you." Stephen read out the GPS coordinates. "A burst of computer comms from grid 913 385."

"We're on our way, ETA 10 minutes."

The elint plane swung in an arc above the valley floor, the wing catching the sun, a reflection bursting in a flash across the windshield of Kazim's truck. Kazim punched off the stereo, in a stupor for a moment. When it dawned on him what had happened, he blanched. How could he be that stupid? They had caught him transmitting. He almost screamed aloud, controlling himself with difficulty.

"Go! Move!" he urged himself. "Hold it, not too fast, not too much dust. I've got to get back."

As he crested the low pass he could see the helicopters rising up the valley floor towards the town.

On board Ears, the elint aircraft, the mysterious civilian in the back was rewinding the video of the first and second passes, cross-referencing GPS coordinates. As he zoomed in on the digital recordings, he saw it—a high-powered antenna in the barn window as plain as day.

"Captain, tell the cavalry it's that barn on the edge of town, on the second floor."

The helicopters were loaded, ready to go 24/7 and, ten minutes after the call, they whop-whopped their way onto the mountaintop, the troops already disembarking and heading for the barn as the birds touched down. But Kazim had prepared for this moment. As they reached the barn, his booby trap went into action, a proximity alarm silently signaling the laptop of the impending danger. The laptop set the timer triggers for explosive devices located around the room and under the laptop itself, and began the process of overwriting its hard drive with random ones and zeros, destroying all of its data. A few minutes later explosions rocked the area, ravaging the troops approaching Kazim's relay station. The helicopter crew carried the dead and wounded back to Mountain Base, calling in the cavalry to take over.

"The repeater was wired. We've got three fatals, two wounded. It had to be receiving from that village, line of sight 126°. The transmitter has to be there. Or maybe the bad guys are holed up in a cave on the hillside across the valley ..."

While all this was going on, Stephen was hard at work in the back compartment, puzzling over the source of the transmission he had picked up. It wasn't obvious, and, as he scrolled through the video, he could see no immediately evident corresponding base for receiving and transmitting. Wait a minute, there, on the truck, on both passes; he could see it, an aerial protruding from the window.

"Captain, I've got something else for them. The transmission was from a truck. It's gone now, but follow that road. It's the only way out of here down the valley."

"What kind of truck?"

"It's beat up, black, looks like a Toyota."

"Mountain Base, Ears. Get some more artillery fired up. A black Toyota half-ton is on the road toward Feyzabad. We're headed there."

The elint plane broke its lazy circle of the village and followed in the direction the truck must have gone, down the winding dirt road, dust still hanging in the still air. The truck was nowhere in sight.

"Mountain Base, there's nothing between us and the town, no place else for him to go. Any chance the local cops could help, maybe a road block?"

Mountain Base was well set up. They had done extensive local liaison, and the call to the local police was made.

Kazim had driven as fast as he dared, careening around the corners, holding his breath as he skidded near the edge, a void falling away below him. He knew that it was a race against time, that the plane would be on him quickly. He pulled under the trees and into the garage, hoping that he had beaten them. But he could hear the police scanner in the truck crackle out a description of the vehicle and, almost before the truck had stopped moving, he was out, running and shouting toward the mosque. As he ran he couldn't miss the unmistakable sound of helicopters descending on the road he had just used to enter the town.

Only minutes before the attack helicopters started to touch down, not knowing where or who to fire at, Kazim was shouting, "Out, out, now! Run! RV at Camp Medina."

The residents ran for their lives, not for the first or the last time. Most just blended in with the local villagers, but Kazim had made special arrangements for bin Laden, his deputy and himself. As the local constabulary did their search of the town, starting at the far edge, a truckload of produce, nicely covered to protect its valuable cargo from the hot sun, drove down the road toward the other end of the village. When the truck reached the hastily erected roadblock, the young policeman looked in the cab at the driver and stepped back. He gave a short salute, and the truck was on its way, courtesy of the local tribal chief.

It was the closest the group had come to disaster since the cruise missiles hit near Jalalabad, but this one was close, too close. Kazim choked on the dust under the vegetables and on the beginnings of a thought that maybe the infidels were not quite as stupid as he would like to think. His risk-taking had almost killed him even though he still was the best computer guy in the universe. He'd show the bastards.

After re-establishing their base, now at their Medina camp Kazim had organized as a backup, a just-in-case, bin Laden asked, "My brother, what went wrong?"

Kazim replied, "The Americans bribed someone in the village to betray us."

He was too ashamed to mention his close call with Stephen and the sophisticated gear in the back compartment of that airplane. He knew, though, that they would now have to establish new arrangements for any and all communications.

Kazim said to bin Laden, "The infidels will use any means to subvert us. They listen to our every word. From now on we must take special precautions when using any electronic devices. The infidels can listen to everything we say."

"So, Kazim, what can we do to protect ourselves against this insidious invasion of our privacy?"

Kazim had already given the problem considerable thought. It was clear that al-Qaeda did not have the ability to overcome the technological advantage held by the US. The American challenge was not in gathering the signals, it was in sorting through the huge maze of data that came to them every minute, 24 hours a day. Kazim knew that anything that al-Qaeda said on the airwaves could be gathered in the wide net that the US had cast.

"We must stop talking."

"But then how will we communicate?"

Kazim knew his history, that the maze of data could work to their advantage. Following World War II, the US had reviewed to exhaustion the intelligence that was on the table before the disaster at Pearl Harbor, all the scraps of information that pointed to the Japanese attack, but determined they'd had no way to link them together into a coherent picture. Now, following 9/11, things weren't much different, even though commissions and inquiries were examining an intelligence system that had failed to link bizarre flight training to bank accounts, immigration visas to known terrorists on watch lists, scraps of intelligence flags from European allies. Agencies still did not talk to each other, did not compare notes. The persistent confusion would give him time and space.

Kazim knew that he had to teach the al-Qaeda leaders not to use their phones, not to use the airwaves, because it was certain that the signals would be picked up. Hearing what was said was bad enough, but it wasn't the worst. What was much more serious was that the signals would give away their locations and invite instant retribution. Kazim's insistence had convinced a reluctant al-Qaeda to cut the US's electronic signals intelligence lifeline. As Kazim thought about all his ingenious work setting up the extensive computer and wireless systems—the extensive network that could no longer function, a source of al-Qaeda power projected worldwide, all lost because of US action—he became even more determined to retaliate against his personal enemy, the US. His *jihad* had become a personal one, nothing to do with bin Laden's Islam.

He had talked with his old friends in St. Petersburg about encryption, but the al-Qaeda organization was too far flung for this to be either affordable or practical. The only way to overcome the huge US advantage was by not providing anything to listen to, or by talking in ways that were not worth listening to.

"The US capacity is now even better than what we had in the Soviet Union in the old days of the Cold War. They have spent a huge treasure to be able to listen to our every word. The only safety that we will find is in not giving the infidels anything to listen to."

"But, Kazim, with our network now covering every continent, how will we lead our *jihad*?"

"By the grace of Allah and your good planning, you have decentralized our operations, so we will not need many links. But we must decentralize even more. We must encourage local cells to continue our quest. We can ensure their financial support through the bank accounts that you have established throughout the world, and by returning to our age-old system for transferring funds, the *hawala,* banking by word of mouth."

"Yes, that is so. Distributing funds will not pose a problem."

"We must stop using the ether for our communications. No cell phones or even satellite phones can be used, and no radios. The infidels are able to locate us through any signal that is transmitted. But we have many couriers who will pass our messages. The groundwork that you have laid through our training camps will now pay us big dividends, with our graduates in place worldwide, and they know how to continue our cause without detailed guidance. You only need to give the word, and *jihad* will be carried to every continent."

"Yes, Kazim, you speak the truth. By the permission of Allah, our philosophy has spread like wildfire around the world. Our brothers can act independently, without our management of each operation. But what about you? You have to lead your plan from here."

"I have a way to reach our brethren in America, and to link to the technical support that I require."

Kazim's background provided the solution to his own communication problem. In fact, it was so easy and straightforward that, among all the sophisticated surveillance systems, no one even looked for it. It was almost foolproof. Hotmail-addressed emails went through intermediaries in several European and hostile Middle Eastern countries, through trojan computers, using anonymous accounts, on dial-up connections and hot spots. They were virtually impossible to trace. In each message all negatives were reversed, so to the recipient "no" meant "yes," the first two digits of each number were increased by one, so telephone number 153-2286 became 263-2286, masculine and feminine were reversed so that "he" became "she," and all players went by western names. Assad was Silvio, Kazim became Bill, along with many other American-sounding names in the chat group. The NSA computers that processed the massive volumes of data from the signals and cyber collectors were programmed to look for key words, anything that might conceivably be linked to terrorism, or *jihad*, or al-Qaeda. Kazim had trained his group well. No key words were used that might trigger the National Security Agency computers to pay special attention. To an observer, Kazim's messages appeared as innocuous emails between American tourists, lost in the millions of inconsequential messages that traveled the internet every day.

And what only bin Laden, some couriers, and a small cell in St. Petersburg knew was that Kazim still had his secure link to the outside world, the one through the Russian's own encrypted diplomatic net.

CHAPTER 11

Now that he was retired and had time to reflect, Jim found that he did his best thinking on the treadmill. It was elevated a few degrees, enough to make him work, and he was sweating, legs starting to burn. "It's time I checked in, called in the big guns." He dialed the number from memory, and clicked on the speaker phone.

"Antonio, it's Jim Buchan."

"Hey, Jim. Long time no see. How ya doing?"

"I'm just fine, Antonio, but I've got something that worries me. How about lunch?"

"For you, Jim, anytime. You want to grab a sandwich at the old deli?"

"How about 11:30?"

"I'll see you in an hour."

As Jim drove to the deli his thoughts roamed back a few years. Antonio Pesquali had been his deputy. They had worked together for years, and Antonio had replaced him when he retired. They had barely spoken over the past years, Jim telling himself that he was taking special care not to interfere in Antonio's show, while not wanting to admit that he couldn't stand being out of the intelligence loop. After so many years of seeing the best, most secret product cross his desk every morning, he was feeling a bit deprived of information, a bit naked. The real reason that he had not stayed in touch was that he could no longer share Antonio's world; without security clearances they had nothing to talk about, nothing in common, and both felt a bit embarrassed. But even though Jim could no longer share his old world he knew that he'd get the straight goods from Antonio.

At 11:30 sharp Jim entered the old German deli, aptly called Franz's, which he and Antonio had so often frequented in the past, a little hole-in-the-wall a few blocks from the Agency headquarters in Langley. The place had the best smoked meat in town—in fact, it was the only thing worth having. Antonio had already taken the liberty of ordering their usual, the 'Mile High', and was seated in the last of the long row of red leather booths. The place had not changed or been redecorated since Jim started catching quick lunches there some twenty-five years ago. As he walked in, Suzie, the veteran waitress, came over, all smiles, greeting Jim like a long lost brother.

"Good morning, sir. Haven't seen you in ages. Welcome back."

It was the first time she had ever really spoken to him personally. In Franz's there was a tacit understanding that you pretended not to know the folks who worked down the street.

Antonio was dressed in the standard navy blue suit, black oxfords and a crisply starched white shirt, the uniform for the headquarters staff, except for his tie. He had always shown his independence with colorful silk ties, this time burgundy with a small pattern in blue. As he approached, Jim could not help but think that the older he got, the more Antonio looked like a character from an Italian mafioso movie—short, squat and a bit swarthy. He was of Italian-American decent, and his dark eyes and olive-colored skin looked right out of southern Italy. When he told jokes he even emulated an Italian accent. Jim had recruited Antonio from the New York police after they had worked together to snare an East German spy hiding under the cover of the UN, and then later moved him in as his 2 i/c, his second in command. They both had the same thorough, somewhat unconventional approach to problem solving and Antonio had easily transitioned to Jim's old position.

Jim slid into the booth, shaking Antonio's hand. In typical fashion, there was some small talk, but not much.

"Thanks for coming. It's great to see you."

"So, Jim, why the call? What brings you here?"

"Well, I do have something that I want to run by you, but it is really good to see you again."

"How's retirement? You surviving?"

"Sure am. You know the old joke, I don't know how I ever had time to work!"

"It's good to hear that, 'cause I'm not too far behind you and I'm starting to get a wee bit concerned."

"Well, we're out of the same mold, and what I find is that I'm enjoying all the things I never had time for. I doubt you have to worry, my friend."

"Family all good, Jim? I do know that that lovely wife of yours is doing well. Boy, her stuff is first class. She must have learned a thing or two from you about analysis. The unclassified assessments are really valuable, especially when we look at them alongside the product that usually crosses our desks. Leigh's papers are highly prized by your old office."

"Thanks, Antonio, I'll pass that on to her. Coming from you I know that she'll especially appreciate it. Needless to say, I agree with you—she's a natural. I find reading the assessments that she brings home keeps me up to speed on things pretty well. But I must say that I sometimes would like to be able to check it against the stuff in your in-basket."

"Yeah, I can understand that, but I can tell you that her product is pretty accurate. The only thing missing is some of the crucial details. How about your youngest, Mark? For a while there you were really worried about his hacking. Has he turned into another Bill Gates?"

"Not quite, but he's on his way with his own cyber security company. In fact, Antonio, that's what brings me here."

By the time the pastramis on rye were on the table the small talk was finished. They were ready to get down to business.

"So tell me, Jim, what's on your mind?"

"What I want to talk to you about is, well, you know that Mark has always been into computers. He and I were talking about the stuff that you're up to your armpits in, al-Qaeda, terrorism, all the threats that keep you up at night. Mark was asking me what I thought the terrorists might do, and I thought about how close Kazim came with the Onion."

Antonio leaned back in the booth, putting his hands behind his head. "Yeah, that was your finest hour. We still use it as a case study at the Farm."

"Well, Mark spent a lot of time looking at stuff and thinks he may have come across something. I've looked at it and it scares me silly. It looks almost like Kazim is back at it, this time with the hydroelectric power systems. I wondered if anyone has this covered?"

"Jim, we're watching it, but not nearly enough. With everything going on, trying to keep a handle on the really high threats, the hard infrastructure, ports, bridges, high-density buildings and things like that, we haven't got the resources to cover everything. We have a couple of young analysts who have talked about cyber terrorism, but they haven't convinced anyone else. The truth is that we are just spread too darned thin."

Antonio saw Jim's eyebrows go up. "Okay, okay, I see the look on your face. And you'd be right. It's more than just resources. The fact is that the high visibility tickets are getting all the attention. Even with the campus recruiting drives that we finally got going again, I'm really hard up for computer folks. And we're so short of linguists that we can't even cover the critical signals intelligence, the sigint.

"The last time we went through rating the threats, some of us were outvoted. The feeling at the top is that the dams are close to invulnerable. They're closed systems and independently operated, so even if someone could figure out how to get in, damage would be limited. The bottom line of all this is that I've had to pull the small team I had on the infrastructure side of things to concentrate on watching the sigint and the internet for terrorist traffic," Antonio said with a frown.

"Do I detect some cynicism there, Antonio? Because you'd be right. I think we have a problem."

"Tell me, Jim, what has Mark found?"

"He spent a lot of time exploring and scanning the many systems. I had suggested that if someone was going to succeed in causing widespread destruction, they'd have to find a common denominator, one that would capture a wide range of the dispersed systems. I think he found one."

"I'd sure hate to see you get involved in an Onion 2 as a civilian, but I know you, and you aren't going to let it go, are you? I must admit, though, that if you and Mark are willing to give it a shot, I'd feel a bit more at ease. It would be good to have someone like you having a look at it."

"Yes, Antonio, I'm not going to sit back and do nothing when I think that Mark is onto something big. And, for sure, Mark is at least as good, maybe even better, than anyone that you could put on it. How about we agree that I'll work the problem and if I find anything definite I'll let you know? I have some thoughts about where to start."

As much as he didn't want a civilian getting involved, Antonio knew that there would be no deterring Jim, that he was beaten. "If you can point us in the right direction, I could divert resources to do the follow-up. What do you have in mind?"

"It's a deal. If I'm in the ballpark on any of this, I'll need to find out what Kazim is up to these days. I've always wanted to show Mark some of Russia. Maybe we'll visit an old friend and see what he has to say. If anyone can find out what Kazim is doing, it's him."

"Jim, you're treading on what might be really dangerous ground. We don't know where this might lead. Tell me you'll contact me the minute you come across even a hint of confirmation."

"Are you kidding? Leigh wouldn't let me do anything else!"

As always, as if by magic, Suzie knew that now was the time. She had long ago guessed that these customers worked in the building down the street, and she made it a point of staying out of earshot until there was a lull in the conversation. The minute that happened she was there. "A refill on the coffee? How about the apple pie, fresh out of the oven?"

Jim and Antonio looked at each other and smiled. They never ordered desert, but they appreciated the discreet service, the intelligent smile.

"Thanks, Suzie, not this time."

She quietly made her way out of earshot back to the other end of the counter.

Antonio had been lost in thought for a minute, mulling over what Jim had told him. It fit with some of the threat assessments that a few of his staff were making, certainly not in the mainstream but close enough to have a ring of truth.

"If you and Mark are doing some traveling, maybe I should put you on a contract, both to cover expenses and to provide you some official status."

"Yeah, that would be good, I guess. You could pick up the airfare. You'll need to make it first class. I'm too old to travel at the back of the bus. Besides, if Mark and I were charging for this it would have to be big bucks."

"You got it. I'll get the paperwork started. If you find you're right about any of this, please shout for help before you get into hot water."

They gave Suzie a wave as they left, Antonio saying, "Jim, it was good to see you and to see you haven't lost your touch. I hope I don't hear from you again on this, but I guess we both know that what you've found is plausible. I can see how it could be done."

"I'll be in touch, Antonio."

When Antonio got back to the office his first call was to Frank Connors, his boss, the Director of Central Intelligence and the head of the CIA.

"Carol, I need to talk to him. Can you squeeze me in? Five minutes."

"He's just about on his way to the Hill—more testimony for the oversight committee. Come up right now and I'll tell him to hold."

Antonio took the stairs two at a time, and as he entered the outer office Carol flashed her radiant smile, blowing him a kiss and waving him in to the DCI's inner sanctum. It wasn't a huge office on its own, but tastefully furnished with a tan wood desk and cabinets, an ordinary-looking computer, and a couple of phones that looked normal but that Antonio knew provided for secure calls to anywhere in the world, including across town to the White House. An adjoining room doubled as a small conference center and a private dining room for special visitors. Many of those visitors who were impressed with the VIP treatment didn't realize that the fancy treatment allowed the Agency to corral them, to limit their access to the rest of the Headquarters building.

"Frank, I've just had an interesting talk with Jim Buchan. He and his son Mark have come across something that I think is worth following up."

"Jim getting back in the business? What's he found? His son is into computers, isn't he?"

"He sure is, in a big way, with his own security business. What Jim's got is about cyber terrorism directed at our hydroelectric system. What really caught my attention, though, is that Jim thinks that Mark has found the tracks of our old nemesis, Kazim."

"Man from the Onion File? That sounds a bit farfetched!"

"Doesn't it, though? Coming from anyone but Jim, I'd say forget it."

"My thoughts exactly. I thought we had agreed that that was a low priority area, but I can understand your concern. If Jim says there's something there, it's almost certainly the case. He wasn't wrong very often."

"That's true, and in this case we're getting the best that money could buy, for free. Well, almost free. Boss, I think they may be onto something. We'd be foolish not to let them have a go at it. You know Jim. He's going to do it with or without us. I told Jim we'd put him on contract to cover expenses. What I didn't tell him was that what I really want to do is give him some legal and financial cover and our life insurance if something goes off the rails. I couldn't face Leigh otherwise if he was out there on his own and something happened."

"Sounds good to me, Antonio. Let's do it."

CHAPTER 12

That evening Jim got a cold bottle of Corona from the fridge, cut a lime wedge and stuck it in the mouth of the bottle, a technique he'd picked up on their last holiday in Mexico. He was in his study, a ten-year-old phone list on his screen, as he thought back to the time several years ago that he had last talked with his Russian colleague. Only a bit more than a decade before, it would have been unthinkable, beyond anyone's wildest imagination, for him to be dialing the number that was now ringing. He had allowed for the time difference, hoping he'd catch the comrade at home before he left for whatever he was doing these days, not sure that he'd still even have the same number. Jim found himself excited in anticipation as the connection went through. He could picture Illyich, a huge man, yet you knew just looking at him that it wasn't his size that was important. It was his personality, so full of life and the storehouse of surprising, sophisticated knowledge that showed itself at every turn. Jim recalled with a smile that first improbable encounter, way back at the height of the Cold War.

As with Jim and the Agency, but on the other side of the Wall, Illyich Makov had spent a productive career in the KGB. Over the years they had run into each other's work, usually through the reports that crossed their desks, always at a distance. Even though they were on opposing sides of a huge divide, each had felt a sort of professional kinship and a healthy respect for the other. Each recognized that the other was in the same business. In the strange days of the Cold War when so little was as it seemed in the world of espionage and deceit, Illyich was surprised to find himself searching the files to see what Agent Buchan had to say on the big issues. And over the years, Illyich had found that his own take on those issues often paralleled Jim's. He had found a brother in arms, one whose words and actions he could take to the bank. Some might have said that the business they were both in was one of mutual destruction, but Jim and Illyich had long ago decided, independently, that what they were really after was just the opposite—to prevent nuclear suicide. Then, as the Cold War era ended with the collapse of the Soviet Union, Jim and Illyich had suddenly and unexpectedly found themselves on the same team, for the same cause.

"Hello Illyich, this is a voice from the past."

The response came without a moment's pause. "Jim Buchan, it has been a long time. How are you?" And continuing his rapid thought process which made him so interesting to talk to, "I know, you're finally calling to take up my offer of a few years ago. It still stands, you know."

After retiring, Illyich had established an international import-export business which, no surprise to Jim, had thrived beyond his wildest dreams. Illyich didn't know the word failure, and he didn't do anything by half measure. He was now a very wealthy man. Jim knew that he had passed up a golden opportunity when he had not accepted Illyich's offer to become a partner in the business, but at the same time he was well aware of the cutthroat capitalism that was emerging in Russia. He had no regrets about his decision.

"Well, Illyich, I'm just fine. A lot older, but not much wiser. The answer to your exciting offer is the same now as it was then. Much as I'd like to be working with you, nothing has changed here. Leigh completed her PhD and has a dream job that I wouldn't have the heart to even suggest she give up. How are you, my friend?"

"Jim, things couldn't be better, and I do know about Leigh. I read her work regularly. In fact, maybe we could really do something big. As you know I'm involved with the Russian-American Institute, and we could sure use two people with your talent and experience. Both of you come. We'd get two of you for the price of one!"

"We appreciate the vote of confidence, old friend."

"But if I know you, Jim, you didn't call me looking for a job, did you? What's on your mind after all these years?"

"Well, I do have something that will catch your attention. Think back to our common enemy, the one that brought us together way back."

"Like yesterday! How could I forget? Don't tell me he's come back to haunt us?"

"Maybe he has. Do you have any idea what he's doing these days?"

"Yes, I do. Not in any detail, but I still keep in touch with my old colleagues. In the business I'm in, being able to assess risks is vital, and these guys are the best. Nowadays I'm able to buy their services, so I'm still connected. This guy's name has come up because we'd still like to finish the job that you and I started. Knowing him as we do, you might guess that he'd still be in business, and you'd be right. We think he's working with the opposition, because we've run across his tracks in Chechnya and in Afghanistan. Why do you ask? What's he up to now?"

Jim paused for a second. "Illyich, this is remarkable, and more than a little worrisome. It's like déjà vu all over again. You remember my son, Mark? He's now twenty-four years old. He was always into computers and he has now turned his hobby into a thriving business."

"I can almost guess what you are going to say!"

"Well, you'd be right. Last summer, Mark and I were watching bin Laden's rant on TV and Mark asked about cyber terrorism. We talked a bit about some old times—enough so that he spent a lot of time and effort figuring out programs to test some of my tall tales. It was Mark who found a signature that I think might grab your attention."

"Unbelievable, Jim, but I guess I'm not surprised to hear that he's back in business. What is it this time? I'd be more than interested to hear about it."

"I'd like to meet with you to discuss some ideas. What would be easiest for you?"

"I'm tied up for a while working on a large deal that I have going on here. I couldn't get away for a week or so. It sounds to me like your timelines might be tighter than that. Why don't you come over here?"

"Yeah, I thought maybe Mark and I would pay you a visit. Where would I find you these days?"

"Well, I'm still at the same dacha. It's a bit bigger now than when you last saw it. You've missed out on some really big bucks not being here."

"I'll check the schedules and see what flights we could get."

"The easiest for you would be to arrange to get into Moscow in time to catch the one o'clock flight to Sochi. It's direct, gets in at four. It's the one I always use."

"Mark and I will be there the day after tomorrow. We'll book through Moscow to make the Sochi connection. Could you pick us up?"

"Sure will. See you then, old friend."

Jim put down the phone with a wry smile on his face, which disappeared immediately when he thought about how he was going to explain this to Leigh.

CHAPTER 13

Illyich had done all the right KGB things. Early duty on the front lines of the Cold War, Berlin and Austria, Eastern Europe during the turmoil of the '60s. Later, as he gained seniority, he had served two tours of duty under the cover of the United Nations in New York, so he knew the US well. He was a student of Russian history and, in the complex world that had emerged from Lenin and Stalin, he often took the long view. That approach to intelligence analysis sometimes did not sit well with some of his colleagues, but it often turned out that his assessments were closest to the mark. Along with all his other traits, his approach to interpreting the often incomplete and ambiguous intelligence set him apart from his colleagues. He stood out in a field of gray. Moreover, he had learned the language and culture of each of the half dozen countries where he had been posted and, after his years with the UN, he spoke English like a New Yorker.

Illyich was like a Russian bear—big, and shambling, over six feet tall and close to 300 pounds. He immediately filled any room that he entered, his thick, black hair crowning piercing brown eyes, almost black, his commanding personality and warmth gathering people in, the smile both charming and disarming. His loping gait fooled a lot of people; he was as quick and nimble as they come, both mentally and physically.

He and Jim had crossed paths at a distance over the years, not personally, of course. They each dealt with similar files, each looking at similar intelligence so painstakingly collected about each other. But then, in the early '70s, an historic event changed all that. President Nixon and Henry Kissinger pulled one of their rabbits out of the hat. They met with Premier Brezhnev, the arch enemy, to start the Strategic

Arms Limitation Talks, SALT, which led to the first agreement on limiting nuclear weapons.

This unlikely set of circumstances brought these two unlikely colleagues face to face. It was 1972, but Jim still marveled that all the formalities and protocol were but one stone in the foundation for the endless rounds of meetings between two wary adversaries, meetings leading to an improbable measure of agreement.

He remembered it like yesterday. Arriving at the formal black-tie affair at the Soviet embassy in Washington, Jim stopped in his tracks. The grand entry was lined with Soviet soldiers, at rigid attention, big, brown, flat hats and dress uniforms giving the distinctive, very military, unmistakably Russian look, and providing each arrival with a fanfare salute. Then he stopped again as he entered the grand ballroom. "What am I doing here?" he wondered.

Several hundred people from the diplomatic, military and spy worlds, were smiling and relaxed, as if meeting across the divide was a normal occurrence. There, the Russian foreign minister in deep conversation with Kissinger, and over there, in the corner, the chiefs of staff of the US and Soviet Union armed forces engaged in conversation as if they had just finished a round of golf.

Jim looked around the room in amazement. The Russians had really pulled out all the stops. A dancer from the Bolshoi pirouetted on the balcony to a trio playing Tchaikovsky. "Man, I wish Leigh could see this!" Jim mused. "What a cast of characters! How could the Cold War be so hot with these decision-makers having drinks like old friends?"

Both Jim and Illyich were there to ensure that the opposing 'bean counts' of strategic weapons stayed honest. Each was responsible for monitoring the other side's arsenal, and over the years Illyich had learned that the US was good at overhead photography. After Gary Powers in his U2 was shot down, the SR71 Blackbird and satellite imaging came along, so the KGB knew that they couldn't hide much. Then, as the Soviet Union gained strategic parity with the US, it became a matter of pride to negotiate as an equal with the enemy. Now that they had surpassed the US in numbers of missiles, warheads and megatons, they not only knew that the US knew this but took great pride in that fact, and they were ready and willing to demonstrate their power, to let the world know of their peaceful intentions, to confirm their status as an equal superpower.

In earlier years, when vodka was the oil that kept the machinery running smoothly, Illyich lived life to the full, easily the one still standing at the end of tough negotiations. Illyich's file on Jim was considerably thicker than Jim's file on Illyich. The KGB made it a practice of knowing their enemy, so the file on Jim Buchan included all the details: Agency position, past postings, wife Leigh, kids, home address, clandestine photos. Given the extent of KGB secrecy over the years, all Jim knew about his counterpart was the name of a Russian bear who had a reputation for hard-driving results. Before the meeting, each thought about the possibility of the other being there. Each knew that the other side would be closely watching the numbers of missiles and warheads that were being bargained, just like a bazaar.

As this introductory reception got underway both men scanned the huge room, Illyich looking for the face that matched the photos in his thick dossier, Jim looking for his counterpart, the bear—without, however, the luxury of photographs. When Illyich spotted Jim, he caught his eye and nodded toward the bar.

Jim thought, as he threaded his way through the crowd, that there could be only one man fitting the description in his file. The bear ambling toward their rendezvous had to be that man, and Jim said, almost aloud, "This should be interesting," his mind racing as he considered the possibilities and risks of meeting Makov face to face. Jim thought, "I need to send a message to him, something that will establish a personal link between us that we can use if the opportunity to cross paths ever happens again." By the time he got to the bar, Illyich already had the shot glasses of vodka full, ready to go.

"Jim Buchan, a toast to our two great nations. *Za vashe zdorov'e*—to your good health."

"And, most important of all, to peace between our two great countries. *Za vas* to you."

As the empty glasses hit the table, Illyich was already pouring the refill.

Jim looked Illyich in the eye. "Illyich Vladimir Makov, I suspect we may have cause to run across each other occasionally over the years. I am familiar with the importance in your country of a toast as a mark of respect, to end a session or to seal a deal. I want to get some personal ground rules straight between us so that there will be no misunderstandings, no offence taken in any future relationships. I will accept with pleasure the first toast, but it will be the only one. You could probably drink me under the table any day, but it's not going to happen. One toast is enough to show my respect and to seal my word. I will know to accept yours by your honoring this one agreement between us."

Illyich thought to himself, "Boy, this guy really thinks he's something. No wonder he has a reputation." But then as he looked into those gray-blue eyes he decided not to argue. And over the next decades that was just how it had worked.

It was some six months later that Jim had confirmation that his message had been received and understood. He found himself at a diplomatic reception, standing beside Andrei Gromyko, the long-serving Soviet foreign minister, who turned to Jim raising his glass.

"Mr. Buchan, one toast, to peace between our two great countries."

"Mr. Minister, I drink to that with respect and with my prayers."

With that toast Jim immediately knew several important things. He knew that Illyich's influence extended to the top levels of his government, but more importantly, that Illyich had accepted his ground rule and his word. The minister's toast was Illyich's reply to Jim. There was to be no double-dealing in their relationship. Jim hoped that his response to Gromyko would confirm to Illyich that same understanding.

CHAPTER 14

By 1989 Jim's professional life had revolved around the old Soviet Union for more than thirty years. Every day started with the overnight take: the little bits of human intelligence gleaned from a closed society, the photography from the Keyhole spy satellites, the signals intelligence picked up from the listening posts along the borders and around the world, the analysts' assessments of Soviet activity, the diplomatic judgments from missions across the globe. He knew the Soviet Union as well as any Westerner could. And yet, overnight the world changed, and all the old dependable facts could not explain what was happening. The most sophisticated, extensive, expensive intelligence system in the world could not predict the internal upheaval taking place in Moscow. The best analysts in Jim's Soviet section could not read the tea leaves. It was not as if the brand of tea had changed overnight, they had switched to coffee.

Over the years Jim and Leigh had developed a routine. Jim was constrained in what he could talk about from work, everything he looked at was classified, but Leigh had figured a way around these legalities. In their long discussions, sitting by the hour on their veranda, enjoying the tranquil views in the heat of Washington summers, discussions that ranged on everything from world affairs to the arts, Leigh did the leading, leaving Jim to agree or disagree on statements of fact. She knew that disagreement meant that Jim understood from his secret files that what she had said was not accurate, and over the years she had developed a pretty broad and detailed picture of US policy and action. Now Leigh was putting this insight to work in her analysis, and getting paid well for her product. US companies were crying out for business and risk assessments worldwide.

One evening in late September, as they enjoyed dinner in their favorite spot, their balcony, the sun just finally setting, the view spectacular, Leigh said, "You know, my love, what I don't understand is how, with such an extensive apparatus to watch the Soviet Union, none of you predicted what's happening over there. How could everyone have missed it? Surely there must have been some signs!"

Their meal was just about finished. Leigh had prepared a simple filet mignon on the barbeque, with a lovely light salad, a perfect meal for a warm clear evening. Before answering, Jim pushed his plate over to the side and rested his elbows on the table. Leigh took the opportunity to refill their glasses with burgundy wine, one of the few remaining good bottles from their wine cellar, stocked on their last posting in Europe some twenty years before. They both knew that this was the time to have one of their enlightened, thorough after-dinner talks.

"Well, you know, Leigh, even the best farmer can only work with the grain that's in the hopper. An intelligence analyst has to work with the information available. There are a couple of principles that people work to. One, as in HR, in the personnel business, is that people tend to behave in the future as they have in the past. Occasionally, people break out of the mold, but not often. And it appeared that the Soviet mold was made out of the concrete poured by Lenin and Stalin. No one could have predicted that Gorbachev would break out of that concrete. Heck, he not only broke out, he broke the mold. We were still counting missiles, which we got pretty good at, but we didn't have people on the ground, listening to the drums. Even today the Russian people themselves, the people who are now beating the drums, don't know what to make of their world."

"Yes, that's true. In the work I'm now doing it's clear that Russia is feeling its way, kind of groping, taking one step, then pausing to see what to do next."

"And, you know, the best satellite photography that I saw every morning didn't tell me that Gorbachev was going to defy history, that a buffoon like Yeltsin was going to find the guts to stand on a tank to turn the tide. The Russians themselves didn't see it coming. People talk about us not foreseeing the collapse of the Soviet Union as an intelligence failure, but the fact is, there simply was no intelligence, nothing to analyze that would have led us to that assessment. Gorbachev himself didn't know where all the changes might lead. He just knew that things needed to change."

"And they still are changing," Leigh sighed. "Now that I'm looking at so much information, I guess I can see what you're saying. We can hardly tell what's happened over there today, let alone what's going to happen next week. Now we have people on the ground, access to the leaders, business people assessing financial risks, tourists, students. In your day you didn't have any of that. I guess I can begin to understand the challenge."

"Yes, and the stakes were higher then. Now it's the risk of some dollars. Then it was a matter of life and death."

Among the many surprises—Gorbachev, Perestroika, Glasnost, the sledgehammers at the Berlin Wall, the breakup of the Soviet Empire—for Jim the biggest surprise of all was finding the respect and friendship that he and Illyich shared for each other. For all those years, since that first toast when the ground rules had been established, they had had a strange relationship, arm's length, watchful, but honest. Now they really were working toward the same objective, often on the same team. And, amazingly enough, that objective was the subject of that first toast, "peace between our two great countries."

CHAPTER 15

The next morning, less than 24 hours before Jim was to leave for Russia, he and Leigh were relaxing over coffee, soothed by the tranquil view over the park and river which masked the urban sprawl that surrounded them. For years, they had enjoyed the leisure of their Saturday mornings together. With Jim now retired and Leigh involved full time at the institute, their roles were reversed. After thirty-five years when Jim was telling the stories, at least those parts of the stories that he could tell, now Jim was eager to hear about Leigh's work. This morning, though, the topic was different.

"Jim, you and Mark have been spending a lot of time together lately. I know you've found some exciting stuff, but where is it taking you? It seems to me that it's almost as if you were back at work, and that worries me." Leigh crinkled her forehead and continued. "Now that you're not bound by all the clearances you used to have, out with it. What's going on? What have you two come up with?"

"Hmm, it's a long story, at least a story that had its beginnings a long time ago. I guess I've been avoiding the issue of talking to you about it. I know about your concern over the years, your stoic bravery, and I haven't wanted to worry you unnecessarily. Now it seems that Mark has found something that really concerns me. Given the work you're doing it isn't surprising that it is just what you predicted when we had that discussion with Mark in the coffee shop. One of the files that I worked on you'll remember well, the computer virus that took me to St. Petersburg."

Leigh visibly recoiled. "When you almost got killed!"

"That's the one. Well, Mark started to look at the risk of cyber terrorism against our hydroelectric power infrastructure. Unfortunately, he found something, and when he showed me what he found I think I recognized the pattern. There's enough there that I want to do some follow-up." Jim leaned over to the side table to refill his cup of coffee.

"But surely the people in your old office should be doing that. After all, they have the experts, the analysts, the equipment and the intelligence. Have you talked to Antonio?"

"Yes, I have. Antonio and I have an agreement that if I find anything definite they'll put resources on it. But right now they have nothing to go on, no place to start. And, you know, Leigh, this kind of thing takes intuition, there's a lot of gut feel involved. On this one I'm the one with the gut. I've been there before, and the people I need to talk to will help because of our personal history, our track record together. Official action by Antonio's people won't cut it, especially in the time frame that I think may be required. Besides, Mark is better on the computer stuff than anyone I ever had working for me. I think between the two of us we might have a good shot at tracking this down. The first thing I want to do is find out if there is any way that what I see could be for real—whether Kazim is even alive, whether he could be involved. Mark and I are going to meet with Illyich in Sochi. He's the one person who might have a chance of finding out what Kazim might be up to."

After a moment of thought Leigh said, "Unfortunately, my love, I think you may be onto something. Everything I see indicates that al-Qaeda has to be planning more devastation, and cyber terrorism is a distinct possibility. But, Jim, it isn't fair for you and Mark to be out front on the firing line on this. I thought we were home free once you retired. And Mark isn't in that sort of business."

"True, but with his computer expertise he will track things down if there's anything there to track."

"Jim, I am not sure I like the way this is sounding. We had a deal that seems to be going up in smoke. All those years I supported your career, no questions. The dangerous trips, the near-death experiences, the time you were shot and had to be airlifted home from St. Petersburg. I didn't ever talk about it, I never complained, never said no, but I worried about you for more than thirty years. This last period has been the first time since our kids were born that we have had real quality time together, time when I could forget about that nagging fear."

"Yes, my dear, but it's different now. Mark and I are just tracking computer stuff, trying to crack what he found. The follow-up that we're doing is pretty straightforward."

"I don't think so. I don't like the sound of it, not one bit." Leigh continued, and there was no stopping her now. "I guess I've gotten used to having you safe. The deal was when you retired, it was my turn. I can't believe you are now proposing to take a trip to Russia and to take Mark along to boot, both of you at risk. And looking for the monster that almost killed you!"

Leigh stormed from the deck, heading for the bedroom, the room that carried so many memories from the past, of Soviet bugs and the real start to Jim's career. After a bit, Jim went in quietly, finding her face down on the bed. Sitting beside her he gently stroked her hair. "Honey, I'm sorry to upset you. I know you worried about me all those years, but this isn't like that. I'm not going to be on the firing line on this one. Mark and I will do the leg work, the research. I promise that I'll call Antonio to take over the minute we have something to go on. Leigh, please look at me."

He cupped her face in his hands. "Honey, I'm so sure about this. I think our nation is in real danger. I can't sit back and do nothing. If Mark and I can do anything to help avert disaster, we have to do it!"

Leigh threw her arms around him, tears flowing down her cheeks. "Jim, I know that. It's just that I love you so much. The thought of you going back, I guess it unlocked all my old fears. You know, every time we made love in the old days, afterward I'd lie there thinking, wondering what I'd do without you. Now we're getting to the point where life is even more precious. I can't bear the thought of anything that might take you away any sooner than what we know we'll eventually have to face. I guess I just don't want to give fate a helping hand."

"I love you, Leigh. And I agree with you, we have a wonderful son and a wonderful life that I wouldn't put at risk for anything."

From the first day that Jim had laid eyes on her, their love had been central to their lives, and later their lovemaking passionate and satisfying. This morning was no different, and as they lay together in bed, Leigh said, "Okay, lover, I guess that I won't go back quite yet to worrying about the wonder of it all. So, what are your plans?"

Jim didn't reply, lost in thought.

"I notice that you've been on the phone a lot more than normal. Where is Illyich? And I've heard Moscow being bandied around. Jim, what exactly have you organized? What have you cooked up?"

"You're right, as always, my dear. You'd think after all these years I would have figured out how to keep a secret or at least to stop trying, even though it's been a habit for so long. We're going to follow up with Illyich in Sochi. He will for sure still be connected in Moscow and if he can't locate Kazim no one can."

"When are you going?"

"We're booked on tomorrow's flight, through Moscow to Sochi, back in four days."

"A fast trip," Leigh responded. "You're sure not giving Mark any time to enjoy the sights!"

"That's true, but we need to move fast. All my experience and intuition tell me that we haven't got any time to spare. Kazim has got to be close to pulling the trigger. We need to be back here so that Mark can keep an eye on his screens."

"Jim, I'm sorry about the outburst. The thought of you going back on the firing line got to me, I guess."

"Shh," Jim said, putting a finger to her lips. "You can burst out anytime if it leads to what we just had, my dear. I kind of enjoyed the results!"

"Okay, enough of that stuff, you old letch. But seriously, Jim, I want you back from this in one piece. Please be careful. Your last John Wayne act almost got you killed."

"We'll be careful. We're doing the footwork, the research. I can't see us getting into glue on this."

"Promise me that you'll call in the cavalry, plus all the close air support in the US Air Force, at the first sign of trouble."

CHAPTER 16

The flight to Sochi was a long one, taking Jim and Mark across the Atlantic, first to Moscow on a brand new Aeroflot Airbus, with smooth flying and comfortable service. Compared to the old days, business class actually meant something on this flight, and the flight attendants looked pretty spiffy in their uniforms.

"Well, Mark, I can tell you that times have changed, at least in this part of the Soviet empire. The old Russian airliners didn't come close to this. They were knock-offs of US aircraft, without the luxuries."

"This one has to be the top of the Airbus line—leather seats, phones, the works. Traveling business class for the first time I have nothing to compare with, but I must say this is awfully nice. And the champagne in the middle of the afternoon, I could get used to this!"

About then the menu for dinner was presented, and Mark just rolled his eyes in amazement.

"Dad, is this the way you spent your life on the road?"

"Only at the tail end, and only when I traveled to a formal meeting. Till then I was with the rest of the peasants, back there," as he pointed his thumb over his shoulder.

They both enjoyed the three-course meal, caviar to start, French-style tournedos with béarnaise sauce and a tossed salad, with a deliciously sweet Russian dessert. Three types of wine accompanied the three servings. First, and surprising to both of them, a French Chablis, then a Napa Valley red, followed by a Russian ice wine with dessert.

When the list of liqueurs was presented, Jim looked at Mark and said to the flight attendant with a smile, "This young man will have your best cognac; it's too good to pass up. I'll take a rain check. Can I reserve mine for the trip home?"

As they pushed the buttons and the seats moved down to full recline, Jim spoke quietly. "I know you are going to find my friend Illyich as fascinating as I do, and we've got a lot of talking to do. Get as much shut-eye as you can. We're going to be busy."

"I have no doubt about that. I really can't wait to see what you have planned for Kazim. I just can't imagine."

"We'll have to be patient, but at the end of all this I'd like to see him brought to justice."

It seemed but short minutes later that the lights came on in the cabin and fresh orange juice was being served. As they started the descent into Sheremetyevo, the airport serving Moscow, Jim said, "I wonder if the Western-style service we're seeing here extends to the airport. I sure hope that they've improved things. Last time I was through it was pretty bad. The Soviet Union never did quite figure out the meaning of customer service, and the facilities were everything you've heard about Soviet architecture—and I was getting VIP treatment then."

"What do you mean, VIP treatment? How did that happen?"

"I was on my way to meet with the KGB. That's the story that I hope you're going to hear in Sochi."

"Aw, man, this is great, Dad!"

Then, as they made their way through to their connecting flight, Mark asked, "It's still pretty bad now. Everyone seems so surly. Has it got any better?"

"Doesn't seem like it to me. Some work's been done, but there's a lot more people traveling now, so things are just as slow. I guess the customer service message hasn't gotten through."

Like airports the world over, this one had construction going on everywhere, the progress never quite keeping up with the demand. But here, as in the old Soviet Union, bureaucracy took precedence over people, obstacles at every turn. After many line-ups and much red tape, they made their connection. This time it was an older model Tupolev 154M, the Russian knock-off of the Boeing 727, but still sleek, fast and comfortable, and the best thing was it took them direct to Sochi, 1500 miles to the south. Even though they were the only English speakers on board, they managed without too much difficulty using the universal sign language, laughing with the flight attendants and other passengers in their awkwardness.

Mark was surprised to find business-class comfort on the aircraft, but Jim's analysis made sense. "This flight carried the old Soviet *nomenclatura*, the Party bigwigs and now the new capitalists, to their dachas in the sun. They weren't about to slum it with the proletariat."

Between naps, Mark was like a five-year-old with his questions. "How come Illyich is in Sochi? It sounds kind of backwoods. I would have thought Moscow, or maybe St. Petersburg would be a more exciting place to retire."

"Illyich had enough excitement in his career to last a few lifetimes, Mark. I don't expect that he's looking for any more, and I know him well enough to know for sure that he will be very well set up. The dacha that he used to live in as a senior member of the *nomenclatura* was pretty comfortable. Some people call Sochi the Russian Riviera. It was the watering hole for the elite long before the upper levels of the Soviet hierarchy commandeered it for themselves. And when you see Sochi, I think you'll agree it's a lovely place to live—beautiful beaches, warm water, mountains, nice weather, lots of good-looking girls in bikinis, most of them without tops—"

"—Too bad you didn't plan more time so I could see for myself!"

"Also, I expect Illyich is well connected, both socially and technically. He was always way out in front of the pack with computers. I'm sure he can run his business empire from home. I doubt that he has to travel anywhere he doesn't want to."

"What's he like? He doesn't sound like the stodgy caricature of a spy that we read about, crumpled suit, baggy trench coat, smelly Russian cigarette."

"You'll see. Probably the most urbane, well-read, quick-witted, charming man you'll ever meet. And honest, straight, brave beyond belief. I've always wondered how he came out of the Soviet mold. He could be a British diplomat or a New York power broker. He just commands attention."

"I can hardly wait to meet him!"

They landed at the fairly small Adler Airport that serves Sochi, and as they emerged from arrivals into the sunlight, Mark said immediately, "That's got to be the guy you used to call the bear. That's got to be Mr. Makov, over there."

"It sure is. And he hasn't gotten any smaller since I saw him last."

"Jim, *privetstvie*," Illyich greeted them. "Welcome to Sochi. It really is good to see you. I see you're still keeping in the same fine shape as always. And this is Mark. Mark, I'd have known you even if you weren't with my friend here. You've got his eyes. Mark, I know your dad, and I know his modesty. He probably hasn't told you how good he is. Maybe while you're here we'll find time for some old war stories."

"Sir, I like you already."

"Don't believe a word of it, Mark," Jim scoffed. "But this guy does spin a good yarn."

"Let's go, you two. After the traveling you've done, I think you need to get comfortable, and I've got just the spot." Jim was happy and excited to see Illyich, once again marveling at how easily he made the transition between cultures and languages, from Russian to New Yorker without missing a step.

It was clear as they approached the parking lot which vehicle had to be Illyich's—there couldn't possibly be two of them in Russia. And, sure enough, as they approached Illyich clicked his key fob, the lights flashed and the doors clicked open. Even knowing Illyich as well as he did, Jim was amazed. "Okay, my friend, there has to be a real story here. How in the world did you orchestrate this?"

Illyich said with a grin, "Large man, large vehicle?"

They were climbing into a real, live, American-made Hummer, the commercial version, leather seats, fully equipped, even to the GPS display. Illyich continued, "Well, you're right, there is a story. I'm in the process of negotiating to import these for the burgeoning nouveau riche market. I've got the first and only demonstrator."

Mark exclaimed, "You've got to be kidding! In Russia?"

"Yes, if all goes as planned, I expect to deliver about 500 a year, starting now. Should make me a few rubles and in the meantime I can get to places in the mountains that have only been visited by donkeys."

As they drove from the airport toward the coast, Mark marveled at the scenery. "Dad, you were right, this is truly beautiful."

Snow-capped alpine mountains behind them on the left stretched down to the Black Sea coast, glimpses of tile roofed estates nestled behind stone walls, fleeting views of blue water flashing in the sun, low hills rising to the horizon on the right. Mark was in the front with Illyich, listening in rapture to the descriptions of the countryside, and then of the city as they arrived in the more densely-populated suburbs.

"Illyich, I'm flabbergasted. Those mountains back there look like ski country. Are they developed? Do people come to ski?"

"We're just starting, Mark. The first heli-skiing got going a couple of years ago, and an extreme skiing movie was filmed last year, which should bring your rich Americans here in droves."

"Things have sure built up since I last visited you," Jim exclaimed.

"They have indeed. You'll only see a bit of it this time—we haven't got too far to go. The airport is 25 kilometers from Sochi, but the city stretches for miles along the coast. I'm about a half-hour north of the center."

"Looking at all the construction going on, it seems that others must have found your hideaway, Illyich. But I see that the big red-and-white tower on the hill still dominates the town. And I remember the port area, really attractive with the harbor against the river. Does it still have that terminal, the Harbor Station with the spire gleaming in the sun?"

"It does, Jim, but now it can hardly meet the demand. The old *nomenclatura* pretty well had things to themselves, but more and more Russians can afford to travel and many have boats. The harbor is crammed with yachts. The long piers have been expanded but they can barely handle the boat traffic, and all the beaches overflow with young people."

"Well, your climate would sure be a draw for Muscovites, a welcome relief from Moscow. Lots of sun, beautiful summers, mild winters and the Black Sea!"

"My friends, that's why I'm here. Easy access, still not too big, an agreeable climate, good living. Now I only travel when I have to."

Illyich swung left off the road onto a short driveway and as they rounded a bend Jim was struck by the changes that had taken place in the ten years since his last visit. While before the dacha had been lavish by Soviet standards, befitting a KGB general, now it was positively opulent.

"Illyich, I see that you have indeed done well over the past few years. But how come you still have access to this place? Didn't that disappear when you retired?"

"It did, but once we were into capitalism I was able to make an offer that couldn't be refused. I own this humble abode, and I live here full time now. Come, I'll show you around."

As they rounded a corner of the house, Jim and Mark stopped dead in their tracks, looking in wonder at the panorama in front of them. The edge of the infinity swimming pool gave the illusion of extending into the sea beyond, the patio around the pool extending into space. A dock stretched out from a pebble beach, a gleaming white yacht moored against it. Mark's eyes roamed the horizon, then closer in, to the pool and grounds. His eyes stopped roving, as Jim and Illyich heard the quick intake of breath. They followed his gaze. Illyich chuckled.

"Mark, you are not the first and you're not likely to be the last to react to that view. Come and meet Katrina."

Katrina stood up as they approached. She was the most striking girl that Mark had ever laid eyes on. Long dark hair framed a chiseled face, brown eyes smiling out at him. As he drew alongside he realized that she came up to less than shoulder height. How could such a mite radiate that much warmth and beauty? In his eyes, she filled the space around her.

Smiling, Illyich put a huge arm around her and said, "This is my girl," winking at Jim as the look of consternation crossed Mark's face. He extended Mark's stunned silence for a bit and then added with a smile, "Mark, she's been my favorite girl since she was born twenty-two years ago. This is my granddaughter, Katrina Makov. Katrina, my old friend, Jim Buchan, and this is Mark, his son."

Katrina turned to Jim. "Mr. Buchan," she stated formally, in flawless English, "I feel I know you well from my grandfather's stories, although we've never met. Mark, it's a pleasure to meet you." Mark felt a jolt of excitement, of pleasure, when she shook his hand, a touch so gentle, like silk. How could it be so electric?

Illyich looked at Mark. "I wouldn't want to tell stories out of school, Mark, but Katrina wasn't so sure that she'd look forward to your visit. I suggested that she come for the weekend, and she doesn't like being told what to do, especially if she thinks she is being set up with a blind date."

"Oh, Illyich, don't embarrass me." But as she looked at the tall beanpole in front of her, glasses glinting in the sun, trimmed auburn hair and mustache—a clean-cut look—a face open and honest, she thought, "Hmm, interesting."

"Clearly, Illyich, this young lady is a chip off the old block," Jim said, looking at Katrina and laughing. "I sure don't mean physically. How could a bear like you have this little beauty as a granddaughter? I'm referring to intellect. She's taken a lesson from you in sophistication and language skills. Where in the world did you learn to speak English like that, young lady, and with a slight British accent?"

"Thanks to Deda, Grandfather, here, my dad was able to send me to international schools. I spent a year in the US and one in England, in your ninth grade and the British General Certificate of Secondary Education, for my eleventh grade."

As they walked, Mark found himself trailing, Katrina by his side. Fortunately for him, she was doing the talking. He was tongue-tied for the first time he could remember.

"Illyich, if memory serves me, your wife died, what, in the '60s?"

"That's right, 1967. My son was twelve years old. He grew up with me, then married early. Katrina came along the next year. Believe me, Jim, when I say she's been the best thing in my life since my wife died."

After touring the beautiful grounds, Illyich led them to a balcony looking out over the coast. Four crystal shot glasses were alone on the table. Illyich proceeded to take the chilled bottle of Stolichnaya vodka out of the ice cooler, cracked open the bottle, and poured four liberal portions. Illyich looked Jim in the eye, turned to Mark and said, "Mark, this toast was the start of a long and fruitful relationship." He raised his glass. "One toast, to peace between our two great countries."

"Illyich, I can hardly believe that we are here to raise our glasses for our toast once again," Jim said. "Way back, that first time in Washington, we could never have imagined, never dreamed, that our world could have changed the way it has. Old friend, we have been blessed."

Mark was fascinated. He had only seen this kind of ritual in movies, and had never drunk pure vodka, straight, and in one gulp. "Hey, wait a minute here," he intervened. "You two have got some explaining to do. What I see here is way more than just a toast, or a professional rivalry, or for that matter even a professional friendship. Maybe this goes a little way to making some sense out of some of the weird stuff I used to hear about when I was a kid. Katrina, do you know what's going on here?"

"To tell you the truth, that's the only reason I agreed to come this week. I thought I might just hear a little about his past. Illyich—I've called him that as long as I can remember—never told me much about his career either."

Mark thrilled at what came next. "But now that we've met, I'm really glad I came. I wouldn't want to miss this," she said, all the while looking directly at Mark, a radiant smile lighting her face.

Jim saw Illyich give a slight wave of his hand and, as if by magic, a large plate of cold meat, cheese and fruit appeared on a side table. Mark and Katrina were so absorbed that they didn't even notice the silent apparition in traditional, flowing gowns that set down a frosted pitcher of ice tea and quietly departed.

"Son, it is a strange world. And the relationship you see here is one of the strangest. Illyich and I spent our working lives as enemies, and at the end it turned out that over all those years we both had had the same objective: not to blow humanity off the face of this beautiful planet.

And it was serious. Radically different philosophies, ideologies, nothing in common as a place to even start dialogue."

Jim paused for a minute, lost in thought. "You know, Illyich, even at the very end, in '89, I was amazed at how far apart we were. Things were changing so fast, with the President and the British prime minister meeting their counterparts on your side of the curtain, some military leaders exchanging visits, things starting to open up, but the word still had not started to filter down to the troops. I remember speaking with the Soviet Air attaché in Washington, and saying how much things had changed in Western Europe, with borders disappearing, people moving freely from Norway to Greece, kids backpacking everywhere. I attributed this openness in large part to a common language, which happens to be English. All the kids have learned it in school, and can communicate in any country in the European Union.

"I was making a point about breaking down barriers, about open borders. To my surprise, in fact even horror, the attaché's response illustrated the divide that was still there, embedded so deeply into the psyche. He said, 'Yes, it's like the cat sitting outside the mouse hole, waiting patiently. But as long as the cat is there, the mouse won't come out. After a bit of thought the cat said to himself, "As long as I'm here the mouse won't budge. But I'll fool it. I'll use another language. If a dog was here the mouse would not be afraid, because if a dog were here a cat wouldn't stick around." So, the cat barked like a dog, and the mouse thought, "Hmm, the cat must have gone." When he came out, he was promptly devoured. Ah, yes,' said the attaché, 'It's very important to learn another language.' And, you know, that little story says a lot about the fifty years of Cold War. We really did approach things from opposite ends of the spectrum. Even at the very end, experts on both sides were still inflexible on the party line, no give at all. It's amazing that Illyich and I ever found each other. And I've always marveled that he survived the Soviet regime. Illyich, you really did come from a different mold."

Katrina chimed in, "I never understood our history. After living and traveling abroad, looking at other people and other countries, and the way the world is going, how could your generation not have figured a way out of the impasse over all those years? How could you have brought the world so close to disaster?"

After a bit more banter, Illyich settled back into his chair. "Jim, I agree with your son. He deserves a history lesson. Katrina and I haven't talked much about our past either. Mark, your dad signed an oath not to reveal the intelligence he spent his life working with. He especially can't talk about the code word part of it—that's the special intelligence that's beyond the normal top secret classification. The work he was in was almost all code word. After all, he was busy looking at what I was doing! I signed a similar oath, but now there's a difference. If your dad breaks that oath, which he would never do, there might be a lawsuit. Over the years the US has occasionally taken action against the rare offender, but generally it has depended on people like Jim here to keep their promise. But I can tell you that, in the old days, if I broke the faith it wasn't a lawsuit, it was a bullet, at least for the lucky ones. Some were tortured beyond belief as a lesson to the rest of us. Others were roasted in the infamous oven. Our Stalinist legacy was unforgiving. Fortunately, those days are gone forever. Now no one could care less what I do. With what we may be embarking on, I think you need to know some background. Certainly you should know what you might be getting into, about the лук, our Onion File. Without you getting all the security clearances that you'd need to have in America, your dad can't tell you about any of it. But I can, so after a decent night's sleep we'll get started."

CHAPTER 17

The next morning over a breakfast of fresh fruit, croissants and dark Russian coffee, Mark said, "I've waited a long time for this. I have to admit that I didn't sleep that well last night thinking about all the questions I want to ask."

Illyich smiled. "Just a minute now. Don't kid me about the cause of those circles under your eyes. I'm a light sleeper and on one of my regular walks around the balcony, I just happened to observe you two deep in conversation out on the bluff. I must say, it gave my heart a stir! It was a beautiful night."

Katrina and Mark looked at each other, eyes sparkling, and said in unison, "Yes, it was."

They had sat talking for hours, the moonlight shimmering on the water, both eager to hear about the other's life. As different as they were, different backgrounds, cultures, history, they were surprised to find that they had so much in common. They liked the same music and literature, had similar outlooks on politics, on values, on goals and the future.

Katrina had seen and done a lot in her twenty-two years of life, and Mark was fascinated—the language skills, the treasure of knowledge and interests. He spoke his thoughts aloud. "Boy, the things I have been missing. I haven't done any of that, Katrina."

"Yes, but you are already established, with your own business, out on your own, and I don't even know what I want to do yet."

As they made their way back to the house heading to their respective bedrooms, Katrina had put one arm around Mark's waist, the other reaching up, drawing his head down for a brief kiss. "Mark Buchan, I think I like you. I look forward to tomorrow."

Mark did indeed have a difficult time getting to sleep. He had never met a girl like Katrina.

"Okay, let's take our coffee to the pool and get started. Jim, you know, I think I may enjoy this as much as our two kids."

Despite the hour of the day, Illyich pulled a bottle of twenty-year-old Stolichnaya Cristall vodka out of the freezer, as if an actual toast was required to bring the story home. Illyich saw the look of amazement streak across Mark's face, and said with his eyes twinkling, "Don't worry, young man. I won't subject you to a toast with breakfast. Your dad called the shots on that almost thirty years ago, and I know better than to argue with him."

And so Mark and Katrina's history lesson started, with the toast and what it had meant to both Jim and Illyich, and the subtle impact that it had had over the years on a much broader set of relationships.

Mark commented, "So, we could say that that toast all those years ago led the two of you to your collaboration on the Onion File?"

"That's right, Mark. Illyich and I would never have gotten together if it weren't for that fateful reception so many years ago in Washington. And, what's more important, we'd never have become friends."

"Illyich, what about this Russian Onion that almost got my dad killed?"

Katrina settled back in her chair, fascinated.

"To start with we should set the scene. Remember, this was at the height of the Cold War, in the late '80s. We had all kinds of plots going on, some of them really down and dirty, like recruiting the executive assistant to the chancellor of West Germany to our cause, or assassinating diplomats. When I say we, I mean the outfit I worked for, the KGB. Most of these schemes were tightly held secrets, compartmentalized, so that only the people involved knew about them, and I can tell you, the KGB knew how to keep secrets."

"I can vouch for that, Illyich. You were pretty hard to break into, and darned effective in some of the programs you ran. I remember one in particular, one we knew all about but couldn't do a damn thing to counter." Turning to Mark and Katrina Jim added, "Just to give you an idea of the cleverness we faced, Europe had a program, TIR, Transports Internationaux Routiers. It was an international agreement to permit trucking across borders, to facilitate trade, so that a TIR licensed truck could cross from country to country. Even at the height of the Cold War there was a fair bit of cross-border activity and we always suspected—heck, we darn well knew—that the Red Army sent their field commanders as second drivers, to scout the territory they would be invading if things turned hot. If they had gone to war those battalion commanders knew exactly what they would face on the ground."

Illyich laughed. "So, you knew about that, did you? You know, it wasn't only the ground commanders. We knew how many aircraft you had on each squadron, what deployment bases were earmarked for use, the forward operating bases. Even our Spetznaz troops, the Special Forces guys that would go in before the invasion, had reconnoitered their targets. They had been over the ground, taken pictures, the nuclear sites, the Rhine bridges, airfields. They knew where they would place the explosives, how much to use and where it would come from. We were amazed that we got away with it! I always wondered how come you didn't try to stop it."

"Well, money counts," Jim said. "The nations valued the trade too much to even think about stopping it, but then, once we realized that we weren't going to stop it, we decided we could live with it. Maybe it wasn't a bad thing that those soldiers knew that they faced a well-equipped and well-trained adversary. Folks, what I find really interesting now is that after all those years of highly classified intelligence, I can talk about it. Heck, Leigh can now find most of this stuff through the internet."

"Jim, you and I should sit down and compare notes, maybe write a book or make a movie, a 'blockbuster' as you call it. We could really have some fun."

Katrina looked at Mark. "They could start with the Onion story. It sounds like it might be a good one. So, Illyich, we can't wait. Let's hear it."

Illyich leaned back in his chair, and folded his arms across his massive torso. "As I said, we worked in cells, compartments. Most of the time the right hand didn't know what the left hand was doing. It turned out that the cell that this guy Kazim ran had developed a software virus to corrupt US financial systems. It was beautiful, elegant. What he did was design a worm that would go into the major credit card and bank databases. He had set the program up by using a hack that garnered the passwords and accounts of bank managers. It was to be activated by a call to Port 5000. When the time came to go, a simple IP address and port number was called, a password entered, and it would then spread through the banking system, erasing all the data in its tracks. I had an inkling that something important was going on, but I wasn't in the loop. I can tell you that if I had known about it at the time I would have thought it was a great plan, brilliant. After all, we were in the business to win against the United States, any way we could."

Mark understood the technical implications of the Onion. "So, until it was activated there was nothing to find, nothing there to see?"

"That's exactly what happened, Mark. I had my people across the US going nuts. But of course, it was a wild goose chase," Jim added.

"But the Soviet Union was in turmoil, coming apart at the seams. Those years after 1989 were a roller-coaster ride. First Gorbachev, and then after the Wall came down, Yeltsin standing on the tank in front of the Duma. Things were changing so fast that no one knew what the outcome would be. No one knew whom to trust, whom to bet their life on. Loyalties were fragile, with a large faction planning to turn the clock back to the good old days, to retain their power."

"Mark, it was at this point that an extraordinary thing happened. Oh, man, Illyich, it's like it was yesterday. I picked up the phone in my office."

"Hello, Mr. Buchan. One toast, to peace between our two great countries."

"Illyich Makov."

"Yes, Mr. Buchan. If our toast is going to come to fruition, we need to talk."

"I'm listening."

"We need to meet, and soon. Prague should be neutral enough ground for both of us."

The pause only lasted for seconds. "When?"

"Tomorrow afternoon, say five o'clock. In front of my embassy."

"I'll be there."

"Mark and Katrina, you can believe it when I say I had some scrambling to do to convince my boss to go along on this one. I mean, in our business it's not as if you just go out and meet with the opposition. This kind of thing only happened in spy novels. I had two major hurdles. The first was to overcome forty-five years of history, to even think about meeting with a senior KGB officer. When I finally got reluctant agreement, the next was to overrule the strong view that I shouldn't do it alone. They wanted to wire me and have a whole battalion backing me up. If it hadn't been for that toast almost twenty years before I wouldn't have done it, and I certainly wouldn't have been able to go it alone. But you know, sure enough, when I arrived in front of his embassy, he was there."

"So, Illyich Makov, we meet again."

"Yes, and after all these years as enemies, this time I come as an ally. You are following what is happening in my country. You know the turmoil, the uncertain future that we face." It was a statement, not a question.

"Yes, and I can tell you, we are not finding it easy to make any assessment, to make any predictions. I'm being pressured to make recommendations, but things are moving way too fast."

"I live there, on the inside, and I don't know what the outcome is going to be. It's too close to call. When you return, you can make your report that Illyich Vladimir Makov says that not even the Kremlin knows what the outcome will be—and those inside are the ones making the decisions. If we are to change history, start a new direction, many things must change. And I find myself with information that will place our relationship with you at risk."

"Mr. Makov, my being here to speak with you goes against all of our history, too. So, tell me, what is this information?"

"I told your dad, Mark, about what he later called the Onion File.

My finding out about it was a stroke of luck, pure chance. Normally I'd never have been aware of it. With all the upheaval going on, though, one of Kazim's people wasn't sure what side he should be on. The lad recognized the implications of the work he was doing, what it would mean for the new détente with the US if the worm was released. He and one of my officers had been to school together and, fortunately for us, he came to my officer for advice. That was the break we needed."

"So, as we walked the streets of Prague, Illyich told me that a sleeper worm might be activated in our financial systems, and that if that happened we could kiss détente goodbye, we'd be back to the bad old days of the Cold War—things were that close. Mark and Katrina, you need to recognize the courage that it took for Illyich to meet me. For him, it was literally life or death. Had the upheaval in the Soviet Union turned out differently it's for sure Illyich would not be here talking about it."

"And of course, Dad, when you set your team loose to try to find whatever it was, they didn't find anything. The worm was in the computer code, but if you don't know what you're looking for, and they wouldn't have known, it becomes a needle in a haystack. It can take thousands of man-hours to debug code."

"You got it, son."

"So, what happened?"

"Well, it didn't take long to realize that Jim wasn't going to make any headway at his end," said Illyich. "I was also working at my end, but it also didn't take long to figure that we weren't going to crack Kazim's team easily. As I said, the KGB worked in tight cells, and he had a lot of support at high level. I started to get some leads and wanted Jim to be part of it when it broke, so that the US would be ready to move fast when the time came."

"That's when Illyich called me to come to Moscow. He thought that things were close to winding up. When I arrived, the next thing I knew we were both on a KGB airplane headed for St. Petersburg."

"Jeez, Dad, I thought they threw enemy agents out of their airplanes?"

"That's right, Mark. I could hardly believe what was happening.

Everything was moving fast, a race against the clock. It was beyond the eleventh hour. I can tell you, all my training didn't cover this."

"Kazim's KGB cell was in St. Petersburg, then still called Leningrad. By the time your dad got to Moscow it was clear that we weren't going to succeed with Kazim through dialogue. Gorbachev was still in power and his rivals were fighting to the finish. It was clear to those of us who were privy to the Onion File that the virus was one of the many things that could make or break the new Russia and would set our new course with the United States. We couldn't allow it to stay in place, and my orders were to fix the problem. Believe me, my employers didn't have the kind of restrictions that your dad's had!"

"Well, Mark, it was critical to stop it. We wound up having to go in shooting."

"Your dad's long-term memory must be getting short," Illyich said with a laugh. "We first had to get in the building. It was a secure facility, still controlled by the old guard. I had to really bend the rules to get the codes to open the door. All hell broke loose when we did get in. That's when the shooting started."

"In all my years with the Agency, Mark, that was the only time that I was involved in a shoot-out. And I can tell you, once was enough! Fortunately, I was with this guy or your mother would have been a widow when you were still a teenager."

Mark looked at Illyich, unable to hide the emotion he felt. "Thanks, sir. We've kind of enjoyed having him around all these years. Sounds like a close thing?"

"That's for sure!" said Jim. "I was always impressed, though, that Kazim's staff kind of held back. I guess they weren't sure about shooting at who they knew were their own people. Some of them knew Illyich and they weren't about to mess with him. It was Kazim who was fighting like a tiger."

"He sure was and, although he lost that battle, I guess from his perspective he didn't lose the war," Illyich added. "After all, we're here talking about him again, just like '89. The important thing was that we had to get somebody out alive to be able to find out how the virus was going to work and it was your dad who did that. He tackled one of

Kazim's programmers, had him pinned to the ground when Kazim took the shot that got him in the leg. Your dad held on and it was this kid that gave us the program. You know, Jim, I've often wondered whether Kazim meant to kill you or Igor, or both. He certainly wouldn't have wanted Igor around to testify!"

"Son, either way, what Illyich left out of the story is that Kazim would have killed me with that shot if he had been one fraction of a second faster on the draw. Illyich's shot got Kazim in the arm just as he fired. He saved my life."

"As it was, your dad was bleeding so badly that we had to airlift him to a hospital, and then home. He's certainly the only enemy agent to have survived an involuntary airplane ride with the KGB!" Illyich laughed.

Mark exclaimed, "No wonder you guys have a special bond between you. Whatever happened to Kazim? Given the reputation of the outfit you worked for, I'm surprised that he's still around for us to be worried about him."

"Kazim is smart. He had his escape plan well worked out. Quickly he was out of our reach, back home in Turkistan, and by then we were on our way out of business. We weren't allowed to go and get him."

"And the guy that you got alive? He was willing to cooperate?"

"That's a good story. Igor was then a young programmer, right out of Moscow University, doing the job he was hired for. Once the dust settled and he understood that his old boss was on the wrong team, he was happy to destroy all the evidence. He showed us how to find the worm. He's now a senior staffer with the FSB, the new KGB. If Kazim is involved, we want Igor on our team for sure."

After a fairly long period of silence, Jim broke into their thoughts. "So, Mark and Katrina, you now know the story. It was pretty hairy. And you now know why we're here. I can see Kazim written all over these computer anomalies. There are just too many similarities. And if I'm right, we need the help that Illyich can organize. We need that young lad, Igor, whom I tackled, to work with you. We need to track Kazim and see what he's been up to for the last few years. And we need to find out what happened to the rest of Kazim's original team. He would have needed some expert help to create a new threat."

Katrina had sat quietly throughout the discussion. Now she said, "I had guessed that this wasn't a simple social visit, Mark. I've always wondered about who your dad was. Illyich never explained, but every now and then his name came up, always as a friend, even colleague, and I could never figure out the relationship. This explains a lot."

"It sure does, Katrina. It seems we have something in common."

"Hmm, after last night, I think it is more than just these two old guys," she said coyly.

Jim and Illyich exchanged happy, knowing glances, feeling the magnetism in the air.

"Jim, for some time I've wanted to tell Katrina something of my life. When you called, I saw this as an opportunity to do that. I hope you don't feel like I've done an end run on you, including her in this."

"Illyich, this has been a wonderful experience, one I never thought I'd have. Like you, I've long wanted to share our story with my son, and meeting Katrina is a delight."

"Well, Jim, now that the history class is finished, and we're moving on to Lies, Spies and Terror 101, are you okay with her being here?"

"You always did have an uncanny knack of reading people's minds, my friend. I was just thinking about that. And I had reached a conclusion, one so foreign to me that I'm astounded. After all those years of everything being classified, 'need to know,' I guess I realize we're on our own on this one. All the security clearances we lived our lives with don't mean a damn at this point. My only concern would be whether she'd be at risk, but I can't see how."

"Neither can I, but before we start we need some sustenance after that light breakfast."

As if by magic, a babushka appeared at his elbow. Nadia had been with Illyich's family from the time she was sixteen, and she now looked timeless in traditional Russian dress, from the patterned headdress to the colorful, embroidered smock that covered her from neck to ankles.

Katrina saw Mark looking with interest. "Rather like turning the clock back a century, isn't it?" she said, smiling with obvious affection at Nadia. "All my life she has been like a grandmother to me."

Nadia announced in Russian that lunch was served, leading them to a patio table loaded with traditional Russian delicacies—plates of zakushki, cold appetizers, smoked fish, caviar, pickled onions, cabbage salad, gherkins, and the most delicious grilled white fish that Jim had ever enjoyed.

"Illyich, you have outdone yourself," Jim said as he surveyed the scene. "Mark, you are seeing Russian hospitality at its very best."

As the meal drew to a close, Illyich switched his conversation from the small talk and humorous stories from his long career that he had been entertaining them with, saying, "Okay, why don't you and Mark start by telling us what you've found, what brought you here?"

"Illyich, I'm sure you are well aware of the al-Qaeda threat back home. After the last bin Laden tape on television last June, Mark and I were talking. I thought back to how close Kazim had come and figured that if I were with al-Qaeda I'd go after our infrastructure, something that would cause lots of damage and destruction. It was Leigh who suggested that the hydroelectric dams might make a good target. Mark, you take it from here."

Mark was excited to finally be the focus of attention. He clearly wanted to impress Katrina, to capture her interest. "I looked at a lot of systems. For a determined enemy, there could be a whole range of opportunity. Dad had made the point that the terrorists would want to see blood on TV, and most of the systems would be limited in scope or geography if someone got at them. He had pointed out that the nuclear facilities were pretty well protected, so I didn't really try them. Mom zeroed in on the hydroelectric dams. If they were going after the power stations' operating systems they'd need to find a way in. The systems are closed. You can't just call them up on the internet. So there'd have to be a portal, a backdoor to allow access. It took me a long time playing around, probing, but eventually I came across a blip, the kind of thing that shouldn't be there."

Mark paused and looked over at Katrina, whom he was pleased to see was sitting on the edge of her chair. "It doesn't tell me anything except that something is there that shouldn't be there. If I hadn't been talking to Dad about it I wouldn't even have noticed. But it is exactly what I would have expected to find if someone was screwing around with the software."

Jim added, "The thing is, Illyich, that I'm convinced that Mark is right. He found what would have to be there for a terrorist to get into the operating systems for the generating stations. They'd have to build a portal, a back door into the program."

"It sounds to me as if you may have found it."

"What I found was what I was looking for, an anomaly in the continuity that could indicate that someone was into the software. That's about all it is. But it's exactly what Dad told me to look for."

Katrina continued to watch Mark, fascinated by the intensity of his presentation. "So, Mark, you've turned your hobby into a business. It seems to me that while you work you're actually having fun!'

"You're right there, I enjoy what I do," Mark beamed. "And it has turned into a good business. My timing couldn't have been better."

"Illyich, if it wasn't for the Onion, we wouldn't be here. It's just that the whole thing is so similar. It seems too real to be a coincidence."

"I agree. The risk is just too high to sit back and do nothing. I think Mark has done outstanding work. Maybe your old outfit should hire him, Jim."

"Not a chance," Jim said with a laugh. "They don't come close to paying enough to afford him."

Mark said seriously, "But I might pay *them* to be able to play with some of the classified toys that you two were brought up with!"

After a laugh, Illyich got right down to it. "Speaking of your old outfit, what's their take on all this? You've talked to them, Jim?"

"Yes, I have. Antonio might agree with me, but his hands are tied. They're so busy trying to protect bricks and mortar, to prevent another World Trade Center disaster, that he can't put anyone on it. The analysts who see a cyber threat are in the minority. If we get any leads, though, the Agency will back us up."

"Okay. Where do we start?"

Jim sat back, grabbed another pickled herring and popped it into his mouth before replying. "We need to start with Kazim. That's why we're here."

"I'll get things rolling." Illyich slapped his thigh. "I've got a lot of markers out there and it's time to call some of them in. I'll ask around with old colleagues and see what I can find. Kazim could do it, but I must say that it's hard to imagine him being able to organize that from wherever he is."

On the way to the airport, Jim and Mark reviewed what they had accomplished.

"Dad, what if we find Kazim? Then what? I don't think there's much time before the disaster that's on the way. We need to think of some way to take control if Kazim pulls the trigger."

"For sure. I'd like to catch him, but maybe I'm letting my emotions run away a bit. On the other hand, you're the one that needs to figure out the computer stuff. I can make things happen, but you need to tell me what to do."

"Yeah, I've got a lot of work to do in a hurry when we get home."

Fifteen long travel hours later, Jim tiptoed into the bedroom. The patio windows were open, a warm summer breeze rustling the curtains, moonlight highlighting Leigh's sensual, still appetizing curves. He stood still for minutes, looking in wonder at his wife, eyes moist as he drank in the view. As he climbed into bed, Leigh rolled over, wrapping herself around him, saying with a mischievous giggle. "Welcome home, lover. I see you like the scene that I set."

"You devil, but, yeah, it isn't bad for an old married woman," as he kissed her, starting at the top.

It wasn't till a fair bit later that Leigh got around to saying, "So, my love, how was the trip?"

"Honey, it was a long trip and way too fast. I'm too old for the fast lane, I can tell you. Things were just fine, but I've got to tell you the most important part first."

"You got a lead on Kazim?"

"No. Much bigger than that."

"But that's what you went over for!"

"My love, Mark has found himself a girl."

Leigh sat bolt upright in bed. "You're kidding. How can that be? You only had your feet on the ground there for a day or so. Tell me about it."

Jim said smugly, "Aw, well, like father like son, I guess. Remember how long it took me to snare you, my dear?"

"Huh, that's the version of the story that I've let you believe over all these years. But it has been rather good, hasn't it?" as she kissed him. "So, what's happened that he could be so lucky?"

"Katrina is Illyich's granddaughter, twenty-two years old and beautiful. I don't so much mean her looks, although she's a knock-out. It's her presence. She's like you and just radiates warmth. They had a good chance to talk and it's clear that they've taken to each other. I thought that you and I and fairytales were the only ones fortunate enough to have that kind of electricity flowing, but I tell you, I could see the sparks!"

"Hmm, we were pretty fortunate with the sparks, weren't we? It sure sounds exciting for Mark. What do you know about her?"

"Mark did a lot of talking on the way back. I've never seen him so pumped about a girl. She's just completed her degree in political science, and is accepted into a master's program at the university in St. Petersburg starting in September. She's traveled and, like her grandfather, speaks languages as if she were born to them. She has Illyich's gift with people, and I can tell you, she had our son tongue-tied."

"Sounds to me like she got to you as well as to our son."

"She sure did! My love, I am convinced that this has the makings of something really good. You just wait till you meet her, and judging by Mark's reaction to her, I'm sure that you will soon."

CHAPTER 18

Kazim bowed low as he entered the abode. The small group had moved from one remote village to another along the Pakistani border and was now in a traditional small hut, indistinguishable from any other on the outside, modest but clean and comfortably appointed on the inside. In appearance, the men were also indistinguishable from the tribesmen who had lived there for generations—their gowns flowing to the floor hiding simple sandals, beards extending to the *thawb*, the turban wrapping their heads. It was no wonder that all the spying that had been painstakingly carried out over the whole region had not succeeded in singling out these outsiders. They blended in with natives of the village.

"Peace be upon you and the mercy of Allah and His blessings."

"And upon you be peace and the mercy of Allah and His blessings," came the response from the men inside.

"And with you my friend. May your work do Allah's bidding. The infidels need another call to God. In the days since our great victory in New York, they have shown us much grief here in Afghanistan with their bombing and attacks. It is time to teach them another lesson in their homeland. I am told that your plan is ready? You are ready to strike?"

The sun was slanting over the rugged mountains of the tribal lands, shading the interior, and as Kazim drew closer he was shocked to see the gray pallor of the leader's face. Although the two weeks of being on the run since September 11 had taken a real toll on bin Laden, the intensity of faith, the stolid determination, the fervent faith in the cause still burned brightly.

"I am humble but proud to be able to tell you that with the support of the Prophet, may the peace and blessing of Allah be upon him, and of your friends, we have the key that we spoke of two years ago."

Kazim continued to marvel at the power that this one man held, despite his weakened state, both in terms of his people and also for the terror that he struck against the infidels across the western world. In the past, many speculated that bin Laden must have been killed or at least neutralized when, as he would periodically remind the world, he had simply chosen to keep a lower profile—planning, waiting patiently.

"We have put in place an Onion whose layers will cause great grief to our enemies as they are peeled back. Praise be to Allah, I am ready to go. I am here to seek your advice and your agreement on when we should unleash our terror."

"It is time for a major strike," replied bin Laden. This discussion was clearly invigorating for the ailing leader, his courage and dignity apparent as ever. "The infidels have been vigilant. Many of our plans have come to nothing. It is time for another success. What is this Onion of yours?"

Now, more than a decade after the first Onion, this Onion 2 was more sophisticated than Kazim's earlier masterpiece.

"My program is ready to be spirited into the automated controls of some of the major power grids, dams, turbines, and floodgates across the US. One touch of a key will initiate a computer call to each of the twenty-eight sites using the Intelligent Solutions & Security software, and my application will start its work."

"But you can do this, my brother?"

"My plan is both simple and complex. Simple: it will be activated by a single password entered into an opening that I have created in their computer system. Complex because the program is so sophisticated and redundant."

Bin Laden was clearly impressed, and Kazim was enjoying the attention.

"I don't understand how this is possible. You could do this by the person that we found in America, your 'key to the Kingdom'?"

"Yes, it has taken much time. My key has created a back door into the closed systems that operate the hydroelectric power facilities. A portal is now ready and waiting to accept a password. My brother, the technical name of the portal is Port 5000. I think that it is fitting that our radio is Radio Al-Islam, channel 5000."

A smile lit up bin Laden's face. "And the Quran says, 'Nay, but if you are patient in adversity and conscious of Him, and the enemy should fall upon you of a sudden, your Sustainer will aid you with five thousand angels swooping down.' You have done the Sustainer's bidding."

Kazim was proud to receive such praise from the leader. "When I make that call, my program will hijack the system, erasing its own tracks in the process."

"And what can we expect to celebrate?"

"Allah willing, and nothing is too great for Allah, after I take control, the major hydroelectric power dams will open, releasing water to cause major flooding across the US. Water is a gift from Allah, a gift which the infidels do not appreciate or deserve. Allah's gift will kill our enemies and when it is gone they will not have enough electricity to survive, their economy will collapse in ruins. They will be forced to withdraw from our lands."

Bin Laden smiled with pleasure. "And when will you turn the key, my brother?"

In Islamic religion the *salat* is communication between the creature and his creator and is one of the five pillars of Islam. *Salat* requires a special communication five times a day: *Fajr*, the dawn call to prayer, *Zuhr* at noon, *Asr* in the afternoon, *Magrib* at sunset, and *Ishha'a*, late night. Kazim had given serious thought to how he would pay special tribute to Allah, and he decided that *Magrib* would lend particular significance to his Onion, sunset, with the lights going out all over America. But then, as he did his planning he realized that to maximize the destruction of the flooding, the gates should open at the busiest of times, with people vulnerable on the roads, activity in the streets, children getting ready for school, shifts changing in factories.

"I have timed this to start at eight o'clock in the morning on the East Coast on a Friday, when the roads will be clogged with commuters. Families will watch the devastation on CNN, that is, until their power goes out. Going into the weekend the infidels will have a difficult time organizing rescue and recovery operations. Osama, the timing is based on our *Magrib*, our evening call to prayer here, so that we can pay special thanks to Allah for his blessings, for the darkness that the infidels will experience. God willing, we will see great death and destruction. The crusaders will suffer."

A glow lit bin Laden's face. He was thrilled at the significance of the timing. What a magnificent message to send to the world! "After the setbacks since the Americans declared war on us after our victory in New York, it will be a joyous day to achieve revenge. You have my blessing. May Allah smile on your endeavors."

"I would also respectfully suggest that our cause would benefit from another of your appearances on Al Jazeera. Each time you have spoken, you have struck fear into the hearts of the infidels. The panic caused by flooding and electrical failure would be doubled by knowing our power to strike, knowing that Allah is with us."

"If I do this, Kazim, we would need to take care not to compromise your mission."

"Everything is prepared. They will not know where to look or what to expect. We know that they are spending all their time and resources on protecting the major shrines to the infidels, their useless symbols of power. We will give them enough time to work themselves into a panic. Their ridiculous color code has been sitting at yellow for some time now. It is time we turned it to red, to cause some terror in advance of the real thing."

Bin Laden knew that Kazim was right. "When would you recommend that I speak? Our enemies do not make it easy for us. When we have the tape you will be the one to have the honor to deliver it."

To ensure his safety, since 9/11 bin Laden only relayed his messages of destruction via videotape. Al-Sahab, the underground video production unit that had prepared all the al-Qaeda tapes for bin Laden and al Zawahiri went to work yet again.

"No, my communication stations have been compromised. Since the invaders blew themselves up at Feyzabad, they have sought out my network. The equipment is gone. We will need three days after making the tape to have it delivered by courier for broadcast. If you could do it over the next week, I will be ready."

"God willing, it will be done."

"*Al salem*—peace."

CHAPTER 19

Seth, the head of security at Intelligent Solutions & Security, poked his head around Dave's door. "Dave, got a minute?"

"Sure, Seth, what's up?"

"Well, I've been playing with this all day, but I don't seem to be getting anywhere. I think someone has been trying to get into our system. I've got all the indications, but I can't seem to nail it down. The scans are coming from different IPs. It looks like a pro at work."

Dave's first thought was, "Oh, oh, now I'm in it." But Seth read the panic that showed momentarily on Dave's face as concern on the part of a loyal chief programmer. Dave recovered quickly. "Well, at least we know they can knock at the door all they want, but they won't get in, will they? What did you find? What do you think we should do?"

"It sure would be interesting to know what's going on, but I'm not getting anywhere. Given the tight timeline on the contract for Germany, I'm not sure I should be spending much time on this thing."

Dave masked his sigh of relief. "Okay, I'll have a look at it myself. It's probably the security people doing their regular checks on our system integrity. Or some clumsy hackers looking to steal credit card numbers. You concentrate on the German contract. We sure can't afford to fall behind on that one. Let me know if you see any more."

As soon as Seth stepped out the door, Dave did a quick check and what he found scared him silly. He knew that with so many different IPs scanning the systems it was not a legitimate security screening that had been doing the fishing, doing their normal checks. Someone else was looking.

Dave was a nervous wreck, near the end of his tether. Along with millions of others, he had watched the television reruns over his breakfast coffee as the plane flew into the first tower, the smoke and flames and terror increasing by the second. Then, incredibly, another one into the second tower, debris showering out the other side. The torture of desperate people tumbling down out of the smoke, people running through the streets, police and firemen emerging, overcome by exhaustion, smoke and fatigue. Then the collapse, first one and then the other, all those people trapped inside, the utter destruction. It had only been a few weeks since this terrible destruction and Dave, like millions of others, shuddered every time he relived it.

Dave knew in his heart what Kazim had done, and at first he had been thrilled that he would avenge the cruelty that had been inflicted on his family and contribute to the fight for all those downtrodden souls in his homeland. But now, after 9/11, he could visualize the destruction below the dams if Kazim's plan came to fruition. It hit him like an epiphany, but what was he to do? It was too late. "Am I now a part of them, these people who have killed thousands, people like me, Americans, earning a living, bringing up families? What about all those children, those orphans? Will they feel as I do? Will they also want revenge? My God, the Koran cannot want that! Where will it end?"

From the time the airplanes hit the towers, Dave had become more and more disillusioned. How could he have done what he did? Now, as he realized that something was about to happen, he was afraid to think what might have been done with the software that he had handed to Kazim. But he knew that he didn't have to think. He asked himself over and over, "What have I done? Have I become one of them, a terrorist, killing people? I cannot live with that on my conscience."

Not long after Seth left the office, Dave dialed the phone. "Hi. Something's happened, we need to speak. I need a coffee. Meet you in thirty minutes?"

"I'll be there." Silvio could tell that Dave was agitated and that his worst fears were about to be realized. Fast action would be needed.

Dave left the building, got in his car, and drove to a small café, one of their regular meeting spots. Silvio was already waiting in their corner booth and, as soon as he saw Dave, his suspicions were confirmed. It was serious, something Silvio knew was coming and something he had been waiting for with dread. He had worried from the beginning that Dave was too straightforward, too honest, too naive to keep their secret under pressure, and to keep the fragile faith that had been so carefully instilled. The instant the airliners hit the towers, Silvio knew that Dave would start to unravel. Even he himself was feeling the heat. He could sense the increasing scrutiny that had been intensifying since 9/11, and he had anticipated that sooner or later the lid would blow off. As Dave slid into the booth, Silvio knew that that time had come. In as casual a voice as he could muster, he said, "Hey, Dave, what's up?"

"Silvio, I'm getting really worried. The longer this goes on, the more we are at risk. My security chief has picked up some probing of our systems."

As the waitress came their way, Silvio put his hand on Dave's arm in warning, saying to the waitress, "One large coffee, strong, please," and as Dave nodded, "make that two."

When she was out of earshot Silvio asked, "What do you mean, probing? What does that mean? You told me there's nothing to find."

"Well, there isn't really. But someone who knew what they were doing might see that something wasn't quite right. I think we need to pay attention. This could be a serious risk."

"Who could be doing this? It must not be that easy."

"Seth thinks he has picked up an official test of our security—a regular audit—but I know it's not, it's a very sophisticated hacker. There are too many different IPs. A security company would use its own. Here is a list of the IPs, the addresses from where the probing is being done. Whoever it is, is good. They might pick up something, and then we're really in trouble."

Silvio's nagging concern turned immediately to worry. The whole thing was taking too long. He had lived easily over the last years without a worry but now, since 9/11 with the huge crackdown on security everywhere, he thought that even he might be watched. And he was having some trouble with his own conscience. In Afghanistan, with a shooting war going on, he had no pangs about pulling the trigger, but now, somehow, seeing those towers in New York made it different. All those people, working in offices, could have been the wife and family he never had.

But he said calmly to Dave, “Don’t worry. Leave it with me. Give me that list that you have from the computer and I’ll send it off for some checking. If there’s any problem I’ll let you know.”

“Well, okay, but pass the word that whatever is going to happen, make it sooner rather than later. This can’t go on forever.”

Silvio was no longer using internet cafés. They asked for ID. He used his own laptop at a hotspot, a free internet site with an account set up using a fake ID. His message to a Hotmail address in Italy was relayed and received in minutes in Afghanistan.

> to- bill115543@hotmail.com
> from- sily456@hotmail.com
> subject- All okay
> Our friend is not at all concerned about your offer. She says no one is interested in the price and that you do not have to look further. There is no rush.
> I have some numbers for you.

Kazim translated the code as he read it: “Dave is concerned. Someone is probing. You need to take fast action.” He couldn’t imagine what the numbers would be, but he knew that he had to connect with Silvio. His reply directed Silvio to a chat room, the same arrangements that he had used to communicate with Dave.

That night Silvio took his laptop computer for a ride downtown. He had scouted out unprotected wireless routers and had found so many that he knew he would not have a problem. It was simply a matter of parking conveniently on a side street and logging on. Once connected he started the encrypted chat application, waiting for it to connect to Kazim’s private mesh, then opened the chat room. Once again Kazim was the only one there. Even though the chances of discovery were miniscule Kazim had taught his people well, and Silvio used their simple code wherever he could.

<Bytes> has entered
<Çå$îm*> to what do we owe the pleasure of your visit today?
<Bytes> we have some good news.
<Çå$îm*> what's that?
<Bytes> our friend gave me some quotes for the deal that we discussed.
<Çå$îm*> excellent. I'll crunch the numbers.
<Bytes> what about her? I give her more than a few days.
<Çå$îm*> let me see your figures and we will discuss her later.
<Bytes> OK. Here are her numbers.
<Çå$îm*> bye for now.
<Bytes> has left.

On Kazim's monitor a box popped up: "Accept file from user Bytes." Çå$îm clicked "yes" and the file opened to display a list of numbers, each one in the distinctive format of four numbers separated by three periods.

As Silvio typed in the code, he knew that he had to wait to hear back from Kazim about Dave. He'd just have to do his best to keep Dave on track and, as he thought about it, to keep his own nerves in check.

On the other side of the world, Kazim immediately recognized the significance of the numbers. They were IPs, addresses that could lead to the source of Silvio's concern. Kazim's decision was made in a heartbeat. All his hard work, his ingenuity, even his reputation was on the line. How could anyone be probing Dave's software company? Who would know to look, and where?

CHAPTER 20

Kazim knew that he must act quickly. The next morning, he arrived at the tribal chief's abode bearing his usual gift of barter, a sack of gold coins.

"May the blessings of Allah be upon you and your people," he said with a slight bow of deference, the sack disappearing as if by magic under the chief's flowing robes. "I wish to again prevail upon your hospitality and good will."

"So, my brother, will this be the usual delivery? I note that your gift is somewhat heavier than our terms."

"You are correct. The delivery is as arranged. However, I would ask that it be made as soon as possible."

"With the Prophet's guidance, it will be there tomorrow."

The package that exchanged hands was quickly relayed by the courier to the same staffer with the Russian mission in Kabul, and from there an encrypted message made its way to the office in St. Petersburg. Kazim's team of rogue programmers started to work immediately to sort through the maze of data that would lead them to the source of the probe that Seth had detected, starting with the IPs that Dave had given to Silvio. It took them only minutes to eliminate the official agencies that might be responsible for the probing. Some of the IPs were spoofed, not even real, but there were many that pointed to anonymous proxies.

One of the team piped up on seeing an IP at the bottom, "Hey we know this address in Bahrain. Kazim's friend operates this anonymous proxy server."

Ten minutes after a phone call, an email came back to St. Petersburg with a list of IPs linked to a domain registered in Washington, a private computer site. A little further digging and a quick search of online databases brought up a company website, an outfit called Buchan Security, registered to a Mark Buchan. One of the team said aloud, "That explains how Buchan could have done it. If he's in the business, he'd have both the equipment and the expertise. I just found his home address at a Georgetown apartment and his telephone number, too."

None of this information meant much to Kazim's men in St. Petersburg. They had accomplished a difficult and complex task that few people could have done, but all the information in the report went back by encrypted message to the wilds of Afghanistan.

As Kazim skimmed the report, he leaped out of his chair, his face livid with anger. "This can't be," he said aloud. "Buchan is not going to do it to me again."

He looked again at the report, remembering 1989. Something nagged at him and, as his anger subsided, he remembered that Buchan's first name was Jim, not Mark. So, could the name Buchan be a coincidence? All his years of training, experience and intuition had taught Kazim not to bet on coincidences. He had to talk with Silvio and, when he did, he'd have to breach his own rules on security.

A Hotmail message made its way to California directing Silvio to the chat room. And again Silvio found his quiet spot to park and log on.

<Çå$îm*> has entered
<Çå$îm*> hey friend, you there?
<Bytes> ready and waiting
<Çå$îm*> i need you to track something down
<Bytes> sure
<Çå$îm*> who is Mark Buchan in Washington? Any relation to Jim?
<Bytes> i'll be back to you by email
<Çå$îm*> OK make it fast
<Çå$îm>* has left

As Silvio drove home he thought, "I don't like this. Kazim never says things right out like that. This doesn't feel right at all! It has to be really serious."

He couldn't stop thinking that trouble was just around the corner and that his neck was on the line.

After several roundabout emails, Silvio's reply told Kazim what he needed to know.

> to- bill115543@hotmail.com
> from- sily456@hotmail.com
> subject- our friend
> She is the daughter of your old friend, now 35. She is of no interest to you at all.

Again, Kazim did the translation as he read. It wasn't a coincidence. Mark was Jim Buchan's twenty-four-year-old son and an immediate threat. Kazim had no doubt that Jim was involved up to his armpits. But how could Buchan have learned about his latest Onion? The first Onion had failed for one reason and one reason only, a traitor in their midst. Kazim was good, but he had a problem. He knew he was good, so good that he could not begin to contemplate that someone like Mark Buchan, untrained in espionage, could stumble onto his software. What would have triggered him to look for it?

Kazim was confident that al-Qaeda's security was tight and he himself had set up the system of couriers. He was sure that loyalty in the camp was firm. But the more he thought about it, the more concerned he became. Could there be a traitor in the camp? A seed of doubt had been planted. His one and only undoing, the one that had peeled his first Onion, had been a traitor in the camp, his programmer, Igor.

Kazim was determined that this time no Buchan, father or son, would ruin his plan. He wanted Mark out of the way both as a guarantee that Mark would not make any progress in his hacking and that Jim would have good reason not to interfere. The next set of emails set things in motion.

> to- sily456@hotmail.com
> from- bill115543@hotmail.com

subject- Vacation
It is not essential that she take her holiday now. It could be within 3 days and then be extended indefinitely. Instructions on timing of extension to follow.

Silvio understood that Mark was to disappear within four days, with further instructions on the timing for his killing. Silvio was worried. The more time that passed the less sure he became. Ever since Lindbergh, kidnapping in the States had been a serious, high visibility offence. Mark's disappearance would be sure to bring the full weight of the law enforcement community down around their ears. And now it was becoming evident to Silvio that Dave was getting very nervous. Dave's newfound faith and his disillusionment with US policy might have brought him to helping the cause, but Silvio also thought that Dave's beliefs might not be strong enough as he thought for long about the potential impact of his actions. It was clear that the plan would not hold together much longer.

Silvio's emails had let Kazim know that Dave was worried and that the risk of detection was growing. Kazim also knew that it might be only a matter of time until Mark's probes might break through his carefully built security ruses. If that happened, the track would lead directly to Dave. And, in any event, as soon as Onion 2 opened the dams, the investigation would also quickly end at Dave's door, opening the trail to Silvio. Either way, Kazim decided that Dave was an immediate threat to Silvio's survival and to the success of the *jihad* he had committed his life to. Something had to be done.

More Hotmails confirmed Kazim's fears. Things were starting to unravel. With so little time to go until his years of hard work paid off, he had to deal with Dave now rather than later.

to- sily456@hotmail.com
from- bill115543@hotmail.com
subject- Your friend
Your friend must not leave immediately, and it must not be forever.

That short email to Silvio sealed Dave's fate.

CHAPTER 21

It was three o'clock in the morning and Mark had spent most of the night wide awake. He couldn't get Katrina out of his mind. He cursed himself for not being on the ball that night on the bluff, but he had been so smitten that he hadn't thought to ask her where she lived. Just as he had decided that he would call his dad in the morning for Illyich's number in Sochi, the phone rang. He had it before the first ring had finished.

"Are you sleeping?"

"No. I've been awake for hours thinking about you."

"Me too. I had to call."

"Good. I didn't know how to call you. How did you do it?"

"Hey, now, you're the computer whiz. I Googled you and there you were."

"Katrina, I'm so happy. If you were with me right now I might be able to get some sleep—well, maybe not right away."

"So I'm talking to a sex fiend?"

"Right now, close to it."

"Hmm, sounds interesting. What are we going to do about it?"

He could just see the wide smile spreading across her face, and he found himself thrilled at her responses. So, what were they going to do?

"First, give me an email address where we can talk or we'll both go bankrupt with telephone bills."

By the time Mark had an email drafted and ready to send, he saw that Katrina had beaten him to it. He laughed out loud as he read it. "Hey, expert, talking like this may be all right for some things, but not for us. Illyich has me on MSN and a web cam and we stay in touch all the time. Show me yours and I'll show you mine."

Mark went back to his draft and added, "I hate to admit that you're way ahead of me, but I'm going to have to go out tomorrow and buy some equipment. I've got enough hardware to start a war, but no cam. I'll remedy that immediately."

So it wasn't long before they were looking at each other as they spoke, not as good as the real thing, but better than the 'you've got mail' option. They quickly picked up the conversation that they had started on that night looking out over the sea in Sochi.

"So, Mark, we decided in the moonlight that we share some ideals, but what about your life? What do you do for fun?"

"You have a blank page to work on, Katrina. For the last few years, computers have been my business and my recreation. I think you'll find me boring, but I'm willing to learn anything. What about you? Sports? Skiing? I'm sure you've tried those mountains I saw in Sochi. I skied for a couple of years as a kid when my dad was stationed in Europe."

"I sure have. I might even be able to keep up with you."

"I bet. I can just hear the chuckle that you're holding down. I have no doubt that you could ski circles around me. But I used to play a mean game of chess with my mother. I might win at that. One thing for sure, I look forward to you showing me the world that I've missed."

"I can hardly wait."

As they got to know one another, comparing notes and ideas, Mark said, "We were sure lucky to have met. Those two are quite the pair, aren't they, your grandfather and my father."

"They sure are—out of the same mold."

"I remember years ago asking my dad how he could work for an organization that did such bad things, like some of the stuff that went on in South America. His answer was interesting, and I think it is what drew the two of them together, kind of soul mates in a difficult world. He said that he was one of the lucky ones, because he didn't have to cross those bridges. He was focused on the Cold War and the rules were set. Some dirty tricks, but they were accepted as part of the ground rules. Each side knew the game, knew what the other was doing."

"Illyich has said the same sort of things, that he respected Jim from the beginning. They share the same stories. But I do think that there'd be some bad stuff in my grandfather's closet. The KGB was ruthless with spies and Illyich gathered his share of them."

"Yeah, in fact I think that was the one thing that really bothered my father, that the frontline guys, the real spies, were expendable, that when the chips were down he couldn't help them."

They checked in every day, sometimes for hours, and it wasn't long till they knew that somehow they had to see each other again, sooner rather than later.

CHAPTER 22

After the last exchange of emails with Kazim, Silvio thought long and hard. He was true to the faith. He had fought in Afghanistan. But now? Was he prepared to take the next steps, to do what Kazim had directed? Afghanistan was different. There they were on a battlefield, at war. Yes, he told himself, but this was also war, a vital part of the *jihad*, wasn't it? These people were infidels and killing infidels was glorious. Besides, Dave had become an immediate threat, not only to the cause, but to him personally. Somewhat reluctantly he concluded that he must do Allah's bidding, not only for the cause, the *jihad*, but for his own skin. He reached for the phone.

"Hello, Dave, I've got some news for you. How about another hike up Elbow Canyon on Saturday?"

"Sure, Silvio. Sounds good."

"Let's go early and avoid the heat and the crowds. I'll need my car later, so could you meet me at the base, say seven o'clock?"

"I'll be there."

Saturday morning was clear, the temperature perfect for walking. Silvio arrived early, parking his car in the second lot, the one serving the trail down the valley floor, then walking back to the entry to the trail up the mountain. When he saw that a few cars had pulled into the lot, he thought, "Hmm, this may be a bit tricky."

As Dave arrived, another car with a young couple pulled in beside him. "Morning. What a beautiful day for a hike! You on your own? Want to join us?"

"No. My friend over there is going with me, thanks."

"Okay. See you on the Elbow. We're going to grab a coffee before we start."

"Damn," thought Silvio. "Just my luck. I didn't think we'd see anyone this early." By the time he walked over to Dave's car, the young couple was entering the coffee shop. Silvio was usually very careful about using any overt Arab customs that might attract attention, but now they were alone.

"Good morning, Dave. May the peace and blessings of Allah be upon you."

"And on you. Great day for our hike. What is this news?"

As they started up the trail it was clear that a few other hikers had beaten them to it. Dave was nervous and anxious to hear what Silvio had to say, but he knew that he'd have to wait until they were alone. As they climbed higher, Silvio maneuvered Dave into the lead, reaching into his backpack and surreptitiously tucking something in his belt under his shirt as another hiker appeared on his way down the trail. He realized that perhaps this was not going to be as easy as he had thought.

Over the past year the two had found peace on the beautiful trail up the mountain. Each time Dave returned home with his faith renewed, his doubts on hold. This morning he needed Silvio's reassurances. The higher they climbed, the more magnificent the vista that unfolded below the narrow path. Eventually they were alone. Silvio could tell that Dave was worried. He was like a flea on a hot brick, as he tugged on a loose strand of hair, looking around as if someone was about to pounce on him.

The discussion had been general as they left other hikers behind, but now Dave said, "Silvio, I'm worried. I didn't know that it would take so long. I think it is only a question of time until something falls apart. We have to run security checks on the system all the time and eventually something will be picked up, some anomaly or a discrepancy in the continuity of the code."

"I understand, Dave. I told you I had some news. We won't have to wait much longer. Everything is going well, and all is in place. You have done a great job."

"But I don't know how much longer I can stand it!"

"Dave, your family will soon be avenged."

"Yes, but my vengeance cannot justify more slaughter. All those innocent people, whole families, entire towns!"

That conversation made Silvio's next task much easier. They were now close to the top, the cliff stretching steeply down to the river far below. As they rounded a bend, with Dave in the lead, Silvio's walking stick flashed between Dave's feet. Dave went over the edge with a gasp.

As Silvio returned down the trail, he pulled the pistol out from under his shirt and stored it in his knapsack, saying to himself, "I'm glad I didn't have to use this. With this many people around the noise would have been heard for miles. Much cleaner this way. There's no way he could survive that fall."

As Silvio walked through the first parking lot toward where he had left his car, he noted that the young couple he had seen speaking to Dave earlier was just leaving. They gave him a wave. "Beautiful morning on the Elbow. Hope you enjoyed your walk as much as we did. Did you lose your friend?"

Silvio just waved to them, thinking, "By Allah, I hate nosy, obnoxious Americans."

Just before midnight the park security guard did the rounds, noting a couple of cars still in the lots. They each received a ticket under the windshield wiper, 'No all-night parking'. The next morning the day guard noted Dave's car, the ticket from the night before still on the windshield. Following park procedure, he called the office to report the car, indicating that someone may have spent the night in the canyon. Just as the incident was being logged at the park headquarters, a hiker walking the riverbed at the bottom of the Elbow was on her cell phone, talking excitedly to the 911 dispatcher.

"I'm hiking along the river. My dog just discovered a body—it's all broken up, horrible, something's eaten part of it."

"Where are you, Miss?"

"I'm just past mile 6, on the river."

"Which river are you on, Miss?"

"Oh, sorry. I'm really shaken up. It's the Elbow Canyon Park. I'm near mile six, on the east side trail."

After logging her name and looking at a map, the dispatcher said, "Sorry to ask you this, Miss, but could you stay there? We'll get the police there as soon as we can—probably in about a half an hour. Please ask anyone else who arrives to stay away from the body."

That evening the local television station carried a public service police announcement. A hiker identified as David MacIntyre had been killed in a fall at Elbow Canyon, a description of his car and its location in the parking lot completing the brief coverage. The police were asking anyone with information that might help the investigation to contact them. Silvio didn't know any of this. He never watched decadent American television, but a young couple having an early dinner did.

"Hey, Marilyn, look at this. That's the car beside us when we did the hike. MacIntyre must be the guy that we talked to. He's the one who's dead."

"Hard to imagine anyone hiking up there falling off, but I guess it must happen sometimes with that many people doing it."

"Remember he said he was with someone? He was meeting a guy just as we pulled in. Maybe we better call the police."

So the initial police report indicated that witnesses said that Dave had been with someone, perhaps Arab extraction, middle-aged, burly, dark black hair. No, they hadn't talked to him, just briefly to Dave MacIntyre. But, yes, the man that Dave had been walking with was leaving at the same time as they were. No, they hadn't seen any sign of Dave when they left, but his car was still parked beside theirs when they drove away.

CHAPTER 23

Jim spent an hour over coffee running through scenarios in his mind. He had become even more convinced that Mark was right, that Kazim was likely to activate his Onion at any moment. Jim had to find a breakthrough. He picked up his cell and pushed the speed dial.

"Mark, when you were looking at the outfit with the software contract, did you get any contacts, any names or phone numbers?"

"Hi, Dad. No, not really. I just know them on the computer. Why?"

"Well, I think it's time we did some checking. We can't wait any longer—we'll have to take the risk of possibly spooking one of al-Qaeda's agents."

Mark said, "Hang on a sec." He leaned over, his fingers flying across the keys. The company web site appeared on the screen, but after 9/11, like many government contracting and high security sites, it had been stripped, altered so that no security-sensitive data like key personnel appeared.

"Nope, there's nothing on the screen. All that stuff has been deleted."

"Well, I'll see if I can come up with some names," Jim said, redialing the phone.

"Antonio, it's Jim Buchan."

"Hi, Jim. Have you made any headway on what we talked about?"

"Antonio, there's too much there to be coincidence. I need you to do something. The outfit in California that has the software contract for the power dams. I need some names and numbers so I can do some quiet checking. Could you get me an org chart for them?"

"Yeah, probably. I'll get the security file from the Bureau. I'll get back to you as soon as I have it."

During the night Jim's fax spat out four pages. There was no title, no indication what they were or where they came from. Jim looked at them and thought, "That was fast work. Let's see what we have here." He looked at his watch and realized that with the time change to the West Coast he'd have to wait a couple of hours. He made coffee and got on the treadmill.

By 11:30 he couldn't wait any longer and he punched in the number for the CEO, hoping that they started at least by 8:30 in California.

"Intelligent Solutions & Security. Mr. Cartwright's office. This is Cathy speaking. How may I help you?"

"Cathy, this is Jim Buchan in Washington. We're doing some routine follow-up to update our security files. Could I speak to Mr. Cartwright for a few minutes, please?"

"Oh, Mr. Buchan, you must be the person I sent the files to yesterday. Could I help you?"

"Well, I'd really like to speak to the boss if I could."

"Sir, he's not in the office today. Could I have him call you when he gets back?"

"When could I expect to hear from him? It is fairly urgent."

"I'm not sure he'll be back in today. In fact, I'm alone here holding the fort."

"What's this, a holiday in sunny California?"

"No, we had a real tragedy a few days ago, and they're all out at a funeral. He could give you a call tomorrow, if that would be okay."

"I'm sorry to hear that, Cathy. What happened?"

"One of our people was out hiking and fell off a cliff. He was dead when they found him at the bottom of the canyon. It's really sad. He was so good. Everyone liked him."

Jim felt the hairs stand up on the back of his neck. "I'm sorry to hear that, Cathy. One of your staff, you say?"

"Yes, our chief programmer, Dave MacIntyre. We're really going to be in a bind. He kind of did everything around here."

"Bingo," Jim said to himself, then aloud, "Don't worry about it, Cathy. We'll get back to you when things settle down. Many thanks for your help."

Jim's next call was to his old office. "Antonio, now I really think I have something for you to go on. I called Intelligent Solutions & Security in California. They're the people who do the programs, the org chart you got for me."

"What did you find, Jim?"

"It seems that their chief programmer just died in a hiking accident. I'll bet you the next round of drinks that his fall was no accident. And when the dust settles, I'll also bet that he provided the terrorists with access to his programs. There's just too much going on for it to be coincidence."

"Jim, I'll get on it right away. If you are right, this is really bad news. But one thing I do agree with you on is that the pattern sure fits."

"Antonio, if I'm right about this, we've got a real problem." Jim took a deep breath before continuing, "You remember the first Onion. There was nothing to find until Kazim pushed the start button. I'm sure it will be the same here. Mark has been working for months trying to find a way in, and so far all he's got is that little ripple that started us on all this."

"I'll put my people to work as soon as we hang up the phone. What do you plan to do now, Jim?"

"Well, Mark and I are going to do some brainstorming, and I plan to touch base with Illyich. We need to find Kazim, and I may be able to do it faster than you can. I'll stay in touch."

Antonio made a call to California, and it wasn't long before the local police were at Dave's apartment. So far, they weren't treating the case as a possible murder. People did occasionally have hiking accidents in that part of the world. As they went through the place, one officer said, "He sure was a tidy soul. Not even a dirty dish in the sink." After a full sweep, he added, "I don't think there's anything to find here, nothing out of the ordinary at all."

"I agree. I wonder what they thought we'd find."

The report of the investigation went into the bin for review by the supervisor, normally done within twenty-four hours, but the person responsible was on sick leave. Anyway, there was no rush. After all, the report didn't say anything. The only thing raising any question was the report by a hiker that MacIntyre may have been with someone that day, and what could they do about that? It wasn't until the police report finally arrived two days later on the desk of the local FBI Bureau chief, Prescott Smith, that the alarms started ringing.

"Hi, Chief. It's Prescott, over at the Bureau."

"What can we do for the Feebs today, Prescott?"

"Well, I'm a little miffed. I just got the file on MacIntyre. You guys sure took your time getting it here."

"We've had a rash of folks down with the flu. I had a look at it and figured there was no rush. There's nothing there."

"You're right on that, there isn't, and that's what's got me worried. I'd like to talk to your officers who did the search."

"Stand by. I'll get one of them right now."

After a pause, "Constable Greyeyes here, sir."

"I've got your report on the MacIntyre apartment in front of me. You didn't find a thing? Nothing touched, tampered with, nothing out of place?"

"Just as I said in the report—nothing." A hint of annoyance in his voice.

"You did a thorough search? Everything? We think maybe he was murdered."

"Well, we sure didn't find any hint of that in his apartment."

"What about the telephone and computer—anything?"

"No, nothing on the answering machine and the computers looked brand new, nothing on them."

"What do you mean, nothing on them? Nothing incriminating?"

"No. Nothing, period. We turned them on and they were blank, never been used by the look of it."

"Jesus. Put the chief back on ... Chief, the only way the computers would be blank is if they had been erased. I'm going to get a team over there."

Prescott's FBI team didn't take long to determine that Constable Greyeyes' report was essentially correct. There was nothing there. But they viewed the scene through a different lens. It wasn't just that the place had been cleaned, it had been sterilized. The most telling evidence was indeed the computers, the desktop unit and a laptop that was on the bureau in the bedroom, both wiped clean, no disks lying around, no evidence of use.

"We'll get these to forensics right away, but I can guess the outcome. It's going to be gibberish. Whoever did this knew what they were doing."

But it wasn't Silvio who had known what to do, it was Kazim. Silvio had just followed Kazim's instructions to the letter, going directly from the hike on Elbow Canyon to Dave's apartment. He had done just what Kazim had told him to, paying special attention to the computers. After all, his neck was on the line.

CHAPTER 24

The next day Jim was back in Mark's home workshop, bringing him up to speed on the events in California.

"Mark, let's review some timing. We started this over Jeannie's cappuccinos in June. The 9/11 hijackers were already in the US by then. You found the Port 5000 anomaly in, what, August? They struck the towers in September. We're now in early October. What can we figure about timing for our Onion?"

"And they've got to be close. Dad, since 9/11 the terrorists haven't had as easy a ride as when they were training to be pilots and making money transfers. I'll bet this MacIntyre guy was killed because he was spooked by all the increased security everywhere. If we're right about this, I think Kazim's plan must be in place and he didn't need MacIntyre any more."

"I'd agree with that."

"And if that's the case, then we are really in trouble. MacIntyre would be the only one with the key. Short of getting into the program, there'd be no way of finding out what he did. And if I had done something like that I'd have built in some safeguards, some diversions, to cover my tracks."

"Exactly, Mark. And, since we don't know the timing, when he plans to pull the trigger, we need to figure out how to stop things even if he does shoot. You've been looking at the system. If Kazim could take control of the program, what could be done to stop it from running?"

"Short of shutting down the whole system I can't think of any way to guarantee that it could be done."

After a thoughtful pause, Jim said, "So, you're saying that if we want to prevent a possible disaster, all the hydroelectric generating sites controlled by this program would need to go off line?"

Mark gave his shoulders a shrug. "Well, that would keep the gates from opening."

"This is going to take convincing some important people. Getting someone to make the decision to shut down that much generating capacity on our say-so will not be easy. I need to figure out a way to make that happen. I guess I'll start with Antonio. You know, Mark, the other thing we really need to do is to find Kazim."

"I'm not sure what Kazim would give us even if he could be found. From what you and Illyich have said, it's not likely that he'd be volunteering information."

"You're probably right on that, but I'd sure like to put him out of business. For the first challenge, getting a directive out to the hydroelectric power stations, you and I need to meet with Antonio. I'll set that up right now. For the moment, I need to make a few calls. I'll be back to you shortly."

"You know, Dad, if this is a sample of the kind of stuff that you did for a living, I guess I can begin to understand why you liked it so much. This is kind of exciting!"

"Hmm, that's true." Jim had been lost in thought. "You know, as I think about this, I don't think we can afford to wait. I think we need to see if Antonio can put some directive into the system immediately, so that if we miss Kazim there'll be some chance of minimizing the disaster. I'll dial. You get on the other phone …"

"Antonio, it's Jim. Mark is with me on the extension. We were talking about the 'what ifs.' What if Kazim activates his program before we can stop him? We need to take some serious precautions, and you are not going to like what we're suggesting."

"Maybe not, but let's hear it anyway."

Mark explained why he thought that if the hack was activated, the power would need to be immediately shut off, to stop the equipment before much damage was done. "I've done a lot of research into the power system and the SCADA, the supervisory control and data acquisition system that runs the programs. There is one built-in safety factor that will be in our favor. The gates on each dam are interlocked, designed so that only one set of gates can open at once. That is for safety, so all the water wouldn't spill at once if something failed, but also because it would take more than the available electrical power to operate all the gates at the same time. What this means is that if the first gate started to open on its own, if the power were cut off, then the next gates in the sequence couldn't open. That way, the volume of water that would be released would be much less than the total potential. It could still be bad, but nothing like the tidal wave and flooding would be if the whole dam was breached."

"So, if I understand what you're saying, you want them to shut down much of the hydroelectric power system across the US. You've got to be kidding! That's way above my pay grade."

"Hear us out, Antonio. If I'm right on this, and I'm pretty sure I am, there could be disaster. We need to convince the right people. If Kazim's program takes control, it's for sure the dams are going to open."

It didn't take too much more talking before Antonio said, "Okay, I'll start the briefings. I don't even know who could make that kind of call, but I'll find out. Thanks a lot, you two."

The next morning at dawn Jim was on the phone. With ten hours difference between Washington and Sochi he said, "How's the sunset over there, Illyich? As glorious as ever?"

"Yes, my friend, it is. However, I am sorry to have to tell you that there is more sun shining on me here than there is on our search. We've tracked him to Afghanistan, but that's as far as we can get. He is as invisible as bin Laden himself. What have you got?"

"Quite a bit, really. I'm pretty sure we've found the guy that held the key that opened the door."

"Hey, that's great news."

"No, actually. He's dead. Supposedly fell off a cliff."

"Well, that certainly looks like our friend, Jim. As you suggested, I've convinced some of my old people to poke around. We have indications that his old cell of agents and programmers is still in business in

St. Petersburg, for themselves this time, working for the highest bidder. Separate from the official inquiries, Igor, the fellow you were holding down when Kazim shot you, is keeping an eye on their computers. He tells me that there is coded traffic, both in and out. My bet is that it is with Kazim. I should know more soon, but in the meantime I was thinking that, given the Islamic connection, if maybe you should talk with your friend from Harvard. He might have a faster route, maybe even the only route, to where you want to be."

Antonio was meeting with the brand new Secretary of Homeland Security and his senior staff. They were in the spanking new boardroom, some confusion with the new organization still evident, people feeling their way with new equipment and relationships, the operations staff quietly doing their thing on the computers ringing the room. Those sitting around the oval conference table at the end of the room had all been around the security bazaar for years in the many disparate intelligence and security agencies. Now they were gathered together for the first time to provide cross-discipline assessments. There were people from the CIA, the FBI, a secondment from the chiefs of police, representatives of the many organizations that had been thrown together to form the new department. Even though most had been in the same business for years, many were meeting for the first time, and the differences in operational and bureaucratic culture were evident. They weren't anywhere close to a smoothly running team, and there was some obvious gamesmanship going on, jockeying for position.

As Antonio wound up his analysis of the Onion and what he was recommending to contain the risks, there was a moment of stunned silence, no one sure who should lead off on the discussion, then everyone babbling at once. Dieter Simpson, the newly appointed director of operations and the nominal chair of the meeting, had been the chief of staff to the Secretary in his previous political position, and he cut off the chatter. "You want us to do what? That many generating stations off line would shut the country down. Can you imagine the havoc? The economic impact would be unimaginable!"

And, as people started to assess or reassess their positions, he continued. "So, Mr. Pesquali, you are saying that you want us to issue an order to pull twenty-eight hydroelectric stations off line, including the biggest in the country, at the first sign of trouble? And this based on an assessment by one of your retired agents and his son who isn't even in the business? Where are you coming from?"

Antonio contained his anger with difficulty. "Let me tell you something, people." He looked directly at the Secretary, sitting quietly to the side, taking everything in. "Jim Buchan knows more about terrorists and risk assessment than the rest of you in this room put together. His son, Mark, was hacking into secure computers when he was fourteen. In 1989, Jim single-handedly averted the biggest cyber terror plot that the nation has ever faced, and came close to being killed for his trouble. If Jim and Mark Buchan say the worm is in the hydroelectric station software, it's there. Guaranteed. It is not a question of whether it will be activated, just when. We'd be nuts not to take precautions."

There was a moment of silence in the room, with those who knew Antonio surprised at the passion of his argument, this from a man known to be as cool as a cucumber.

After a few minutes more discussion, a voice from the back of the room, an FBI operations guy who had done frontline duty with Interpol in Europe and really understood the threat, spoke up in a laconic, southern drawl.

"Wait a minute here, folks. Why are we even discussing this? Think back to that day a few weeks ago that we'll never forget, that September day when time stood still for so many of us. Remember the FAA guy who was on duty? No precedents, no contingency plans, no time to seek advice and no one to get permission from, on his own, making that fateful decision to land every airplane in the US, to divert all those transatlantic flights to Canada. He had a lot less to go on than we have, he had nothing, and his ass was on the line, hanging out a mile, all by itself. If he was wrong he'd have had to move to Mongolia. He didn't have the luxury of sitting around arguing the case as we do. He just did it. And he did the right thing. He's a hero. We need to be at least as gutsy as that guy. We shouldn't be arguing about this at all. Antonio's evidence makes sense to me. It's the most solid intelligence we've had about a threat since 9/11. Let's just do it, now."

After a moment of silence it was clear that the discussion was over. The Secretary made the first big, coordinated decision of his new behemoth. "Okay, draft it up and I'll set things in motion. This is going to have huge political implications. I'd better brief the National Security Advisor before we send this out."

Since 9/11, no one was taking chances. No one was going to leave themselves open to a charge that not enough was done, that intelligence was overlooked. When the Secretary called for a meeting, the answer from the National Security Advisor was immediate. "Come on over."

Convincing the chain of command turned out to be easy. "We can't afford not to do it. And this is better, more specific intelligence than we've had to date from anyone. You say this is one of our retired agents and his son? The Agency must be a little ticked, to be preempted like that."

"No, as I understand it this guy's reputation carries a lot of weight. He evidently found a similar plot way back in the Cold War, the Onion File, something to do with a virus in the financial system. So this time people are listening."

"Sounds like something out of a movie. Even more reason we have to pay attention, I guess. Can you imagine if he's right? My God, the country would be flooded."

"The other side of the coin is, if he turns out to be wrong, it's no harm done—and we're seen to be doing our jobs."

"Okay, do it. I'll brief the President tomorrow morning, so he's not caught flat-footed if this guy turns out to be right."

That afternoon a fax went to every power station using the Intelligent Solutions & Security software. Every operator coming on shift read, and signed as having read, the notice that warned of a potential attack on the dam control systems. The instructions were clear. If it looks like something is wrong, don't take a chance, don't stop to try to analyze the anomaly, turn off electrical power to the equipment. Then immediately alert all the other dams on the list to do the same. Most operators had complete confidence in their systems and their training, and most were skeptical that they would ever be faced with a situation critical enough to demand such radical action. But they all read and thought about that extraordinary order. Beth Simmons, the operations chief at the dam in Woodhaven, said to herself, "And who's going to be the jackass?"

Jim was spending more time in Mark's home office than he could ever have imagined, and they were once again reviewing what they knew, what else they should be doing.

"Well, Mark, the orders have gone out across the country, to every station using the Intelligent Solutions & Security software."

"That's good. Hopefully no one is going to have to pull those switches, but if they do let's pray that they do it fast enough so that not too many floodgates are opened. That way the damage from flooding at least should be limited. Where do we go from here?"

"I need to take two trips. I'd like you to come to California with me, to talk to the folks at the computer company. We should do that right away."

"Okay, I agree. I can go anytime. And what's the other trip?"

"Mark, I went to grad school with an Arab sheik. We became good friends, and we've traded some pretty big favors over the years. I think he might just be able to pull off another one. I'm going to find out where he is and go to talk to him. Now that I think about it, if I know him, he's likely to be in Sardinia at this time of year."

"Jeez, Dad, why go all that way? Can't you ask him on the phone?"

"Son, here's a little lesson in the Jim Buchan theory of international human nature, especially in the Middle East and around the Mediterranean. The personal touch, respect, is everything. What I'm going to ask Mo, that's what I call him, has to be done face to face. He'll have to use all his contacts throughout the Middle East to locate Kazim. This will put him at considerable risk. I need to show my respect, to demonstrate the importance of my request, to honor him by the effort I have made to seek his assistance. Doing it by phone just won't cut it."

The next morning in the Oval Office, the National Security advisor had just completed the last item in the President's daily brief, an item that in the grand scheme of things was a relatively minor security matter, a contingency plan. President Walker had a busy day ahead and until now had been silent, but this one caught his attention. He was a man who liked action, who listened to the facts and made decisions, and who had surrounded himself with people who didn't beat around the bush.

"So, you're saying that if this virus starts messing up the system, we're going to shut down a good portion of our electricity?"

'That's correct, Mr. President. It really is just a precaution."

"Well, for sure, better safe than sorry." He turned to his chief of staff. "Have some speaking notes drawn up just in case. Tell the people to keep up the good work. Hmm, I'm sure they're doing it anyway, but we should have some plans of action prepared on the off chance that there is something to this."

"It's being done as we speak, sir. One thing that was clear immediately when the staff started to look at this is that if it happened, we'd be in a world of hurt. Flooding would be serious enough even if limited by turning off the power to the dam gates, but the loss of capacity would take enough generating systems off line that the economy would essentially be shut down. We'd have to take the major electrical consumers off line to be able to manage a minimum distribution of the remaining power for emergency uses."

"You'd better brief me on contingencies so that we've got the bases covered. If this turns out to be right, the Agency must really have their ears to the ground. Good work on their part."

"Mr. President, the word I hear is that it's some retired guy and his son who are leading on this, so I really feel that it is pretty unlikely."

CHAPTER 25

Today was like many other October days in Southern California, blue sky, light breeze, temperature warming after a cool night. The trees lining the entry were losing leaves but there was still a lot of green. The palms waving gently, flowers still blooming, the whole atmosphere looking almost tropical and very exotic to an Easterner. The road ran along bluff, high mountains to the left, the Pacific below on the right.

"Kind of neat," Mark said, expressing his thoughts aloud. "I could take this."

Jim and Mark had rented a car at the airport and driven straight to the small complex. As they arrived at the gate, Wally, the guard, raised the barrier, saying, "Welcome to Intelligent Solutions & Security. Mr. Cartwright is expecting you. Please park in the Visitors spot just at the entrance, right over there." He pointed to the front of the one-story high-tech looking building, glass glinting in the sun.

As they walked through the door, a trim young woman greeted them. "Good morning, Mr. Buchan, I'm Cathy. We spoke on the phone. Please come this way."

Jim thought, as they made their way down the short hallway, "Hmm, at least he runs an efficient operation."

Cathy gave a knock on the open door to the office, announcing, "The Buchans are here, Mr. Cartwright."

As they entered the clean, business-like office, Jim did a quick visual: modern desk and chairs, efficient equipment, no paper lying around, no fancy trimmings, impressive in its simplicity. He extended his hand, saying, "Mr. Cartwright, we spoke on the phone. I'm Jim Buchan, this is my son, Mark. Thanks for seeing us on such short notice."

"I'm glad you're here, Mr. Buchan. Your man in Washington, Mr. Pesquali, briefed me. This whole thing is just terrible. If you are right about this, poor Dave. I mean it's so hard to imagine him being involved in terrorism with all the precautions that we take. I just don't understand how it could happen. I've checked the files and he passed all his security checks just fine."

"That may be so, sir, but the fact is that for whatever reasons, he more than likely has corrupted the software. I'm sure the reasons will all come out in the wash."

"Mark, Antonio—Mr. Pesquali—tells me that you're the one who discovered this?"

"Well, it was kind of both of us, Mr. Cartwright, but, yes, I did spend a lot of time looking, with some pretty sophisticated equipment. I'd like to speak with whoever backed MacIntyre up. And also, could we speak with your security guy to see what can be done fast?"

"He's one and the same. We're not a big outfit. It's Seth Patterson. He's ready and waiting." Mr. Cartwright punched a button on his desk. "Cathy, ask Seth to come in, please."

The young man who walked through the door was dressed in a tee shirt, sawed-off jeans and sandals. He had a ponytail, a scruffy beard, massive tattoos on each arm, and an earring dangling from one ear. He was clearly under stress.

"This is Seth, our chief of security. Seth, these folks are from Washington, Jim Buchan and his son, Mark. They are the ones who discovered irregularities and believe Dave has helped set up a virus."

Mark's eyebrows rose quizzically as he saw his father's face crease with a smile. "What could be funny about this?" he asked himself.

"Mr. Cartwright, Seth, when you walked in it reminded me of a story from my past that I think I should take a minute to tell. It might help to put some perspective into this sorry state of affairs, set us off on the right foot. A colleague of mine retired and was hired as the CEO of an outfit not unlike this one. They made stuff for the satellites and they had similar security checks to what I'm sure you are subjected to. One of the visits from the counterintelligence people included a briefing on who to hire, the type of people. After all, everybody knows you need to be careful about these hippy types—I mean, who could trust them? My friend smiled to himself as the Washington bigwig said this, and with a straight face to boot, because he knew what was coming. They left the briefing room and, as they started the walk around for the physical check of the plant, ran into a hippy-looking guy, about like you, Seth. My friend said, 'Gentlemen, I'd like you to meet Dr. Ahmed Abdul, our chief scientist. He designs the product that we make for you. His PhD is in thermodynamics from MIT.' Seth, I've been around long enough to know both not to judge a book by its cover and that the most careful security checks are just one part of the puzzle. You are going to be key to recovering from this mess and, even though I may look pretty straight to you, know that we consider us all to be on the same team. We're 100% on your side here. You have the expertise and the knowledge that's needed to start to fix this. Now, let's get down to business."

The CEO sat back, with a pause and a quizzical look. Only then did he burst into nervous laughter. "That was a good thing you just did, Mr. Buchan, breaking the ice like that. I know that Seth is worried sick about all this, and I can tell you, I'm not far behind."

"The important thing now is to figure out how to prevent the disaster that Mark and I think is imminent."

Mark started. "Over the last while, was there anything out of the ordinary, anything different that you noticed, anything that caught your attention?"

Seth was ready for this. He had lain in bed at night going over and over in his mind how it could have happened. He knew enough to know that whatever Dave had done had to be really complex, really sophisticated.

"Yes, there was, but it didn't register at the time. Since Dave's death, I remembered it. A while ago, I picked up what looked like a probe of our systems. When I reported it to Dave, he got a really worried look, then told me he'd handle it. I never heard any more and just forgot about it, thinking that it was the security people checking us out. Now that I think about it, his look was more than just concern. He must have realized that the probing was real."

"That was no doubt my tracing that you picked up, Seth. I was on your system for a long time. Tell me, you run a security program regularly, to check for continuity, for corruption?"

"Sure do. The contract requires that it be done at least weekly. I ran it yesterday and everything seems fine."

"Dave did all the high-level programming, didn't he?" As Seth nodded his head, Mark continued, "So he also wrote the security program, the one you use to check the system?"

Seth's look of horror said it all. "Oh, Lord, of course. If Dave had corrupted the software, he would have written a program to cover it up, to indicate that everything was all right!"

In the silence that followed, everyone recognized what must have happened.

Cartwright was the first to speak. "I agree. We have a potential disaster on our hands. At best, going all out, it's going to take Seth and me at least five days to work through the codes, the software. Dave was so good that he did it pretty much by himself. We'll get going right away. Mr. Buchan, maybe we should be doing something in case we run out of time?"

"I hope that that's been taken care of. Orders have gone out across the country to turn the power off to all the equipment at the first hint of trouble."

"Okay, Seth, let's get at it. Mr. Buchan, Mark, we owe you a huge vote of thanks. I'll be in touch with Antonio Pesquali in Washington as soon as I know anything."

Jim and Mark spent most of the trip back to Washington trying to catch up on sleep. "One thing traveling with you, Dad, you sure don't allow much time for sightseeing along the way. I don't know how you did it all those years."

"I agree, this whole thing has been kind of rushed, and for sure, we aren't finished yet. One thing I have decided, though, is that when this is over, your mother and I are going to take a few excursions. Certainly to Sochi, but also to Sardinia to see the old friend, the one I hadn't thought about for a few years."

"He's the sheik you mentioned the other day, Dad? I don't understand what triggered Sardinia now, with so much going on. You said he might be able to track Kazim?"

"I would guess he's our only possibility, especially if Kazim is with bin Laden in Afghanistan, which all the indicators point toward. Anyway, when all this is finished and we settle down to our normal routine, maybe you'd want to come along, especially back to Sochi."

"Dad, Katrina and I have been in serious touch on the net. If I go anywhere, she's coming with me."

"That's great. She's a very impressive girl, and I'd sure like your mother to meet her."

"Well, I've been thinking about that. Katrina thought that maybe she'd come for a couple of days and I think we'll see what we can do. Mom spoke to me the other day and I told her that this was serious. For sure, I've never felt this way about anyone before."

After a brief silence Mark added, "I guess Mom's a bit anxious about what we're doing. I told her not to worry, but I'll give her a call tonight."

CHAPTER 26

The minute Mark got home he was on his computer. He got straight to the point. "I've been away with my dad, a fast trip to California, and I've missed you, Katrina. I want to see you, soon. I can't get over there for a while, so could you come here? I've got to see you again."

Her smiling face glowed at him out of the lens. "Ha! You just want to finish what we didn't quite get done that beautiful night in the moonlight! I'm not that easy, you know."

"No? Are you going to pretend that you haven't thought about it?"

"I've thought of little else. I can't wait."

"So, good. I'll complete the reservation I have on hold. You leave at ten in the morning. I'll email you the ticket and see you tomorrow afternoon. Two days won't be enough but it'll be better than the virtual life we've been having on the internet! Might be okay to learn to fly on a computer, but it sure doesn't cut it for what I need."

Mark had lived on his own for a few years and, as the cleaner from Trim'n Tidy kept reminding him, he wasn't the best of housekeepers. He looked around at the chaos and decided he'd better spend some time straightening up his apartment. Some flowers in a vase on the hall table, fresh linen and towels, the table set for two with crystal glasses and china that Leigh had given him several years ago, now out of the boxes they came in for the first time, the CD set to play Diana Krall. He did some fast shopping, steaks, salad stuff, a bottle of California sparkling, as well as white and red wine.

As Katrina stepped out of customs, she saw Mark's head above the crowd, dropped her one carry-on bag and from a running start jumped up, arms around his neck, legs around his hips, the kiss that they had discussed in detail on the net now the real thing.

One of the other passengers picked up her bag and with a smile tapped Mark on the shoulder. "Looks like she won't need her clothes on this visit, but here's her undies for her return flight."

Katrina grinned at the remark. "Mark, if you live more than a half an hour from here we're going to need a motel. Let's get going."

About the only thing that Katrina noticed on the drive home was the car they were in. "For a computer nerd you're ritzier than you look. I just knew there was something more behind those horn-rimmed glasses. Hmm, and I can feel that there's more here, too."

They were peeling off each other's clothes before they even made it to the bedroom.

About nine o'clock Katrina woke to the smell of broiling steak. By the time she wrapped herself in a towel, Mark was serving, handing her a glass of sparkling wine, salad on the table, steak just about done.

"Kats, I love you."

"Hmm, nice. The sex isn't bad either, is it? If I had known how good it is I would've tried it sooner!"

"You're a devil," he laughed, pulling off the towel.

Over dinner Mark said, "You met my dad. I told him you were coming and my mother has asked us to dinner tomorrow. That okay with you?"

"This is sounding serious! Just kidding. I'd love to. And tomorrow you could take me to a park somewhere near here. I remember visiting it when I was here at school."

"Probably Rock Creek Park. We'll do that on the way to Dad's."

"Mark, this is how I remember it, just beautiful. I can imagine it in the spring with everything in bloom. And the trees—majestic! What a pleasure for the people of Washington."

People were strolling, young mothers pushing baby carriages, others of all ages gliding by on roller blades, school kids lining up for the zoo, the creek running slowly under an arched bridge. Mark and

Katrina walked hand in hand for an hour, past the Old Stone House and the Pierce Barn, talking of American history, lost in the joy of being together, then somewhat reluctantly returning to the Corvette for the drive to dinner.

Leigh met them at the door, arms outstretched to both of them and, with a twinkle in her eye, looked at Katrina. "So, you are the girl who has stolen the hearts of both my husband and my son. But if you are the granddaughter of Illyich Makov, I can understand why."

"She is, in spades," Mark said with a laugh. "Just a bit smaller and a lot more beautiful."

The relaxed dinner, tranquil setting and soft conversation didn't hint of the fast approaching danger. When Mark and Katrina said their reluctant farewells at the airport the next morning, they had no idea how soon she would be back in Washington, nor why.

CHAPTER 27

"Well, my dear," Leigh stated as they got out of bed. "You're doing more running around now than you did before you retired. It must be kind of strange, touching base with old colleagues that you haven't spoken with in years."

"It sure is. This will be a fast trip, back in a couple of days. Mo's arranged my flight from Paris to his place."

Leigh put her arms around Jim as they kissed. "Say 'hi' to him from me, and come back in one piece. I'm starting to be more than a little concerned about all this."

"Don't be, dear. One way or another it's going to be over soon."

Jim slept all the way to Paris where, true to his word, the sheik had sent his personal aircraft to meet him. As Jim left customs he was met by a uniformed chauffeur who drove him across the airfield to a Learjet, where he climbed the few stairs to find himself the only passenger in the opulent interior. A woman as exotic as if she had just stepped out of *A Thousand and One Nights* welcomed him.

"We are ready to go when you are, Mr. Buchan. I understand you know the sheik, so you will know that his orders are to look after you well," she said with a radiant smile. And then with a laugh, "My name is Fatima and, as they say, your wish is my command."

It wasn't long before the sleek jet leveled at 45,000 feet, heading due south, 180°, alone in the sky at that high altitude. When he went to the washroom Jim wasn't surprised to find it tastefully equipped. He just knew that the gold sink and taps must have cost more than his house. Looking out the window at the view Jim got the same thrill as the first time he had traveled this route years ago. As they crossed over

Dijon, in France, the cloud underneath dissipated, the view changing from the cool gray of north Europe to the hot haze of the south, the more arid, southern, rolling, tropical coloring of the French Midi, the Rhone meandering down the center. The snow-capped Alps glistened on the left, the Matterhorn and Mont Blanc lifting up from the crags and snowfields, with the Pyrenees on the horizon on the distant right.

Fatima served him a delicious shrimp salad, Perrier water and a glass of chilled Alsatian Gewürztraminer to top it off. Then, as the southern coastline of France slid into view, the turquoise Mediterranean shimmered from the Italian Riviera on the left around to the Costa Brava of Spain on the right, white surf ringing the beaches far below. Jim thought again that it was about as spectacular a view as it gets. Just as they started their descent into Elmas, the airport at Cagliari in Sardinia, he could just make out the coast of North Africa glowing through the haze. Jim forced himself to concentrate on the file, to read again the Agency briefing that Antonio had put together for him, what was known about bin Laden and al-Qaeda. This wouldn't be the first time Jim had bent the rules in sharing intelligence with Mo. It would be done as a gesture of respect.

"We sure don't know a whole hell of a lot after all this effort," he said to himself. He thought about his friend, Sheik Mohammed, and what he was about to ask him to do, something that all the US effort and dollars had not yet accomplished.

As the steps of the plane touched the ground, Jim saw a smartly-dressed pilot striding toward him.

"Mr. Buchan, Sheik Mohammed sends his greetings. I am Captain Farhouq. It is my honor to fly you to the villa. Your bags are being looked after. Please join me in our helicopter."

Jim followed the captain to a very trim-looking Jet Ranger, recognizing the same racing green-and-white striped livery as the jet that he had just stepped out of, clearly the sheik's racing colors. He smiled at the thought.

"Here you go, sir. Sit up front with me and I'll give you the VIP look at the city and the coast. It's kind of special."

Jim had barely strapped in when the helicopter lifted off and swung east along the coast, the old city of Cagliari stretching out on the left, looking like a page out of a medieval album. Then the long white sand of the Poetto, said by some to be the most beautiful beach in the world, sunbathers lazing in the afternoon heat. It wasn't long until Jim spotted the huge complex that he recognized from the photos Mo had emailed him. The palace took up several miles of rugged coastline, with tiled walkways leading to secluded beaches lapped by turquoise water.

Jim and Sheik Mohammed became close friends while spending a year together doing graduate work at Harvard in the '70s. Mohammed—Mo to Jim—was a Saudi who bridged East and West, secular and Islam. With his many contacts throughout the Middle East, and the stature provided by both birth and wealth, he had unique access to people and places who would not have welcomed Jim or, for that matter, anyone from the western world. They had spent hours discussing the Middle East, Islam, the Holy Land, and had coauthored a paper on the Palestinian situation, feeling out each other's philosophy and belief, becoming good friends in the process. The sheik had long recognized the fragile political and cultural balance on which his country teetered precariously and had come down firmly on the side of the West. Over the years he had quietly but firmly supported US policies and actions in the Middle East and provided Jim with critical intelligence on key issues. Mo had played a hand in helping Illyich track Kazim back to his home in Turkistan in 1989 after the first Onion was wrapped up, and Jim now hoped that he could do the same again, help him find Kazim in the wilds of Afghanistan.

By the time the rotor blades wound down after the compulsory two-minute cooling period, the sheik was there to greet Jim. In his flowing robes, Mohammed looked larger than life. Although he was short and rotund, the Arabian goatee and sunglasses were just like those in the pictures of the royal family seen regularly in the western media. No doubt about it, he projected confidence and power.

As Jim stepped down from the cockpit he extended a hand to the pilot. "Thanks for the millionaire buggy ride. I enjoyed it."

Turning to the sheik he said, "Well, Mo, you've built yourself quite a place here. What a view coming in! You look great as ever, my friend."

"Jim, good to see you. I'm sorry that we had to wait for whatever mission you are on. Sometime you and Leigh should visit when you haven't got the fate of the world resting on your shoulders. But let's get to that later. Let me show you around."

Mohammed led Jim along a slate-tiled, palm-shaded pathway that looked out over the azure blue of the Mediterranean. Steps led down to a white sand beach nestled between rock outcroppings, protecting it from waves and wind. As they rounded the bluff Jim could see the main complex nestled in the hills along the rugged coastline. "Got to be at least 15,000 square feet," he thought to himself. "Man, what a place!"

"We'll sit out here on the patio."

Jim surveyed the scene. The wide terrace, stretched out to the water below, with tent-like silk draped to break the hot afternoon sun. Wicker chairs with luxurious cushions surrounded a large, etched glass-topped table, and when Jim sat down he found himself settling deeply into their comfort. As iced tea arrived in crystal glasses, a sprig of fresh mint nestled in the ice, Mohammed said, "Okay, Jim, let's get down to business. Since you wouldn't tell me anything on the phone I gather that you're not as retired as you're supposed to be."

"Mo, I can hardly believe it myself, but it's as if the clock got turned back. I think Kazim is at it again. This time it's Onion 2."

"I must say I'm not too surprised, given his history. How bad is it this time?"

"Well, bad enough, for sure. We're pretty sure he's found a way to get into our power system, the hydroelectric dams. It's going to be difficult, if not impossible, to sort it out without information that only he could provide. I know it isn't likely that we could get at him, but I'd like to try."

Twenty minutes later, after describing the situation, Mo asked Jim, "What can I do to help? I could probably guess what's coming."

Jim said, "You'd be right, of course. Once again, Mo, I need a favor, one that only you could give me. I need to find Kazim. I don't expect we'd get lucky enough to get to him, but I want at least to try to get a message to him. We do have a head start. We believe he's in the mountains of Afghanistan, along the Pakistani border, with bin Laden. That, of course, is why I'm here. I think that you are perhaps the only person who might be able to get close. If we can find him, Illyich might have a way to reach him, to get him to show himself. The message that I want to get to him would be from Illyich. You are the only person I know who might be able to get it delivered."

"Jim, you know the tightrope we are on and have been for all these years. I can tell you that the wire is now stretched to the breaking point. The bin Laden family has disowned their wayward offspring, but he still has many friends and sympathizers ready to provide support. My country is caught between your proverbial rock and a hard place. Bin Laden may achieve what he wants for my country without having to fire a shot. He has young people ready to fight to the death."

Jim agreed. "Yes, that's for sure. I recognize that. I think that's one of the major reasons bin Laden is still out there, creating havoc around the world. There is no doubt he has considerable financial backing, despite what your government may be doing to slow it down, and he can see the popular support for change, violent or otherwise."

"What you ask, Jim, could take some doing. I expect I could know pretty quick about the chances of getting a message on its way, but the delivery itself would be problematic. How long do we have? You're staying overnight anyway. I'll see what might be possible, whether there would be any chance."

"Go to it, Mo. I could use a good night's sleep. I'm booked out on the morning flight tomorrow to Rome. Depending on what you can do for me, I'm either heading east from there to Russia, or west to home."

"How about dinner and a swim before bed?"

"I was well looked after on the meager chariot that you provided, but, yes, I could use a bite. First though, the Med looks awfully inviting. How about you show me your favorite spot?"

Mo led Jim down gentle stone steps to a stunning white sand beach, about 200 feet wide, nestled between rock outcroppings, turquoise water glistening in the setting sun. Then, as the sun set, they had a supper of fish and salad on the same silk-draped veranda.

"Mo, the decision is made. I need to bring Leigh to see your piece of paradise."

The sun was rising and, with the new light of dawn streaking in the window, the bedroom looked even more sumptuous than when he had fallen instantly to sleep. Even with the change in time zones Jim was awake, drinking in the luxury of it all, as the quiet sounds of servants watering planters and the myriad of other morning chores went on outside. A knock at the door and Fatima entered, placing a caftan for Jim to wear on his bed, saying, "Good morning, sir, at your service as always."

Jim laughed delightedly. "Your boss knows me well. I'm sure he's enjoying pulling my chain. Perhaps it is my loss, but he knows me too well. He knows you're safe with me. I have a wife who would cut them off if I even thought about what that service might be."

"Hmm, yes, that is what he told me," she said with a chuckle and a radiant smile, leading him down the wide marble stairs. "The sheik awaits your pleasure for breakfast."

Mo was waiting for him, comfortably lounging on a chaise lounge wearing a caftan similar to the one that had been brought to Jim earlier.

"Good morning, Jim. I trust you slept well."

"How could I not in such comfort? I especially enjoyed the special offering this morning, though, Mo, it's the thought that counts!"

"Yes, Fatima and I did have a little fun with that. She's a great girl, and takes every opportunity to get away with me, out of the confines that still bind women in my country. She especially likes the clothes she can wear when we're away."

"I must say, Mo, I've never understood how an educated woman like Fatima can reconcile her life to the milieu in which she lives." Jim said this knowing that Mo would not take offence. They had spent many hours discussing and arguing these kinds of social and religious issues those many years ago at Harvard.

"It gets more difficult every year to keep the lid on. It is lifting, but slowly. And our people are divided, with a huge and increasing number coming down on the side of Islam. Fatima with her western clothes may be in the minority. We still have many in power who will fight any change to the bitter end. If I were writing one of our scholarly papers now, I would conclude that the outcome is still quite uncertain."

After a thoughtful pause, Mo continued. "Jim, I've taken the liberty of ordering your old favorite, eggs, poached, on toast, sausage and coffee. Note that I do keep sausage in the freezer so my infidel friends will feel at home, a foot in both camps, you know. Come in and join me. You will be pleased to know that I have some news to accompany your breakfast."

Jim knew Mohammed well enough to know that the sausage had nothing to do with keeping a foot in both camps. It was simply Mo's excellent hospitality and cosmopolitanism.

"Mo, with this kind of service, and these kind of digs, you might never get rid of me. I'll definitely return soon with Leigh. She'd enjoy seeing you again. It's truly beautiful. Tell me, though, what were you able to find for me?"

"Of course, you were right. There's not a chance of getting to bin Laden. You are also right about Kazim. He is more than likely holed up with tribes along the border with what's left of the al-Qaeda hierarchy. Even with the multimillion price on it, no one is delivering that head on a platter. There'd be no way of physically getting to Kazim as long as he's with bin Laden. But I think we might be able to get a message to him. It will have to go through many hands and might take some time to get there."

"Outstanding! I appreciate the markers that you must have called in for that. I'll get the message to you as soon as I can. In fact, I'll have our Russian friend speak directly to you when it's ready."

"Tell Illyich to get his message to me and I'll put in motion the delivery system. As I said, it might work, but I expect the only way you'll know is when your trap is sprung—and I don't want to know what it is that you have planned. The fewer that know, the better. I do wish you success, though. It would ease things for us if you succeed. Jim, it doesn't sound to me like you are old and retired!"

"You know, it's kind of ironic," Jim responded. "This all happened by accident. I can tell you, I sure didn't plan to be here under these circumstances. I can also tell you though, Mo, it is good to see you again."

"I know you, and I can guess that you aren't going to take time to laze around in the sun, are you? The helicopter is ready anytime you are."

"Before I leave, let's touch base with Illyich to set things up. Can we give him a call?"

"Of course. You have some numbers?"

Within minutes Jim had briefed Illyich, and had handed the phone to Mo. "I'll get the message drafted as soon as I can confirm with the key player that we're okay with what I have in mind. I'll be back to you as soon as I can, Mo, and as always, thanks. Let me speak to Jim for a minute before we disconnect …"

"Jim, I'll put things in motion and speak to you when you get back. This is going to be tricky, just like old times!"

With that, the sheik clapped his hands to signal to his staff that Jim was ready to depart.

"I think we're all set. Thank you for your usual magnificent hospitality. Leigh and I will take you up on your offer to visit just as soon as this is over."

"Anytime, my friend."

"As always, it was worth the long trip, and I'll be in touch as soon as I know anything. I'm going to head west from Rome and I'll call you from home. Goodbye, my friend."

"May God be with you."

CHAPTER 28

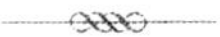

Between emails to Kazim and phone calls to Washington, Silvio had been a busy man, but he had the operation organized. Kazim's contact in Washington had been doing the surveillance so they'd be ready to move. Kazim had warned Silvio that he had to be very careful using the telephone, so the few calls made were from different pay phones a few blocks from his apartment, and the conversation was innocuous enough not to set any tracking computers running. The one to Washington was short and to the point, no names, no small talk: "You are ready?"

"Yes."

"Monday?"

"Yes."

When he arrived in Washington he met with Chavez, the man he had spoken to on the phone. Chavez was originally from Algeria and, like Silvio, had been in the States for years doing surveillance and some banking: receiving and transferring funds for the cause. On instructions from Silvio, he had spent the last few days quietly watching their target, and by the third morning he had it aced, he was ready to go. Chavez had checked Silvio into a motel under a fictitious name, and had paid in advance in cash. As he dropped Silvio off, he said, "Here are the keys, it's the second on the left. I'll pick you up at 4:00 tomorrow morning. This shouldn't take long. He's regular as clockwork. May Allah be with you."

Mark didn't need his alarm. At five o'clock he jumped out of bed, grabbed a glass of orange juice, pulled on his sweats and hit the trail, as he did five mornings a week. And every morning he thought the same thing, "Life doesn't get much better." He had selected the condo not only because it was in a neighborhood where he had gone to school and which he loved, but because he could step out the door onto the five-mile path, tree-lined, quiet, ideal for a yuppie single guy. "Hmm," he thought, "not single for much longer." Good thing he had recently upgraded to a larger two-bedroom to accommodate his expanding computer stuff, though it was already getting crowded.

It was early morning, the start of a beautiful day, with the joggers few and far between, just as he liked it. He headed down the street and onto the Whitehaven Parkway. Mark did his best, most creative thinking on his morning runs among the trees of Whitehaven. This morning he was lost in thought about Kazim's program and what else he could be doing to prevent disaster.

As he overtook another early bird he said, "Hi, Dorothy. How come you're out so early? I thought you had switched to the evening for your workout."

"I'm leaving on a trip so I have to get my licks in now, Mark," she said as he sped by. Neither Mark nor Dorothy noticed the two men quietly sipping their coffee on a nearby bench.

Silvio said, "Now what? I thought you said the place was deserted when he ran."

"Don't worry, tomorrow's another day." On the three previous mornings there hadn't been another soul in sight. "This is the first time anyone else has been on the trail. We'll try again tomorrow morning."

Bright and early the next morning their car was parked beside the same jogging path. They waited on the same bench, again appearing to enjoy their coffee, two men relaxing before starting their day's work. It turned out to be incredibly easy. The place was deserted.

As Mark came along the path, sweat trickling down his face, the men stood up, one saying, "Just a minute, Mark." As Mark came to a surprised stop he found himself looking into the muzzle of a gun.

"Please get in the car."

In less than a minute, the dark blue Grand Marquis was on its way, Mark on the floor, handcuffed, feet tied, gagged and a hood over his head. He tried to keep track of where they were going and in the beginning he thought that the car had gone south and crossed the Potomac River.

After almost an hour on what seemed to Mark to be a highway, the car came to a stop. He thought that they had made it to somewhere in the countryside, yet he could still hear the morning traffic heading into Washington and what sounded like airplanes, likely near an airport. He was hustled up some stairs to a landing and into a house, and then he was shoved roughly down a set of steep stairs. He guessed he was in a basement just outside the city.

CHAPTER 29

With the time zone change, Jim was home from Sardinia in time for dinner. Leigh had prepared a fillet on the barbeque and tossed salad. They were settled on the balcony, enjoying the remainder of the bottle of wine, one of their favorites, an Oregonian Merlot that they had shared over dinner. Jim marveled at the last rays of sun catching the light in Leigh's still auburn hair. The view from the balcony was as satisfying but so different from the one he had just left on the other side of the world.

"You know, my dear, we really must go to Sardinia soon. Mo's place is incredible. Lavish, as you'd expect with that kind of money, but tasteful, as you'd expect from Mo, and he is as warm and hospitable as always. He genuinely would like to see us."

Leigh closed her eyes, smiled, and dreamily responded. "That sounds smashing. I'd love to go. So, tell me, your trip was successful? Mo can help?"

"I'm really asking a lot, but he thinks so. With his wide range of contacts it's likely that he can at least get a message on the way. Only time will tell if it gets to its destination. And we'll have to see what Illyich can come up with. I really can't imagine how he could craft a message to Kazim that would be strong enough to lure him out of hiding. Kazim is so wily, and this will not be the first trap that has been set to snare him."

"When I think about Mo and Illyich, you sure picked up your share of interesting friends along the way. It is an unusual set of circumstances that would take you to Sardinia, to an Arab sheik, to link to an ex-KGB spy to find a terrorist who is bent on our destruction, hiding out in tribal lands that no country controls. What next, my husband?"

"Leigh, I do have a lot of activity underway. I just hope the steps that we've taken are enough to head off whatever disaster Kazim has planned for us."

"I'm not sure what more you could be doing." Leigh paused for a moment before continuing. "You've got the whole US security apparatus cranked up, with precautionary action orders to the right people. How dangerous is this for you and Mark? What if Kazim knows you are intent on foiling him again?"

"I don't think there's much to worry about personally. After all, I'm retired," he said with a smile.

"Good. I've been following the commentary and the unclassified assessments about the terrorist threat. I think that, as usual, your analysis is right on the money. There is a huge risk to the nation in all of this. It must be driving your old colleagues wild not knowing where to look."

"I'm sure it is. With the work you're doing, what's your assessment of al-Qaeda? Where would you be looking?"

"Well, in the material I read every day I see a lot of different opinions about what should be done, about where the counter terrorist resources should be concentrated. I can tell you though, Jim, that my read of the situation is different from that of at least some of your old colleagues. Of course, they're looking at a lot more information than I'm seeing."

"Yeah, but I used to see the same stuff they do and I didn't always agree either. Let's hear your thoughts."

"I think that the war that we are waging has changed the character of the threat. What bin Laden put together in the Taliban lands of Afghanistan is in retreat. It couldn't withstand the intense onslaught of so many Northern Alliance troops with our air support. But what little we see from the Intel agencies and from testimony in the congressional committees indicates that at least some of your old colleagues seem to believe that al-Qaeda is still a cohesive conglomerate, centrally controlled and led, planning and directing operations."

"And you don't agree?" Jim asked thoughtfully.

"No, I don't," Leigh sank back into the chair before continuing. "I think that bin Laden has morphed into the rallying messiah, encouraging the faithful, keeping hopes alive with the occasional message of encouragement and promise. His character galvanizes the faithful. His austerity, living in caves, just enhances his probity and dignity in the Muslim world. But I just can't believe that he could lead the charge from a cave in the tribal lands. I think that what we will now see is the action of *jihadists* who have come out of the millions of disillusioned Islamists from across the Islamic world."

"I think I'd agree with you about bin Laden. He may be more of a figurehead now than an operational leader. If you are correct on that, then catching him may make a symbolic difference—a big one to be sure—but the terrorist activity may not skip a beat. Now there's a scary thought!"

Leigh said reflectively, "It is, indeed, but that is what many of us think. We really need to pay attention to the other stuff that has been around all these years, like Palestine, like the religious dictatorships that marginalize people, the oppressive regimes. Until these issues start to be resolved, I'm not sure that catching bin Laden will make that much immediate difference to the threats we face."

"Well, my dear, you may be right. At least in this case, the one Mark and I are spending so much time on. No doubt this Onion is Kazim's personal mission, his baby, with or without bin Laden's command. It fits nicely with al-Qaeda, but this could be Kazim's personal *jihad*, with resources provided by bin Laden. And I also think you're right about my ex-colleagues. Antonio can't say much, but I know that he is really concerned and frustrated. At least now some action is underway to handle this particular threat. Mark has sure done good work."

"I'm still really worried, Jim. These people are desperate. Who's to say what they might do to see their plan through?"

After a thoughtful pause Leigh said, "Jim, I wanted some quiet time together to talk, to get caught up, before I handed you this. It arrived special delivery this afternoon. It looks official. Maybe from Antonio?"

The envelope that Leigh handed to Jim was marked "Top Secret. Eyes Only. To be opened personally by J. Buchan."

Jim thought as he opened the package, "That's peculiar, it's not Agency." Then, as he read the contents, the expression on his face turned to one of horror.

"Jim, what's wrong? What's happened?" In all their years of marriage, even when he had been involved in intrigue and danger, she had never, ever, seen the look that was now on Jim's face.

"Oh, Leigh, I was wrong. I'm so sorry. They've got Mark."

"What do you mean? Where's Mark?"

He handed Leigh the letter.

> *Jim Buchan,*
> *You know that you can trust my word when I say that your son will survive only if you stop all activity on my Onion. I will know immediately if you do not obey. My next shot will not miss the way the first one did.*

The letter did not need a signature. The photo that accompanied the note was of Mark, duct tape over his mouth, holding a day-old *Washington Post*.

Leigh caved in, distraught. "Oh, Jim, how could you have gotten us into this? I've been so worried. I could feel the danger in the pit of my stomach. I should have insisted you stop. What are we going to do?"

"First, we're going to call in every damn IOU that I've got out there," Jim said as he reached for the phone.

CHAPTER 30

Antonio had worked overtime that day and just got home after a long and tension-filled meeting with emergency security agencies, trying to work out jurisdictional boundaries and intelligence-sharing arrangements. It wasn't going to be easy overcoming years of bureaucracy, turf and vested interest, every player loath to relinquish position in a city where information often equaled power. The one small bit of optimism, a small beacon of light in the long afternoon, had come not from new arrangements or agreements, but from the past. Over many years a quiet, unofficial liaison that Jim had initiated and nourished with his FBI counterpart had blossomed under Antonio's gentle hand. Oscar Delormier had replaced Jim's counterpart at the FBI and had agreed with Antonio that they should continue a good thing, perhaps not fully legal according to the tight rules that both agencies worked under, but effective when the chips were down, when the pressure was on.

Oscar had started in the bad old days of J. Edgar Hoover and had soon recognized that he wasn't happy spying on activists and peaceniks, kids like his own son. When he made it into the senior ranks he was quite happy to bend the rules a bit to keep things honest. He was appreciative to be able to cross-check with the spies to be sure that the internal enemy that he was after was the real thing. Now, after 9/11 when the bureaucracy everywhere was being arm-twisted to cooperate, Antonio and Oscar had the working model, one that Jim had wrestled his conscience with over the years when the CIA was not allowed to compare notes with the FBI.

The phone rang as he walked in his front door. Antonio picked up the one on the hall table, calling, "I'll get it, Honey."

"Antonio, they've got Mark." Jim was clutching the phone so hard his hand was turning white.

"Whoa, slow down there, Jim. What's happened? Who's got Mark?"

"Kazim had Mark kidnapped. He's told me to back off from Onion. That means he's got to be really close to activating the program."

"Hold on, don't do anything. I'm on my way."

Leigh and Jim were on the sofa, arms around each other, Jim trying his best to be practical, Leigh saying, "My worst nightmares have come true. Jim, what are we going to do? Kazim is ruthless."

"Yes, that's true, but he needs Mark alive." Then he added to himself, *but for how long? How much time do we have before it's too late?*

When Antonio arrived he had his wife, Susan, and two of his agents with him. Susan hugged Jim then put her arms around Leigh.

"Let's go somewhere quiet, maybe upstairs?"

"No, Susan. I appreciate the thought, but I'm part of this now. This isn't business, this is personal. Antonio, I'm staying right here. I want to know what's going on."

"By all means. Both of you stay. Okay, Jim. Let's start with the letter."

It didn't take long to bring everyone up to date. There wasn't much to say.

Antonio had his cell phone out before they were finished.

"First, we need to bring the Bureau into this right now." And into the phone, "Oscar, it's Antonio. We've got something big coming down. Can you get your best guy over to Jim Buchan's house right away?"

"Sure will, Antonio. What's up?"

"Mark Buchan, the Buchan's son, has been kidnapped. We know who did it and why."

"That's a real good start. They're on the way."

As Antonio put down the phone, Jim said, "After all these years, you aren't telling me that the Agency and the Bureau are talking to each other, are you?"

"Jim, Oscar and I continued where you left off, but now it's legal so we can do it openly. We're not only talking, but cooperating. After 9/11, the Attorney General laid down the law and anyone who wanted to stay employed listened carefully. So if there's any chance of finding Mark, turf wars aren't going to get in the way."

By the time they were joined by Oscar's agents, they had an idea of what they had to do. Jim said, "We need to find who killed Dave MacIntyre. He's got to be the key. He must be Kazim's man here on the ground."

Oscar's team lead said, "Jim, we have a lot better shot at it now than we would have had before 9/11. The new rules mean that now we can keep tabs on the bad guys, and we've got a good database to get us started. After New York, we started pooling our information on people with any connections to al-Qaeda. We'll get our West Coast people on it right now. I'll call you the minute I have anything."

After the agents left, Antonio and Jim continued their discussion. "When we catch the guy, Jim, I have an idea how we might handle it. We've got a whole lot more latitude under the new legislation. Special procedures to deal with terrorists. I'll check with Oscar and our legal counsel. I want to put some flesh on my thoughts."

"Antonio, I'm sure glad you're with us on this, and that times have changed. Having the Bureau alongside us makes me feel a bit better. It's going to be tough waiting, though."

"Susan, thanks for coming over," Leigh said. "Antonio, I think I know where you're coming from on this. I'm up to speed on the issues, the arguments about how we are handling the terrorist prisoners that we've got locked up, the concerns about civil liberties. I can tell you that now that it's us directly involved, if the controversial measures help get our son back, you'll have a convert. I know you'll do your best for us."

"I agree," Jim added. "There isn't much I can do, and I can't just sit and wait. I'm going to go ahead with Illyich to see if we can find Kazim."

"Susan and I will get out of your hair. I'll check in with you tomorrow. You both know that you'll get the best support that we can give."

Back in his office Antonio was on the phone. "Oscar, this is all linked to the al-Qaeda stuff that Jim has been working on. Mark's kidnapping indicates that he must have been on the right track. If we get lucky and get a break, I think we need to be ready with the authority to take really strong action."

"I agree with you. I'll set up a meeting with the AG people and get this into the terrorist side of the house. We'll need to brief the Attorney General, because with what we might find ourselves in, we'll really be pushing the legal envelope. I'll try to get the authority to squeeze whoever we may come up with. I'll likely need you for a briefing on what you have."

"Good. I'm ready as soon as you can get the right people together."

While all this was going on, the FBI and the local police were undertaking a full operation, now just winding up. Mark's apartment had been searched with fine tooth combs, Buchan Security sealed, computer experts going through everything, neighbors questioned, and at the end of all this the only lead they had was that maybe Mark had gone for his morning jog. He hadn't been in to his office, but that wasn't so unusual as he often worked from home. The shiny black Corvette was in its spot in the underground parking garage. There was simply nothing to find, no leads to follow.

As Oscar read the reports he thought, "We're not going to get anywhere fast enough with this stuff. Certainly not in time, there's nothing here to go on."

His next call was to California. "Pull out all the stops, guys. There's nothing at this end at all. Our only hope is with you out there. Go over everything again. What about MacIntyre? I assume that his home and office have been thoroughly searched."

"Yeah, but we'll have another look."

CHAPTER 31

"I'd better phone Illyich to let him know what's happened. He's still working on tracking Kazim, and now it's even more urgent."

"That's for sure. We need all the help we can get if we hope to see our son alive."

Leigh was numb with fear. Jim was sick with remorse. How could he have been so stupid? He knew Kazim, but like almost every other American even after 9/11, he couldn't believe it could happen here. Now Jim's determination was visible, palpable. He was going to see Kazim in Hell.

He dialed the phone. "Illyich, I've been so stupid. I should have seen it coming."

"Slow down there, Jim. What's happened?"

"Kazim somehow got to Mark. They've grabbed him and have him hostage. I got a note from Kazim telling me to back off from Onion or Mark will be killed."

"Jim, what's happened?"

"He must have tracked Mark somehow, and his organization reaches far enough that the note is his personal message to me. From the wording, there's no question that it is him, personally."

After a short silence, neither saying anything, Illyich said reflectively, "I guess this shouldn't surprise us at all. We both know that they will stop at nothing to achieve their goals."

"We were both asleep at the switch," Jim said bitterly. "But this confirms my worst fears. It also tells us that we're on the right track and that we're getting close. Illyich, I'm calling to try to figure out how they got onto Mark. Unless our phones have been tapped, I'm not sure how the trail could have led to him."

"I can tell you, as sure as it's possible to be, that there is no problem at this end. With the large-scale corruption and crime over here, I have all my communications swept regularly. They're clean. And with the security that you've had going on over there since 9/11, I doubt whether even al-Qaeda would risk trying to break into your systems. They'd know that doing that would leave them exposed."

"So that leaves us with the hacking that Mark has been doing. For someone to have tracked Mark through his computer probing would be quite a trick. Even Kazim couldn't do that from the wilds of Afghanistan. He has to have had help."

"That's for sure," Illyich replied.

"I know that you've had Igor keeping an eye on those fellows in St. Petersburg. Could you see if he's picked up anything unusual?"

"I'll call him right now."

"Illyich, I know that Mark and Katrina are really serious. In the two days she was here they weren't apart for one minute and they spend a lot of time together on the internet. Do you think that maybe she should know about this?"

"Oh, boy." After a pause, "Yes, I better tell her. She'd never forgive me if I didn't. Jim, I'll make those calls now. Be back to you as soon as I hear from Igor."

Less than an hour later, Illyich was back on the phone.

"You are probably right, Jim. Igor noted a huge jump in computer traffic last week. It went on for hours. Unfortunately, they are using a high-tech encryption system that even we can't get into, so we can't tell what they were doing, but Igor says that the pattern fits a wide search of systems. They could have been looking for whoever was trying to tap into the programs at Intelligent Systems."

"And that would explain how they knew someone was looking and why they decided to eliminate Dave MacIntyre. Does Igor think that they could have found Mark through his hacking?"

"For sure. These guys used to do that kind of thing for a living with us, and now they have the best equipment money can buy."

"Illyich, we're so close and yet so far from being able to head off the disaster that has got to be coming."

"We are close. Don't give up hope, Jim. Your priority now is Mark."

"I feel pretty helpless. And, of course, Leigh blames me for getting us into this, and she's right. I never should have involved Mark."

"Come on now, Jim. Even knowing Kazim as well as we do, neither of us thought that he'd be able to pull off something like this, with the screws being tightened after the atrocities in New York and Washington.

"That may be true, but it doesn't make me feel any better. The only good thing about any of this is that the agencies have pulled out all the stops. I'm hoping against hope that we have the time to find him." He didn't need to add what they were both thinking—*before it's too late*.

"Jim, I talked to Katrina. She wants to go back to Washington. Would that be okay with you and Leigh?"

"I'm sure it would. Tell her to let us know and we'll meet her flight. She'll stay with us."

"I'll work with Mo to try to get that message to Kazim. I've got a good idea of how we'll frame it to try to draw him in."

"I can't imagine what that could be, Illyich. He's so crafty. But I can tell you, if I wanted to get him before, now it's personal. We need to stop him."

"We'll see. I'll keep Igor working on the St. Petersburg connection. Please let me know when something breaks."

"I will. Thanks, old friend."

"Honey, we're going to have a visitor. Katrina wants to come, and I told Illyich that it would be all right."

"By all means. She should stay with us. I guess she's really serious about our son. Jim, I'm so worried, I'm at my wit's end." Leigh's face crinkled up, and the tears began to flow. "In all our years, this is the worst time we've ever had."

"That's for sure, but, Honey, we can't give up."

Jim moved towards Leigh, giving her a large hug. "We've got the best people and the best support that can be put together. If anyone can find him it's Oscar and his team, and Antonio has let me know that they may be getting close."

CHAPTER 32

It was another sunny morning in California. The two men dressed in lightweight summer suits were not the average apartment hunters or tourists. But as they approached the building a casual observer might have thought that they could be potential buyers as they gave it a thorough inspection, noting with professional eyes the five stories, ramp to basement parking, windows indicating about five units per floor.

"Decent enough building," one remarked. "But nothing special, not expensive. Could use a paint job. If he did something other than programming computers it wasn't for the money."

"Yeah. He could afford to live here even on a modest salary."

"Okay. Let's do it." They rang the buzzer for the building manager.

After a fairly long wait they had just started to ring again when the door opened. A man in his seventies, balding, shirt sleeves rolled up, open neck, blue shorts and running shoes greeted them with a smile as he wiped his hands on a rag.

"Sorry for the wait. I was in the parking area cleaning up an oil spill."

"Good morning, sir. Are you the apartment manager?"

"And good morning to you. I am. You just may be in luck. I have a very nice one bedroom that is just coming available."

The badges and an official-looking paper appeared. "I expect that's the apartment that interests us, but it's not for the rental. We have a search warrant for Mr. Dave MacIntyre's apartment. Would you open it for us, please?"

As they walked down the hallway, the manager chatted nervously. "This is most unusual. Nothing like this has ever happened here before. The police have already visited twice." After a pause, "But you're not the city police, are you?" he said, as he looked at the civilian clothes and thought about the badges that hadn't really registered on the fleeting glimpse that had been offered. "Who are you?"

"Sir, we are with the FBI. We want to do some follow-up to the previous visit."

"Mr. MacIntyre was such a nice young man, quiet, no visitors, never a problem. It is a real tragedy. Do you suspect that it wasn't an accident? The apartment has been sealed since you were here the last time, you know."

One of the men said, "Thank you. We'll let you know when we're through." The door swung closed in the manager's face.

"Well, here we go again. Only this time it's not a needle in a haystack—there's no haystack to look in. Let's hope we get lucky."

It took a while, but lucky they were. They had both done plenty of searches and had worked together for years. "Let's start with a survey of the space. If there's anything to find it's got to be well hidden."

"Yeah, the place has already been gone over once, twice, if you count the local fuzz. We know for sure that whoever went through to scrub it knew what they were doing. The report back from forensics says that the computers were cleaned, nothing but random 0's and 1's."

"You know, in the inventory there wasn't much personal stuff. Whoever sanitized the place must have cleaned house pretty well. Our guys didn't find anything. If there is something here to find it's going to be in a personal space, well hidden, one designed for hiding stuff. When they went through it the last time, they weren't looking in the walls."

"So we're talking wall panels, ceiling openings, plumbing, the kind of places people search out to stow their pornography. This place has central air. Let's start with the ducts."

They started in the kitchen. "Nothing here."

But only minutes later they hit pay dirt in the living room, a grate to an air duct behind the sofa. They pulled out several packets of files, and after a short silence, both started talking at the same time.

"Here's a photo of MacIntyre and a guy. On the back it says, "Silvio and me on the Elbow, May 2001." That's where he went off the cliff.

Silvio looks like he might be Middle Eastern. I bet he's the guy that young couple saw on the Elbow when he went over the side."

"And look at the gold mine I've got. This little file explains it all. His parents were Iraqi. He must have been adopted. There are even photos."

"This is just what our people in Washington need. With any luck at all this should break the case wide open."

The cell phone was already out, reporting in to their bureau chief. "We're at MacIntyre's. There's a fax machine here. I'm going to send you the front and back of a photo. Plug it in and see if this guy shows up. And call Oscar in Washington to stand by for a conference call in, let's see, one hour. We're coming in with a file that'll blow the lid off this. We'll brief you when we get there."

By the time they got back to the office, the computer had spewed out the information on Silvio—not a lot but enough. He had first appeared on the watch list a year ago as a possible al-Qaeda sympathizer. His movements had been tracked. To no one's surprise, the information immediately available indicated that he had just returned from Washington and the date corresponded with Mark's disappearance.

With the photograph of Dave and Silvio on the Elbow Canyon trail and a little old-fashioned foot work, the link between the two over the years at the coffee house was established. A few hours later, Marilyn, the hiker who had reported seeing Dave the day he was killed, said, "Yes, that could be the man we saw him talking to."

Dave's time with the imam at the local mosque was tracked back to two years earlier, to an era when no one was looking for terrorists born and living in California.

CHAPTER 33

The slightly tinny sound of the speakerphone interrupted the conversation around the table in the FBI Ops Center in Washington.

"Hello, Oscar. Are we ready to roll? I've got all the people we need on the line at this end."

"Okay. Let's hear what you've got. Our friends are here, Antonio and a couple of his people. And Mark's dad, Jim Buchan, is sitting in."

It didn't take long for the people on the West Coast to describe the events of the last twenty-four hours.

"Dave MacIntyre was sure an innocent, roped into a situation way beyond him. He had only taken the most rudimentary precautions, almost nothing to cover his tracks. We found letters and photos in his apartment that tell the story as if he had written it out for us. His parents were Iraqi. His whole family was killed by one of our bombs in the no-fly zone in Iraq. I assume that's how al-Qaeda snared him. Their contact here is a guy goes by the name of Silvio. Real name Assad. We're pretty sure he's a sleeper agent—been here for years. Fortunately, we had put him on the watch list and, sure enough, he made a trip to Washington at the same time Mark disappeared."

Jim's voice came through the speakers. "Man, this is truly impressive. We were good in my day, but we couldn't have pulled off what you guys have done so quickly. Thank you all very much. What's next?"

"Oscar, it's your call. Do we pick Silvio up?"

"Yes, right now. Antonio and I have been doing some fast work with the Justice people. They agree that we could hold him as an enemy combatant. This gives us a lot more latitude to squeeze whatever we can out of him. We've worked out a deal, a plea bargain, ten years' jail time here in the US in return for information, so I've got the go-ahead to pressure him. I have an idea how we might convince him to give us information about Jim's son. Keep him on ice till I get there. It'll be early tomorrow morning. Good work, guys."

Oscar turned to his staff. "Coordinate with the police. Have the best SWAT team that we've got ready to go by eight o'clock tomorrow morning. If what I have planned works, they'll know where to go … Come on, Antonio, we have a redeye flight to catch. Hope it's a smooth flight so we can get some shut-eye. Tomorrow's going to be a busy day."

CHAPTER 34

It was the middle of the night in California, but Silvio didn't know that. He had been in isolation since being shoved into the tiny cell twelve hours ago. Despite his protests no one had told him anything and he had spent the night stewing, wondering what they knew, what trail had led to him? Since 9/11 he knew the US authorities were seriously pissed, that there would be no screwing around. Word had filtered back from Afghanistan that the Americans were having some success in rounding up a few key al-Qaeda and Taliban leaders who had simply disappeared. As he wondered if that was to be his fate, the door to his cell swung open. Two men stepped in, one moving directly in front of him.

"Good morning, Assad. My name is Oscar." Turning to the other man standing quietly to the side, "This is Antonio. I trust you slept well on the last comfortable night you will ever have."

"My name is Silvio. Please call me by my name."

"Sorry, Assad, you gave up the right to be called Silvio when you joined Kazim and became a terrorist. You do know that America does not look kindly on terrorists these days. You do not leave us very much time, so we are going to make this short."

It was only then that Silvio really looked at the two men. He had been trying to look bored but now he knew he was really in trouble. These weren't ordinary cops. Both were in suits; the one at the door looked like a heavyweight enforcer, the gray-haired one doing the talking, lean and tough, dressed like an executive.

"I demand to see a lawyer. I will not speak to you."

"That's okay, Assad. You are not going to have a lawyer and you only have to speak one word. To save your life you just have to listen.

And I'm only going to explain this to you once. I'm sure that you read the newspapers occasionally. I am sure you know about our new laws, the laws that have been passed since your friends' atrocities in New York. You have heard about Padilla and Hamdi, both Americans, both, like you, charged with being terrorists, with being enemy combatants, both beyond lawyers, both in military brigs, both facing military tribunals for their crimes against the United States."

"Surely you are not suggesting that I am like them?"

"No, you are right. I am not suggesting you are like them. I'm saying you are much worse. Because you are already a murderer. You see, we know that you killed Dave MacIntyre, and we know that you would soon have killed Mark Buchan. We know of Kazim's plan and your role in it. Your fate is sealed. There will be no grandstand defense, no lawyers, no front-page coverage in the newspapers, no one rising to your defense. You are the only one who can change that certain fate."

Silvio sat quietly. How did they know all this? About Kazim, about Mark Buchan, about Dave? What else did they know?

"My friend, I'm going to lay it out for you. You will have one hour after we stop talking to decide whether you will live or whether you will die. Your choice is clear. You can choose to cooperate now and live. Or you can die. If you do not cooperate, your first stop will be with our friends in the Middle East who will be very interested in talking to you. If you live through that, you will be returned to us, to be sentenced to death as a murderer, a terrorist and a traitor by a military tribunal. Think about that as I make my offer."

Papers were laid out on the table. Silvio could see that they looked official, with stamps and seals and, at the end, a place for a signature—his.

"Assad, here's the deal. I don't need to know about your friend in Afghanistan, nor your role in the Onion computer systems virus. That has all been taken care of. We know about MacIntyre's fall, we have witnesses and evidence, and can charge you with murder, if we wish. What you do need to tell me is where you are holding Mark Buchan and what arrangements have been made. For the deal I am offering, Mark Buchan must be alive."

The silence stretched to two minutes, neither saying anything. Then, "And if I agree? What do I get?"

"Your life. Not in freedom, but with a fixed term of ten years in an American jail, with three meals a day. Otherwise you may be making a trip to our allies in the East and their unpleasant ways to make you talk. You have sixty minutes left to decide. Remember, life or death. Where is Buchan?"

The men left the room as abruptly as they had entered. Silvio was left alone, just he and the chair he was sitting on.

For one hour, Silvio sat without moving. How had Kazim's plans unraveled so quickly? It was clear to him that they knew everything. He was a devout Muslim, a strong supporter of the al-Qaeda cause. It was right and just to fight to restore Islam to its rightful glory. Yet, he had lived most of his life in the United States. He honored those who chose martyrdom in the name of Allah, yet now that he found himself face to face with the choice, black and white, live or die, he was not sure he was ready to join their ranks. He knew with certainty that martyrdom or agreement to the Americans' terms were the only choices offered by these serious men.

Kazim's plan had somehow been uncovered. They knew all about it. The dams were not going to open. He might be willing to become a martyr for Allah if it meant something, if it furthered the cause, his duty to *jihad*. But if America was not going to suffer, his sacrifice would count for nothing.

As Silvio knew it would, the door opened one hour to the second after it had closed. The man called Oscar spoke only one word, "Well?"

"I agree to your terms. I will tell you where to find Buchan. You will honor your agreement with me if I do this?"

"Our agreement will be honored if we get Buchan alive."

"But I cannot control whether Buchan survives whatever you intend to do."

"Then you had better pray to Allah that we succeed. We will only succeed if the information that you give us is complete and accurate. Your life is in your hands."

"He is in the basement of a house in West Washington."

"The address?"

"It is 14340 Shean Terrace."

"How many guards?"

"Two."

"Remember, Assad. Your life depends on the accuracy of your answers."

"There are two, I swear."

"Their names?"

"I know only one. It is Chavez."

The microphone in the lapel pin on Oscar's jacket transmitted the proceedings to the team in the next room. The whole interrogation had been videotaped and recorded, the transmission link to Washington open the whole time.

In Washington the FBI team was already at work, the Ops Center a beehive of activity. This is what they had trained all their lives for, and this one was personal. Every one of them knew Mark was part of the team fighting the terrorists. The information from the open phone line was already being plugged into the computers. One of the agents was working the screen with the map of Washington.

"Okay. I've got it. About 20 miles, off highway 267 near Dulles Airport, a bit of a suburb by the looks of it. Oh, oh, looks like the right neighborhood for these guys, at least two mosques in the area."

By now the team chief had walked over and was looking over his shoulder. "Good. Can we seal off the area? How close are the next houses?" Then he addressed the team. "Reg, you're on approaches. Work out how we go in, front and back."

Looking around he pointed. "Marion, get the helicopters rolling. We need downlinked pictures. Now."

"I scrambled them as soon as we had the address. They're already getting airborne, just waiting for the word."

"Good work."

Norm, the liaison from the Washington Police, was focused on the screen. "I'll coordinate with the local police to get the area sealed off.

It looks like we could get in from the adjoining streets, some cover in the back. And there's only one way in. It's a dead-end street."

"Tell your people to tread as lightly as they can. We need complete surprise, full shock and awe, if we're going to get Buchan out alive."

Silent police cars began the process of sealing the streets and securing the nearby houses. The SWAT team did a final briefing, studying the live video feedback from the helicopter, working out the best approaches, planning the entry, covering each team member's position every step of the way, leaving nothing to chance. Weapons were stripped, assembled and loaded, the quiet tension and confidence building as the time approached.

In California, Antonio had not said a word the whole time, standing at the door of the cell watching Oscar's interrogation. As they walked out the door, he looked at Oscar. "My friend, that performance was worth an Oscar, pardon the pun. That was the best I've ever seen. Magnificent."

CHAPTER 35

At 7:30 in the morning, the members of the SWAT team in Washington were about the only people who missed what most of the rest of the world was watching on television. A videotape had been delivered to Al Jazeera, the Arabic-language television channel, during the night and was being rebroadcast to hundreds of millions of viewers. Bin Laden was again railing against the infidels, America and Israel, warning of martyrs and disaster. He said, "And Allah will smite our enemies from sea to shining sea."

Radical Islam cheered in anticipation. Americans everywhere wondered where al-Qaeda would strike next. The duty officers in the new Homeland Security Operations Center cranked up the already high-activity levels, trying to determine where they should focus. And Jim Buchan called his friend Antonio, only to be told that Antonio was out of town. His next call was to the CIA Ops Center.

"Could I speak with the duty officer, please?"

After a bit of necessary explaining, verifying his credentials, he said, "This has got to be it. The 'sea to shining sea' has got to be Onion 2, the dams."

"Sir, we're already on it. We've got it covered."

As Jim put down the phone, it rang.

"Jim, it's Antonio. I'm on my way back to Washington. We've got some good breaks and should know something soon on Mark. And we're making sure that everyone on shift at the dams across the country has that directive, the memo of instructions, in their hands."

At the same time, Leigh was at the airport, and as her eyes met Katrina's they fell into each other's arms without a word. After a few minutes, Leigh spoke first.

"Katrina, let's go home."

"What has happened? Is there any news on Mark?"

"No. We're worried sick. I know that the FBI has something going on. All they'd tell me is that they have new information and that we should have some news soon, but we haven't heard anything yet."

"When we were fighting in Chechnya this kind of kidnapping happened, but I didn't think it would in America. I hope he's all right!"

"So do we, Katrina. So do we."

They arrived home just as Jim was answering the phone.

It was a classic hostage rescue operation. The team had practiced time and time again. A dozen black-clad figures spread out around the house, while police fanned out quietly through the neighborhood, the streets around the block sealed. Communication was by hand signal, but very little was needed. They knew exactly what they were doing. It was a small single house, one storey, separated from the neighbors by hedges. Records showed that it had been rented for a year, but some fast checking of phone and hydro billings indicated that it couldn't have been used much. The team lead voiced his thoughts, "Likely a safe house, in case it was needed."

The front and back doors were covered. With the team in place, the lead's arm went up, every eye watching, alert, each of the team like a coiled spring, the tension palpable. The arm dropped and everyone began moving at once. Stun grenades went in through the front and back windows at the same time as the doors blew in. The first man through each door rolled to the left, covering for a teammate. Corporal Sandra Willox raced in the back, scanning the room. As she ran toward what had to be the basement door, a shot from the hallway in front caught her right in the center of her chest. Her teammate rolled out of the line of fire, shouting into the mike on his headset, "Officer down. Shots coming from the front of the house."

The team through the front door was on it. Rapid return fire meant that if Silvio's confession was accurate there should be only one terrorist left to take care of. Silvio turned out to be right. They found the second man cowering behind a sofa in the living room and quickly had him spread eagle on the floor, a machine pistol pointing right between his eyes. At the same time, the medics were bending over their teammate: "Easy, Sandra, we'll have you out of here in a minute."

"I don't need out of here, I need out of this straight jacket. It's killing me. Thank God for Kevlar but I can hardly breathe. I never realized there'd be such a kick!"

The key was in the basement door. As he opened it, the team leader called down, "Mark, this is the police. We've looked after the bad guys. Don't move until we can confirm there are no traps or triggers for explosives. I'm coming down."

As soon as the duct tape was pulled from his mouth, Mark was talking.

"I can tell you, I am sure glad to see you guys. They were watching TV just now and I heard them say, 'That's the signal. We do it tonight and we're out of here.' For sure, they were going to kill me. Can we get word to my dad and mom? They must be worried sick."

"Your parents are being told as we speak. The mike on my helmet broadcasts to a truck parked just outside. We'll debrief you and have you on the way home as quickly as possible."

The intense activity had been quick, all of eight minutes from the doors blasting in to steaming coffee being poured from the back of the command truck. But for the members of the SWAT team, the tension and activity felt like it might have taken hours. They were drenched in sweat from excitement and exertion, wrung out. For Mark, after he heard the first stun grenade explosion, time stood still. He had no idea how long it had taken. For the news reporters and television crews scrambling to catch up, it was over and the site sealed off before they even knew it had started.

Jim was on the phone as Leigh and Katrina walked through the front door. Leigh took one look and said quietly, "Thank God." She threw her arms around her husband. Katrina broke out in tears of joy and relief.

"They just got him out. He's fine. I've asked them to come straight here."

Jim put his arms around Katrina. "It's a little early in the relationship for a hug like this, but I have to tell you that you are going to have one seriously happy camper on your hands in a few minutes. I'm glad you came."

As Mark walked through the door, his eyes fell on Katrina. They were instantly in each others arms, Katrina finally breaking the long silence. "I'm not sure I like the smell, but the whiskers kind of suit you, a bit bohemian."

The elation, the relief and the happiness overwhelmed them all. Leigh and Jim embraced their son, everyone talked at once.

"I didn't think I was going to make it. What a miracle you people pulled! It's good to be here. How long can you stay, Katrina?"

"Well, you know, Mark Buchan, I was thinking on the way here that if I ever saw you again I might not let you go. So when you ask how long I can stay the answer is, maybe forever? But first tell us what happened."

Mark had been debriefed by the FBI SWAT team leader on the way home, and he repeated the story now. It wasn't a long one. "The kidnapping happened so fast. In seconds I was on the floor of a car, tied up and blindfolded. I had no idea where we were. Kazim is dangerous—he's got to be stopped. First he almost gets you, Dad, and now me. That's a bit too scary."

Leigh looked from her husband to her son. "It sure is!"

"Okay, Mark, you need to take a bath, because once we get going you're not going to have time for anything but me," said Katrina. "First thing tomorrow you can take me to the National Gallery. The only time I saw it I was fifteen years old and I didn't realize till much later how much I had missed. I can keep you busy for a long time, Mark Buchan, so you won't be thinking about this Kazim monster."

"You're on, we'll do the sights. Dad, how in the world did they find me? I really thought I didn't have a chance."

"The FBI tracked down Kazim's man in California—the one who killed Dave MacIntyre and who organized your kidnapping. Somehow they got him to reveal where you were being held. After that it was up to the SWAT team."

"When I heard the explosion and guns and then the basement door opening, it was sure a relief to hear that it was the SWAT leader on the stairs. Any news about the Onion—do we know when it will be triggered?"

"We don't know the timing but we've got a play in motion to get Kazim. I'll call you tomorrow if anything breaks. Best you two go home now and relax," he said, walking them to the door. "I expect the FBI will have undercover agents discreetly guarding you until this Onion is resolved."

Jim had his arms around Leigh as sobs racked her body, "Jim, I was blaming you. I couldn't stop myself."

"Shh, my love. You weren't alone in blaming me. I knew I got us into this."

Behind them they could hear Katrina. "Okay, bearded one, let's get going. We've got things to do."

But as it turned out, Mark and Katrina didn't have much time to enjoy the attractions of Washington. Fate, in the name of Kazim, would get in the way.

CHAPTER 36

"Hey, Illyich. First the good news. Mark is home. They found him, and a SWAT team just got him out. Katrina and Leigh were walking in the door as I got the call."

"Aw, that's wonderful, Jim! Give Leigh a hug for me. And a special one for my granddaughter. You know, we really need to go after this bastard. If he's left on the loose, he'll be back at it with a vengeance."

"Well, that's the bad news. You saw bin Laden this morning? It's almost a certainty that Kazim is ready to crank up his program. The damn thing is that we can't do much till he does. They're going full out on searching the software, but Kazim is so good that it'll take time to sort it out. It's almost as if we have to wait for it to happen before we can do anything about it. We can't afford to shut the whole system down in advance."

"Good luck. At least you know that with the precautions you've put in place the damage will be minimized if he does succeed."

"Yeah, but if the gates at all those dams do open even part way, there could still be hundreds, even thousands killed and it's driving me nuts."

"I've given considerable thought to how we might lure our friend out into the open. It will take longer than you've got for your immediate problem, for your Onion 2, but if we don't get him, he'll be back."

"What do you have in mind?"

"Jim, you remember Olga, in St. Petersburg?"

"How could I forget? Anybody as good-looking as she is isn't easily forgotten. And what an agent!"

"That's for sure. They don't come any better. She is willing to give us a hand. She'd be the only lure that Kazim might bite on. I'm headed to St. Petersburg today to meet with her, see what kind of a story we can dream up."

"That's great, Illyich."

"If we could draw him in, we'd need to think carefully about where we'd want to get him to. He certainly wouldn't come to the States or back to Russia, but maybe we could bring him to neutral ground."

"The lure would have to be really good, but Olga might be able to pull it off. She'd be willing to put herself in danger like that? That's asking quite a lot."

"Yes, she would. She's got her own reasons to help bring him down—good personal reasons."

"And if we got him, what would we do with him?"

"Well, if he went to you people, you'd likely put him in some military prison. Then you'd agonize for a few years about what to do with him. Then he'd have a media trial circus, a field day for some high-priced lawyers. Better he come here to Russia, where we already have the charges drawn up and approved, left over from the first Onion."

"Sounds good to me, Illyich. What do you have in mind?"

"I'll draft a message and get it to Mo. Give me a day to put things in motion."

CHAPTER 37

The group that was gathered in the shade of a low stone abode in the mountains was much smaller than it had been a few years earlier at that first planning meeting for 9/11 and for Onion 2. They had been on the move frequently and many had fallen under the onslaught of the US war on terrorism. Key losses in Europe and in the Far East were not easily replaced and the new US travel security arrangements had nipped several al-Qaeda actions in the bud. Travel and communications were difficult; the trusted inner circle had shrunk to just six. But, despite the US attacks, the price on his head, the mostly ineffectual Pakistani efforts in the wild tribal lands, bin Laden had survived, moving from camp to camp in the border mountains, invisible to the intense surveillance.

And over the years both the leader and al-Qaeda had changed. The leader still saw himself as the humble follower of Mohammad, living in a cave, wearing the traditional *thawb* gown. But now, when he appeared on Al Jazeera, the gown had become a gold-fringed robe to suit his stature as the messenger, the personal envoy for *jihad*. The Base, al-Qaeda, had also evolved and grown. Bin Laden was the *Mahdi*, providing inspiration and guidance to the faithful. The training camp graduates had returned home, ready to continue the *jihad* on their own, with spiritual leadership and only occasional guidance from the leader. It had been some time since the inner circle had discussed the details of an operation, and, as Kazim finished outlining his Onion, broad smiles welcomed the news.

"Your broadcast will have the infidels running in circles. They are raising their alert status, which in itself will spread fear across the land

and cost them billions in treasure. With Allah's blessing, we will succeed with our attack."

"You are ready as planned, Kazim?"

"The call has been made and the program to take control of the dams is activated. We will soon see victory in another battle of our holy war. This attack will fulfill your prediction. Thanks be to Allah, it will spread devastation from sea to shining sea."

A look of intense satisfaction spread across bin Laden's gaunt face. "With Allah's blessing, this time we will succeed."

CHAPTER 38

Mo did not look at the content of the message that he was given. He thought it best to remain only the messenger. But many of the dozens of couriers on the relay team did steal a surreptitious glance as it passed through their hands. The response was always the same: an uncomprehending shake of the head and wonder at what could be so important about such a strange message. Eventually it reached the hand it was meant for. A frown crossed Kazim's face as he read it.

> *My dearest lover,*
> *We must meet. I have information vital to your cause and to your leader. You have four legs in your camp. Our spot in Istanbul, 7:00 p.m. on the 25th.*

Even without seeing a signature, Kazim's shocked face indicated that he understood both the author and the content of the letter. There was too much history, too much emotion for the message to be anything but genuine.

Kazim and Olga had both been KGB agents in St. Petersburg in the late '80s, and for a while they had even been assigned to the same files. Despite the differences between them, they had become passionate lovers, afraid to think about where fate would carry them. And the differences were huge. Olga was Russian through and through, with the deep-seated love of the *rodina*, the motherland, that many Russians carry in their souls. Although Stalin had stamped out the formal trappings of religion, Olga, like many of her countrymen, was a devout Russian Orthodox just below the surface. Olga had been blessed with vitality from birth. She bubbled with enthusiasm, which developed into a measure of mischievous irreverence as she grew through her teens, irreverence which at first tended to get her in trouble in an authoritarian society. Even though she had learned to keep that trait in check, it was always just waiting to escape, and it was that enthusiasm that had caught the attention of her ever watchful future employers. Besides, she was good-looking enough to catch anyone's attention in a drab society.

What only the KGB recognized was that this effervescent exterior covered a deep patriotism. Olga had joined the KGB to do her part to protect Mother Russia against her enemies, enemies that had time and time again stormed across her borders. Olga, like every Russian, had lost many members of her family over several generations to invaders, and her personality made her especially effective as a spy. After all, who could suspect that this one could be one of them, those surly, beefy guys in the baggy suits?

Kazim's motives were vastly different. From a southern republic, a scratch of his surface uncovered an Arab with a radical Muslim's hatred of the infidels. His motive for his KGB employment was opportunistic, to get an education, to squeeze the system for all he could get, to work toward freedom for his homeland. That he had found such outstanding sex with such a voluptuous woman was an unexpected bonus.

The one thing that they had in common, other than the passion that they felt for each other, was a love of literature. After making love they would lie together and read—poetry, classics, anything that they could get their hands on in the huge St. Petersburg library. And then they would discuss what they had read. One of these discussions was the origin of the enigmatic message that had passed through so many uncomprehending hands. And this was why it meant something only to Kazim. As they lay in bed after a particularly satisfying encounter, they had read Homer's story of the Trojan horse. The subsequent discussion had led to an impassioned argument over the merits of such a ruse. After the Greek siege that had gone on for ten years, how could Troy have fallen for such a trick? How could they have let Odysseus into their camp?

Kazim was adamant. "Well, my lover, the system that we work for, this glorious Soviet Union, can by its very nature expect the occasional horse in its midst, the occasional enemy inside the camp. There are too many disparate interests, too many differences to be held in check by force and fear alone. Only a society of strong central beliefs, beliefs that have the strength of religion, can be safe from Trojan horses."

Olga disagreed. Her patriotism did not permit her to think it possible that any Soviet citizen would have the courage to disagree with Soviet doctrine or policy. Moreover, she knew in her heart that no Soviet citizen would dare to bring a Trojan horse into the camp, when the certain result was the Gulag.

"And what kind of society would this be, Kazim? We have these strong beliefs that you speak of, and in the Soviet Union fear alone would scare any horses away. What is this society you dream of, with religion powerful enough to overcome Trojan horses?"

Without thinking, Kazim replied, "My homeland is such a place."

Much later Olga thought back to that conversation, only to realize that Kazim had been talking about himself, about his own beliefs, his own religion, an Islamic world, and that he himself was the Trojan horse that they had been speaking about, working not for the Soviet Union but for his own homeland.

This discussion, then, was behind the message that Kazim received in the wilds of Afghanistan. He believed the message, because Olga was telling him he had a four-legged traitor, a Trojan horse, in his closed society, an event which he had argued could not happen. But if Olga was correct, then bin Laden was in imminent danger. And that would explain how Buchan had started to look for his Onion. The seed of worry that had been planted when Kazim received the news that someone named Buchan had tracked his virus now burst upon him full blown. Yes, Olga's warning must be right. They had an enemy in their camp. Kazim's loyalty to the cause and to its leader would not allow him to ignore this warning. He would have to risk the trip to Istanbul to learn the traitor's identity.

That evening after dinner, Kazim approached the lone figure reading the Koran by candlelight.

"I must travel to Istanbul. I have received a message of utmost importance to our cause and to your safety."

"But, my brother, this trip will be very risky. What could be that important? We need you to complete your operation."

"Osama, this information will be given only to me in person. I must go. I will take precautions so that no one will recognize me. If this is a trap I will either survive or die. I will not give the infidels the satisfaction of capturing me alive. The Onion is now in place and will proceed as planned. I will get a message to you. If that message is a warning, you must follow the instructions that I give you immediately. Your life will be in danger."

"May you travel with Allah at your side."

Thinking back to discussing the Trojan horse with Kazim many years earlier, Olga pondered about the fundamental differences in outlook that had opened like a chasm between them. She wondered, "How could I have loved him? He was out for himself only. My homeland was never his, and he was always fighting against us!"

She learned that Kazim's main project, the Onion File, had been wound down, with Kazim finding himself in the wrong camp. Soon after Kazim fled from Russia, reports started trickling in through her old employer about turmoil in the republics, with Kazim's name central to the plots for independence. By the time he joined al-Qaeda, Olga had reconciled herself to the fact that Kazim had used her—for legitimacy within the KGB, for information, and for the sex that they had both enjoyed. When Illyich called to ask for her assistance to lure Kazim, she did not hesitate. She thought about Kazim's betrayal of Mother Russia, her homeland, her strong sense of patriotism overcoming any hesitation and found that she was ready to do her duty both for her motherland and because she realized that she hated Kazim for what he was, for what he had done.

CHAPTER 39

"My God," Beth said aloud, as she pulled the main power switches, "this must be what that order was all about. Someone must have had some warning that this would happen."

She was already reaching for the emergency phone.

"We've got gates opening, uncommanded. The operations room is frozen, no gauges or dials are working. The SCADA system is locked and unresponsive. I've lost all control. I've pulled the power switches. The floodgates are already open. We've got water flowing out."

"Hang on, Beth. I'll be back to you right away. I need to implement the emergency plans."

The first call was to sister stations across the country. All the power switches were pulled at all the stations on the watch list. The next was to FEMA, the Federal Emergency Management Agency, to implement disaster plans starting in the Woodhaven Valley.

But it was too late for poor little Chloe. She would never get the swing promised to her at lunchtime by her dad.

"WKTN, Tim Baker speaking."

"Hello, this is Otis Davenport at CNN New York. Understand you've got some excitement going on up your way."

"You're not kidding. We sure do. A major flood!"

"Have you got a crew who can feed to us till we can get set up?"

"Yeah, I think we could do that. Something's gone haywire with the Woodhaven Dam. A wall of water came rolling down the valley, taking out everything in its path. We've got a reporter and cameraman there now. We could tie you in."

Tim Baker, the anchorman for WKTN had just settled in his chair to watch his stringer get her few minutes of fame. The screen on the main TV flashed "CNN – Breaking News" in tickertape, as Davenport said: "We've got Cindy McNeil from WKTN reporting on the flood that is happening in the Woodhaven Valley. Cindy, can you tell us what's happening?"

"A huge wall of water crashed through this town just below the Woodhaven Dam. There are five confirmed dead so far, with many more missing. Given the destruction that I see everywhere in front of me, it is impossible to say what the toll will be when things are sorted out. Whole houses have been swept away, cars are buried in mud."

"What about downstream, Cindy? Is there still a steady stream of water flowing or has it let up? Are there more towns in the flood's path?"

"Well, the water seems to be slowing down a bit now, and the valley opens up, so one hopes the front wave won't be as fast or as deep when it hits the towns downstream."

"When did this happen? How long ago?"

"It was just after 1:00 o'clock. We got word about half an hour ago."

"Cindy, is there any indication of what caused the flood? Did the dam break? Of course, at the front of everyone's mind these days, what everybody worries about, is terrorism. Do we know what happened, what's behind this disaster?" Davenport was using his most earnest, anchorman voice that he saved for disasters such as this.

"No, we don't have any information. All I've heard so far is that one of the main gates fully opened unexpectedly. I don't know what happened. The authorities haven't said anything at this point."

"Do you have any indication of how many more may have died in the flood?"

"Not yet, but I just spoke to a very distraught Selma Thorpe who is afraid that her husband, Jeremy, may have been swept away in his car. Selma says he is not at the bank where he works and his car is evidently not in his parking spot."

"That was Cindy McNeil of WKTN, reporting live from Woodhaven.

We'll continue to update you on this emerging disaster as events unfold—"

Tim Baker interrupted, "—We are going to cut now to Washington where a live news conference with an official from Homeland Security is about to get underway."

The trailer on the news screen indicated 2:05 p.m. Eastern time.

"Good morning from Capitol Hill. The Assistant Secretary of Homeland Security, Jonathan Goodpastor, is just starting a news conference concerning the tragic events in New England."

The camera switched to the podium.

"I want to open this statement concerning the events at the Woodhaven Dam by assuring everyone that the situation is under control. Immediate steps have been taken to minimize the flooding, and the water spillage from that dam is now under control. When the first report of the malfunction was received, authorities implemented contingency plans to isolate all other hydro facilities that might have been at risk, and there have been no reports of malfunctions at any other station across the country. We do not yet know for sure, but officials believe that this might have been a terrorist act. Therefore, as a precautionary measure many generating stations across the country have been taken off line. The power stations that have been shut down will be brought back into service as soon as this can safely be done. In the meantime, the electrical generating…." He came to an abrupt halt as the producer spoke aloud into his microphone, cutting into the presentation.

"Sir, I have to interrupt you. We're just receiving a report from one of our affiliates in Wisconsin. Evidently there's a flood going on there as well. The dam at St. Javier has given away."

"We will get back to you with information as soon as possible. The other dams were supposed to be isolated, off line, so for the moment I cannot elaborate." Jonathan Goodpastor hurriedly closed his binder and exited through the side door, abruptly cutting his news conference short, muttering to an aide, "What the Christ is going on?"

And in Washington at the main terrorist assessment center: "Okay, people, what's happening here? I thought we had this licked. Another dam opened?"

A voice spoke up. "Somebody didn't pull the switch."

The Secretary of Homeland Security was again in the Ops Room, the same room where the decision had been taken a week before to issue warning orders across the country. This time the quiet aura of confidence was replaced by pandemonium, the fifty analysts frantically huddled over their phones and computers looking for information, with none forthcoming, the screen the size of a movie theater covering one full end of the room where all eyes were focused essentially blank. The staff did not have the facts to begin to sort through the confusion, to start to figure out what should be on the big screen.

"Do we know this as fact that someone screwed up? Is that what's gone wrong?"

"Sir, we don't know from shit. We're not getting any information. No one knows what's happening."

"Oh, boy," the Secretary said, looking at his watch, "and the President is just about to start his press conference, telling everyone that things will be fine. I better let them know." He dialed the White House.

The president's chief of staff's response was immediate.

"No, we can't cancel it. He needs to be seen leading the country. You told me that things were under control. So what are you saying now?"

"We thought we had it, but somehow another dam opened. We're just not sure. We're working on it and should have more info fairly soon. If you can't shut the conference down, better at least put a note of caution in what he says."

"Okay, I'll try to get something to him before he starts speaking. Will Grady is with him. I'll try to catch him before he starts."

On a rural road a couple of miles south of St. Javier, campers at the Sunset Vale campground lined the high banks of the river watching the show as the water rushed down the valley. Three drenched but exhilarated kayakers had just pulled themselves out of the raging torrent, saved by an eddy below the campground.

"Awesome, what a ride! What the fuck happened?"

"I've done some good rivers but after this, I can tell you, the Snake is lame."

"Christ, unreal! After that first curl I thought I was gone. We sure didn't expect that on this river."

Kazim would have been very disappointed to know that he had made three crazy kayakers ecstatic over their downstream adventure. There was nothing for miles below that dam to destroy.

An hour later, however, Kazim would have been thrilled at the results of his efforts further west, because there was a lot more than kayakers in the valley below that dam. The largest gate on the giant dam on the Upper Missouri River in Montana opened. The main turbines disintegrated as the rushing water hit them, the big power station below the dam disappeared in the wall of water, the electricity to three states flicked off in an instant, communications cut. The turmoil and destruction in the cities and towns below the dam were beyond belief, and for long minutes no one in the world outside the devastation zone even knew that it had occurred. There were no telephones, no television showing the chaos, no breathless reporters describing the incredible scene, just a roaring silence from a communications black hole.

Jim was frantically trying to reach Mark, who wasn't answering either his cell phone or his phone at home. Jim had left messages both for Mark and for Seth out in California.

As soon as Mark walked in the door and got the message, he was on the phone. "What's up, Dad? Katrina and I were just out shopping for a gas generator to help in the brown-out. We thought we had best get one before the rush."

"So, you haven't heard?"

"Heard what? What's happening?"

"Evidently a dam in Wisconsin called the St. Javier has opened."

"I can't understand how that could happen. Unless they didn't shut off the power. But that was over an hour ago. Everyone in the country must have heard about Woodhaven. How could they miss it?"

"Mark, maybe it's us who're missing something. Remember, Kazim is smart. He would have gone through every scenario. Is there anything you could have missed, anything in the programming?"

"I have been wondering how come only the Woodhaven opened, Dad. If all the dams have code that is infected why didn't any others start opening at the same time? Surely Kazim would have wanted a bigger disaster than only the Woodhaven?"

"You're right. My gut tells me there's more to this threat—there must be more layers to this Onion."

"I'm going to talk to Seth, see if we can walk this through."

"Try him at his office."

"Hey, Seth, it's Mark."

"Geez, Mark, what's happened? I just heard. This is terrible!"

"That's what I'm calling about, Seth. I can't believe that the operators at St. Javier wouldn't have pulled the switch. Let's assume that the power was off. How could the gates have opened?"

"Well, they couldn't. They need power to operate the motors."

"Yeah, I agree. So where did they get the power?"

"I wonder if somehow the auxiliary power was used. Each of the stations has a full emergency generator to back up the main power." Seth continued, thinking aloud, "But, with the main switch off, the auxiliary should be isolated. It shouldn't switch on."

"But if it was on, it would power the gates?"

"Well, sure, I guess."

"Kazim must have somehow foreseen the possibility of a fast response by the operators. He must have built his software to keep the auxiliary on line if the main switch was pulled. Could he do this?"

After a pause, Seth, lost in thought, jumped up in his seat as it hit him.

"It would be pretty ingenious, but, yes, I think he could. He'd have to build his program to bypass the normal switch for the auxiliary and to bring it on line. Yes, I think he could have done that!"

"And if he did this, then all the other dams could open under auxiliary power. Seth, I've got to get to my dad real quick. I'll be back to you."

Mark dialed frantically and was talking as soon as the connection was made. "Dad, it has to be the auxiliary power that opened St. Javier. We've got to get the word out to isolate the auxiliaries at all the stations. We're on our way to your place."

"No, I'm headed to the Agency Ops Center. Go there and I'll arrange to get you in. Call Antonio in, say, five minutes on your cell. This is the unlisted number. Call it as you arrive and someone will meet you at the front entrance. We'll get you in."

The calls had gone out from the Homeland Security Ops Room to Wisconsin Power. The dam at St Javier was remotely operated. The caretaker had been instructed to physically check the equipment, which took time for him to get in his truck, drive to the dam and open the building. When he did call in from the control station, what he had to say was a surprise to everyone.

"Sir, the main power is off, but everything is up and running and the top gates are open."

A hush fell over the ops room. Everyone inside understood that this was disastrous news, news which immediately got worse as information started to trickle in from the western states that had been so silent for the past few critical minutes.

Below the big dam in Montana on the Upper Missouri River, Sally Beckwith had watched in horror as the house right next to hers disappeared, the raging water rushing just outside her back door. Her television was on in the background, and as she turned to it to find out what was happening she realized that it had gone blank. She picked up the phone. Nothing, no dial tone. Her kids had slept over at her sister's house and, in a panic she ran across the street, meeting the new residents who had moved in just two days before as they stepped out the door.

"My God, that house just disappeared," said the man. "Look at that water! My God, Audrey, why did we move here?"

"Can I use your phone? I need to phone my kids." Sally was distraught.

"Sure, it's right here." But when she picked it up, it too was dead.

Sally ran back to her house and grabbed the brand new satellite phone that her husband had just bought, dialing her sister's number—nothing. She punched in the numbers for her mother in Florida.

"Mom, it's terrible. The flood is taking everything down the river. I can't get through to Sis and the kids are there. I'm okay, but I don't know what to do!"

"What do you mean you're okay? What's wrong?"

"You haven't heard about the flood?" Sally said breathlessly.

"Yes, there's been one up north, in New England, but what are you talking about?"

"No, Mom, it's not over there, it's here. Everything is flooded!"

"We haven't seen anything about that on the news. Are you sure?"

"Mom, I'm looking at a vacant hole in the ground where my neighbor's house used to be. There's water running everywhere. I can't find the kids."

The emergency crews below the dam were frantically trying to get organized, but it was close to impossible. Those who could make it to the rallying points found most of the rescue equipment gone, disappeared in the waterlogged, muddy rubble. There were no communications systems to give or get direction even if there were anyone to give or take that direction. All over the area people were heroically rescuing people from drowning, pulling them bare-handedly out of the debris, comforting panicked people who were wandering glassy-eyed through the remains of homes. It was some time before anyone's immediate priority became letting the world know what had happened.

When the news started to make its way out of the Midwest, it was by satellite phone, by ham radio nets, and then, as emergency generators started to pick up some of the slack, by the odd radio and television channel. People across the country who still had power slowly became aware that it wasn't just a pretty little town in New England that had a problem. As the reality sunk in, Americans discovered that many people must have died in the Upper Missouri River Valley and that everyone else in that area would be numb with hurt for some time to come.

As the first news of the anguish, death and destruction made its way to a computer in the wilds of Afghanistan, Kazim ran to bin Laden.

"From sea to shining sea—*bada'a*—it has begun. Thanks be to Allah, we have succeeded. The infidels are dying in their homes, just as our people do when they bomb us. The electricity will soon be off all over America. We will bring them to their knees."

Guns started to fire into the air, celebrating the success of Kazim's Onion. Six excited voices were talking at once. Bin Laden said quietly, "It will tell the world of our success. Two great attacks on their homeland in two months. It will reinvigorate our *jihad* on every continent. My brother, by the permission of Allah, you have brought our *jihad* to the infidels' homes."

In his car, Jim was agonizing over what had gone wrong.

"Leigh, I don't understand. I thought we had this aced. Mark and I were sure that once the power was turned off on the first one, the others would be isolated. To have another one open an hour after the first doesn't make sense."

"You know, the Islamic fundamentalists have managed to bend the Koran in ways that mainline Islamic scholars believe is way out of line with what the Muslim religion is all about. Bin Laden and his disciples use the Koran for their *jihad*," Leigh mused, thinking aloud. "I wonder whether Kazim might have tried somehow to tie the dam openings to the call to prayers, to the *Salah*?"

"That could explain why the dam at St. Javier opened later, but why one hour?" Jim said reflectively, "If he had tied it to the call to prayers that happens five times a day, wouldn't that mean a delay of several hours? And that would spread the threat over too long a time and we'd have time to react."

"Yes, that makes sense. Maybe it's a time zone issue," Leigh said with a sigh of frustration.

Jim thought about that for a second. "My God, you might have something there! I'll get Mark working on that idea."

It took Jim quite a while and a lot of cajoling to get through to the Ops Center.

"I'm sorry, Mr. Buchan, things are pretty tense here as you can imagine. They've left orders that they'll only take calls related to the flooding. They're on the phones with our people across the country."

"Jennifer, trust me on this. Antonio needs to talk with me. Put me through."

"Just for you, sir. Tell him not to shoot me."

"Thanks, Jen. When Mark calls, put him through, right away …"

"Antonio, it's Jim."

"Hey, Jim, as you can imagine, we're up to our armpits. Hope you've got something good."

"Mark and I are on the way over. No, don't argue. Make arrangements to get us in. You need Mark. He's giving you a call from his car. Listen to him."

Katrina had listened to Mark's end of the telephone calls and, as she started to ask what was going on, Mark cut her off. "We've got a problem with the dams. I'm going to meet Dad. I'll call you later."

He ran out the door, tore down the stairs to the garage, and started his Corvette, revving the engine. He was thankful for the power as he tore up the ramp to the road, only to screech to a stop. He couldn't even get to the street, stopped vehicles were everywhere.

"Jesus, now what am I going to do?" he muttered. "You can't move in this jam. Streets clogged, and with the power going off, most traffic lights are out."

He had spent years in the area and bicycled all the back streets when he was at university so he knew the area well. He raced backwards down the ramp to his parking spot. Once out of the car, he grabbed the dirt bike that had a lot of rough miles on but hadn't been fired up for a long time, yanking off the cover.

"Okay, baby. Let's see if you've still got it." He kicked down on the starter pedal. It caught. He threw on the helmet still covered with mud from his last outing, then stopped to pin his BlackBerry on his belt, plugging in the cord for the helmet phones and mike. The front wheel lifted off the ground as he accelerated onto the ramp then out of the garage onto the side walk.

His mind was split, half concentrating on squeezing the bike around stalled cars and making tight corners, the other half reviewing what he knew. Somehow Kazim had anticipated the power being shut off. "He's sure a smart one."

Brakes locked, the bike skidded as it swerved up onto the sidewalk while Mark accelerated around a dozen vehicles. Thoughts flashed through his mind: most of the big dams using Intelligent Solutions & Security software were out west. None of them had opened at the same time as Woodhaven. They were shut down now, but why didn't Kazim open everything at the same time? And how come the one in St. Javier opened exactly one hour after Woodhaven—probably under auxiliary power?

He knew that the bridges would likely be plugged so he took a left onto Canal Way, hitting the sidewalk at the corner of 29th, practically running over the traffic cop shouting and waving for him to stop, on a bike that had no license, not even street legal, onto the Francis Scott Keys bridge, again on the sidewalk. Over the river, he turned right using the verge to pass the slowly crawling highway traffic on the George Washington Memorial Parkway heading north.

"Got to do with time zones," he said to himself, echoing his mother's thoughts, and after another few minutes, "Oh, man, most dams are on Pacific Time, three hours after the East Coast. That leaves only about 45 minutes. We were lucky with the two so far. They're nothing to what those biggies out there will do if they open any gates."

Mark knew that some of the larger western dams, the Grand Coulee and the Hoover, would make the earlier ones look like ripples on pleasant country streams. He reached down, clicked the button on his BlackBerry and spoke into the mike. "Call number."

"The number, please," came the robotic response.

He spoke the number he'd been given. Antonio had instructed the staff to put Mark through the instant he called, and when the call came the Agency director stopped what he was doing.

Mark was sweating to keep the bike in control while he spoke into his mike, talking the instant Antonio answered. "Somehow Kazim managed to bypass the system and get the auxiliary power to open the dam. We need to get the other sites using the software to isolate the auxiliaries, the alternate power units. I think they'll turn on one hour after the last one."

"Everyone here is blaming the idiot who didn't pull the switch! How did you come up with this, Mark? Aw, never mind. You've been right on this all the way."

"Let's discuss the finer points later, Antonio. Right now, we need to get those units turned off. Judging by the sequencing so far, we really need to get to this before the big ones out West open. We can't let this happen with the Hoover and the Grand Coulee. If they let loose, I don't even want to imagine what it would be like."

"You've got it. We'll make the calls from here."

"Antonio, Dad should be there shortly. I'm about five minutes out on my motor bike. I need to be there. Tell Security to let us in."

A few moments after the exit to 123, he pulled off onto the ramp to the CIA, skidding up to the gate, the guard hollering at him through the window to follow the sedan with the flashing lights that led him to the building entrance. Mark left the bike where it fell at the bottom of the steps, ran up to face a serious-looking guard stepping in his path with a machine pistol aimed right at the center of his forehead.

"I'm Mark Buchan. Antonio Pesquali is waiting for me."

Another guy in a suit appeared as if by magic. "Thanks, Joe. I'll take it from here."

Half a block away, Jim had already rushed out his car door, saying, "Leigh, you stay here. There's not a chance that they'd let you in over there anyway. It's going to be hard enough for Antonio to get me and Mark in. Give Katrina a call at Mark's to see what's happening there. We'll check back in with you as soon as we have something to report—reasonably soon I would think."

It was only then that the news from the Upper Missouri River Valley started to reach Washington.

CHAPTER 40

The television camera provided a close-up of the familiar face of the commentator as he spoke.

"We are waiting for the President to enter the briefing room where he will address the nation about the flooding in Woodhaven and St. Javier. Many of the hydroelectric power stations across the country have been shut down as a precautionary measure, and factories and businesses all over this land will not be able to operate. There will be major inconveniences for everyone. The reserve power that is available will last only so long and then the bulk of the nation could be thrust into silent darkness. There is real concern whether the nation can survive the economic consequences of this. Sources tell us that this is definitely an act of al-Qaeda and that the other hydroelectric stations have been taken off line as a precaution. The disaster in Woodhaven is serious. So far ten people are reported to have lost their lives in Woodhaven alone. We don't know yet about St. Javier. But even with all this, it sounds like the tragedy could have been much worse. The President is entering the room now, walking to the podium."

Suddenly the deputy national security advisor rushed towards the President, thrusting a single sheet of paper into the president's hands.

"He seems to have paused, speaking to an aide. He's looking at what must be a report with the latest information. Ah, yes, now he's ready to start the conference."

President Walker walked towards the familiar podium, with the official seal of the Office of the President of the United States prominently posted on the front. He looked drawn, pale, his face lined with worry, and he pulled his fingers through his thick hair before putting on his trademark gold spectacles. After grasping the podium earnestly with both hands, he began to speak.

"My fellow Americans, the tragedy that we are experiencing this morning seems to have been brought to us by al-Qaeda, by a senior lieutenant of Osama bin Laden. We know so far that twelve Americans are dead, killed in their homes, in their cars. Our hearts and prayers go out to those who have lost loved ones. Our thoughts are with those whose homes, businesses, places of worship, have been swept away. We are just now receiving reports of two other dams that have partially opened, one in Wisconsin and one on the upper Missouri River in Montana. We do not yet have enough information to report the extent of damage. However, we do know that the electrical power is out in several areas of the Midwest. Authorities will provide more information as soon as it is known. I have directed that the National Guard be fully activated in all those states experiencing difficulty to help restore vital communications links.

"We are fortunate that our intelligence agencies were vigilant, and that plans were in place to limit the damage if our hydroelectric power system was attacked. This action has taken a number of our hydroelectric stations off line. Work is underway now to contain any further disruption, and I pray that these efforts will succeed.

"The terrorists had planned on a much greater disaster than they accomplished today. Through the Federal Emergency Management Agency, FEMA, federal and state assistance will help the communities that were flooded to recover, but only our prayers can help the families who are in mourning.

"What I wish to speak to you about now is how we intend to deal with and recover from the situation that has been caused by this terrorist action, including the destruction that many of our citizens have experienced, and the disruption to our electrical generating system. I am declaring a state of emergency in the areas that have been directly affected by flooding, and the National Guard is being called out to assist in recovery and in keeping the peace in our time of difficulty."

The president looked directly into the eyes of every American who still had a working television, speaking from the heart. "I appeal to every American. Even with a significant reduction in our generating capacity, the United States has enough electrical energy to look after essential services, such as hospitals, emergency equipment and necessary refrigeration. The authorities tell me that the generating stations will be back on line within a few days at most, with full capacity returned in perhaps one week. Until that happens, we need to conserve energy to ensure that we have enough electricity to keep critical systems operating. We do not have the capacity to continue life as normal, such as air conditioning homes and leaving electrical equipment on when not in use or doing daily chores that could be put off for a week or so. We will need to take serious measures to conserve energy. To save lives in hospitals and in critical care homes, we will need to take our high usage systems off line wherever this can be done without risk to human life. Make no mistake. We all need to chip in, to sacrifice comfort and convenience to conserve our electricity for those whose lives depend on it.

"Today, I am asking Americans across our great nation to turn off the switch, to think about how you can save kilowatts. If each of us conserves energy, there will be enough to keep essential services on line. We will have won this battle with the terrorists. We will have demonstrated our resolve.

"Over the next few hours and days, our experts and authorities will advise you on what we all must do to recover our full electrical capacity, and to let the terrorists know that they cannot win in their cowardly war against our great nation. I ask each of you to do all you can to get America back on our feet as quickly as possible.

"Thank you, and God bless America."

The news anchor's voice spoke over a montage of video clips from Woodhaven and St. Javier: "The President has laid out his instructions, calling on all Americans to do their part. I can commit this station and all our affiliates to do what we can to help. Authorities across the country are discussing how to deal with the crisis with the least harm to everyone. Our panel of experts tells me that we will need to shut down some factories and high users of electricity to avert a human disaster in our hospitals and critical care facilities, and that this will need to happen immediately. We'll bring you the up-to-date information as we have it."

The President was back in the Oval Office, his Secretary of Homeland Security briefing on the latest disaster.

"Communication reports are few and unconfirmed. It's going to be a while before we know the extent of damage, but it looks huge. The dam opened and the water just rampaged down the valley."

"Have all the emergency procedures been activated? I want on-the-ground support out there right now."

"We're talking with Governor Patterson. The National Guard is being activated. I should have an inventory of what we can do in the next few hours."

"Let's not wait. We know it's bad. Just start moving food, drinking water and medical supplies from the Army warehouses. Tell your people to get medical assistance organized. I'll talk with John Patterson to clear the way."

The problem was that Governor Patterson didn't know much more than they knew in Washington. It was total confusion. As in any disaster, the first response was only as good as the officials on the ground, but these folks were caught up in the havoc. The response ranged from ineffectual to heroic.

In this case the National Guard had already decided to take action. Colonel Kenny Johnson, a reservist and surgeon at the local hospital, had been in tight situations before, including a tour in Iraq, and knew his business. He immediately tracked down his second-in-command.

"Captain, we're going to need everyone and every piece of equipment that we can round up. See what you can do to get the transport organized. I'll work on the people. We'll set up in the high school."

It wasn't long before the colonel had the beginnings of a field hospital up and running, with the captain and his guardsmen rounding up casualties.

CHAPTER 41

They were at the conference table at the end of the Agency Ops Center. Mark looked around wide-eyed. Getting in, they had run a gauntlet, armed guards leading and following. Jim caught Mark's eye, giving him a wink as Antonio met them. The full screen television at the end of the wall was tuned to CNN. Other wall-sized screens displayed the little snippets of information as they arrived. Computers and analysts were everywhere, banks of colored phones lining each desk.

"You can imagine the strings I had to pull to get you two in here. Bad enough for you, Jim. Your old buddies would walk through fire for you, but this guy with no clearances at all! Let's get you two up to date. It appears that a big dam on the Upper Missouri in Montana has opened, at least enough to knock all the power out in three states. The first info is just starting to come in, but it could be bad."

Mark looked as if he had been hit with an electric shock. "Aw, shit. I should have known that the Upper Missouri dam would open next. I was so focused on the big ones on the Colorado and Columbia Rivers, I didn't think about it. Montana is on the same power grid, but it is on Mountain Time."

"You can't blame yourself for that, Mark. You're the only one who's been ahead of the power curve at all on any of this," Antonio said. He continued, "The draw on the power loop is starting to feed back, bumping the breakers up the line, so we've got electric outages or brownouts all over. Lots of phone and internet lines are down. We're not getting enough info. We know that there are some fair-sized cities in the valley below that dam. The President just spoke. He's declared a state of emergency and called out the National Guard. We're linked into the Homeland Security people. They're getting the new instructions to the hydroelectric stations out West. It's a good thing you were onto this. They had just found out about the auxiliary power at St. Javier. It would have taken more time than we have to figure things out without your help."

Mark said reflectively, "I'm kicking myself. I should have figured this out before. The Upper Missouri dam is one time zone over from the Javier in Wisconsin, so it must have failed at 3 p.m. our time, right? Local time there would be one o'clock! I don't understand why Kazim would have done this but he's timed his attacks at 1 p.m. local time in the first three time zones. And if the main power is shut down, he's programmed the back-up power to open the gates.

"Tell me, Antonio, are the Homeland Security people going to let us know that they've got through to Hoover and the other western dams to disable their auxiliary power? With so many systems going down, there will be real communications problems and a lot of confusion out there. It would be good to have confirmation that they've succeeded in passing the word."

"Good point, Mark. No confirmation yet but, in all the confusion, maybe they forgot to brief us. I'll do some checking."

As the Buchans talked to Jim's old colleagues, Antonio was on the phone. When he put it down he turned to them, his face streaked with worry.

"They're having a hell of a time. With so much of the power out, comms are failing all across the country as switching networks go down. Some of the main phone switches are out. They think they've got to most of the dams, but the really big one, the Hoover in Nevada, is isolated. They haven't been able to get through."

They all looked at the nearest wall clock: 1541 hours Eastern.

"That's 12:41 p.m. Pacific Time. Less than 20 minutes," Jim exclaimed. "This is going to be close!"

"Dad, we can't wait. I have an idea. Seth has a secure phone in his office because of the security stuff that they deal with. Antonio, any chance of getting through on that? It would use different circuits with back-up power and satellite links for redundancy."

"That's right. They're on their own grid. It's sure worth a try." He turned to an ops guy on a computer. "Julio, do your magic. Link us to Intelligent Solutions & Security in California."

It took almost ten minutes to make the connection.

"Seth, it's Mark. Listen fast. I think the Hoover Dam is going to open in less than 10 minutes."

"But surely they've been warned! Shit, how—?"

"No, Seth, just listen to me. You have several dedicated lines to the main power sites. I saw them in Dave's office. Is there one to the Hoover?"

"Yes, we have a 24/7 response requirement with all our stations. Those are dedicated lines, for emergencies."

"This is the biggest emergency we'll ever have, Seth. Phone Hoover and tell them to isolate the auxiliary so it can't come on. Do it now!"

The phone went dead. It was 1554 hours Eastern Time.

Seth had never used the emergency phones in Dave's office.

"Where the hell's the phone book?" When he found it in Dave's file cabinet, Seth's hand was shaking so badly he could hardly turn the pages. "Okay, here it is. Let's see, Hoover … Hoover."

It was 12:57 p.m. local time when the red phone rang in the Ops Room at the Hoover Dam.

"Hoover? Listen, we've only got seconds."

"Who's this? What are you doing on this line?"

"You've got to believe me. Your dam's going to open in less than three minutes unless you can get the auxiliary shut off."

"What do you mean? It isn't on."

"It will be turning itself on—at one o'clock! You need to pull the switch manually. It's like St. Javier. The virus will switch it on and it will open the gates. For Christ's sake, do it now."

"How do I know who you are?"

"I'm in my boss's office at the company that supplies the software. My boss was the bastard who put the virus in the system. He's dead now. This is his phone. Don't take the chance. Pull the damn switch!"

"Jeez, that's about one minute from now. It's across the room."

"Run!"

Seth heard the phone drop and waited. It seemed like hours, Seth holding his breath. The digital clock on the wall flipped over to 1:00 p.m.

Then, finally, a breathless voice said, "Oh, God, that was close! The motors just started turning over as I got to it. Whoever you are, I'm sure glad you got through to me."

But the people in the valley below the Hoover didn't know that the switch had been pulled. The news from the communications void in the Upper Missouri Valley one time zone over from them was scattered, but once it got to Nevada the word spread like wildfire. What if it could happen here?

"Hey, Sam, Julie just got a call from her sister on her sat phone. The dam above her place was blown up. Some place on the prairies. The whole valley is flooded, just like the one in the East. We're out of here, right now."

The response was immediate. "My kids just ate lunch and are ready to go back to school. Give me a minute to get organized. We'll follow you."

All anyone below the Hoover knew was that a dam somewhere in Montana had opened, one that sounded just like theirs. Of course, they knew that it couldn't possibly be as big, but if that one had opened just like that puny little thing in New England, then what about theirs? As they looked up at the massive, familiar face of the dam, panic set in, people running, but to where? Families loading into every available vehicle, driving, to where? Julie and her neighbor Sam raced out of town, panicked, only to find the highway clogged, traffic grinding to a halt.

"What do we do now?" Julie leaned out her van window and shouted to Sam.

"We should try for high ground. The road back there goes up the valley to the lookout. Let's try that."

They swung the cars around, roaring back the way they had come, only to find others had beaten them to it. The lookout road was blocked, leaving no way out.

In the town, scattered rioting had already started. People were cleaning out the grocery stores, carrying cartons of bottled water on their shoulders, anything that could be carried away. Looting began as homes emptied. The police were overwhelmed and bewildered. Rumors ran rampant, many people certain that the giant Hoover was rigged with terrorists' explosives and about to open wide. They did not know where to go or what to do.

CHAPTER 42

Discussion in homes across the country was quickly turning from fear to outrage and anger. Brownouts became power failures as the overloading of circuits rippled through the grids. All eyes were glued to those televisions still functioning, ears tuned to the battery-operated radios being pulled out of basements and garages, stereos on in every car and truck on the roads, everyone looking for news, but in the absence of news, rumors carried the day. Then, a can-do attitude began to emerge.

The regulars coming off shift at the big plant in Detroit were gathered at the local watering hole, a big screen television still miraculously droning away in the corner. The shift changes involved thousands of workers in plants across the country in an industry that just ate up electricity. The regulars at Joe's Bar and Grill watched the news, saw the President appealing to Americans to do their part to recover from the disaster the bastards had done to their country. Many of them were veterans, all strong union members.

One of the popular union leaders enjoying his beer spoke up. "You know, guys, I have a brother over in the desert, getting shot at fighting al-Qaeda. There's not much we can do from Joe's Bar and Grill, but I'd be willing to contribute to getting back at the terrorists who did this to us. The President has asked for our help. He says we need to shut down electrical use all over the US. Listening to this guy talk about the electrical energy crisis gives me an idea. We can help."

"I'd like to get the bastards. What you got in mind, Tom?"

"Well, if enough of our guys agree, we could shut our plants down for a while."

After another round and a lot of talk the consensus was clear: "Let's do it."

The idea spread within hours across the country, from worker to worker, union shop steward to union shop steward, factory to factory. It wasn't long before the idea moved up to the boardrooms of both union and corporation. The union executives were gathered around the conference table, now littered with empty coffee cups. Coordinating with locals across the country had taken some time, but there was overwhelming agreement to the idea. The union president looked around at his colleagues.

"All right then, all agreed?"

There were no dissenting votes.

"My friends, if we can pull this off, it should give us enough brownie points to last us through the next round of bargaining."

"Yeah, it's not often that we can make an offer that they can't refuse."

"We'll be like Lech Walensa in Poland. We'll save the country."

"Let's get things moving. I'll call the CEO now and put it to him."

The lines of authority and power between management and labor had evolved over decades, with few surprises in the bargaining process. The phone in the corporate head office rang and when the union president called, he got through, without question. George's secretary transferred him to the inner office immediately.

"Sir, Jed Highwater is on line 1. Will you take the call?"

"Yes, I've got it." George Greeley paused before picking up the phone. Leaning back in his big chair, he sighed deeply and asked himself, "Why would the president of the union be calling me now? Must be to do with the electrical crisis. We sure can't survive any more disruption than we've already got."

He punched the button and said in as normal a voice as he could muster, "Good morning, Jed. What's up?"

"George, we're just winding up an emergency meeting of our executive. I'm on the speaker phone in the conference room."

"This sounds serious, Jed. What's going on?" And he thought to himself, "We've got enough of a crisis going on without looking for another one."

"Well, George, we've been dealing with a wildcat vote that our members have just taken. I have an offer that we don't think you'll want to refuse."

George's thoughts quickly ran through the scenarios: "Don't tell me they're going to try to hold us over a barrel while they think we're vulnerable with the power shortages that are on the way." His voice, now considerably icier, indicated his displeasure. "So, Jed, what's this wonderful offer?"

Jed looked around the table, winked, and mouthed, "May as well draw this out and have some fun!"

"George, you are going to have a hard time without enough electricity to run the plants across the country. Our membership is not going to put up with layoffs or shutdowns. We want to put you on notice of what the membership has voted."

"Aw, here it comes," thought George. Aloud he said, "Okay, Jed, let's have it."

"George, the members across the country have been watching the news. It's clear we have a serious situation, one that is surely going to get worse before it gets better. I don't know if you caught the press conference, the one that the guy from Homeland Security gave, and then the President asking everyone to do our part, to conserve electricity. We figure that if our plants weren't running for a while, that would go a long way to eliminating the shortfall."

"And what is it that you are suggesting, Jed?"

"George, Americans are a patriotic people. It reminds me of when I was in England at a labor conference as the Falklands War got underway. The Royal Air Force had tried for years to put an air-to-air refueling capability into their Vulcan bombers, without success—too costly, too technically difficult. The government was fighting with the unions, and the unions wouldn't give an inch on anything like rolling back overtime. Well, the war started, a Vulcan arrived at the plant on Friday, and took off with a load of bombs on Monday, non-stop, air refueling, to drop bombs on the bad guys. There was no hassle about overtime, shift limits or collective agreement clauses. The union members just did it. They worked full out all weekend to do what couldn't be done."

"That's a good story, Jed. Where is it taking us?"

"You know, George, I'm bloody proud to be an American. Our members have just voted overwhelmingly to shut everything down for a day, or for however long it takes to get the power systems back up. They want to forego their pay to see our country through the crisis. We figure that with all our company's plants off line, the power companies could stagger the shutdowns to match the need, so there should be enough power to see the nation through.

"There's more. Next week, or whenever the power is fully restored, our members will put in some voluntary, unpaid overtime to get production caught up."

George sat back in his chair, a look of wonder crossing his face. It took about ten seconds for his response. "Jed, give me a half an hour to figure out how to make it happen. And I think we should organize a press conference. Workers and companies in other manufacturing sectors will likely follow your plan. This is one time when I'll be happy to give you all the credit."

"No, George. Let's both give credit where it's due—to the great Americans who dreamed this up."

CHAPTER 43

Jim and Mark were in Antonio's office, reviewing what they knew, trying to figure out what else should be done.

Antonio summed up, "Thanks to you two, we were lucky. Only three dams opened. Can you imagine just how bad it could have been? And what about the hour difference between each of them? Even with that, we sure got off light compared to what could have happened if you two hadn't made that order to shut off the power go out to everyone. Or Mark, if you hadn't figured out how to get to the Hoover in the nick of time."

"Yeah, that really was quick thinking," Jim added.

Mark said, "While I was spending so much time on the systems, I had to do a lot of research on the dams themselves. They are designed so that only one gate can open at a time, so pulling the power switch stopped the sequence. But Kazim was smarter than I was. He built in a Plan B with the auxiliary power, so even with the mains turned off, the auxiliary motors would open the gates."

"Well, you couldn't have suspected that."

"My guess as to why only the three dams opened is that it had something to do with the program, some mistake on timing. I have no doubt that Kazim wanted them all to go at once, especially the big ones out West. As it is, I'm pretty sure that Woodhaven is the only one controlled by the Intelligent Solutions & Security software that is in the Eastern Time zone. The St Javier is one time zone over and it opened one hour later. The third, the Upper Missouri, two hours later. The rest of the dams are out West, in the Pacific zone. It took me a while to recognize that. All I can think is that Kazim must have made a huge mistake on his timing."

After a thoughtful silence, Antonio replied, "I expect you are right. It would be good to know how he screwed up."

"Antonio, I think we need to ask our unofficial, unpaid, volunteer computer expert here to do a little more work. Mark, how about asking Seth to look to see if he can find what kind of timing Kazim had programmed for?"

"Yeah, that would be interesting to know. I'll call him right now ..."

"Seth, it's Mark Buchan in Washington. Now that the dust is settling, let me tell you how well you did. That was too close for comfort with Hoover. It's great that you know your systems as well as you do and were able to make that call."

"Making the call was easy. It was convincing the guy that answered to believe me. For a bit there I wasn't sure he'd pull the switch."

Antonio interrupted, "Seth, this is Antonio Pesquali. You'll no doubt be hearing from folks in Washington, and so will your boss. That was a fine job. I can tell you that, as far as I'm concerned, you just saved the country's and your company's ass."

"I'm sure glad it worked. I just hope and pray that I never have to cut anything as fine again, I can tell you."

"Seth, I know you are up to your eyeballs in work, but we have a question that we'd like answered."

"Sure, Mark, what is it?"

"We'd like to know how come only three dams responded to Kazim's order to open. I would have thought he'd want them all to go at once. But only three opened, and they were in different time zones, one on Eastern Standard Time, one on Central, one on Mountain. I think that what you need to look at is the timing sequence in the code. It should be fairly easy to spot."

"I'm onto it. I'll call the minute I find anything."

Mark didn't know how right he was about the timing. In all the complexity and sophistication of the Onion, Kazim had overlooked one small but critical detail, and he had two problems, one philosophical and one technical. What he didn't know or think of, and what Dave MacIntyre didn't think to tell him when Kazim's St. Petersburg technicians were hacking the Intelligent Solutions & Security software, was that each facility operated on local time. This was so because the facilities, spread across the US, controlled water flow and power generation according to local demand, and that demand varied across the time zones due to local weather conditions. The clocks at the dams were set to local time, and those clocks controlled the computers. Kazim's philosophical challenge was that he had been trained in a military system, in a nation of eleven time zones, where uniformity was law. The thought did not cross his mind that infrastructure as important as a nation's electric power would be left to individual managers to manage. He just assumed that, of course, the system would be centrally controlled and would, therefore, operate on UTC, Coordinated Universal Time, the old Zulu time, Greenwich Mean Time. It was beyond his frame of reference to think that the clocks at each of the dam sites would do their own thing, converting UTC to local time. The technical side of his challenge was that he also didn't know that his team in St. Petersburg had cut corners by using timing code plagiarized from the Russian systems which were, of course, in UTC.

And Dave MacIntyre had no reason to think about it. His only role was to provide the keys to the kingdom, the back door to the computers, a copy of the software, and then to turn a blind eye as Kazim inserted his code into the system, into the software updates. He did not allow himself to think about what had been done to the application. But he didn't really want to know, and in all the plotting the flaw went unnoticed.

Mark had been lost in thought, exhausted, the tension finally draining out of him. He looked at his dad. "You know, I've never really thought about it before, but how come the time zones now are in UTC? I guess it stands for Coordinated Universal Time. What happened to the good old GMT initials, Greenwich Mean Time, which were once used?"

Jim laughed. "Well, I kind of like the unofficial, politically incorrect explanation."

"What's that? What do you mean?"

With a smile Jim said, "In the days of the British Empire, with the world map pretty well painted red, it was fine to have time start and end in Greenwich, England. France, of course, always knew that that wasn't the case because, after all, Paris is the center of the universe. So at the first opportunity GMT was renamed UTC, which is neutral, a compromise between CUT, coordinated universal time and TUC, *temps universel coordoné*. So now that every time a Frenchman looks at his watch he doesn't have to be reminded that the world starts in that little town in England."

"And what's the official reason?"

"The invention of highly accurate atomic clocks, which everyone agreed to use as standard the world over—Coordinated Universal Time."

By the time Mark got back to his apartment there was a message on the answering machine.

"Mark, it's Seth. You were right. As plain as day. But we'd been looking in the wrong code entirely. It seems that the terrorists must have changed the program version here, then let it automatically update all the dam sites. Then they replaced the code here with the old version. When I couldn't find any references to this timing sequence anywhere in our code on the server, I logged into the control program at one of our clients and immediately found their virus.

"This Kazim guy apparently wanted all the dams to open at 1300 hours UTC, which is 1 p.m. in England and 8:00 a.m. local time on the East Coast. So what he did is set the timing for them all to open at 1:00 p.m. But our operations control program takes its timing from the clocks on the dam's computers, which are all set for local time. That would mean that in each time zone coming west, the virus kicked in one hour later. That's why the dams opened exactly 60 minutes after each other. And why we just got to the big ones out here in the nick of time. If we didn't have the delays, we wouldn't have figured out about the auxiliary power danger in time to prevent nation-wide disasters. Boy, there must be some disappointment in the bad guys' camp these days. If Kazim hadn't screwed up, if the dams had all opened simultaneously, we would have had a major catastrophe especially below the really big ones. As it was, I guess things are pretty bad for those poor people below the ones that did open.

"By the way, Mark, you'll be pleased to know that we're making good headway repairing and confirming the software now that we know which version was corrupted. We should be back on line sooner than we thought. Talk to you later."

CHAPTER 44

"Jim, it's Illyich. You Americans sure know how to do it. Your major hydroelectric stations go off line and there's hardly a ripple in your economy. Of course, how was al-Qaeda to know or understand that all those exploited workers in the biggest unions in the country would decide to save your bacon?"

"Yeah, that was really something, wasn't it? And it was all their idea. By workers agreeing to shut down the heavy industry, the power companies are able to distribute what power they have to keeping people alive, to keep the country ticking over. I can tell you, I'm not a union guy, but I sure take my hat off to them on this one. So, Illyich, any news on your special delivery?"

"That's why I'm calling. I think there is a better than even chance that delivery has taken place. Whether Kazim takes the bait is the big question."

"Well, we've got a few days to figure out what we're going to do if he does."

"Now that your crisis is almost over, I don't suppose I could convince you to let it go, leave it to us over here?"

"Illyich, you know me better than that. I wouldn't miss out on this for anything! Kazim and I go back a long way. And Mark now has a personal stake in the action. We'll both be there. Besides, I have an idea that I want to explore with you."

"That's what I figured you'd say. What's the idea?"

"You had said that Igor had picked up encrypted traffic from Kazim's people, so he must have been in contact with his old team in St. Petersburg. Otherwise, how else would he have found Mark?"

"Yes, that's true. Hmm, I think I see where you're heading."

"Yeah. If those encrypted messages were going to Kazim, how did they get to him? The only plausible answer to that question is that Kazim has access to a computer with the encryption keys at his end of the chain. That sure as hell wouldn't be in a cave in the mountains. Unless I miss my bet, the answer to that question lies with your old outfit. If Kazim was sending and receiving those messages wherever he is in Afghanistan, we would have picked up the signals, even if we couldn't read them. I'm sure the NSA has that covered, they've got to be listening to every squeak into or out of that whole region."

"But you wouldn't know it if they had picked up anything, would you?"

"No, you're right. I'm way out of that loop. I'm surmising. I'm assuming that if they had anything, bin Laden would be locked up or bombed to pieces by now. Since he isn't, then I'd guess all the listening hasn't borne fruit. This would mean that Kazim is getting through some other way."

"Oh, my God! Of course! With signal traffic that wouldn't lead to him, traffic that went somewhere it was expected to go. Your listeners may have heard it but it wouldn't have raised alarms."

"Bingo, you got it! He has to be linked in through one of your normal destinations, a Russian station that would normally receive coded message traffic. I bet you'll find that he has a wireless connection across the street tapping into somebody's router or something."

Jim didn't know how right he was. That is exactly what Kazim had been doing until the US security net in Afghanistan got so tight that he couldn't drive into town to pick up the message traffic. That's when he set up the courier arrangements with the tribal chief.

There was a moment of silence while Illyich thought through the possibilities. "Jim, I think you're right. Kazim is good enough to do that, and he clearly still has the right contacts in Russia. I'll get Igor onto it right now."

"Okay. Back to our friend. What do you have in mind? What's the plan?"

"Jim, I think we need to meet in Istanbul in, say, about three days.

Olga and I will come, along with one agent who will do the dirty work."

"One thing for sure, Illyich, we can't fool around there. We need the Turks on side, if for no other reason than, if something goes off the rails, I sure don't want to spend time in a Turkish jail."

"I have some thoughts about how to handle the Turkish end. Things have changed over the last few years. We're now doing a fair bit of trading along the borders, the ones that had been sealed for all those years, practically all my life. You remember all the roads were cut, so even if you had wanted to you couldn't drive across the border. It was pretty well impenetrable to anything but donkeys. Well, those roads have all been rejoined, and truck traffic is heavy. The biggest problem now on both sides is smuggling of arms, drugs and black market goods. There is good coordination by the authorities on both sides when it comes to dealing with that."

"How the world turns! What do you have in mind?"

"I know the head of Turkish intelligence. We've done some work together. If we had information on one of our big smugglers, that he was going to be in Istanbul on, say, the 25th, and we were willing to run a joint operation to catch him, we might find the Turkish authorities quite happy to lend a hand. And then if we offered to take the problem off their hands by removing him to Russia, they wouldn't have the trouble and expense of prosecuting him. It would save them a lot of hassle."

"Illyich, if you could pull that off it would certainly provide the cover that we'd need. How will we go about it? It seems to me that Olga is the key. She'll need to be there, visible, to lure him in. We won't even know what he'll look like until he reveals himself. When I think of how he's slipped through the fingers of your old outfit, this will have to be really good!"

"You're right. We won't be able to pick him up before the meet. Almost for sure he'll be on a clean passport. And you're also right, it's not likely that we'd be able to recognize him. He's short by Russian standards but that's typical of millions of people in that region. He'll be well disguised, so we'll have to wait until he identifies himself. Now that I think about it, I'll add some reinforcements, put some people in place now in case he has some reconnaissance under way."

"We'll all come over. That will work out well for Katrina to get home. She can join us on this little jaunt. I'll make the travel arrangements at this end. Will you look after Istanbul?"

"Sure will. As I say, I've got some good contacts there. Give Katrina my love. How are they doing?"

"Unbelievable, my friend. They haven't been out of each other's sight for more than five minutes at a time, but Mark has been busier than he'd like with Kazim's bug. I can tell you, he's done a fantastic job. I would like to have had someone like him on my staff in the late '80s. As far as our kids are concerned, Illyich, if I was to make an intelligence assessment based on too little information, I'd say that what they have going is serious. Fate is sure a wonderful thing sometimes."

"I can't think of anything better, Jim. See you in Istanbul."

CHAPTER 45

"Leigh, I think we need a holiday. Illyich is going to be in Istanbul before the end of the month. We could go to Turkey, see the sights around Istanbul, meet Illyich there, then go with him in his boat to his dacha on the Black Sea. Knowing him, I expect that boat is suitably comfortable. We could ask Mark if he'd take a break and come with us. That would work well for Katrina as well. How does all that sound?"

"Sounds great. Mark hasn't seen Istanbul, and I'd love to see Illyich's place. From all you've told me, it's worth seeing. But you know Jim, in all our time together, I can't remember having a vacation that wasn't linked in some way to your work. Knowing what we've just been through, you may as well come clean. This has to do with Kazim, doesn't it? What have you two dreamed up?"

"Honey, I didn't really believe I'd get away with it. Habit, I guess. Well, to be completely honest that's not why I wasn't being forthcoming. You were right to worry, and, yes, it is about Kazim. Illyich hopes to lure him to Istanbul, nab him, then take him back to Russia. I'd like to be there to see it happen, to be there to close the story, and I think that Mark should be part of it."

"And what about the danger? I can't imagine Kazim going quietly."

"This'll be Illyich's operation, his and the Turkish authorities. There is no way that Illyich would put Katrina at risk. We'll be on the sidelines, with a ringside seat to see the action. The Turks will be in charge. With all I've been through with Kazim, I really don't want to miss the final chapter. I have to go."

"You know that I won't stand in the way. And I guess that Mark would like to be part of it, especially with his new love. Boy, is their life together ever starting with a bang! It should be a good trip for both of them. Also, Mark now has some personal baggage with Kazim. We are talking minimal risk here, right?"

They flew into Frankfurt and were on the connecting flight to Istanbul.

"Mark, you are going to enjoy Istanbul. It is truly fascinating. It is a remarkable spot that marks the divisions in the world, a crossroad of civilizations."

"You mean like Kipling's 'Oh, East is East, and West is West, and never the twain shall meet'?"

"Exactly. Except this is where they do meet, where East meets West, where Asia meets Europe, where Arab meets Caucasian. And, perhaps most important of all, where Islam meets Christianity," said Jim. "You will see it in the teeming humanity and in the bazaar, which, by the way, is unbelievable. And the history! After all, this was the center of the Ottoman Empire for some seven centuries—and that was after Byzantium. The Bosporus has been a strategic crossroads for millennia. Now, in a Turkey that is struggling with its history, you can see Ataturk's influence at every turn, a secular society delicately balancing the Muslim world and economic growth, what has been a military regime with democracy. It's edging its way into the European Community, history still in the making."

Katrina had listened with interest, and eagerly added, "I agree with your father, Mark. I spent some time there two years ago with Illyich. It is fascinating and I can show you around. This is going to be great!"

"I'm really looking forward to it. But, Dad, what about the reason for coming? Is everything on track?" Mark's voice had dropped to a whisper.

"We'll find out in a few hours, but knowing Illyich, I'm sure it will be."

"What possible bait could you two have dreamed up that would lure Kazim out of his hiding place? I can't imagine anything being powerful enough to convince him to take a risk like that."

"One of Illyich's people from the old days worked with Kazim.

They became lovers, there's evidently some deep emotional issues there, to do with loyalty and love. It's about the only bait that might work. As I understand it, she has designed the trap—in fact, I guess she is herself part of the bait."

Katrina broke into the hushed conversation. "That must be Olga. I've met her, and I can tell you, she's some bait. A very sexy woman. Not someone a young man would ever forget, even decades later."

Jim thought about that for a minute. "She must be a brave woman too, putting herself on the line like this. There must really have been a powerful link for her to do this."

Mark said thoughtfully, "Yes, for Olga for sure. But what about Kazim? He's the one with everything to lose. To lure a monster like him, the enticement must be about fear and power, as well as lust and love."

As they emerged from the aircraft at Ataturk Airport, a young Turkish naval officer saluted Jim. "Mr. Buchan, General Erkat sends his regards. He has asked me to accompany you to the Orduevi where accommodation has been arranged. Mr. Makov is already there. Your luggage will meet you at your suite."

"But what about customs and immigration?"

"The general has taken care of those formalities, sir."

"Lieutenant, this is an unexpected pleasure. When Mr. Makov told me that he had made arrangements, I had no idea that we would have the honor of staying in your Officers' Club. I hope that we will have the opportunity to express our appreciation to the general."

As they made their way into the city and then started the climb to the highest point, Mark marveled at the sights, a teeming multitude of people, of dress, of races, all set in a backdrop of architecture rich with history. Katrina was a tour guide, pointing out the sites. And then, when they reached the Orduevi, the Officers' Club, all four gasped in awe. They looked down, Istanbul spread out as far as the eye could see, the Topkapi gleaming in the setting sun and the long suspension bridge across the Bosporus linking Europe and Asia.

Jim said, "If I'm not mistaken, that's the roof of the Sheraton Hotel that we're looking down on. These are some digs!"

"Dad, you sure were right. What an exciting city. Boy, do I look forward to this!"

Katrina gave him a gentle poke in the ribs. "Hmm, and I look forward to being your tour guide."

The two-bedroom suite came with a houseboy, ready to do their bidding. The message from Illyich asked them to meet in the dining room at 2000 hours for dinner, and for Katrina to join him. The note closed with the news that Jim was so anxiously waiting for: 'All is ready.'

CHAPTER 46

"Illyich, you outdid yourself this time. Relationships between Turkey and Russia must really have changed for you to be able to pull this off!"

"Jim, I told you, I do a lot of business with these people. The general was happy to oblige if it will help with the smuggling problem."

"I can't believe the houseboy right outside the door to the suite, on standby for all our needs," Leigh said.

Illyich laughed. "Leigh, I hate to destroy your illusion, but that 'houseboy,' as you call him, is there to keep an eye on you. There's a machine gun within easy reach, and his boss is an intel officer, not a concierge. Your every move will be monitored, not only to ensure that you don't cause trouble, but also to make sure that no one causes you trouble. They want you out of here, quietly and in one piece, when this is over."

"Dad, all this gets more and more interesting by the minute."

"Yes it does, Mark. What I have to tell you now, though, is not good. Jim, Igor tells me that all the computer activity in St. Petersburg stopped cold yesterday. He had seen a lot of encrypted activity over the past week, but it's stopped completely. Kazim's old colleagues had been under surveillance, but I'm told they disappeared off the face of the earth last night. This can mean only one thing: Kazim has reinforcements on the way. Former KGB agents with no allegiance or respect for anyone or anything except money."

"Well, Illyich, I must say I'm not at all surprised. We didn't expect this to be a cakewalk. On the other hand, it probably means that Kazim took the bait. So, what's the plan?"

"The Turks plan to put a gun in his back, load him on a boat in the harbor, motor up the Bosporus into the Black Sea, and transfer him to us at their territorial limit. The Russian navy will have a patrol boat in place to meet them and complete the transfer. We discussed doing it by air or road, but both of those options were rejected. Given the distance to the border and the state of some of the roads, that choice was not practical, just too risky and too long. I would have preferred to do it by air, but the Turks want to keep control until Kazim is out of their country, and they do have pretty tight control of the strait. They know everything that floats, anything going in or out of the Black Sea. This way means that we are not operating on their soil. Sovereign control is important to them."

"No question, we do it their way, and I agree, they control the Bosporus really well. I can remember toward the end of the Cold War your navy was building its first real aircraft carrier, the *Kuznetsov*, in the Nikolayev shipyards on the Ukrainian Black Sea coast. There was a raging debate in the naval world about whether Turkey would let it through the strait to the Med, because the Montreux Convention of 1936 outlawed the passage of that class of warship. Through some quiet back channels we asked the Turks what they were going to do when the request arrived on their desk. The answer that came back was interesting: 'You mean that large deep-sea fishing vessel with the flat deck? Of course, we will grant permission for its passage.' The Turks know how to finesse an impossible situation, they know the practical limits of sovereignty, and they know what goes in and out of the Black Sea."

Illyich said with a laugh, "I can tell you, Jim, we laid the groundwork for that before we even started building the ship, and we provided Turkey with the right kind of motivation to grant permission for passage. There was no question, it was heading for the Atlantic—if it had ever been completed."

Katrina and Mark smiled. "We'll sure need to spend time with these two when we start writing our spy thriller," she laughed.

"Illyich, I'd like to have a look at the meeting spot, sort of case the joint, and we need to find a safe ringside seat for us spectators."

"That's for sure—someplace *very* safe, well out of the line of fire,"

Leigh added. “We’ve already been closer to Kazim than I want any of my family to ever be again. I can’t imagine how Olga is going to feel. She will be really vulnerable, right out in the open like that, Illyich.”

“Yes, that is true. She is a very brave woman. As you know, security in this country is always tight, lots of soldiers visible on the streets, all armed. These days, between the terrorist threat and the Kurds, the security is even more obvious than usual, especially around the big tourist attractions. And the meet is set up to take place at one of the biggest. For the next week, those soldiers that we are going to see lounging around the square where the meet will take place will all be crack security troops trying to look like bored conscripts.”

“Your friend must owe you something big time. It sounds to me like they’ve really covered the bases on this one!”

“That’s true, Jim. They’re going all out to make this work, but it isn’t because of me. They desperately want the country in the European Union, and among the conditions they have to meet is the need to tighten up control of what comes in and out of the country. They want to be seen to be dealing with the border problems.”

“What’s the plan, once Kazim is loaded on the navy boat?”

“I’ve got my boat here from Sochi. The five of us will follow them out to the transfer point, then we’ll head across the Black Sea to home. I thought we’d take a leisurely trip along the coast, stop in the Crimea and show our kids here some history, Sevastopol and Yalta.”

“Sounds great. After all the excitement we could use a nice break. What about Kazim? Where is he going?”

“We’re not taking any chances there. The patrol boat will go into the navy yard at Novorossiysk, on Russian territory, and then he’ll be taken on to Moscow. He’ll wind up in a place he knows well from his KGB days, the basement at Lubyanka, but this time on the receiving end.”

CHAPTER 47

For the next few days, while Jim and Illyich organized the operation, Leigh, Mark and Katrina thrilled at the sights of Istanbul. "I can sure see what my dad meant when he described this city. It is truly exciting."

"Yes," said Katrina, "and you haven't seen the most fascinating piece of it yet. To most Westerners, the Kapali Carsi, the Grand Bazaar, or to most people the Covered Bazaar, is the most foreign of all. Let's spend tomorrow there."

They had spent hours at the Topkapi, the famous palace, amazed at the jewels, so big, so numerous, that they looked fake. And the history! The Basilica of St. Sophia, with its splendid dome almost 180 feet high, dating from Constantine the Great and rebuilt by Justinian in the sixth century and the Blue Mosque from the early seventeenth.

"Really puts things in perspective, doesn't it, Mom?"

The next day found them wandering the narrow alleys in the Covered Bazaar, magnificent Oriental carpets piled floor to ceiling in never-ending rows like cordwood, sellers with long poles like shepherd's crooks to pull them down. Goats and donkeys walking over the carpets that had been hooked down for the viewing. Rows and rows of tiny stalls, packed with more gold than most people would see in a lifetime. And then, one section over, the same thing again, only this time silver, each stall in the bazaar only about eight feet wide, everything tightly arranged like sardines in a can.

"Katrina, I don't understand the finances of all this. It boggles my mind. They seem to accept any currency, any form of payment. They know the exchange rates for anything in their heads! And the value of the stuff inside this city block must be astronomical, fortunes in gold, silver, carpets. How do they do it?"

"These people have been in the business since the dawn of civilization. They know human nature, values, prices. They've never had banks or financial institutions, most have little or no education, they don't need computers—they count with those sliding beads, the abacus, have done for centuries, and they seem to do it faster than I can enter the numbers into my calculator. You may think you're getting the best deal of the year, but they know to the lira what their bottom line is. You will walk away thinking you got the better of the bargain and that is exactly what they want you to think. They are masters at the art of trading. It's a big part of the pleasure and fascination of the place."

By this time they had found themselves in an alley with copper of every description as far as the eye could see. Leigh had bargained for a large bean pot, just the one she wanted, but she didn't like the price. Hours later, they found themselves back in the same place, in the stall just across the alley, which had a bean pot almost, but not quite, like the one she wanted. The shopkeeper listened with interest to the discussion. Should she pay that much for the one she wanted? Should she settle for less and just buy this one? As Katrina realized what was about to happen, a smile creased her face. She nudged Mark, whispering, "Watch this. This is going to show you the bazaar at its very best."

"Well, if you prefer that one over there, then you should go and buy that one," the shopkeeper said to Leigh, with a wave of his hand in dismissal. He was squat and fat and gave the impression of being almost as wide as he was tall, his robe accentuating the effect, the fez on his head and gold chain around his neck completing the exotic appearance.

Leigh exclaimed in frustration, "But he wants too much for it!"

"No, that cannot be. How much is the robber asking?"

"After heavy bargaining he wants 200 million liras. I don't want to pay that much and he won't budge."

"Ho! Robber!" The stubby little shopkeeper was getting more and more excited. He continued in his squeaky high voice, almost shrill at this point. "You should pay not a lira more than 150 million. You go and bargain." As she hesitated he said, "Here, wait a minute," reaching in his pocket for a small coin. "Take this with you to give to him to seal the deal."

So while Leigh went into the ring to bargain, the stall keeper poured Mark and Katrina a tea, giggling gleefully the whole time. He stood between Mark and Katrina—Mark a giant beside him—and reached up to wrap his arms around their shoulders. For the funny little shopkeeper, this was the best sport in the world.

The three stood eight feet across the alley to watch the fun, the other customers in his little stall forgotten in the age-old pleasure of watching the making of a deal.

"So, sir, what was the significance of the coin you handed my mother?"

"It is to seal the agreement. He will come down in price more than he would like, and that lira, given after the price is settled, shows honor for a hard bargain and saves face for having agreed to such a ridiculously low price. Look, she has it." He shook as he giggled. "The deal has been made, the coin is passed, and now the shake of hands between worthy adversaries."

With that, he grabbed Mark's and Katrina's hands and danced with them in a circle, his robes jiggling with the movement. The other customers had stood with their mouths open watching the show, the people in the alleyway mesmerized, all breaking into applause, the shopkeeper and Leigh smiling with delight.

As they walked away in triumph, Mark was deep in thought. "You know, Mother, that was a once-in-a-lifetime lesson in cross-cultural relations. A little thing like that really brings home the challenge of thinking that we know what's right for the world! We can't even begin to understand those thousands of years of culture and history. I'm beginning to understand the hurdles Dad must have faced all those years in trying to look into his crystal ball at the Soviet Union. I feel like a school boy—all this new experience."

Katrina smiled at him, "Mark, it's going to be fun traveling with you, and this is just the start. You're so enthusiastic. Wait till I show you St. Petersburg!"

Leigh turned away so they wouldn't see the huge grin that spread across her face. This was quite a woman that Illyich had brought into their lives!

Illyich knocked on the door.

"Come in. It's open."

"Jim, I just got a call from our guy here in Istanbul. I've called a driver to take us over there."

"Interesting. I didn't know that Russia had anything here," Jim teased.

"We've done it quietly over the years. The strait is way too important for us not to have an ear close to the ground."

"So, you've heard from Igor?"

"Yup, let's go. We'll do our talking in the vault."

At the small Russian mission they were met by the head of post, whose real job was as the local FSB station chief. His name was Vladimir Andropovich and he had been in this post for three years, a long time by KGB standards, but it meant that he knew his way around. Vladimir led the way to the basement, to the SCIF, the sensitive compartmented information facility, a room completely shielded by copper to prevent any unwanted electronic emanations, either in or out. The only people allowed in the room were those with the special clearances to handle the highly classified intelligence. The good news about the 'chamber of silence' as they called it was the silence. The bad news in this case was that the air conditioner was not keeping up with the heat generated by the bank of secure communications equipment. The place was stifling.

Illyich smiled as he poked Vladimir in the ribs. "I see that our supply system has not improved with our new capitalist society."

"No, sir. The new air conditioning unit has been on order for a month now. Things never change."

Jim said, "It's the first time in ages since I was in one of these. For sure, I never expected to be in one of yours, Illyich. It's hard to believe."

"Well, I must say, I didn't expect to be using one of these again either, but we need to be here to answer the question that we posed to Igor. What do you have, Vladimir?"

"First, let me say that this is most unusual." Despite the intense heat, Vladimir was clearly used to the environment. He was barely breaking a sweat. "There has never been anyone in here without clearances. Illyich, your reputation with your old colleagues is remarkable. I regret not having had the opportunity to work with you while you were active."

"Thank you for that. We did have our moments. What does Igor have to say?"

"They've managed to track the message traffic from St. Petersburg," Vladimir explained. "As you suspected, the receiving station is our mission in Kabul. What they're doing is hiding it in the normal diplomatic traffic, using the same patterns and circuits."

"So, Kazim still has friends in the right places. Someone in Kabul is on his payroll." He looked at Jim. "Since your countrymen have tightened the screws, I doubt that Kazim can just walk in and pick up his messages. I expect that from there they must use local runners to carry them to their camps."

Jim said, "I guess that would be relatively easy. There are a lot of Taliban still out there, ready to do anything for the cause."

"Did Igor indicate where to from here? Did he say what they plan to do?"

"Yes, they've put a watch on Kabul. It shouldn't take long to find the guy. Once that link is cut, Kazim will be out of business. He couldn't operate without the technical support he's been getting from St. Petersburg."

Both Jim and Illyich looked at each other, eyebrows raised.

"You're reading my mind, Illyich. This is an opportunity like no other. We need to bring in the big guns."

"Yeah, you may never get closer."

Vladimir was looking from one to the other quizzically. "What are you two talking about?"

"Vladimir, can you link us with Igor on secure voice? We need to talk with him."

"Sure can. Get on those extensions. I'll make the connection."

Moments later, Igor greeted Illyich in Russian.

Illyich promptly switched to English: "Igor, Jim is on the line with me."

"Hey, Jim, just like old times, eh? Only next time we meet in person I hope it's not in a wrestling match, with people shooting at us again. How are you?"

Vladimir was stunned. How could Igor possibly be on a first name basis with an enemy agent?

"Just great, Igor. Good work on the tracking of that message traffic."

"Igor, Jim and I have an idea that's too good to pass up. Vladimir tells us that your people are going to pick up the contact in Kabul when they identify him."

"That's the plan, yes."

"Igor, Kazim is almost certainly with bin Laden. That contact and the couriers could lead us to the motherlode. We can't pick him up. We can't lose this opportunity."

"Illyich, I understand. This will be quite an operation."

Jim had been lost in thought for a moment. "Illyich, we've got to link your people with the US. We've got the resources in theater, the Special Forces boots on the ground. Igor, could you get a name for a contact in Washington? I'll arrange for Antonio to connect at that end."

Illyich stepped in. "I agree with Jim. It's time to call in reinforcements. Igor, you set things up at your end. Make sure they don't spook the courier. Get a name at our embassy in Washington to work with the CIA, and get the guy briefed so he knows what's going on when Antonio gets in contact. Jim, can you set things up at your end?"

"Give me a day, Igor. Vladimir will let you know when we're ready."

"Working with you two the last time almost got us all killed. I'm not sure I'm ready for this again! Seriously, though, I'll get things set up right away, and wait to hear from you, Vladimir."

Jim said, "Thanks again for the good work, Igor. We'll be back in touch fairly soon." Jim turned to Vladimir, "I need to speak to our guy here in Istanbul. It used to be the cultural attaché. Any ideas?"

Vladimir's long-standing posting was coming in handy. "It still is. His name is Lowell Westerby. I could call him."

"Please do."

Vladimir dialed the number. "Lowell, Vlad here. Just fine, thanks. I have someone here who needs to talk with you."

Jim reached for the phone. "Lowell, I don't think we ever had the pleasure of meeting. I'm Jim Buchan. I was with the Agency."

"Sure, I know of you, sir. What can we do for you?"

"Well, you can do something out of the ordinary but important. I need to speak with your boss, Antonio, on a secure phone. I'd like you to set it up. Call him and he'll okay it. And, by the way, I'll have a retired KGB general with me. Antonio will understand. If you could get things going, we'll get a ride over to your place, say, in half an hour."

"Mr. Buchan, I cannot imagine the circumstances that would allow you and a KGB officer into my vault, but I'm onto it. As long as Antonio approves, I'll have things arranged for you when you get here."

Jim put down the phone, and stood up. "Come on, Illyich. Let's head over to make that call. Vladimir, thanks for the good service."

As Vladimir escorted them out, he looked at Illyich in admiration. "Mr. Makov, I see why you have the reputation that you do. We've all heard stories, but now I think I could believe them. I would be honored to invite you for dinner, but with one condition—that you tell me how you ever linked with Mr. Buchan here."

"I'd be pleased to accept, but not this time. We'll be a bit busy for the next while."

A short ride later, Lowell met them at the front door, under a sign that read 'Welcome to the Consulate of the United States of America,' another sign underneath announcing 'You are now entering US soil.'

"Well, gentlemen, this was easier than I ever thought it could be. I've been told to treat you two like royalty or," with a smile, "maybe like US senators would be more accurate. Let's go downstairs."

As they entered their second vault of the day, Jim and Illyich looked at each other and burst out laughing. Lowell looked on in astonishment, not seeing anything humorous about any business that went on in that high security room.

Jim said with a grin, "Lowell, it's just that we spent our years on opposite sides during the Cold War. For us to be going from the most secure room on the Russian side directly to the most secure room on the US side, and holding hands as we do it, is just so far from anything we could have ever conceived, not in anyone's wildest dreams."

Lowell was not sure what to make of this two-ringed circus, but recalled Antonio Pesquali's instructions. He also knew the reputations of the two men following him into the room. "I must say what we're doing here catches one's attention. Let's make that call …"

"Hello, Antonio, thanks for the arranging."

"Jim, I have no doubt that this is going to be good. What in the world are you two up to?"

"Antonio, we have an idea that's too good to pass up. You know that Illyich and I are tracking Kazim. As part of that we had Igor in St. Petersburg—he was the young KGB programmer that was with us on Onion."

"Yes, I remember the name."

"Well, Igor tracked some encrypted message traffic that was going to Kazim. The destination was the Russian mission in Kabul. The Russians have things under surveillance and planned to pick up whoever it is on the receiving end. Illyich has managed to put that on hold until you get in the act. The point is, Antonio, that I'm pretty sure Kazim is with bin Laden."

"Oh, man, this might be the break we've been praying for. Right now, we're at a dead end. Every time we get close, he slips through our fingers."

"So, to close the loop, Igor is briefing their Washington contact who will be in touch with you, Antonio. Illyich, you can now let Igor know Antonio is ready. And, just to be sure, Antonio, why don't you contact Igor if you don't hear anything within twelve hours, so that nothing goes off the rails."

Antonio spoke up. "Illyich, how would I get in touch with Igor?"

"I think the best way would be through our man in Washington. I expect you know who that is?"

"Sure. Could you lay some groundwork, smooth the way?"

"Yes," replied Illyich, "we can. I'll have our man here, Vladimir, get the word to him."

"Jim, it seems that I'm saying thank you a lot these days, but it will have to be a lot more than that if this works out."

"Good luck!"

As they were walking out of the building, Lowell said to Jim, "Sir, I've heard about you, of course, but to meet you here, and with Mr. Makov, a KGB general—this is one story that I'll have to save for my grandkids! And here I thought you two guys were retired."

Jim and Illyich looked at each other, grinning from ear to ear.

"We are," said Jim. "It just doesn't look that way."

CHAPTER 48

About the same time that Leigh and Jim were bargaining for a beautiful Caucasian carpet, one that Leigh had picked out on her first day at the bazaar, and Mark and Katrina were walking hand in hand along the Golden Horn, a man with an Algerian passport was making his way through Customs and Immigration. He was conservatively dressed, Panama hat, neatly trimmed beard and moustache, nothing remarkable, nothing to draw anyone's attention.

The paperwork and passport raised no alarms. He was traveling light, just one small, expensive tan leather overnight bag. Those who did look at him thought what they were supposed to think, just one of thousands of successful businessman coming to the crossroads of the world.

Kazim stepped out of the airport into a taxi. "Take me to the Hotel Metropole."

The taxi driver responded as they all did, "Inshallah."

Kazim smiled to himself. He was a devout Muslim, but he had always found it ironic that the success of a taxi ride depended more on God being willing than on good driving. He had thought about staying in the Sirkedje, but had quickly realized that if this was a trap that would be the first place they'd look. It was there that he and Olga had had such a wonderful weekend—so long ago, but it seemed like only yesterday.

The meeting was to be in the plaza in front of the Sirkedje Railway Station, the one made famous in the Western world as the destination of the old Orient Express. He and Olga had watched the Agatha Christie play, and then replayed the murder as they sat over drinks at 'their' table, the one where his fate was to be decided in four days.

His thoughts stirred deep memories, and he found excitement flowing through his veins. "Careful," he told himself, "this is no time to become sentimental." But the more he thought about Olga, the more he wanted to see her. Kazim had forgotten that those emotions had ever existed. He had been determined to bury them forever.

Each day for the next four, the 'Algerian' roamed the plaza between six and seven o'clock. Each day he was a different man, unrecognizable as the same person. Each day he watched the chaos on the plaza, milling crowds, lounging soldiers, peddlers, people of every color, dress and culture, a tumult of languages, hurrying into the train station and across the plaza. And each day he saw no change in the chaos, no cause for alarm. He would be there to see if Olga kept her word and would identify the Trojan horse in bin Laden's camp.

It was six o'clock on the 25th when Olga took a seat at a patio table in front of the Sirkedje. She was simply but elegantly attired in a gray, calf-length dress of light linen, white mid-heel shoes, a white Pashmina shawl draped over the arm of her chair, a huge, floppy hat of fine natural fiber shading her eyes.

Despite now being 40, she looked serene and inviting, causing male heads to swivel to admire the view. She was stunning.

As Kazim looked toward their table he stopped dead in his tracks, his thoughts racing back a dozen years. She was a bit heavier, but still voluptuous, striking, breathtaking. He felt a tightness in his chest, an emotional jab he had not felt for a long time. He stood looking at her, marveling that she still thrilled him, wondering what might have been in a different world.

A small twinge of fear and doubt ran up his spine. That uneasiness had become more insistent in the days since he received the enigmatic message in the wilds of the tribal lands. The impossible must have happened. Olga must be right. There had to be a traitor in their midst—that was the only thing that would explain Buchan's interference, how Jim Buchan would have even known to start looking for him. The internal debate that he had been wrestling with since receiving her message ended as soon as he saw her. He looked around carefully and, his decision made, swiveled and started towards her.

Illyich was nowhere in sight. The sheer bulk of him was impossible to hide even with the best of disguises.

Leigh, Mark and Katrina were in a darkened hotel room with Jim, sipping tea, looking out over the scene below. Olga was sitting quietly, not a care in the world, soldiers lounging around the square, tourists milling and gawking. People everywhere, Western, Eastern, Muslim, Orthodox, Christian, hawkers displaying their wares, in a ballet of organized chaos. How were they ever going to pick Kazim out of that crowd? They had no idea what they were looking for; indeed they were not at all sure that Kazim would take the bait.

Jim was starting to despair. How could they succeed, Olga so vulnerable out there on her own?

"She sure has guts," he said aloud. "Kazim could have ordered her killed."

Leigh, and next to her Katrina and Mark, hardly dared to breath. "Jim, how are they going to get him in that sea of humanity? What if he puts up a fight? I can't see any police or security people at all."

Anyone who looked carefully at Jim, and no one could in the privacy of their room, might have noticed that he had an earplug in one ear and a small microphone pinned to his shirt.

"My dear, you're not supposed to see anything out of the ordinary. They're there, and there's no sign of him yet. But I agree the tension is heavy."

He caught his breath and pointed to the far left side of the square, "Wait, over there!"

Something had caught his eye. His mind flashed back. He was lying on the floor, blood streaming out of the wound in his leg, trying to hold onto Igor. Kazim spun around so fast that Jim didn't see his face, but an image was there, a brief picture that Jim had not registered at the time. But there it was again. He had just seen that picture repeated, in the sea of humanity spread out below. That man, there, the one in the tan outfit had spun around, the same pirouette that Jim had seen a dozen years ago, almost like a dancer.

Jim was talking into his mike. "I've got him. He's about a hundred feet out, toward the train station. He's got a tan suit, graying hair, short beard and moustache. Walking towards her now … About fifty feet."

The security team was impressive to watch. No one seemed to rush; none of the hundreds of people in the immediate vicinity even knew that something was going on. Olga was looking around casually, to any observer a tourist interested in the fascinating scene surrounding her.

Her face suddenly registered surprise, and then Kazim saw a look of shock leap into her eyes as she recognized him. That brief look gave Kazim almost enough warning, almost, but not quite. As he started to turn away, he found himself looking into the barrel of a machine gun. Two soldiers, one on either side, steered him to the sidewalk where a black, unmarked Mercedes staff car was pulling up.

Leigh, Mark and Katrina sat in stunned silence.

"Jim! How could you have done this all those years? I can hardly breathe."

Jim shook himself, trying to slough off the tension. "Let's go. I see Illyich's man has Olga. We're going to meet at the Sirkedje Hotel."

Mark and Katrina's fingers were so tightly entwined that their knuckles were white.

They now leaned out the window, still staring down in awe as Kazim neared the car. The guard turned him around to back him into the seat. As Kazim glanced to heaven, to Allah, his eyes stopped suddenly, locking onto Jim's. A look of recognition, of defiance and perhaps triumph crossed his face. He had been right. Jim Buchan had done it to him again.

Leigh gasped in horror. "My God, Jim, he recognized you. Did you see the look on his face? This is really scary."

Jim mused aloud, "How could fate have arranged that glance? Thank goodness he's on his way to Russia!"

They hurried to a shaken Olga. Illyich was already there, an arm around her. She was speaking in fast Russian, the words spilling out of her mouth.

"Illyich, I almost blew it. When I saw him, he was so close I thought you must have missed. I think he must have interpreted my shock as a warning and was starting to leave. I have to admit, despite being briefed and prepared, getting myself psyched up, I was just plain scared, petrified!"

"Olga, you did well. It's over now. We waited a long time for this. Let's get you out of here."

As the two walked to the hotel, Olga couldn't stop talking. "Illyich, I don't know what to think. We were so passionately in love. And I grew to hate him. When I saw him turn toward me I knew it was him. But for a moment there I saw that old look, the one I fell in love with all those years ago. How can someone so bad have that kind of effect on me?"

"Olga, Kazim has survived through charisma, guile, playing on people's emotions. He is a master. You are not the only one to have been ensnared in his web, but you should be the last. Without you we would not have caught him."

"Yet it is going to take me a long time to get over the shock of seeing him there …"

Katrina greeted them in English. "I've seen a lot of good theatre, but I've never seen a performance like that, Olga. You were magnificent. Mark, you and I really do need to write a book about this."

"All right, everyone, we need to move. I took the liberty of pulling some strings. We are dining in the general's suite at the Orduevi. We can hash over old times with a drink. And, Olga, this is one time you can really let off steam. You may still be a working girl, bound by the rules, but I can tell you those rules don't exist in this company. We've got a car waiting for you. Mark, why don't you and Katrina keep Olga company on the drive over? Katrina, you could start the research for your novel with a real live spy!"

The dinner in the general's suite was just what everyone needed. The furnishings were an old world mix of Western and Eastern, heavy embroidered drapes open to a cooling breeze, the city stretching for miles below, ottomans lining the walls, high-backed chairs around the white linen table loaded with exotic foods from East and West, discreet servants keeping the glasses and plates full. Mark and Katrina were deep in conversation with Olga, hanging on her every word. As always, Illyich was at his best, charming Leigh with stories and jokes. Jim enjoyed seeing his wife and son relaxed after all the tension of the past weeks.

No one had noticed the three Russian tourists, sitting a few tables over from where Olga had been, as they laid lira on the table to cover their bill, calmly stood up and faded into the crowd. As they walked with the flow of pedestrians, one said quietly, "We go to Plan B."

CHAPTER 49

Kazim had not survived all those years without exceptional cunning. He did not undertake any operation without plotting for contingencies, without a Plan B to kick in if Plan A was foiled. His loyalty and commitment to al-Qaeda did not permit him to ignore the chance that Olga's message was a sincere warning that the leader and the cause were in grave danger from within. He knew that it could be a trap, but he had to go. Plan B was the contingency in case of a trap.

Plan B had cost a lot of Turkish lira, Bulgarian leva and Russian rubles. It had three components: by land, by air or by sea. Kazim had always worked on the premise that someone could be found who could be bought—not everyone, but at least one. And it was not always necessary to actually make a purchase. Like the old saying about the warlords in Afghanistan, they couldn't be bought, just rented until the next better offer. In Istanbul, he only needed a temporary rental of someone's loyalty, just time enough to learn how he would be transported if the meeting with Olga was not what she said it was.

Contingency arrangements were in place for all three possibilities. The land component would be easy. It was a long drive to Russia from Istanbul, with many possibilities for ambush. The air option would be more difficult. It would require action either at the departure end or at the destination airport. The departure end in Istanbul would be tricky, but with a good network still in place in Russia, there would be some chance of payoffs at the landing site, which undoubtedly would be Moscow. He had no doubt about the final destination: It could only be the basement on Dzerzinski Square.

Kazim's old cell of agents and technical specialists in the KGB had been known as the 'dirty tricks office' and they had often worked with

Bulgarian agents who had done some of the KGB dirty work abroad. They had murdered KGB targets in London, and it was this cell that had dreamed up the infamous poisoned umbrella assassination, giving the job to their agents, the Bulgarian secret police. Now the team from St. Petersburg looked to their Bulgarian friends to cover the sea component of Plan B.

On the morning of the 25th, the day of Kazim's meeting with Olga, a dockworker in the navy yard reported to Kazim's St. Petersburg friends that a naval gunboat was being prepared for a classified mission the next day. The sea component of Plan B went into action.

Oblivious to impending danger, a gleaming white cruiser sailed along the Bosporus, keeping easy pace with the Turkish navy gunboat. Illyich was at the cruiser's helm. Four people sat comfortably in deck chairs watching with interest as the remarkable panorama rolled by. Mark focused on the sights unfolding in every direction, and Katrina kept up a running dialogue. The scenery was spectacular, Asia on the right, Europe on the left, overhead the long suspension bridge that spanned East and West, linking the two continents. Ships of every description, every nation of registry, from small fishing boats to huge freighters and tankers. Above the throb of the engine they could hear snippets of what sounded like every language in the world floating across the water.

The trip to the Black Sea took two-and-a-half hours. Jim and Illyich's eyes constantly swept the horizon. When they were in open seas an hour beyond Turkish territorial limits, the gunboat was met by a Russian fast patrol boat. The transfer of their prisoner took place in minutes, professionally accomplished. The Turkish navy boat swung around and headed for home. The captain on deck saluted Illyich as it cruised by the yacht.

At about the same time that the gunboat had slipped its moorings at the navy dock in Istanbul, a big, black, ocean-racing cigarette boat quietly left a secluded dock near Ahtopol, a small resort and fishing village on the southern coast of Bulgaria.

Both Jim and Illyich watched through binoculars as Kazim was taken aboard the Russian ship and then, as the Turkish boat passed them, a Russian Hind helicopter appeared overhead.

Illyich smiled, "I'm glad to see they've got an escort—not leaving anything to chance. Kazim will be locked up in a Russian jail by tomorrow night."

The Turkish gunboat returning to Istanbul was just a speck on the horizon when Illyich said, "We part company with Kazim's chariot here. They've got about 400 miles to go into Novorossiysk. We'll take our time and head north to the Crimea."

They were having a final look before turning 30 degrees to port for their new course to the Crimea when Jim exclaimed, "Illyich, something's happening here. Look at that boat smoking in from the left."

The five people on the yacht were no longer lounging in the deck chairs, but on their feet, speechless at the drama unfolding in front of them. Illyich and Jim had binoculars glued to their eyes. They watched in horror as six shoulder-fired missiles were launched from the big cigarette speedboat. Two were Russian SA-18 Igla surface-to-air missiles. Before the Russians even realized they were in trouble, the Hind helicopter exploded in a massive fireball. The other four were aimed at the Russian patrol boat. The AT-13 Metis-M anti-tank missiles were charged with armor-piercing high explosives and phosphorous. One took out the bridge, the captain and officers instantly incinerated. One caught the operations room, one the superstructure, with the last exploding in the jet turbine engine and igniting fuel spraying from the flailing lines. Everything above the deck disappeared behind smoke and flames.

There was no crew in sight left to put up a fight as the cigarette boat drew alongside the burning hulk. It was difficult to see what was happening through the black pall, but the watchers could hear gunshots and small explosions across the water.

"Sounds like Simtex. Likely blowing open the doors looking for him," Jim exclaimed, the others looking on, mouths agape.

There was a flurry of activity as several figures leaped onto the deck of the cigarette boat, already casting off and getting underway. It was about a hundred yards off when a huge explosion erupted, the remains of the Russian boat splitting into pieces, flames leaping out of the water. By the time the Ukrainian marine rescue aircraft from Yalta arrived overhead, there was nothing to see but some floating debris and an oil slick.

Illyich, Jim, Leigh, Mark and Katrina stood in stunned silence on the yacht deck, looking out to where, only minutes ago, the final leg of Kazim's journey to justice had been prematurely ended, not as planned, in the basement of the building on Dzerzinski Square in Moscow, but in a black cigarette boat speeding to the Bulgarian coast. There seemed to be nothing to do or say.

They were quiet as the yacht slowly cruised north. Eventually Mark broke the ice. "How could Kazim have survived that? Or better still, how could they have taken the chance that he would—shooting missiles at the patrol boat like that?"

"Well, son, Kazim is a risk-taker. He calculates the odds, and in this case it was all or nothing. The only way there'd be any chance of getting him out would be by using overwhelming force so that no one could fight back. I expect that they counted on him being locked up below deck, so if their aim was good, there would be some chance that they'd get him out."

"And with the missiles that they used, they could hardly miss. Your dad's right, Mark. Kazim knew his survival was on the line, all or nothing. I expect his instructions were to either get him out or make sure he did not survive if they couldn't. Clearly, he wasn't going to be taken alive. Unfortunately, it looks like he survived."

"We blew it," Jim said with obvious frustration. "We had him alive and may never get as good a chance again. The next time will be even more difficult."

"Now, wait a minute here, you two. What's this I'm hearing about the next time?" Leigh interrupted. "This may not be the end of Kazim's story after all, because one way or another, he'll be back. But let's agree now that you are retired. Leave it to the people who are paid to do the job. And I would think that you, Mark, will have had enough excitement to allow you to get back to your business in peace. You've all done more than your duty and you've done a fantastic job."

Mark agreed, almost. "I sure do need to get back to business, if there's anything left to get back to after all this time I've spent on Kazim. But I'll tell you, this has been almost as exciting as a good breakthrough on the computer. What a story! What an experience!"

They cruised in silence, each lost in the enormity of what they had seen. Then Jim and Illyich began running the scenarios through, wondering what they should have done differently, what would come next.

Katrina had been absorbed in thought. As they started to settle down after the intense excitement, small talk finally getting underway, Katrina really broke the ice.

"Illyich, I'm glad I was here for this." Katrina saw them look at her in surprise. "No, not glad for what we saw, for what happened, that's not what I mean. It's because Mark and I are just starting our lives together, and we've spent these last weeks running on fast forward. What we just saw really brings home how precious life is. The things that have happened since Mark and I met—I mean, all this has kind of speeded things up. It has certainly brought life into focus. We would have gotten here anyway, but I realize now that I don't want to wait for fate."

She looked at Mark. "I guess this kind of sounds like a proposal, doesn't it? I hope you agree?"

"Well, well, now you see it. You folks are getting the abbreviated introduction to my granddaughter's wishy-washy personality," said Illyich with a grin. "You can see she never knows what she wants—just can't make up her mind!"

But by this time, Mark wasn't listening. He was too busy, with Katrina folded in his arms, Katrina saying, "Come below and ask me to marry you."

CHAPTER 50

For a few minutes the adults sat in silence, a bit numb from the intensity of events, the horror and the implications of the explosions, and then the wonder of the fate that had brought their offspring together. Then Katrina and Mark re-emerged on the stairway to the upper deck. Mark had a silver tray, with champagne glasses and a bottle, only the best would do—a Moet & Chandon, Brut, Nectar Imperial.

"I hope you don't mind, Illyich, but we've helped ourselves to what Katrina tells me is your best bottle of bubbly. You and my dad have a tradition, one that we now feel we can be part of. I have told Katrina that I accept her proposal, and we'd like to propose a toast." Katrina's arm was around Mark's waist.

By the time he finished speaking, tears were running down Leigh's cheeks, and Jim and Illyich were grinning from ear to ear. In a rare display of affection, Illyich grabbed Jim and gave him a huge bear hug, lifting the smaller six-footer off his feet.

"Our toast is closer to home, more personal, than yours," Mark continued. "*May we have as long and as wonderful a relationship as Jim and Leigh Buchan.* Thank you, Illyich, for this wonderful woman you brought into my life."

As the glasses were raised, the tears really flowed.

After cruising toward the Crimea for an hour, Jim turned in his chair. "Illyich, I'm feeling a little uncomfortable. We've got the other half of this equation still going on. With what has happened here, I'd like to get in touch with Antonio. Looking at the antennas that you've got on this little barge, I don't suppose we could do it from here, could we?"

"I can talk to the world from here. Mind you, you'll wake him up a little early! It would be four in the morning in Washington. Let's give him an hour."

So, at 5:00 a.m., Antonio rolled over and picked up the phone. "Man, whoever this is, I hope it's worth it."

"Antonio, I think it is."

"Jim!" Despite the hour Antonio was immediately bolt awake, sitting up in bed. "I thought you were sailing on the Black Sea."

"I am. I'm calling from Illyich's yacht in the middle of it. Sorry to wake you, old friend, but we've got some bad news and a thought."

"Jeez, Jim, what happened? But it's the thought that really worries me. They always seem to lead to big trouble. First what's the news?"

"You'll probably have some traffic across your desk today from your Russian friends. There was an ambush with loss of a Russian patrol boat and a helicopter. It was more than dramatic, and our target has vamoosed."

"Jim, that's terrible. I'll pick up the story at the office."

"On the other thing we spoke about, you probably need people to pay special attention. If my hunch is right, I would guess that something will go on the air in the next while. I think he'll want to let the right people know about the excitement."

"I'm with you. I'll make that call right now. What are your plans? Are you guys going to laze around Sochi for a while? There are some folks here that want to talk to you. Once you know your schedule, give me a day or two warning for when you'll be home."

"We'll do that, Antonio. It'll be about five days."

As they cruised toward the Crimea there was agreement that they would pass on the stop at Sevastopol. They all felt drained after the traumatic excitement of the last few days. None of them felt like tourists out for more adventure. Illyich, however, insisted that he was stopping at Yalta.

"Yalta is right on the way. We need to take on fuel."

Illyich saw Jim's eyebrows flick up. "Well, to be truthful, that's not the real reason I want to stop. Jim knows darn well we could make it home with what we've got in the tanks. But I have something which

I'd like you to see, something that puts some meaning into our lives, Jim."

They took in the sights and history of Yalta, and Illyich knew his history. As they entered Livadia Palace he said, "This is what we're here to see, what put Jim and me in business. This is where it all started."

"The Yalta conference?" Mark asked.

"You got it! This was the palace of Czar Nicholas. The conference took place here in February 1945."

Katrina asked, "What do you mean, it put you in business?"

"This is the spot where Stalin, Roosevelt and Churchill met to divide up Europe. The battle lines were set, the line was drawn through the center of the map of Europe. Remember, this was where Germany was divided, where Eastern Europe fell into the Soviet sphere, where what Churchill would later call the Iron Curtain was forged."

Mark was fascinated."You know, I've read some books about Yalta, revisionist history I guess, that question Roosevelt and Churchill's judgment. Standing here now, it seems to me that those authors forgot the balance of power at that critical juncture."

"So, Mark, yes indeed, you'd be right. Stalin had twelve million soldiers on the march. He was through Poland and into the heart of Germany. Eisenhower had about 4.8 million, barely to the Rhine. Churchill and your president were not bargaining from strength against Stalin, who was ruthless, who knew what he wanted and what he could get. Our history books say they never had a chance. Some of yours blame Roosevelt for caving in to Stalin. But as both Roosevelt and Churchill agreed, they had played the cards as best they could with the hands they were dealt. In his typical prescient fashion, though, Churchill got it right, he foretold the future. The Iron Curtain had descended across Europe."

After a thoughtful pause, Jim said quietly, "You know, Illyich, I had never really thought about all those years of the Cold War like that. But you're right. This is where it all started, isn't it? This is why you and I spent most of our lives as adversaries."

The cruise from the Crimea to Sochi was idyllic, calm seas, sun shining, 78 degrees, all five passengers happy to relax. Mark and Katrina had spent long hours talking.

"What are you going to do your grad studies in, Katrina?" Mark asked, almost afraid of what she might answer. Now that he had found her, he could not bear the thought of her being in St. Petersburg while he was in Georgetown.

"You remember what I told you that first night? It seems so long ago, time has gone so fast. I said I didn't know what I wanted to do, but that you did. You have a good life organized for yourself."

Mark held his breath, not daring to move.

"Well, now I know what I want to do. I want to be with you."

He threw his arms around her in a bear hug, so full of joy and relief that he couldn't speak for a long moment, and then he said, "I've been afraid to talk about it. I didn't want to influence your decision, but I've been hoping against hope that you would say that, and I have given it a lot of thought."

"I could see the wheels turning in there, my dear. Tell me what you've been thinking."

"Katrina, my little business is getting bigger than I could ever have hoped or imagined. I've farmed out all the accounting and everything else I can, but I'm turning down some good contracts. I have to spend too much time away from the computers. You told me that you were going to take either political science or business admin. How about you come to the States and join me in the business? I need help and was wrestling with hiring someone. You'd be that someone, starting slowly enough while you go to school for an MBA."

They looked at each other in silence, Mark wondering what she was thinking, Katrina wondering whether she could do this. But her thoughts were not the sentimental ones that Mark imagined, whether she wanted to give up her life in Russia, the privileged position that her grandfather put her in, the prestige of university in St. Petersburg. Katrina's thoughts were much more practical than that. Was she up to an MBA in the States? She knew about the competitive selection process, the demanding curriculum. Would she be accepted? Could she run Buchan Security in the free market world? Could she make her home the United States? She thought about Illyich, so brave and free-thinking, not in the cookie-cutter mold that his Soviet Union had demanded, not hesitating to break out, and she immediately recognized that she knew the answers to any questions concerning her decision. In fact she had subconsciously already made it. She looked at Mark with a twinkle in her eye, a twinkle that Mark was quickly learning meant that he was about to have his leg pulled.

"Mark Buchan, we will do this under one condition."

But Mark was already ahead of her, recognizing that twinkle. "Any condition you could set would be acceptable, just so long as you're with me. So, what's the condition?"

"That I become the other partner in Buchan Partners Security. After all, if I'm going to run the business I have to have a stake in the action."

"Done," as he put out his hand to shake on the deal, grinning from ear to ear. "You Russians strike a hard bargain when you have a position of strength."

As they were approaching the dock at Sochi, sunning themselves on deck, Katrina announced, "Mark and I have made some decisions. Illyich, I hope you won't mind too much. I know you had your heart set on me going to St. Petersburg in January."

"I did, but I'm not surprised to see changes to my grand plans. Indeed, I'd be surprised if you weren't making changes. What have you two cooked up?"

"I'll try to transfer to a university in the Washington area for an MBA. I'm going to join Mark in his business, in fact, he says I'm going to run it, so no doubt I'll be calling on you to bail us out before too long," she said with a smile.

"Somehow, my dear, I don't think so," Illyich replied. "Nevertheless, I am always at your service."

"Leigh, Mark tells me that you are involved at Georgetown University? Would I want to take an MBA there?"

"Yes, Katrina. My PhD is from Georgetown. I do a little teaching there. The big question would be—"

Mark interrupted, knowing exactly what she was thinking. "Mom, I've already asked the question. Her marks are straight A's. Academically, she should be accepted with flying colors."

"Well then, we could give it a try. Yes, they have a super School of Business, and you'd love the campus, if you ever have time to enjoy it."

"That would put me close enough so that I could work with Mark in his business, maybe even use it as a case study in the academic program." Katrina was clearly excited about the prospect.

"Have a look at their web site when you get home. I think you'll find that the school might be just what you are looking for." Then, with a note of caution, Leigh added, "It will take some fast work to get through all the hoops to get accepted, though. I'll be pleased to lend a hand with the application process, the mechanics, at the Washington end."

"That would be wonderful, Leigh. Thanks."

"Granddaughter, I couldn't be more pleased," Illyich said smiling. "But I can tell you, I'm going to miss you."

Leigh put an arm around his oversized waist. "That'll give you a good excuse to visit us."

Illyich looked at Jim. "With all the changes since 9/11, the tightening up of your immigration laws, will that pose a problem for Katrina?"

"I really don't know these days, but we can sure start the process the minute we get home. Maybe there are a few markers I can call in at the Agency to help."

Mark said, "This is going to be a challenge. Let's move really quickly to make it happen."

The day after their arrival at Illyich's dacha, Jim and Leigh were soaking up the sun on the beach patio when Illyich joined them, a tray of drinks in his hands. Mark and Katrina had disappeared for the day to explore Sochi.

"I thought we might need these as I bring you up to date on our friend."

Leigh voiced what they were all thinking. "We haven't heard the last of him, have we?"

"Well, Leigh, I expect you are right. He's disappeared off the face of the earth. The cigarette boat was found abandoned on a beach at Bourgas in Bulgaria. It had been stolen from the marina at Ahtopol three days before, but the owners were away and didn't report it until yesterday. The trail ends there. Kazim hasn't lost his touch nor his contacts. This operation took a lot of organizing, a lot of money and a lot of help. Tracking all that down should keep both of our old outfits busy for some time to come."

"Illyich, even though we lost Kazim—which seems to be getting to be a habit with us—I think we are justified in calling for a toast. After all, we did once again save a lot of grief for a lot of people. How about a toast?" Then, with a smile creasing his face, "In fact let's break the rules, let's make it more than one this time, to continuing peace and, now that our two offspring are together, let's drink to their happiness. May our children live in interesting times."

"I'll drink to that," Leigh said with a smile, "but please don't make those times too interesting."

The following day Illyich dropped them at the airport for the long flight home. Katrina and Mark were in deep conversation, and just as deep an embrace.

"I'll miss you, Katrina. Get that paperwork in process so that you can come quickly. I'll ask Mom to see if she can make sure the university has everything they need. And Dad has said he'd ask the embassy in Moscow to watch for your student visa application."

"I'll be there just as soon as I can. In the meantime, though, I put you on notice, fair warning."

"What's that, you devil?"

"No one else in that black car of yours! That seat is mine now."

CHAPTER 51

"Morning, Jim. It's Antonio. Glad to have you back. That must have been some exciting over in Turkey and the Black Sea—and talk about ringside seats! I can hardly wait to get your personal briefing."

"It did kind of catch one's attention. I'd like to get together, though, and get caught up on the other chapter in the story. Any progress?"

"We'll talk about it tomorrow. I just had an interesting call. Hope you, Leigh and Mark are available tomorrow, early. There'll be a car by to pick you up, 6:00 a.m. sharp. Or is that too early for you old, retired folks?"

"Sure, that's fine. What's up?"

"We'll pick Mark up first at 5:30. Could you let him know?"

"Yes, I'll do that. What's going on, Antonio?"

"Someone wants to say thanks. Wear a tie. See you bright and early. Bye now."

The phone went dead.

"I wonder what this is all about, Jim. I'm not up for many more surprises."

"Leigh, I expect that somebody at the Agency has been told to express the thanks of a grateful nation. I don't care about formalities but it would be nice for Mark. He deserves some kudos. I'll call him."

He pushed the speed dial button on his cordless phone.

"Hi, Mark. We're on tap first thing in the morning. You up for that?"

"Sure, Dad. What's going on?"

"Antonio is picking your mother and me up at 6:00. They're going to swing by your place first, at 5:30. Antonio tells me we should dress up, so find a tie to wear."

Dawn was just breaking as they got into the limo. Jim paused momentarily when he saw what they were climbing into. He knew immediately that this was no ordinary limo. Indeed, it was the President's back-up limo. He resisted the temptation to tell his family, because he guessed from the get-go where they must be heading, and it wasn't the route that he could do with his eyes closed, the commute to the office.

"Okay, Antonio, where are you taking us?" Mark soon asked, barely able to contain his excitement.

"You'll see soon enough, my friend," as he gave Jim a wink.

Mark said excitedly, "Dad, we must be going to Capitol Hill."

But they didn't make the turn that would take them there. Then, after another few minutes of driving, "Dad, I don't believe this!"

Beating Antonio to the punch, Jim exclaimed, "Believe it, guys. In a few minutes we're going to be in the Oval Office."

The limo did not take the usual entrance reserved for diplomats and heads of state. It went directly to the West Wing and was waved immediately through the fortified guardhouse, with the guard snapping to attention and saluting the limo. Everything ran as smooth as silk. As the doors of the limos opened, uniformed marines at attention, armed guards escorted them through the metal detectors. Mark noted the discreet but visible security arrangements and thought, "Just as it should be."

Minutes later they were being whisked into the Oval Office, the introductions made. It was impressive, even for Jim who had seen it before, but Mark and Leigh could hardly believe what was happening. Mark looked around at people that he knew by sight from watching television, but here he was, in person, in the same room! And what a room! The National Security Advisor, the Director of Central Intelligence, the Director of the FBI, the new Secretary of Homeland Security, and the president's Chief of Staff were all present. Antonio took a discreet seat at the end of a sofa.

"Jim, Leigh and Mark." President Walker spoke directly to them, looking right into their eyes. “These people have briefed me on the Onion Files, both of them.”

The President was considerably more relaxed than he had appeared in his last major address to the nation. He rose from behind the famous desk, and approached his guests.

“Jim, you’ve had quite a career. And you two have gone through some recent excitement. It’s very good to have you here with us this morning, Mark. I’m aware of what you have done and I wanted to thank you personally. I understand that it was your quick thinking which got the word to the Hoover in the nick of time. It’s quite a story! This terrorist action was bad enough, but without your initiative and quick action, it would have been devastating.”

Mark spoke up, saying, “Mr. President, there was a lot of luck involved, and we had a lot of help.”

Leigh thought with pride, “Like father, like son.”

“You know, I hear a lot of that these days. People like you, not even on the payroll, who step in to do the right thing. All those thousands of workers willing to reach into their own pockets to help us through the electricity crisis. Without them it would have been far worse. The rescue workers in New York who gave their lives for others. This is the America I know and love—and I see it every day!”

Leigh spoke up. “Mr. President, Jim and I thank you and these people here for rescuing our son, Mark. He would not be here if it weren’t for the coordinated approach to dealing with terrorists and the cooperation between agencies. We are very thankful that they did such outstanding work.”

Jim said, “Mr. President, we appreciate the thanks, but I have to agree with my son. There was a lot of luck involved. We came very close to the wire.”

The President smiled warmly. “Jim, having people like you on our side has nothing to do with luck. And I can tell you that in the past months, I’ve been overwhelmed by the way our people have gotten things done, both here in our country and over in Afghanistan where our forces are wiping out the Taliban and al-Qaeda. There’s no doubt that several al-Qaeda plots have been nipped in the bud. You could call it luck, but it has more to do with the quality and the initiative of people like you and Mark. If that directive to shut down the power to the equipment hadn't been issued, God only knows how much worse the damage would have been. The hundreds of people who lost their lives and the millions in damage are bad enough, but just imagine if those power switches hadn't been pulled. That, sir, had nothing to do with luck. That was to do with your good work. It may sound corny, but when I say thank you on behalf of a grateful nation, it comes from the heart."

Leigh said with emotion, "Mr. President, after what we went through with Mark's kidnapping, your words mean more to me than you know. We thank you."

"In that case Mrs. Buchan, you will be pleased and proud to know that I have decided to award the Presidential Medal of Freedom to your husband and to your son. Their actions were extraordinary. That is the least that we can do to thank you."

On the way back in the limo, Antonio said, "Well, I guess you have to be old and retired to get invited to the White House to meet the President—or young and clever like Mark. I tell you I had no idea about the medals, but I agree with the President, you both deserve it. That was really something. And I'll tell you, I feel the same as he does. That was some job you two did. Leigh, it is nice for you to see Jim recognized like this. Of course, you and Mark may have guessed this anyway, but that's the way Jim performed for his whole career with the Agency. I feel privileged to have learned from the best."

"Okay, Antonio, enough of that stuff," Jim said, his modesty coming to the fore.

Mark looked at his father. "Isn't the Presidential Medal of Freedom the highest honor that can be given to a civilian?"

"You'd better believe it, son. If I was still working I wouldn't even be eligible."

"This is unbelievable. Wait till I tell Katrina!"

"For sure, it is an outstanding honor for all of us," Jim added thoughtfully. "As I think about the President's words, it scares me to think about how close we came, and despite the President's kind words, how big a part luck did play. On the first Onion, if détente hadn't happened and if Illyich hadn't called me, the first we'd have known we had a problem would have been when it was too late. Now this time around, on Onion 2, but for a couple of acts of fate, a huge chunk of the US would have been under water."

"That's true, Dad. If we hadn't been talking the day that we saw bin Laden on TV, we would not even have started looking."

"What's even more frightening is that what really saved us, what made the difference, was Kazim's one little mistake, when he messed up the time zone business. If he had adjusted for the time zones rather than inadvertently programming it all for 1:00 p.m. local time, all the dams would have opened at the same time. We wouldn't have had time to figure out the auxiliary motors. Even with the order to pull the switches, major flooding would have occurred. It was that close."

"Kazim made one critical error, on the timing, but I did too. I should have picked up the auxiliary power scheme. That's a lesson learned the hard way!"

Antonio spoke next, "You know, Jim, I'm not sure where this leaves us. How do we train our young people to think outside the box, the way you two did? To use their imagination, the way you and Mark did? Jim, when you first came to me with this, with all the other huge threats taking precedence, threats of more explosions or hijacked airplanes, I couldn't get anyone interested. It took someone like you to recognize what needed to be done—and then get on and do it."

"Yes, but, of course, I had the advantage of having been there before!"

Antonio turned to Mark. "I know that you wouldn't be interested in a job offer, Mark, but don't be surprised if you get a call for the occasional expert advice."

Seeing the look of consternation on Leigh's face he added, "No, no, Leigh, this would be for computer stuff, nothing on the firing line. I could even convince the agency to pay your exorbitant hourly rates!" he said with a grin.

Leigh had been listening with interest. "You mean like this time, just computer stuff, where Kazim came so close? But I must admit that you need people with his skills, and having lived all these years with my husband here," poking him in the ribs, "I could understand why Mark is likely to answer the call when it comes. As to the challenge of looking into the crystal ball, making intelligence assessments, as I watch the new intel structures emerge, I'd say that at least we're on the right track, with an intel center that has access to intelligence from all the sources, people who can look at everything. The ability to mesh the foreign counterintelligence information with what is gathered internally in the US should make a huge difference."

"Oh, it will for sure. But at the end of the day, we still face the same challenge—how to guess what the bad guys are going to do from what will always be fragmented, contradictory and incomplete intelligence. This part of the job hasn't changed since you left, Jim. One aspect that has, though, is the volume. It was huge while you were around. Now it's unmanageable. In addition to what you used to wade through we've now got all the computer stuff, internet and email."

As Antonio stopped talking, Leigh said thoughtfully, "I can imagine that it must be almost overwhelming. And you need to wrestle with the legal issues. In my work, I see a lot of commentary about the balance between civil liberties and security, and I must say that I've been on the side of civil liberties. We need to be really careful not to throw the baby out with the bathwater in a democracy. But now, I'm not sure what to think, because this time I'm just thankful that you people were able to do what you did. This time we got it right. That Mark is with us is proof enough for me! Antonio, thank you for everything, and thank you for this fine honor that we just received for my husband and my son."

EPILOGUE

Sergeant Timothy K. Leary had been with his special forces squad as the bombs rained down around Mazari Sharif and Jalalabad where all the satellite photography, the signals intelligence and some tightly held human intelligence told them they would find their target. As they watched the B-52s' vapor trails streak the sky overhead and the patterns of explosions tear through the land, one of the soldiers said in awe, "How could anyone survive that onslaught?"

But after it was all over and Sgt. Leary and his team raked through the rubble, there was nothing to be found.

It wasn't long after Specialist First Class Paderewski was heard to say, "We must have got him," that bin Laden was once again on television, vowing vengeance against the modern crusaders.

Now, only short weeks later, Tim Leary and his team were in different terrain, but to them it might as well have been yesterday. The scenery had changed, the quarry was the same. This time, operating as a detached squad from Team 5, they were more heavily camouflaged and more lightly armed as they tracked the courier from the Russian mission in Kabul.

They worked in relays, reinforcements dropping in from helicopters every second day. Tim knew that he had plenty of backup. He just couldn't see them. He also knew that when he spoke the code words 'the Alamo' into the mike on his headphone that the gun ships would be firing in minutes. But all this didn't change the fact that he knew his ass was hanging way out. They were in really hostile territory, in the Pashtun tribal lands, lands that over the millennia the best armies in the world had failed to conquer. Tim remembered reading that even

Alexander the Great's victory had been fleeting, the Pashtun still speaking with pride about their resistance some 2500 years before.

The two robed men looking down on the thin trail exchanged glances, one saying quietly, "There he is, Abdul, just as scheduled. You take the first tail. I'll drop in two kilometers back."

Each of the men had new short-range walkie-talkies, the kind that many American families issue to their kids on the ski hills or golf course. The range of these was limited, just enough to call in their friends. These friends lined the hills on either side of the trail as it became narrower and steeper, and these friends not only had walkie-talkies but heavy artillery as well. The courier and his two trailing friends crept along a trail as familiar to them and to the tribesmen lining the hills as it had been to generations of forefathers fighting to defend their homeland from invaders.

The courier didn't look around as he drew close to his destination, but he felt a deep sense of reassurance and relief. He knew that once he reached within twenty kilometers of the camp he would pick up a tail to cover his backside, just the first in a series of tight security precautions that Kazim had put in place.

A few hours later Tim's advance man reported in. "We've got a tail between us and the target."

After another hour of hard slogging and some discussion with his captain in the lead backup helicopter, Tim started to really worry. "Ignacio, I don't like this. We're in ideal ambush country. The valley's narrowed down to where the helicopters could hardly maneuver if we needed them. If they've arranged one tail for this guy, what if they have a double tail, one that fell in behind us? I get the strong feeling these guys are leading us into a dead end."

Within seconds, he was proven right. The firing started, Tim shouting into his mike, "The Alamo, the Alamo. We're under intense fire."

As the helicopter gun ships raced up the valley, the canyon walls erupted, shoulder-fired missiles lashing out at targets so close they were hard to miss. Sgt. Timothy Leary and his squad fought valiantly, surviving for about five minutes.

On the other side of the world, Jim was relaxing on the deck, halfway through the *Washington Post* when his cell phone did its quiet ring.

"Jim, it's Antonio. I've got some news—not good, I'm afraid. Can I come over?

"Sure thing. When? Now?"

"That would be good. Mark might want to be in on this."

"Let me call him …"

"Mark, Antonio just called. Can you come over?"

"Oh boy, he must have some news. Did they catch bin Laden? Be there in half an hour, Dad."

Jim's next call was to Leigh. She wasn't going to miss this for the world. "Hi, honey. Antonio just called. He has some news. Can you come right away?"

Jim had the balcony chairs arranged by the time they all arrived, coffee ready to go. The welcoming hellos were brief, everyone on the edge of their seats, waiting for the news.

"I must say, Antonio, judging by our brief conversation, I don't like the sound of what's coming."

"Well, you'd be right, Jim. But probably not surprised. You've dealt with Kazim before. Man, we were that close!" He held up his thumb and forefinger squeezed almost together. "You were right on the money, all the way. After we linked with Igor and their people in Moscow, there was very little message traffic from St. Petersburg to the Russian mission in Kabul. That must have been the period when Kazim was traveling to Istanbul. Then, two days after your call from Illyich's yacht, there was one encrypted transmission, the same encryption as they had picked up before. They had the building and everyone in it under as tight surveillance as you could get. It took two days to pick up a slight variance in routine. One of the Afghan employees booked off sick and, sure enough, a day later was on the road. We've always thought that bin Laden was moving around in the Pashtun tribal lands on the border with Pakistan, and that's where the courier headed. Our Special Forces people were with him all the way."

Mark couldn't contain himself. "So, what happened?"

"You know, it's hard to conceive the type of loyalty we see in al-Qaeda and in the fundamentalist groups, people willing to die for the cause. And the security arrangements were simple and sophisticated at the same time. As the courier got closer, it turns out that they had arrangements to cover their backside. A rear guard tribesman fell in behind the courier. Our team spotted him. What they didn't think of till too late was that another tribesman fell in a couple of kilometers behind the first. That one identified our team and, believe me, our guys were the best. But they didn't see what was coming until the last minute."

He paused to sip his coffee. "It was too late. The ambush was successfully executed. In the firefight our guys got a few of them, but in the end, none of those crack Special Forces troops survived. All five of them died."

"What about backup? Surely the five of them weren't out there on their own!" This was Leigh.

"They sure weren't. The helicopters were there in minutes, all over the place. Two of them were blown out of the sky."

Leigh and Mark spoke as one, "That's terrible."

"Many of the people guarding bin Laden died in the firefight. When our people got to where bin Laden probably was, he had vanished, just disappeared into thin air."

"Just like in the caves right at the beginning of all this," Jim added. "You know, even though he's running out of places to hide and the net is closing, he's got people of Kazim's cunning on his side. We may be at this for some time yet."

Antonio was quiet for a few minutes, then said, "Yes, and I have saved the worst for last. They have also located a message from Kazim."

"Well, tell us, Antonio, what is it?" Mark blurted out.

"Jim, I wasn't sure how to handle this, but you've all been involved in this sad affair from the very beginning, so I decided you should all hear it right away. When the troops got to the bin Laden camp, one of the few things left intact had been placed outside the main complex, as if it had been put there on purpose, so that it would survive the onslaught and be found."

No one said a word, waiting for Antonio to break the suspense.

"It was a laptop computer. Our people know from bitter experience the danger of playing with that before the explosives experts have cleared it as safe. When that was done, to everyone's surprise, it had not been wired to blow up in their faces. It was clean. They turned it on expecting to find it blank. It wasn't. There was one page showing on the screen at start-up."

"What was on it?" Mark blurted.

Antonio reached for a folder that he had put on the table beside him, withdrawing a single sheet of paper. He handed it to Jim. Jim glanced at it and, without a trace of emotion showing in his face, turned the page so that the others could see. It said:

ЛУК

JIM AND MARK BUCHAN

TILL THE NEXT TIME

ABOUT THE AUTHOR

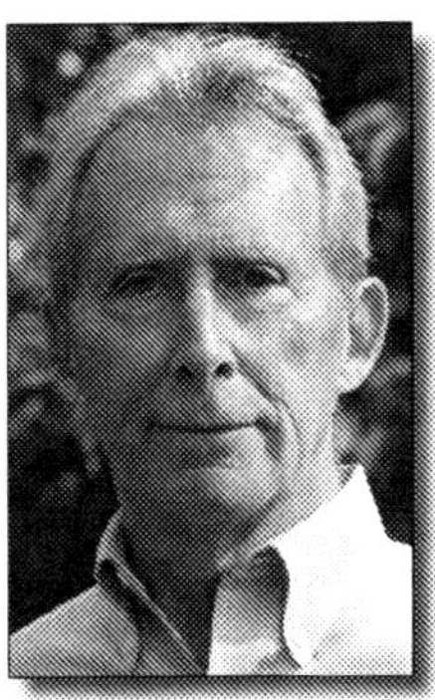

VAL PATTEE

Val Pattee is a retired Canadian Air Force major general, a jet fighter pilot on the front lines of the Cold War who spent his last years in the military as Chief of Intelligence and Security for NATO in Europe and for Canada. Val had unprecedented access to the most secret intelligence of sixteen nations as the Cold War drew to a close. He met one-on-one with the Director of Central Intelligence in the CIA building in Langley, VA, and with the boss inside the National Security Agency at Fort Meade, has been briefed in the inner sanctum of the Defense Intelligence Agency in the Pentagon and at MI5 and MI6, the British Security and Secret Service agencies, in London, at GCHQ, the British Signals Intelligence organization, in Cheltenham. He also worked in Paris at the height of Action Direct terrorism in France and in the bunker nestled in the hills outside Bonn while the Red Army Faction were creating havoc. Val has done business with the J2s, the Chiefs of Intelligence, in Oslo and Copenhagen, in Amsterdam and Brussels, in Athens, Ankara and Istanbul, Lisbon, Madrid, and Rome. He met with the GRU (Russian Military Intelligence) in Moscow and with the People's Liberation Army in Beijing.

After retiring from the military, Val was the senior official for policing for a Canadian province. Val and his wife Joan reside in Victoria, B.C. This is the first book in a series Val is writing while he and Joan winter in Mexico.

Val's website is www.valpattee.com.

Printed in the United States
92326LV00011B/13-33/A

9 781897 435069